KT-527-881

SPIN

**ROBERT
CHARLES
WILSON**

TOR®

A TOM DOHERTY ASSOCIATES BOOK
NEW YORK

NOTE: If you purchased this book without a cover, you should be aware that this book is stolen property. It was reported as "unsold and destroyed" to the publisher, and neither the author nor the publisher has received any payment for this "stripped book."

This is a work of fiction. All the characters, organizations, and events portrayed in this novel are either products of the author's imagination or are used fictitiously.

SPIN

Copyright © 2005 by Robert Charles Wilson

"Infant Innocence" by A. E. Housman is quoted by permission of The Society of Authors as the Literary Representative of the Estate of A. E. Housman.

All rights reserved.

A Tor Book
Published by Tom Doherty Associates, LLC
175 Fifth Avenue
New York, NY 10010

www.tor-forge.com

Tor® is a registered trademark of Tom Doherty Associates, LLC.

ISBN 978-0-7653-4825-8

First Edition: April 2005
First Mass Market Edition: February 2006

Printed in the United States of America

20 19 18 17 16 15 14 13 12 11 10

SPIN

Everybody falls, and we all land somewhere.

So we rented a room on the third floor of a colonial-style hotel in Padang where we wouldn't be noticed for a while.

Nine hundred euros a night bought us privacy and a balcony view of the Indian Ocean. During pleasant weather, and there had been no shortage of that over the last few days, we could see the nearest part of the Archway: a cloud-colored vertical line that rose from the horizon and vanished, still rising, into blue haze. As impressive as this seemed, only a fraction of the whole structure was visible from the west coast of Sumatra. The Archway's far leg descended to the undersea peaks of the Carpenter Ridge more than a thousand kilometers away, spanning the Mentawai Trench like a wedding band dropped edge-up into a shallow pond. On dry land, it would have reached from Bombay on the eastern coast of India to Madras on the west. Or, say, very roughly, New York to Chicago.

Diane had spent most of the afternoon on the balcony, sweating in the shade of a faded striped umbrella. The view fascinated her, and I was pleased and relieved that she was—

after everything that had happened—still capable of taking such pleasure in it.

I joined her at sunset. Sunset was the best time. A freighter heading down the coast to the port of Teluk Bayur became a necklace of lights in the offshore blackness, effortlessly gliding. The near leg of the Arch gleamed like a burnished red nail pinning sky to sea. We watched the Earth's shadow climb the pillar as the city grew dark.

It was a technology, in the famous quotation, "indistinguishable from magic." What else but magic would allow the uninterrupted flow of air and sea from the Bay of Bengal to the Indian Ocean but would transport a surface vessel to far stranger ports? What miracle of engineering permitted a structure with a radius of a thousand kilometers to support its own weight? What was it made of, and how did it do what it did?

Perhaps only Jason Lawton could have answered those questions. But Jason wasn't with us.

Diane slouched in a deck chair, her yellow sundress and comically wide straw hat reduced by the gathering darkness to geometries of shadow. Her skin was clear, smooth, nut brown. Her eyes caught the last light very fetchingly, but her look was still wary—that hadn't changed.

She glanced up at me. "You've been fidgeting all day."

"I'm thinking of writing something," I said. "Before it starts. Sort of a memoir."

"Afraid of what you might lose? But that's unreasonable, Tyler. It's not like your memory's being erased."

No, not erased; but potentially blurred, softened, defocused. The other side effects of the drug were temporary and endurable, but the possibility of memory loss terrified me.

"Anyway," she said, "the odds are in your favor. You know that as well as anyone. There *is* a risk . . . but it's *only* a risk, and a pretty minor one at that."

And if it had happened in her case maybe it had been a blessing.

"Even so," I said. "I'd feel better writing something down."

"If you don't want to go ahead with this you don't have to. You'll know when you're ready."

"No, I want to do it." Or so I told myself.

"Then it has to start tonight."

"I know. But over the next few weeks—"

"You probably won't feel like writing."

"Unless I can't help myself." Graphomania was one of the less alarming of the potential side effects.

"See what you think when the nausea hits." She gave me a consoling smile. "I guess we all have something we're afraid to let go of."

It was a troubling comment, one I didn't want to think about.

"Look," I said, "maybe we should just get started."

The air smelled tropical, tinged with chlorine from the hotel pool three stories down. Padang was a major international port these days, full of foreigners: Indians, Filipinos, Koreans, even stray Americans like Diane and me, folks who couldn't afford luxury transit and weren't qualified for U.N.-approved resettlement programs. It was a lively but often lawless city, especially since the New Reformasi had come to power in Jakarta.

But the hotel was secure and the stars were out in all their scattered glory. The peak of the Archway was the brightest thing in the sky now, a delicate silver letter U (Unknown, Unknowable) written upside down by a dyslexic God. I held Diane's hand while we watched it fade.

"What are you thinking about?" she asked.

"The last time I saw the old constellations." Virgo, Leo, Sagittarius: the astrologer's lexicon, reduced to footnotes in a history book.

"They would have been different from here, though, wouldn't they? The southern hemisphere?"

I supposed they would.

Then, in the full darkness of the night, we went back into the room. I switched on the room lights while Diane pulled the blinds and unpacked the syringe and ampoule kit I had taught her to use. She filled the sterile syringe, frowned and tapped out a bubble. She looked professional, but her hand was trembling.

I took off my shirt and stretched out on the bed.

"Tyler—"

Suddenly she was the reluctant one. "No second thoughts," I said. "I know what I'm getting into. And we've talked this through a dozen times."

She nodded and swabbed the inside of my elbow with alcohol. She held the syringe in her right hand, point up. The small quantity of fluid in it looked as innocent as water.

"That was a long time ago," she said.

"What was?"

"When we looked at the stars that time."

"I'm glad you haven't forgotten."

"Of course I haven't forgotten. Now make a fist."

The pain was trivial. At least at first.

I was twelve, and the twins were thirteen, the night the stars disappeared from the sky.

It was October, a couple of weeks before Halloween, and the three of us had been ordered to the basement of the Lawton house—the Big House, we called it—for the duration of an adults-only social event.

Being confined to the basement wasn't any kind of punishment. Not for Diane and Jason, who spent much of their time there by choice; certainly not for me. Their father had announced a strictly defined border between the adults' and the children's zones of the house, but we had a high-end gaming platform, movies on disk, even a pool table . . . and no adult supervision apart from one of the regular caterers, a Mrs. Truall, who came downstairs every hour or so to dodge canapé duty and give us updates on the party. (A man from Hewlett-Packard had disgraced himself with the wife of a *Post* columnist. There was a drunken senator in the den.) All we lacked, Jason said, was silence (the upstairs system was playing dance music that came through the ceiling like an ogre's heartbeat) and a view of the sky.

Silence and a view: Jase, typically, had decided he wanted both.

Diane and Jason had been born minutes apart but were obviously fraternal rather than identical siblings; no one but their mother called them twins. Jason used to say they were the product of "dipolar sperm penetrating oppositely charged eggs." Diane, whose IQ was nearly as impressive as Jason's but who kept her vocabulary on a shorter leash, compared them to "different prisoners who escaped from the same cell."

I was in awe of them both.

Jason, at thirteen, was not only scary-smart but physically fit—not especially muscular but vigorous and often successful at track and field. He was nearly six feet tall even then, skinny, his gawky face redeemed by a lopsided and genuine smile. His hair, in those days, was blond and wiry.

Diane was five inches shorter, plump only by comparison with her brother, and darker skinned. Her complexion was clear except for the freckles that ringed her eyes and gave her a hooded look: *My raccoon mask,* she used to say. What I liked most about Diane—and I had reached an age when these details had taken on a poorly understood but undeniable significance—was her smile. She smiled rarely but spectacularly. She was convinced her teeth were too prominent (she was wrong), and she had picked up the habit of covering her mouth when she laughed. I liked to make her laugh, but it was her smile I secretly craved.

Last week Jason's father had given him a pair of expensive astronomical binoculars. He had been fidgeting with them all evening, taking sightings on the framed travel poster over the TV, pretending to spy on Cancun from the suburbs of Washington, until at last he stood up and said, "We ought to go look at the sky."

"No," Diane said promptly. "It's cold out there."

"But clear. It's the first clear night this week. And it's only chilly."

"There was ice on the lawn this morning."

"Frost," he countered.

"It's after midnight."

"It's Friday night."

"We're not supposed to leave the basement."

"We're not supposed to disturb the party. Nobody said anything about going outside. Nobody will see us, if you're afraid of getting caught."

"I'm not afraid of getting caught."

"So what *are* you afraid of?"

"Listening to you babble while my feet freeze."

Jason turned to me. "How about you, Tyler? Want to see some sky?"

The twins often asked me to referee their arguments, much to my discomfort. It was a no-win proposition. If I sided with Jason I might alienate Diane; but if I sided too often with Diane it would look . . . well, obvious. I said, "I don't know, Jase, it *is* pretty chilly outside . . ."

It was Diane who let me off the hook. She put a hand on my shoulder and said, "Never mind. I suppose a little fresh air is better than listening to him complain."

So we grabbed our jackets from the basement hallway and left by the back door.

The Big House wasn't as grandiose as our nickname for it implied, but it was larger than the average home in this middling-high-income neighborhood and it sat on a bigger parcel of land. A great rolling expanse of manicured lawn gave way, behind it, to an uncultivated stand of pines bordering a mildly polluted creek. Jason chose a spot for stargazing halfway between the house and the woods.

The month of October had been pleasant until yesterday, when a cold front had broken the back of Indian summer. Diane made a show of hugging her ribs and shivering, but that was only to chastise Jason. The night air was merely cool, not unpleasant. The sky was crystalline and the grass was reasonably dry, though there might be frost again by morning. No moon and not a trace of cloud. The Big House was lit up like a Mississippi steamboat and cast its fierce yellow glare across the lawn, but we knew from experience that on nights like this, if you stood in the shadow of a tree, you'd disappear as absolutely as if you had fallen into a black hole.

Jason lay on his back and aimed his binoculars at the starry sky.

I sat cross-legged next to Diane and watched as she took from her jacket pocket a cigarette, probably stolen from her mother. (Carol Lawton, a cardiologist and nominal ex-smoker, kept packs of cigarettes secreted in her dresser, her desk, a kitchen drawer. My mother had told me this.) She put it to her lips and lit it with a translucent red lighter—the flame was momentarily the brightest thing around—and exhaled a plume of smoke that swirled briskly into the darkness.

She caught me watching her. "You want a drag?"

"He's twelve years old," Jason said. "He has enough problems. He doesn't need lung cancer."

"Sure," I said. It was a point of honor now.

Diane, amused, passed me the cigarette. I inhaled tentatively and managed not to choke.

She took it back. "Don't get carried away."

"Tyler," Jason said, "do you know anything about the stars?"

I gulped a lungful of cold, clean air. "Of course I do."

"I don't mean what you learn from reading those paperbacks. Can you *name* any stars?"

I was blushing, but I hoped it was dark enough that he couldn't see. "Arcturus," I said. "Alpha Centauri. Sirius. Polaris . . ."

"And which one," Jason asked, "is the Klingon homeworld?"

"Don't be mean," Diane said.

Both the twins were precociously intelligent. I was no dummy, but they were out of my league, and we all understood that. They attended a school for exceptional children; I rode the bus to public school. It was one of the several obvious distinctions between us. They lived in the Big House, I lived with my mother in the bungalow at the east end of the property; their parents pursued careers, my mother cleaned house for them. Somehow we managed to acknowledge these differences without making a big deal of it.

"Okay," Jason said, "can you point at Polaris?"

Polaris, the North Star. I had been reading about slavery and the civil war. There had been a fugitive slave song:

> *When the sun comes back and the first quail calls,*
> *Follow the Drinking Gourd.*
> *The old man is waiting to carry you to freedom*
> *When you follow the Drinking Gourd.*

"When the sun comes back" meant after the winter solstice. Quail winter in the south. The gourd was the Big Dipper, wide end of the bowl pointed at Polaris, due north, the direction of freedom: I found the Dipper and waved my hand hopefully in that direction.

"See?" Diane said to Jason, as if I had proved a point in some argument they hadn't bothered to share with me.

"Not bad," Jason allowed. "You know what a comet is?"

"Yes."

"Want to see one?"

I nodded and stretched out next to him, still tasting and regretting the acrid tang of Diane's cigarette. Jason showed me how to brace my elbows on the ground, then let me hold the binoculars to my eyes and adjust the focus until the stars became blurred ovals and then pinpricks, many more than I could see with the naked eye. I panned around until I found, or guessed I had found, the spot to which Jason had directed me: a tiny node of phosphorescence against the merciless black sky.

"A comet—" Jason began.

"I know. A comet is a sort of dusty snowball falling toward the sun."

"You could say that." He was scornful. "Do you know where comets come from, Tyler? They come from the outer solar system—from a kind of icy halo around the sun that reaches from the orbit of Pluto halfway to the nearest star. Out where it's colder than you can possibly imagine."

I nodded, a little uncomfortably. I had read enough science fiction to grasp the sheer, unspeakable largeness of the night sky. It was something I sometimes liked to think about, though it could be—at the wrong time of night, when the house was quiet—a little intimidating.

"Diane?" Jason said. "You want to look?"

"Do I have to?"

"No, of course you don't have to. You can sit there fumigating your lungs and drooling, if you prefer."

"Smartass." She stubbed the cigarette into the grass and held out her hand. I passed over the binoculars.

"Just be careful with those." Jase was deeply in love with his binoculars. They still smelled of shrinkwrap and Styrofoam packing.

She adjusted the focus and looked up. She was silent for a time. Then she said, "You know what I see when I use these things to look at the stars?"

"What?"

"Same old stars."

"Use your imagination." He sounded genuinely annoyed.

"If I can use my imagination why do I need binoculars?"

"I mean, think about what you're looking at."

"Oh," she said. Then: "Oh. *Oh!* Jason, I see—"

"What?"

"I think . . . yes . . . it's God! And he has a long white beard! And he's holding up a sign! And the sign says . . . JA-SON SUCKS!"

"Very funny. Give them back if you don't know how to use them."

He held out his hand; she ignored him. She sat upright and aimed the binoculars at the windows of the Big House.

The party had been going on since late that afternoon. My mother had told me the Lawtons' parties were "expensive bull sessions for corporate bigshots," but she had a finely honed sense of hyperbole, so you had to take that down a notch or two. Most of the guests, Jason had said, were aerospace up-and-comers or political staffers. Not old Washington society, but well-heeled newcomers with western roots and defense-industry connections. E. D. Lawton, Jason and Diane's father, hosted one of these events every three or four months.

"Business as usual," Diane said from behind the twin ovals of the binoculars. "First floor, dancing and drinking. More drinking than dancing at this point. It looks like the kitchen's closing up, though. I think the caterers are getting ready to go home. Curtains pulled in the den. E.D.'s in the library with a couple of suits. Ew! One of them is smoking a cigar."

"Your disgust is unconvincing," Jason said. "Ms. Marlboro."

She went on cataloguing the visible windows while Jason scooted over next to me. "Show her the universe," he whispered, "and she'd rather spy on a dinner party."

I didn't know how to respond to that. Like so much of what Jason said, it sounded witty and more clever than anything I could come up with.

"My bedroom," Diane said. "Empty, thank God. Jason's bedroom, empty except for the copy of *Penthouse* under the mattress—"

"They're good binoculars, but not that good."

"Carol and E.D.'s bedroom, empty; the spare bedroom . . ."

"Well?"

But Diane said nothing. She sat very still with the binoculars against her eyes.

"Diane?" I said.

She was silent for a few seconds more. Then she shuddered, turned, and tossed—*threw*—the binoculars back at Jason, who protested but didn't seem to grasp that Diane had seen something disturbing. I was about to ask her if she was all right—

When the stars disappeared.

○ ○ ○

It wasn't much.

People often say that, people who saw it happen. It wasn't much. It really wasn't, and I speak as a witness: I had been watching the sky while Diane and Jason bickered. There was nothing but a moment of odd glare that left an afterimage of the stars imprinted on my eyes in cool green phosphorescence. I blinked. Jason said, "What was that? Lightning?" And Diane said nothing at all.

"Jason," I said, still blinking.

"What? Diane, I swear to God, if you cracked a lens on these things—"

"Shut up," Diane said.

And I said, "Stop it. *Look*. What happened to the stars?" They both turned their heads to the sky.

∘ ∘ ∘

Of the three of us, only Diane was prepared to believe that the stars had actually "gone out"—that they had been extinguished like candles in a wind. That was impossible, Jason insisted: the light from those stars had traveled fifty or a hundred or a hundred million light-years, depending on the source; surely they had not all stopped shining in some infinitely elaborate sequence designed to appear simultaneous to Earthlings. Anyway, I pointed out, the sun was a star, too, and *it* was still shining, at least on the other side of the planet—wasn't it?

Of course it was. And if not, Jason said, we would all be frozen to death by morning.

So, logically, the stars were still shining but we couldn't see them. They were not gone but obscured: eclipsed. Yes, the sky had suddenly become an ebony blankness, but it was a mystery, not a catastrophe.

But another aspect of Jason's comment had lodged in my imagination. What if the sun actually *had* vanished? I pictured snow sifting down in perpetual darkness, and then, I guessed, the air itself freezing out in a different kind of snow, until all human civilization was buried under the stuff we breathe. Better, therefore, oh definitely better, to assume the stars had been "eclipsed." But by what?

"Well, obviously, something big. Something fast. You saw it happen, Tyler. Was it all at once or did something kind of move across the sky?"

I told him it looked like the stars had brightened and then blinked out, all at once.

"Fuck the stupid stars," Diane said. (I was shocked: *fuck* wasn't a word she customarily used, though Jase and I were pretty free with it now that both our ages had reached double digits. Many things had changed this summer.)

Jason heard the anxiety in her voice. "I don't think there's anything to be afraid of," he said, although he was clearly uneasy himself.

Diane just scowled. "I'm cold," she said.

So we decided to go back to the Big House and see if the news had made CNN or CNBC. The sky as we crossed the lawn was unnerving, utterly black, weightless but heavy, darker than any sky I had ever seen.

○ ○ ○

"We have to tell E.D.," Jason said.

"You tell him," Diane said.

Jase and Diane called their parents by their given names because Carol Lawton imagined she kept a progressive household. The reality was more complex. Carol was indulgent but not terribly involved in the twins' lives, while E.D. was systematically grooming an heir. That heir, of course, was Jason. Jason worshipped his father. Diane was afraid of him.

And I knew better than to show my face in the adult zone at the boozy tag-end of a Lawton social event; so Diane and I hovered in the demilitarized zone behind a door while Jason found his father in an adjoining room. We couldn't hear the resulting conversation in any detail, but there was no mistaking E.D.'s tone of voice—aggrieved, impatient, and short-tempered. Jason came back to the basement red-faced and nearly crying, and I excused myself and headed for the back door.

Diane caught up with me in the hallway. She put her hand on my wrist as if to anchor us together. "Tyler," she said. "It will come up, won't it? The sun, I mean, in the morning. I know it's a stupid question. But the sun *will* rise, right?"

She sounded absolutely bereft. I started to say something flippant—*we'll all be dead if it doesn't*—but her anxiety prompted doubts of my own. What exactly had we seen, and what did it mean? Jason clearly hadn't been able to convince his father that anything important had happened in the night sky, so maybe we were scaring ourselves over nothing. But what if the world really was ending, and only we three knew it?

"We'll be okay," I said.

She regarded me through pickets of lank hair. "You believe that?"

I tried to smile. "Ninety percent."

"But you're going to stay up till morning, aren't you?"

"Maybe. Probably." I knew I didn't feel like sleeping.

She made a thumb-and-pinky gesture: "Can I call you later?"

"Sure."

"I probably won't sleep. And—I know this sounds dumb—in case I do, will you call me as soon as the sun comes up?"

I said I would.

"Promise?"

"Promise." I was thrilled that she'd asked.

o o o

The house where I lived with my mother was a neat clapboard bungalow on the east end of the Lawton property. A small rose garden fenced with pine rails braced the front steps—the roses themselves had bloomed well into the fall but had withered in the latest gush of cold air. On this moonless, cloudless, starless night, the porch light gleamed like a beacon.

I entered quietly. My mother had long since retreated to her bedroom. The small living room was tidy save for a single empty shotglass on the side table: she was a five-day teetotaler but took a little whiskey on the weekends. She used to say she had only two vices, and a drink on Saturday night was one of them. (Once, when I asked her what the other one was, she gave me a long look and said, "Your father." I didn't press the subject.)

I stretched out on the empty sofa with a book and read until Diane called, less than an hour later. The first thing she said was, "Have you turned on the TV?"

"Should I?"

"Don't bother. There's nothing on."

"Well, you know, it *is* two in the morning."

"No, I mean absolutely nothing. There are infomercials on local cable, but nothing else. What does that mean, Tyler?"

What it meant was that every satellite in orbit had vanished along with the stars. Telecom, weather, military satellites, the GPS system: all of them had been shut down in the blink of an eye. But I didn't know any of that and I certainly couldn't have explained it to Diane. "It could mean anything."

"It's a little frightening."

"Probably nothing to worry about."

"I hope not. I'm glad you're still awake."

She called back an hour later with more news. The Internet was also missing in action, she said. And local TV had begun to report canceled morning flights out of Reagan and the regional airports, warning people to call ahead.

"But there have been jets flying all night." I'd seen their running lights from the bedroom window, false stars, fast-moving. "I guess military. It could be some terrorist thing."

"Jason's in his room with a radio. He's pulling in stations from Boston and New York. He says they're talking about military activity and airport lockdowns, but nothing about terrorism—and nothing about the stars."

"Somebody must have noticed."

"If they did they're not mentioning it. Maybe they have *orders* not to mention it. They haven't mentioned sunrise, either."

"Why would they? The sun's supposed to come up in, what, an hour? Which means it's already rising out over the ocean. Off the Atlantic coast. Ships at sea must have seen it. *We'll* see it, before long."

"I hope so." She sounded simultaneously frightened and embarrassed. "I hope you're right."

"You'll see."

"I like your voice, Tyler. Did I ever tell you that? You have a very reassuring voice."

Even if what I said was pure bullshit.

But the compliment affected me more than I wanted her to know. I thought about it after she hung up. I played it over in my head for the sake of the warm feeling it provoked. And I wondered what that meant. Diane was a year older than me and three times as sophisticated—so why did I feel so suddenly protective of her, and why did I wish she was close enough that I could touch her face and promise everything would be all right? It was a puzzle almost as urgent and nearly as disturbing as whatever had happened to the sky.

o o o

She called again at ten to five, when I had almost, despite myself, drifted off to sleep, fully dressed. I groped the phone out of my shirt pocket. "Hello?"

"Just me. It's still dark, Tyler."

I glanced at the window. Yes. Dark. Then the bedside clock. "Not quite sunrise, Diane."

"Were you asleep?"

"No."

"Yeah, you were. Lucky you. It's still dark. Cold, too. I looked at the thermometer outside the kitchen window. Thirty-five degrees. Should it be that cold?"

"It was that cold yesterday morning. Anyone else awake at your place?"

"Jason's locked in his room with his radio. My, uh, parents are, uh, I guess sleeping off the party. Is your mom awake?"

"Not this early. Not on a weekend." I cast a nervous glance at the window. Surely by this time there ought to be some light in the sky. Even a hint of daylight would have been reassuring.

"You didn't wake her up?"

"What's she going to do, Diane? Make the stars come back?"

"I guess not." She paused. "Tyler," she said.

"I'm still here."

"What's the first thing you remember?"

"What do you mean—today?"

"No. The first thing you can remember in your life. I know it's a stupid question, but I think I'll be okay if we can just talk about something else besides the sky for five or ten minutes."

"The first thing I remember?" I gave it some thought. "That would be back in L.A., before we moved east." When my father was still alive and still working for E. D. Lawton at their startup firm in Sacramento. "We had this apartment with big white curtains in the bedroom. The first thing I really remember is watching those curtains blow in the wind. It was a sunny day and the window was open and there was a breeze." The memory was unexpectedly poignant, like the last sight of a receding shoreline. "What about you?"

The first thing Diane could remember was also a Sacramento moment, though it was a very different one. E.D. had taken both children on a tour of the plant, even then positioning Jason for his role as heir apparent. Diane had been fascinated by the huge perforated spars on the factory floor, the spools of microthin aluminum fabric as big as houses, the constant noise. Everything had been so large that she had half expected to find a fairy-tale giant chained to the walls, her father's prisoner.

It wasn't a good memory. She said she felt left out, almost lost, abandoned inside a huge and terrifying machinery of construction.

We talked that around for a while. Then Diane said, "Check out the sky."

I looked at the window. There was enough light spilling over the western horizon to turn the blackness an inky blue.

I didn't want to confess to the relief I felt.

"I guess you were right," she said, suddenly buoyant. "The sun's coming up after all."

Of course, it wasn't really the sun. It was an impostor sun, a clever fabrication. But we didn't know that yet.

COMING OF AGE IN BOILING WATER

People younger than me have asked me: Why didn't you panic? Why didn't *anyone* panic? Why was there no looting, no rioting? Why did your generation acquiesce, why did you all slide into the Spin without even a murmur of protest?

Sometimes I say, *But terrible things did happen.*

Sometimes I say, *But we didn't understand. And what could we have done about it?*

And sometimes I cite the parable of the frog. Drop a frog into boiling water, he'll jump out. Drop a frog into a pot of pleasantly warm water, stoke the fire slowly, and the frog will be dead before he knows there's a problem.

The obliteration of the stars wasn't slow or subtle, but neither, for most of us, was it immediately disastrous. If you were an astronomer or a defense strategist, if you worked in telecommunications or aerospace, you probably spent the first few days of the Spin in a state of abject terror. But if you drove a bus or flipped burgers, it was all more or less warm water.

English-language media called it "the October Event" (it wasn't "the Spin" until a few years later), and its first and most obvious effect was the wholesale destruction of the multibillion-dollar orbital satellite industry. Losing satellites meant losing most relayed and all direct-broadcast satellite television; it rendered the long-distance telephone system unreliable and GPS locators useless; it gutted the World Wide Web, made obsolete much of the most sophisticated modern military technology, curtailed global surveillance and reconnaissance, and forced local weathermen to draw isobars on maps of the continental United States rather than glide through CGI images rendered from weathersats. Repeated attempts to contact the International Space Station were uniformly unsuccessful. Commercial launches scheduled at Canaveral (and Baikonur and Kourou) were postponed indefinitely.

It meant, in the long run, very bad news for GE Americom, AT&T, COMSAT, and Hughes Communications, among many others.

And many terrible things *did* happen as a consequence of that night, though most of them were obscured by media blackouts. News stories traveled like whispers, squeezed through transatlantic fiber-optic cables rather than ricocheted through orbital space: it was almost a week before we learned that a Pakistani Hatf V missile tipped with a nuclear warhead, launched by mistake or miscalculation in the confusing first moments of the Event, had strayed off course and vaporized an agricultural valley in the Hindu Kush. It was the first nuclear device detonated in war since 1945, and, tragic as that event was, given the global paranoia ignited by the loss of telecommunications, we were lucky it only happened once. According to some reports we nearly lost Tehran, Tel Aviv, and Pyongyang.

○ ○ ○

Reassured by sunrise, I slept from dawn to noon. When I got up and dressed I found my mother in the living room, still in her quilted robe, staring into the television screen and frowning. When I asked her if she'd eaten breakfast she said she hadn't. So I fixed lunch for both of us.

She would have been forty-five years old that fall. If I had been asked to choose a word to describe her it might have been "solid." She was rarely angry and the only time in my life I had ever seen her cry was the night the police came to the door (this was back in Sacramento) and told her my father had died on the 80 near Vacaville, driving home from a business trip. She was, I think, careful to show me only this aspect of herself. But there were others. There was a portrait on a shelf in the étagère in the living room, taken years before I was born, of a woman so sleek, beautiful, and fearless before the camera that I had been startled when she told me it was a photo of herself.

Clearly she didn't like what she was hearing from TV. A local station was doing nonstop news, repeating shortwave and ham radio stories and fuzzy stay-calm statements issued by the federal government. "Tyler," she said, waving me to sit down, "this is hard to explain. Something happened last night—"

"I know," I said. "I heard about it before I went to bed."

"You knew about this? And you didn't wake me up?"

"I wasn't sure—"

But her annoyance waned as quickly as it had come. "No," she said, "it's all right, Ty. I guess I didn't miss anything by sleeping. It's funny . . . I feel like I'm *still* asleep."

"It's just the stars," I said, idiotically.

"The stars and the moon," she corrected me. "Didn't you hear about the moon? All over the world, nobody can see the stars and nobody can see the moon."

○ ○ ○

The moon was a clue, of course.

I sat awhile with my mom, then left her still fixed in front of the TV ("Back before dark this time," she said, meaning it) and walked to the Big House. I knocked at the back door, the door the cook and the day maid used, though the Lawtons were careful never to call it a "servant's entrance." It was also the door by which, on weekdays, my mother entered to conduct the Lawtons' household business.

Mrs. Lawton, the twins' mother, let me in, looked at me

blankly, waved me upstairs. Diane was still asleep, the door of her room closed. Jason hadn't slept at all and apparently wasn't planning to. I found him in his room monitoring a short-wave radio.

Jason's room was an Aladdin's cave of luxuries I coveted but had given up expecting ever to own: a computer with an ultrafast ISP connection, a hand-me-down television twice as big as the one that graced the living room at my house. In case he hadn't heard the news: "The moon is gone," I told him.

"Interesting, isn't it?" Jase stood and stretched, running his fingers through his uncombed hair. He hadn't changed his clothes since last night. This was uncharacteristic absent-mindedness. Jason, although certifiably a genius, had never acted like one in my presence—that is to say, he didn't act like the geniuses I had seen in movies; he didn't squint, stammer, or write algebraic equations on walls. Today, though, he did seem massively distracted. "The moon's *not* gone, of course—how could it be? According to the radio they're measuring the usual tides on the Atlantic coast. So the moon's still there. And if the moon's still there, so are the stars."

"So why can't we see them?"

He gave me an annoyed look. "How should I know? All I'm saying is, it's at least partly an *optical* phenomenon."

"Look out the window, Jase. The sun's shining. What kind of optical illusion lets the sunshine through but hides the stars and the moon?"

"Again, how should I know? But what's the alternative, Tyler? Somebody put the moon and the stars in a sack and ran away with them?"

No, I thought. It was the Earth that was in the sack, for some reason not even Jason could divine.

"Good point, though," he said, "about the sun. Not an optical barrier but an optical *filter*. Interesting . . ."

"So who put it there?"

"How should I—?" He shook his head irritably. "You're inferring too much. Who says *anybody* put it there? It could be a once-in-a-billion-years natural event, like the magnetic poles reversing. It's a big jump to assume there's some controlling intelligence behind it."

"But it could be true."

"Lots of things could be true."

I had taken enough gentle ribbing about my science-fiction reading that I was reluctant to say the word "aliens." But of course it was the first thing that occurred to me. Me, and plenty of other people. And even Jason had to admit that the idea of intervening extraterrestrials had become infinitely more plausible over the course of the last twenty-four hours.

"But even so," I said, "you have to wonder why they'd do it."

"There are only two plausible reasons. To *hide* something from us. Or to hide *us* from *something*."

"What does your father think?"

"I haven't asked him. He's been on the phone all day. Probably trying to put in an early sell order on his GTE stock." This was a joke, and I wasn't sure what he meant by it, but it was also my first hint of what the loss of orbital access might mean for the aerospace industry in general and the Lawton family in particular. "I didn't sleep last night," Jase admitted. "Afraid I might miss something. Sometimes I envy my sister. You know, *wake me when somebody figures it out*."

I bristled at this perceived slight of Diane. "She didn't sleep either," I said.

"Oh? Really? And how would *you* know?"

Trapped. "We talked on the phone a little bit. . . ."

"She called you?"

"Yeah, around dawn."

"Jesus, Tyler, you're blushing."

"No I'm not."

"Yes you are."

I was saved by a brusque knock at the door: E. D. Lawton, who looked like he hadn't slept much either.

Jason's father was an intimidating presence. He was big, broad shouldered, hard to please, easily angered; on weekends he moved through the house like a storm front, all lightning and thunder. My mother had once said, "E.D.'s not the kind of person you really want attention from. I never did understand why Carol married him."

He wasn't exactly the classic self-made businessman—his grandfather, retired founder of a spectacularly successful San

Francisco law firm, had bankrolled most of E.D.'s early ventures—but he had built himself a lucrative business in high-altitude instrumentation and lighter-than-air technology, and he had done it the hard way, without any real industry connections, at least when he started out.

He entered Jason's room scowling. His eyes lit on me and flashed away. "Sorry, Tyler, but you'll have to go home now. I need to discuss a few things with Jason."

Jase didn't object and I wasn't especially eager to stay. So I shrugged into my cloth jacket and left by the back door. I spent the rest of the afternoon by the creek, skipping stones and watching squirrels forage against the coming winter.

o o o

The sun, the moon, and the stars.

In the years that followed, children were raised who had never seen the moon with their own eyes; people only five or six years younger than myself passed into maturity knowing the stars mainly from old movies and a handful of increasingly inapt clichés. Once, in my thirties, I played the twentieth-century Antonio Carlos Jobin song *Corcovado*—"Quiet nights of quiet stars"—for a younger woman, who asked me, eyes earnestly wide, "Were the stars *noisy*?"

But we had lost something more subtle than a few lights in the sky. We had lost a reliable sense of place. The Earth is round, the moon circles the Earth, the Earth circles the sun: that was as much cosmology as most people owned or wanted, and I doubt one in a hundred thought more about it after high school. But they were baffled when it was stolen from them.

We didn't get an official announcement about the sun until the second week of the October Event.

The sun appeared to move in its predictable and eternal manner. It rose and set according to the standard ephemeris, the days grew shorter in their natural precession; there was nothing to suggest a solar emergency. Much on Earth, including life itself, depends on the nature and amount of solar radiation reaching the planet's surface, and in most respects that hadn't changed. Everything about the sun we could see with the naked eye suggested the same yellow class-G star we'd been blinking at all our liyes.

What it lacked, however, were sunspots, prominences, or flares.

The sun is a violent, turbulent object. It seethes, it boils, it rings like a bell with vast energies; it bathes the solar system in a stream of charged particles that would kill us if we weren't protected from it by the Earth's magnetic field. But since the October Event, astronomers announced, the sun had become a geometrically perfect orb of unwaveringly uniform and unblemished brightness. And news came from the north that the aurora borealis, product of the interaction of our magnetic field with all those charged solar particles, had shut down like a bad Broadway play.

Other lapses in the new night sky: no shooting stars. The Earth used to accrete eighty million pounds of spaceborne dust annually, the vast majority of it incinerated by atmospheric friction. But no more: no detectable meteorites entered the atmosphere during the first weeks of the October Event, not even the microscopic ones called Brownlee particles. It was, in astrophysical terms, a deafening silence.

Not even Jason could offer an explanation for that.

o o o

So the sun wasn't the sun; but it went on shining, counterfeit or not, and as the days passed, days layered and stacked on days, the bewilderment deepened but the sense of public urgency ebbed. (The water wasn't boiling, it was only warm.)

But what a rich source of *talk* it all was. Not just the celestial mystery but the immediate consequences of it: the telecom crash; the foreign wars no longer monitored and narrated by satellite; the GPS-guided smart bombs rendered irremediably stupid; the fiber-optic goldrush. Pronouncements were issued with depressing regularity from Washington: *We have as yet no evidence of hostile intent on the part of any nation or agency* and *The best minds of our generation are working to understand, explain, and ultimately reverse the potential negative effects of this shroud that has obscured our view of the universe*. Soothing word salad from an administration still hoping to identify an enemy, terrestrial or otherwise, capable of such an act. But the enemy was stubbornly elusive. People began to speak of "a hypothetical controlling intelligence." Unable to see past the walls of our prison, we were reduced to mapping its edges and corners.

Jason retreated to his room for most of a month after the Event. During this time I didn't speak to him directly, only caught glimpses of him when the twins were picked up by the Rice Academy minibus. But Diane called me on my cell almost every evening, usually around ten or eleven, when we could both count on a little privacy. And I treasured her calls, for reasons I wasn't quite ready to admit to myself.

"Jason's in a pissy mood," she told me one night. "He says if we don't know for sure if the sun is the sun, we don't really know anything at all."

"Maybe he's right."

"But it's almost a religious thing for Jase. He's always loved maps—did you know that, Tyler? Even when he was very little, he got the idea of how a map worked. He liked to know where he was. It makes sense of things, he used to say. God, I used to love to listen to him talk about maps. I think that's why he's so freaked now, even more than most people. Nothing's where it's supposed to be. He lost his map."

Of course, there were already clues in place. Before the week was out the military had begun to collect debris from fallen satellites—satellites that had been in stable orbits until that night in October but had plunged back to Earth before dawn, one and all, some leaving wreckage that was invested with tantalizing evidence. But it took time for that information to reach even the well-connected household of E. D. Lawton.

○ ○ ○

Our first winter of dark nights was claustrophobic and strange. Snow came early: we lived within commuting distance of Washington, D.C., but by Christmas it looked more like Vermont. The news remained ominous. A fragile, hastily brokered peace treaty between India and Pakistan teetered toward war and back again; the U.N.-sponsored decontamination project in the Hindu Kush had already cost dozens of lives in addition to the original casualties. In northern Africa, brushfire wars smoldered while the armies of the industrial world withdrew to regroup. Oil prices skyrocketed. At home, we kept the thermostat a couple of degrees under comfortable until the days began to grow longer (when the sun came back and the first quail called).

But in the face of unknown and poorly understood threats the human race managed not to trigger a full-blown global war, to our credit. We made our adjustments and got on with business, and by spring people were talking about "the new normal." In the long run, it was understood, we might have to pay a higher price for whatever had happened to the planet . . . but in the long run, as they say, we're all dead.

I saw the change in my mother. The passage of time calmed her and the warm weather, when it finally came, drew some of the tension from her face. And I saw the change in Jason, who came out of his meditative retreat. I worried, though, about Diane, who refused to talk about the stars at all and had lately begun to ask whether I believed in God— whether I thought God was responsible for what had happened in October.

I wouldn't know about that, I told her. My family weren't churchgoers. The subject made me a little nervous, frankly.

o o o

That summer the three of us rode our bikes to the Fairway Mall for the last time.

We had made the trip a hundred, a thousand times before. The twins were already getting a little old for it, but in the seven years we had all lived on the property of the Big House it had become a ritual, the summer-Saturday inevitable. We skipped it on rainy or swelteringly hot weekends, but when the weather was fine we were drawn as if by an invisible hand to our meeting point at the end of the long Lawton driveway.

Today the air was gentle and breezy and the sunlight infused everything it touched with a deep organic warmth. It was as if the climate wanted to reassure us: the natural world was doing all right, thank you, almost ten months after the Event . . . even if we were (as Jase occasionally said) a *cultivated* planet now, a garden tended by unknown forces rather than a patch of cosmic wildwood.

Jason rode an expensive mountain bike, Diane a less flashy girls' equivalent. My bike was a secondhand junker my mother had bought for me at a thrift shop. No matter. What was important was the piney tang of the air and the empty hours arrayed before of us. I felt it, Diane felt it, and I think Jason felt it, too, though he seemed distracted and even a little embarrassed when we saddled up that morning. I put it down to stress or (this was August) the prospect of another school year. Jase was in an accelerated academic stream at Rice, a high-pressure school. Last year he had breezed through the math and physics courses—he could have taught them—but next semester he was signed up for a Latin credit. "It's not even a living language," he said. "Who the hell reads Latin, outside classical scholars? It's like learning FORTRAN. All the important texts were translated a long time ago. Does it make me a better person to read Cicero in the original? Cicero, for god's sake? The Alan Dershowitz of the Roman Republic?"

I didn't take any of this too seriously. One of the things we liked to do on these rides was practice the art of complaining. (I had no idea who Alan Dershowitz was; some kid at Jason's school, I guessed.) But today his mood was volatile, erratic. He stood up on his pedals and biked a little way ahead of us.

The road to the mall wound past deeply treed lots and pastel houses with manicured gardens and embedded sprinklers that marked the morning air with rainbows. The sunlight might be fake, filtered, but it still broke into colors when it cut through falling water and it still felt like a blessing when we rolled from under the shading oaks onto the glittering white sidewalk.

Ten or fifteen minutes of easy riding later the top of Bantam Hill Road loomed ahead of us—last obstacle and major landmark on the way to the mall. Bantam Hill Road was steep, but on the other side it was a sweet long glide to the mall's parking lot. Jase was already a quarter of the way up. Diane gave me a mischievous look.

"Race you," she said.

That was dismaying. The twins had their birthdays in June. Mine was in October. Every summer they were not one but *two* years older than me: the twins had turned fourteen but I was still twelve for another frustrating four months. The difference translated into a physical advantage. Diane must have known I couldn't beat her up the hill, but she pedaled off anyway and I sighed and tried to pump my creaking old junker into plausible competition. It was no contest. Diane rose up on her gleaming contrivance of etched aluminum, and by the time she reached the upslope she had gained a ferocious momentum. A trio of little girls chalk-marking the sidewalk scurried out of her way. She shot a glance back at me, half encouraging, half taunting.

The rising road stole back her momentum, but she shifted gears deftly and put her legs to work again. Jason, at the peak, had stopped and balanced himself with one long leg, looking back quizzically. I labored on, but halfway up the hill my ancient bike was swaying more than moving and I was forced to sidle off and walk it the rest of the way up.

Diane grinned at me when I finally arrived.

"You win," I said.

"Sorry, Tyler. It wasn't really fair."

I shrugged, embarrassed.

Here the road ended in a cul-de-sac, where residential lots had been sketched with stakes and string but no houses built. The mall lay down a long, sandy decline to the west. A pressed-earth path cut through scrubby trees and berry bushes. "See you at the bottom," she said, and rolled away again.

o o o

We left our bikes locked to a rack and entered the glassy nave of the mall. The mall was a reassuring environment, chiefly because it had changed so little since last October. The newspapers and television might still be in high-alert mode, but the mall lived in blessed denial. The only evidence that anything might have gone askew in the larger world was the absence of satellite dish displays at the consumer-electronics chain stores and a surge of October-related titles on the book-store display racks. Jason snorted at one paperback with a high-gloss blue-and-gold cover, a book that claimed to link the October Event to Biblical prophecy: "The easiest kind of prophecy," he said, "is the kind that predicts things that have already happened."

Diane gave him an aggravated look. "You don't have to make fun of it just because you don't believe in it."

"Technically, I'm only making fun of the front cover. I haven't read the book."

"Maybe you should."

"Why? What are you defending here?"

"I'm not defending anything. But maybe God had some-thing to do with last October. That doesn't seem so ridiculous."

"Actually," Jason said, "yes, it *does* seem ridiculous."

She rolled her eyes and stalked ahead of us, sighing to her-self. Jase stuffed the book back in its display rack.

I told him I thought people just wanted to understand what had happened, that's why there were books like that.

"Or maybe people just want to pretend to understand. It's called 'denial.' You want to know something, Tyler?"

"Sure," I said.

"Keep it secret?" He lowered his voice so that even Diane, a few yards ahead, couldn't hear him. "This isn't public yet."

One of the remarkable things about Jason was that he often did know genuinely important things a day or two in advance of the evening news. In a sense Rice Academy was only his day school; his real education was conducted under the tute-lage of his father, and from the beginning E.D. had wanted him to understand how business, science, and technology in-tersect with political power. E.D. had been working those an-gles himself. The loss of telecom satellites had opened up a vast new civilian and military market for the stationary high-altitude balloons ("aerostats") his company manufactured. A niche technology was going mainstream, and E.D. was riding the crest of the wave. And sometimes he shared secrets with his fifteen-year-old son he wouldn't have dared whisper to a competitor.

E.D., of course, didn't know Jase occasionally shared

these secrets with me. But I was scrupulous about keeping them. (And anyway, who would I have told? I had no other real friends. We lived in the kind of new-money neighborhood where class distinctions were measured out with razor-sharp precision: the solemn, studious sons of single working mothers didn't make anyone's A list.)

He lowered his voice another notch. "You know the three Russian cosmonauts? The ones who were in orbit last October?"

Lost and presumed dead the night of the Event. I nodded.

"One of them's alive," he said. "Alive and in Moscow. The Russians aren't saying much. But the rumor is, he's completely crazy."

I gave him a wide-eyed look, but he wouldn't say anything more.

o o o

It took a dozen years for the truth to be made public, but when it was finally published (as a footnote to a European history of the early Spin years) I thought of the day at the mall. What happened was this:

Three Russian cosmonauts had been in orbit the night of the October Event, returning from a housekeeping mission to the moribund International Space Station. A little after midnight Eastern Standard Time the mission commander, a Colonel Leonid Glavin, noted loss of signal from ground control and made repeated but unsuccessful efforts to reestablish contact.

Alarming as this must have been for the cosmonauts, it got worse fast. When the Soyuz crossed from the nightside of the planet into dawn it appeared that the planet they were circling had been replaced with a lightless black orb.

Colonel Glavin would eventually describe it just that way: as a blackness, an absence visible only when it occluded the sun, a permanent eclipse. The rapid orbital cycle of sunrise and sunset was their only convincing visual evidence that the Earth even existed any longer. Sunlight appeared abruptly from behind the silhouetted disc, cast no reflection in the darkness below, and vanished just as suddenly when the capsule slid into night.

The cosmonauts could not have comprehended what had happened, and their terror must have been unimaginable.

After a week spent orbiting the vacuous darkness beneath them the cosmonauts voted to attempt an unassisted reentry rather than remain in space or attempt a docking at the empty ISS—to die on Earth, or whatever Earth had become, rather than starve in isolation. But without ground guidance or visual landmarks they were forced to rely on calculations extrapolated from their last known position. As a result the Soyuz capsule reentered the atmosphere at a perilously steep angle, absorbed punishing G-forces, and lost a critical parachute during the descent.

The capsule came down hard on a forested hillside in the Ruhr Valley. Vassily Golubev was killed on impact; Valentina Kirchoff suffered a traumatic head injury and was dead within hours. A dazed Colonel Glavin, with only a broken wrist and minor abrasions, managed to exit the spacecraft and was eventually discovered by a German search-and-rescue team and repatriated to Russian authorities.

After repeated debriefings the Russians concluded that Glavin had lost his mind as a result of his ordeal. The colonel continued to insist that he and his crew had spent three weeks in orbit, but that was obviously madness. . . .

Because the Soyuz capsule, like every other recovered piece of man-made orbital gear, had fallen back to Earth the very night of the October Event.

o o o

We ate lunch at the food court in the mall, where Diane spotted three girls she knew from Rice. These were older girls, to my eyes impossibly sophisticated, hair tinted blue or pink, wearing expensive bell-bottoms that rode low on their hips and tiny gold crosses on chains around their pale necks. Diane balled up her MexiTaco wrapper and defected to their table, where the four of them ducked their heads together and laughed. Suddenly my burrito and fries looked unappetizing.

Jason evaluated the look on my face. "You know," he said gently, "this is inevitable."

"What is?"

"She doesn't live in our world anymore. You, me, Diane, the Big House and the Little House, Saturday at the mall, Sunday at the movies. That worked when we were kids. But we're not kids anymore."

Weren't we? No, of course we weren't; but had I really considered what that meant or might mean?

"She's been getting her period for a year now," Jason added.

I blanched. This was more than I needed to know. And yet: I was jealous that he had known it and I had not. She hadn't told me about her period or her friends at Rice, either. All the confidences she had offered over the phone, I suddenly understood, had been kid confidences, stories about Jason and her parents and what she had hated at dinner. But here was evidence that she had hidden as much as she had shared; here was a Diane I had never met, blithely manifesting at a table across the aisle.

"We should go home," I told Jason.

He gave me a pitying look. "If you want to." He stood up.

"Are you going to tell Diane we're leaving?"

"I think she's busy, Tyler. I think she found something to do."

"But she has to come back with us."

"No she doesn't."

I took offense. She wouldn't just dump us. She was better than that. I stood and walked to Diane's table. Diane and her three friends gave me their full attention. I looked straight at Diane, ignoring the others. "We're going home," I said.

The three Rice girls laughed out loud. Diane just smiled embarrassedly and said, "Okay, Ty. That's great. See you later."

"But—"

But what? She wasn't even looking at me anymore.

As I walked away I heard one of her friends ask whether I was "another brother." No, she said. Just a kid she knew.

o o o

Jason, who had become annoyingly sympathetic, offered to trade bikes on the ride home. I didn't really care about his bike at that point, but I thought a bike trade might be a way to disguise what I was feeling.

So we worked our way back to the top of Bantam Hill Road, to the place where the pavement stretched like a black ribbon down into tree-shaded streets. Lunch felt like a cinder block embedded under my ribs. I hesitated at the end of the cul-de-sac, eyeballing the steep incline of the road.

"Glide on down," Jason said. "Go ahead. Get the feel of it."

Would speed distract me? Would anything? I hated myself for having allowed myself to believe I was at the center of Diane's world. When I was, in fact, a kid she knew.

But it really was a wonderful bike Jason had lent me. I stood on the pedals, daring gravity to do its worst. The tires gritted on the dusty pavement but the chains and derailleurs were silky, silent except for the delicate whir of the bearings. Wind sluiced past me as I picked up speed. I flew past primly painted houses with expensive cars parked in their driveways, bereft but free. Near the bottom I began to squeeze the hand brakes, bleeding momentum without really slowing down. I didn't want to stop. I wanted never to stop. It was a good ride.

But the pavement leveled, and at last I braked and keeled and came to rest with my left shoe on the asphalt. I looked back.

Jason was still at the top of Bantam Hill Road with my own clunky bike under him, so far away now that he looked like a lone horseman in an old western. I waved. It was his turn.

Jason must have taken that hill, upslope and down, a thousand times. But he had never taken it on a rusty thrift-shop bike.

He fit the bicycle better than I did. His legs were longer than mine and the frame didn't dwarf him. But we had never traded bikes before, and now I thought of all the bugs and idiosyncrasies that bike possessed, and how intimately I knew it, how I had learned not to turn hard right because the frame was a little out of true, how you had to fight the wobble, how the gearbox was a joke. Jason didn't know any of that. The hill could be tricky. I wanted to tell him to take it slow, but even if I had shouted he wouldn't have heard me; I had zoomed too far ahead. He lifted his feet like a big gawky infant. The bike was heavy. It took a few seconds to gather speed, but I knew how hard it would be to stop. It was all mass, no grace. My hands gripped imaginary brakes.

I don't think Jason knew he had a problem until he was three quarters of the way down. That was when the bicycle's rust-choked chain snapped and flailed his ankle. He was close enough now that I could see him flinch and cry out. The bike wobbled but, miraculously, he managed to keep it upright.

A piece of the chain tangled in the rear wheel, where it whipped against the struts, making a sound like a broken jackhammer. Two houses up, a woman who had been weeding her garden covered her ears and turned to watch.

What was amazing was how long Jason managed to keep control of that bike. Jase was no athlete, but he was at home in his big, lanky body. He stuck his feet out for balance—the pedals were useless—and kept the front wheel forward while the back wheel locked and skidded. He held on. What astonished me was the way his body didn't stiffen but seemed to relax, as if he were engaged in some difficult but engaging act of problem-solving, as if he believed with absolute confidence that the combination of his mind, his body, and the machine he was riding could be counted on to carry him to safety.

It was the machine that failed first. That dangerously flapping fragment of greasy chain wedged itself between the tire and the frame. The wheel, already weakened, bent impossibly out of true and then folded, scattering torn rubber and liberated ball bearings. Jason came free of the bike and tumbled through the air like a mannequin dropped from a high window. His feet hit the pavement first, then his knees, his elbows, his head. He came to a stop as the fractured bike rotated past him. It landed in the gutter at the side of the road, the front tire still spinning and clattering. I dropped his bike and ran to him.

He rolled over and looked up, momentarily bewildered. His pants and shirt were torn. His forehead and the tip of his nose had been brutally skinned and were bleeding freely. His ankle was lacerated. His eyes watered from the pain. "Tyler," he said. "Oh, uh, uh . . . sorry about your bike, man."

Not to make too much of this incident, but I thought of it

occasionally in the years that followed—Jason's machine and Jason's body locked into a dangerous acceleration, and his unflappable belief that he could make it come out right, all by himself, if only he tried hard enough, if only he didn't lose control.

○ ○ ○

We left the hopelessly broken bicycle in the gutter and I walked Jason's high-end wheels home for him. He trudged beside me, hurting but trying not to show it, holding his right hand over his oozing forehead as if he had a bad headache, which I guessed he did.

Back at the Big House, both Jason's parents came down the porch steps to meet us in the driveway. E. D. Lawton, who must have spotted us from his study, looked angry and alarmed, his mouth puckered into a frown and his eyebrows crowding his sharp eyes. Jason's mom, behind him, was aloof, less interested, maybe even a little drunk by the way she swayed when she walked out the door.

E.D. examined Jase—who suddenly seemed much younger and less sure of himself—then told him to run in the house and clean up.

Then he turned to me.

"Tyler," he said.

"Sir?"

"I'm assuming you're not responsible for this. I hope that's true."

Had he noticed that my own bike was missing and that Jason's was unscathed? Was he accusing me of something? I didn't know what to say. I looked at the lawn.

E.D. sighed. "Let me explain something. You're Jason's friend. That's good. Jason needs that. But you have to understand, as your mother understands, that your presence here comes with certain responsibilities. If you want to spend time with Jason, I expect you to look out for him. I expect you to exercise your judgment. Maybe he seems ordinary to you. But he's not. Jason's gifted, and he has a future ahead of him. We can't let anything interfere with that."

"Right," Carol Lawton chimed in, and now I knew for a

fact that Jason's mom had been drinking. She tilted her head and almost stumbled into the gravel berm that separated the driveway from the hedge. "Right, he's a fucking genius. He's going to be the youngest genius at M.I.T. Don't break him, Tyler, he's fragile."

E.D. didn't take his eyes off me. "Go inside, Carol," he said tonelessly. "Do we understand each other, Tyler?"

"Yessir," I lied.

I didn't understand E.D. at all. But I knew some of what he had said was true. Yes, Jason was special. And yes, it was my job to look after him.

TIME OUT OF JOINT

I first heard the truth about the Spin, five years after the October Event, at a sledding party, on a bitterly cold winter night. It was Jason, typically, who broke the news.

The evening began with dinner at the Lawtons'. Jason was home from university for Christmas break, so there was a sense of occasion about the meal even though it was "just family"—I had been invited at Jase's insistence, probably over E.D.'s objections.

"Your mother should be here, too," Diane whispered when she opened the door for me. "I tried to get E.D. to invite her, but . . ." She shrugged.

That was okay, I told her; Jason had already stopped by to say hello. "Anyway, she's not feeling well." She was in bed with a headache, unusually. And I was hardly in a position to complain about E.D.'s behavior: just last month E.D. had offered to underwrite my med school tuition if I passed the MCAT, "because," he said, "your father would have liked that." It was a gesture both generous and emotionally false, but it was also a gesture I couldn't afford to refuse.

Marcus Dupree, my father, had been E. D. Lawton's closest (some said only) friend back in Sacramento, back when they were pushing aerostat monitoring devices to the weather bureau and the Border Patrol. My own memories of him were sketchy and had morphed into my mother's stories about him, though I did distinctly remember the knock at the door the night he died. He had been the only son of a struggling French-Canadian family in Maine, proud of his engineering degree, talented, but naive about money: he had lost his savings in a series of stock market gambles, leaving my mother with a mortgage she couldn't carry.

Carol and E.D. hired my mother as a housekeeper when they moved east, in what might have been E.D.'s attempt at a living memorial for his friend. Did it matter that E.D. never let her forget he'd done her this favor? That he treated her thenceforth as a household accessory? That he maintained a sort of caste system in which the Dupree family was conspicuously second class? Maybe, maybe not. Generosity of any kind is a rare animal, my mother used to say. So maybe I was imagining (or too sensitive to) the pleasure he seemed to take in the intellectual gap between Jason and myself, his apparent conviction that I was born to be Jason's foil, a conventionally normal yardstick against which Jason's specialness could be gauged.

Fortunately both Jase and I knew this was bullshit.

Diane and Carol were at the table when I sat down. Carol was sober tonight, remarkably, or at least not so drunk that it showed. She had given up her medical practice a couple of years back and these days tended to stick around the house in order to avoid the risk of DWI charges. She smiled at me perfunctorily. "Tyler," she said. "Welcome."

After a few minutes Jason and his father came downstairs together, exchanging glances and frowning: obviously something was up. Jase nodded distractedly when he took the chair next to mine.

Like most Lawton family occasions, dinner was cordial but strained. We passed the peas and made small talk. Carol was remote, E.D. was uncharacteristically quiet. Diane and Jason took stabs at conversation, but clearly something had

passed between Jason and his father that neither wanted to
discuss. Jase seemed so restrained that by dessert I wondered
whether he was physically ill—his eyes seldom left his plate,
which he had barely touched. When it was time to leave for
the sledding party he stood up with obvious reluctance and
seemed about to beg off until E. D. Lawton said, "Go ahead,
take a night off. It'll be good for you." And I wondered: a
night off from *what*?

We drove to the party in Diane's car, an unassuming little
Honda, "a my-first-car kind of car," as Diane liked to describe it. I sat behind the driver's seat; Jase rode in the passenger seat next to his sister, his knees crowding the glove
compartment, still glum.

"What'd he do," Diane asked, "spank you?"

"Hardly."

"You're acting like it."

"Am I? Sorry."

The sky, of course, was dark. Our headlights swept past
snowy lawns, a wall of leafless trees as we turned north. We'd
had a record snowfall three days ago, followed by a cold snap
that had embalmed the snow under a skin of ice wherever the
plows hadn't been. A few cars passed us at a cautious speed.

"So what was it," Diane asked, "something serious?"

Jason shrugged.

"War? Pestilence? Famine?"

He shrugged again and turned up the collar of his jacket.

o o o

He wasn't much better at the party. Then again, it wasn't
much of a party.

It was a gathering of Jason and Diane's ex-classmates and
acquaintances from Rice, hosted by the family of another
Rice alumnus home from some Ivy League college. His parents had tried to arrange a dignified theme event: finger sandwiches, hot cocoa, and sledding on the mild slope behind the
house. But for the majority of the guests—somber preppies
who had skied at Zermatt or Gstaad long before their braces
came off—it was just another excuse for clandestine drinking. Outside, under strings of colored lights, silver flasks cir-

culated freely; in the basement a guy named Brent was sell-ing gram weights of Ecstasy.

Jason found a chair in a corner and sat scowling at anyone who looked friendly. Diane introduced me to a big-eyed girl named Holly and then deserted me. Holly struck up a mono-logue about every movie she had seen in the last twelve months. She paced me around the room for most of an hour, pausing now and then to snatch California rolls from a tray. When she excused herself for a bathroom visit I scooted over to Jason's sulking place and begged him to go outside with me.

"I'm not in the mood for sledding."

"Neither am I. Just do me a favor, okay?"

So we put on our boots and jackets and trudged outside. The night was cold and windless. A half dozen Rice scholars stood huddled in a haze of cigarette smoke on the porch, glaring at us. We followed a path in the snow until we were more or less by ourselves at the top of a low hill, looking down on a few halfhearted sledders skidding through the cir-cus glow of the Christmas lights. I told Jason about Holly, who had attached herself to me like a leech in Gap clothing. He shrugged and said, "Everybody's got problems."

"What the hell is wrong with you tonight?"

But before he could answer, my cell phone rang. It was Di-ane, back at the house. "Where'd you guys go? Holly's kind of pissed. Abandoning her like that. Very rude, Tyler."

"There must be someone else she can aim her conversa-tion at."

"She's just nervous. She hardly knows anyone here."

"I'm sorry, but how is that my business?"

"I just thought you guys might hit it off."

I blinked. "Hit it off?" There was no good way to interpret that. "What are you saying, you set me up with her?"

She paused for an incriminating second or two. "Come on, Tyler . . . don't take it like that."

For five years Diane had been coming in and out of focus like an amateur movie, or so it seemed to me. There had been times, especially after Jason left for university, when I had felt like her best friend. She'd call, we'd talk; we shopped or saw movies together. We were friends. Buddies. If there was any sexual tension it appeared to be entirely on my side, and I was careful to keep it hidden, because even this partial intimacy was fragile—I knew that without having to be told. Whatever Diane wanted from me, it didn't include passion of any kind.

E.D., of course, would never have tolerated a relationship between me and Diane unless it was chaperoned, essentially infantile, and in no danger of taking an unexpected turn. But the distance between us seemed to suit Diane, too, and for months at a time I would hardly see her. I might wave at her while she waited for the Rice bus (when she was still at Rice); but during those lapses she wouldn't call, and on the rare occasions when I was brazen enough to phone her she was never in a mood to talk.

During these times I occasionally dated girls from school, usually timid girls who would (often explicitly) have preferred seeing a more conspicuously popular guy but who had resigned themselves to a second-string social life. None of these connections lasted long. When I was seventeen I lost my virginity to a pretty, startlingly tall girl named Elaine Bowland; I tried to convince myself I was in love with her, but we drifted apart with a combination of regret and relief after eight or nine weeks.

After each of these episodes Diane would call unexpectedly, and we'd talk, and I wouldn't mention Elaine Bowland (or Toni Hickock, or Sarah Burstein), and Diane would never quite get around to telling me how she'd spent her spare time during our hiatus, and that was okay because pretty soon we were back in the bubble, suspended between romance and pretense, childhood and maturity.

I tried not to expect more. But I couldn't stop wanting her company. And I thought she wanted mine. She kept coming back for it, after all. I had seen the way she relaxed when I was with her, her spontaneous smile when I came into a room, almost a declaration: *Oh, good, Tyler's here. Nothing bad ever happens when Tyler's here.*

"Tyler?"

I wondered what she'd said to Holly. *Tyler's really nice,*

*but he's been dogging my heels for years now . . . you two
would be great together!*

"Tyler?" She sounded distressed. "Tyler, if you don't want
to talk—"

"Actually I don't think I do."

"Then put Jason on, would you please?"

I gave him the cell. Jason listened for a moment. Then he
said, "We're up the hill. No. No. Why don't you come out
here? It's not as cold as all that. No."

I didn't want to see her. I started to walk away. Jason
tossed me the phone and said, "Don't be an asshole, Tyler. I
need to talk to you and Diane both."

"About what?"

"About the future."

It was an annoyingly cryptic remark. "Maybe you're not
cold, but I am." Freezing.

"This is more important than whatever problem you're
having with my sister." He looked almost comically serious.
"And I know what she means to you."

"She doesn't mean anything to me."

"That wouldn't be true even if you were just friends."

"We *are* just friends." I had never really talked to him
about Diane; this was one of the places our conversations
weren't supposed to go. "Ask her yourself."

"You're pissed because she introduced you to this Holly
person."

"I don't want to discuss it."

"But that's just Diane being saintly. It's her new thing.
She's been reading those books."

"What books?"

"Apocalyptic theology. Usually from the best-seller shelf.
You know: C. R. Ratel, *Praying in the Dark,* the abnegation
of the worldly self. You need to watch more daytime television, Tyler. She wasn't trying to insult you. It's some kind of
gesture."

"That makes it okay?" I took a few more steps away from
him, toward the house. I started wondering how to get home
without a ride.

"Tyler," he said, and there was something in his voice that made me turn back. "Tyler. Listen. You asked what was bothering me." He sighed. "E.D. told me something about the October Event. It's not public yet. I promised I wouldn't talk about it. But I'm going to break that promise. I'm going to break it because there are only three people in the world who feel like family to me, and one of them is my father, and the other two are you and Diane. So could you possibly bear with me just for the next few minutes?"

I caught sight of Diane working her way up the slope, still struggling into her snowy white parka, one arm in, one arm out.

I looked at Jason's face, grievously unhappy in the dim holiday light from below us. That frightened me, and despite what I was feeling I agreed to hear what he had to say.

o o o

He whispered something to Diane when she reached the gazebo. She looked at him wide-eyed and stood back from both of us. Then Jason began to talk, softly, methodically, almost soothingly, delivering a nightmare as if it were a bedtime story.

He had heard all this from E.D., of course.

E.D. had done well after the October Event. When the satellites failed, Lawton Industries had stepped forward with plans for an immediate, practical replacement technology: high-altitude aerostats, sophisticated balloons designed to hover indefinitely in the stratosphere. Five years later E.D.'s aerostats were carrying telecom payloads and repeaters, doing multipoint voice and data broadcasts, doing almost anything (apart from GPS and astronomy) a conventional satellite could have done. E.D.'s power and influence had grown apace. Lately he had formed an aerospace lobby group, the Perihelion Foundation, and he had consulted for the federal government on a number of less public projects—in this case, NASA's ARV (Automated Reentry Vehicle) program.

NASA had been refining its ARV probes for a couple of years now. The initial launches had been designed as investigations of the October shield. Could it be penetrated, and could useful data be retrieved from outside?

The first attempt was almost literally a shot in the dark, a simple ARV payload atop a refurbished Lockheed Martin Atlas 2AS, flung into the absolute darkness over Vandenberg Air Force Base. It had looked like a failure almost immediately. The satellite, which had been designed to spend a week in orbit, dropped into the Atlantic Ocean off Bermuda moments after its launch. As if, Jason said, it had hit the Event boundary and bounced back.

But it *hadn't* bounced. "When they recovered it they downloaded a full week's worth of data."

"How is that possible?"

"The question isn't what's *possible* but what *happened*. What *happened* was, the payload spent seven days in orbit and came back the same night it left. We know that's what happened because it happened with every launch they tried, and they tried it repeatedly."

"*What* happened? What are you talking about, Jase? Time travel?"

"No . . . not exactly."

"Not *exactly*?"

"Just let him tell it," Diane said quietly.

There were all sorts of clues to what was really happening, Jason said. Ground-based observation seemed to suggest that the boosters actually accelerated into the barrier before they vanished, as if they had been drawn into it. But the recovered onboard data showed no such effect. The two sets of observations couldn't be reconciled. As seen from the ground, the satellites accelerated into the barrier and then dropped almost immediately back to Earth; the satellites themselves reported that they had progressed smoothly into their programmed orbits, remained there for the allotted span of time, and returned under their own power weeks or months later. (Like the Russian cosmonaut, I thought, whose story, never officially confirmed or denied, had become a sort of urban legend.) Assuming both sets of data were legitimate, there was only one explanation:

Time was passing differently outside the barrier.

Or, to turn the equation around, time on Earth was passing more slowly than in the universe at large.

"You understand what that means?" Jason demanded. "Before, it looked like we were in some kind of electromagnetic cage that was regulating the energy that reaches the surface of the Earth. And that's true. But it's really only a side effect, a small part of a much bigger picture."

"Side effect of what?"

"Of what they're calling a *temporal gradient*. You grasp the significance? For every second that passes on Earth, a whole lot more time passes outside the barrier."

"That doesn't make sense," I said immediately. "What the hell kind of physics would that involve?"

"People with a lot more experience than me are struggling with that question. But the idea of a time gradient has a certain explanatory power. If there's a time differential between us and the universe, ambient radiation reaching the surface of the Earth at any given moment—sunlight, X rays, cosmic radiation—would be speeded up proportionally. And a year's sunshine condensed into ten seconds would be instantly lethal. So the electromagnetic barrier around the Earth isn't *concealing* us, it's *protecting* us. It's screening out all that concentrated—and, I guess, blue-shifted—radiation."

"The fake sunlight," Diane said, getting it.

"Right. They gave us fake sunlight because the real thing would be deadly. Just enough of it, and appropriately distributed, to mimic the seasons, to make it possible to raise crops and drive the weather. The tides, our trajectory around the sun—mass, momentum, gravitation—*all* these things are being manipulated, not just to slow us down but to keep us alive while they do it."

"Managed," I said. "It's not an act of nature, then. It's engineering."

"I think we'd have to admit that," Jason said, "yes."

"This is being done *to* us."

"People are talking about a hypothetical controlling intelligence."

"But what's the purpose, what's it supposed to achieve?"

"I don't know. No one knows."

Diane stared at her brother across a gap of cold and motionless winter air. She hugged her parka and shivered. Not because of the temperature but because she had come to the fundamental question: "How *much* time, Jason? How *much* time is passing out there?"

Out there beyond the blankness of the sky.

Jason hesitated, visibly reluctant to answer her.

"A lot of time," he admitted.

"Just tell us," she said faintly.

"Well. There are all kinds of measures. But the last launch, what they did was bounce a calibration signal off the surface of the moon. The moon gets farther away from the Earth every year, did you know that? By some minuscule but measurable amount. If you measure that distance you have a kind of rough calendar, more accurate the more time has passed. Add that to other signifiers, like the motion of nearby stars—"

"*How much time,* Jason?"

"It's been five years and a couple of months since the October Event. Outside the barrier, that translates into a little over five hundred million years."

It was a breathtaking number.

I couldn't think of anything to say. Not a single word. I was rendered speechless. Thoughtless. At that moment there was no sound at all, nothing but the crisp emptiness of the night.

Then Diane, who had seen straight to the scary heart of the thing, said, "And how long do we have left?"

"I don't know that either. It depends. We're protected, to some degree, by the barrier, but how effective is that protection? But there are some unavoidable facts. The sun is mortal, like every other star. It burns hydrogen and it expands and gets hotter as it ages. The Earth exists in a sort of habitable zone in the solar system, and that zone is moving steadily outward. Like I said, we're protected, we're okay for the time being no matter what. But eventually the Earth will be inside the heliosphere of the sun. Swallowed up by it. Past a certain point there's simply no going back."

"How *long,* Jase?"

He gave her a pitying look. "Forty, maybe fifty years," he said. "Give or take."

4×10^9 A.D.

The pain was difficult to manage, even with the morphine Diane had purchased at ridiculous cost from a pharmacy in Padang. The fever was worse.

It wasn't continuous. It came in waves, clusters, bubbles of heat and noise bursting unexpectedly in my head. It made my body capricious, unpredictable. One night I groped for a non-existent glass of water and smashed a bedside lamp, waking the couple in the next room.

Come morning, temporarily lucid again, I couldn't remember the incident. But I saw the congealed blood on my knuckles and I overhead Diane paying off the angry concierge.

"Did I really do that?" I asked her.

"Afraid so."

She sat in a wicker chair next to the bed. She had ordered up room service, scrambled eggs and orange juice, so I guessed it was morning. The sky beyond the gauzy drapes was blue. The balcony door was open, admitting wafts of pleasantly warm air and the smell of the ocean. "I'm sorry," I said.

"You were out of your mind. I'd tell you to forget about it. Except you obviously *have*." She put a soothing hand on my forehead. "And it's not over yet, I'm afraid."

"How long—?"

"It's been a week."

"Only a week?"

"Only."

I wasn't even halfway through the ordeal.

○ ○ ○

But the lucid intervals were useful for writing.

Graphomania was one of the several side effects of the drug. Diane, when she was undergoing the same ordeal, once wrote the phrase *Am I not my brother's keeper* in hundreds of nearly identical repetitions over fourteen sheets of foolscap. My own graphomania was at least a little more coherent. I stacked up handwritten pages on the bedside table while I waited for the fever to launch a renewed offensive, rereading what I'd written in an attempt to fix it in my mind.

Diane spent the day out of the hotel. When she came back I asked her where she'd been.

"Making connections," she told me. She said she'd contacted a transit broker, a Minang man named Jala whose import-export business served as cover for his more lucrative emigration brokerage. Everybody on the docks knew Jala, she said. She was bidding for berths against a bunch of crazy-utopian kibbutzim, so it wasn't a done deal, but she was cautiously optimistic.

"Be careful," I said. "There might still be people looking for us."

"Not as far as I can tell, but . . ." She shrugged. She glanced at the notebook in my hand. "Writing again?"

"It takes my mind off the pain."

"You can hold the pen okay?"

"It's like terminal arthritis, but I can deal with it." *So far,* I thought. "The distraction is worth the discomfort."

But it wasn't just that, of course. Nor was it simply graphomania. The writing was a way to externalize what felt threatened.

"It's really very well done," Diane said.

I looked at her, horrified. "You *read* it?"

"You asked me to. You begged me to, Tyler."

"Was I delirious?"

"Apparently . . . though you seemed fairly rational at the time."

"I wasn't writing with an audience in mind." And I was shocked that I had forgotten showing it to her. How much else might already have slipped away?

"I won't look at it again, then. But what you wrote——" She cocked her head. "I'm amazed and flattered you felt so strongly about me, way back then."

"It could hardly come as a surprise."

"More than you might think. But it's a paradox, Tyler. The girl on the page is indifferent, almost cruel."

"I never thought of you that way."

"It's not your opinion that worries me. It's mine."

I had been sitting up in bed, imagining this was an act of strength, evidence of my own stoicism. More likely it was evidence that the painkillers were temporarily in charge. I shivered. Shivering was the first sign of a resurgent fever. "You want to know when I fell in love with you? Maybe I should write about that. It's important. It was when I was ten——"

"Tyler, Tyler. Nobody falls in love when they're ten."

"It was when St. Augustine died."

St. Augustine was a lively black-and-white pedigreed springer spaniel who had been Diane's particular pet. "St. Dog," she had called him.

She winced. "That's just macabre."

But I was serious. E. D. Lawton had bought the dog impulsively, probably because he wanted something to decorate the hearth at the Big House, like a pair of antique andirons. But St. Dog had resisted his fate. St. Dog was decorative enough, but he was also inquisitive and full of mischief. In time E.D. came to despise him; Carol Lawton ignored him; Jason was fondly bemused by him. It was Diane, who had been twelve, who bonded with him. They brought out the best in each other. For six months St. Dog had followed her everywhere except the school bus. The two of them played together on the big lawn summer evenings, and that was when I first noticed Diane in a particular way—the first time I took pleasure in simply watching her. She would run with St. Dog until she was exhausted, and St. Dog was always patient while she got her breath back. She was attentive to the animal in ways none of the other Lawtons even tried to be—she was sensitive to his moods, as St. Augustine was to hers.

I couldn't have said why I liked this about her. But in the uneasy, emotionally charged world of the Lawtons it was an oasis of uncomplicated affection. If I'd been a dog, I might have been jealous. Instead it impressed on me that Diane was special, different from her family in important ways. She met the world with an emotional openness the other Lawtons had lost or never learned.

St. Augustine died suddenly and prematurely—he was still hardly more than a pup—that autumn. Diane was grief-stricken, and I realized I was in love with her. . . .

No, that *does* sound macabre. I didn't fall in love with her because she mourned her dog. I fell in love with her because she was *capable* of mourning her dog, when everyone else seemed either indifferent or secretly relieved that St. Augustine was finally out of the house.

She looked away from the bed, toward the sunny window. "I was heartbroken when that animal died."

We had buried St. Dog in the wooded tract beyond the lawn. Diane made a little mound of stones as a monument, and she built it up again every spring until she left home ten years later.

She also prayed over the marker at every change of the seasons, silently, hands folded. Praying to whom, or for what, I don't know. I don't know what people do when they pray. I don't think I'm capable of it.

But it was my first evidence that Diane lived in a world even bigger than the Big House, a world where grief and joy moved as ponderously as tides, with the weight of an ocean behind them.

o o o

The fever came again that night. I remember nothing of it apart from a recurring dread (it came at hourly intervals) that the drug had blanked more memory than I would ever recover, a sense of irretrievable loss akin to those dreams in which one searches futilely for the missing wallet, watch, prized possession, or sense of self. I imagined I felt the Martian drug working in my body, making fresh assaults and negotiating temporary truces with my immune system, establishing cellular beachheads, sequestering hostile chromosomal sequences.

When I came to myself again Diane was absent. Insulated from the pain by the morphine she had given me, I got out of bed and managed to use the bathroom, then shuffled out onto the balcony.

Dinner hour. The sun was up but the sky had turned a duskier blue. The air smelled of coconut milk and diesel fumes. The Archway glimmered in the west like frozen quicksilver.

I found myself wanting to write again, the urge coming on like an echo of the fever. I carried with me the notebook I had half filled with barely decipherable scribbling. I'd have to ask Diane to buy me another one. Maybe a couple more. Which I would then fill with words.

Words like anchors, tethering boats of memory that would otherwise be scuttled by the storm.

RUMORS OF APOCALYPSE REACH
THE BERKSHIRES

I didn't see Jason for several years after the sledding party, though I kept in touch. We met again the year I graduated from med school, at a summer rental in the Berkshires about twenty minutes from Tanglewood.

I had been busy. I had done four years of college plus volunteer time at a local clinic and had started prepping for the MCAT a couple of years ahead of writing it. My GPA, the MCAT results, and a sheaf of recommendation letters from undergraduate advisors and other venerable worthies (plus E.D.'s largesse) had bought me admission to the SUNY medical campus at Stony Brook for another four years. That was done, behind me, finished, but I was still looking at at least three more years of residency before I was ready to practice.

Which put me among the majority of people who continued to conduct their lives as if the end of the world had not been announced.

It might have been different if doomsday had been calculated down to the day and hour. We all could have chosen our motifs, from panic to saintly resignation, and played out human history with a decent sense of timing and an eye on the clock.

But what we were facing was merely the strong likelihood of eventual extinction, in a solar system rapidly becoming unfit for life. Probably nothing could protect us indefinitely from the expanding sun we had all seen in NASA images captured from orbital probes . . . but we were shielded from it for now, for reasons no one understood. The crisis, if there *was* a crisis, was intangible; the only evidence available to the senses was the absence of the stars—absence as evidence, evidence of absence.

So how do you build a life under the threat of extinction? The question defined our generation. It was easy enough for Jason, it seemed. He had thrown himself into the problem headlong: the Spin was rapidly *becoming* his life. And it was, I suppose, relatively easy for me. I had been leaning toward medicine anyway, and it seemed like an even wiser choice in the current atmosphere of simmering crisis. Maybe I imagined myself saving lives, should the end of the world prove to be more than hypothetical and less than instantaneous. Did that matter, if we were all doomed? Why save a life if all human life was due to be snuffed out? But physicians don't really *save* lives, of course, we prolong them; and failing that, we provide palliative care and relief from pain. Which might prove to be the most useful skill of all.

On top of that, college and med school had been one long, relentless, grueling, but welcome, distraction from the rest of the world's woes.

So I coped. Jason coped. But many people had a much rougher time. Diane was one of them.

o o o

I was cleaning out my one-bedroom rental at Stony Brook when Jason called.

It was early in the afternoon. The optical illusion indistinguishable from the sun was shining brightly. My Hyundai was packed and ready for the drive home. I had planned to spend a couple of weeks with my mother, then drive across country in a lazy week or two. This was my last free time before I started interning at Harborview in Seattle, and I intended to use it to see the world, or at least the part of it bracketed between Maine and the state of Washington. But Jason had other ideas. He barely let me get out a hello-how-are-you before he launched into his pitch.

"Tyler," he said, "this is too good to pass up. E.D. rented a summerhouse in the Berkshires."

"Did he? Good for him."

"But he can't use it. Last week he was touring an aluminum extrusion plant in Michigan and he fell off a loading platform and cracked his hip."

"I'm sorry to hear that."

"It's not serious, he's recovering, but he's on crutches for a while and he doesn't want to ferry himself all the way to Massachusetts just so he can sit around and suck Percodan. And Carol wasn't that enthusiastic about the idea to begin with." Not surprisingly. Carol had become a career drunk. I couldn't imagine what she would have done in the Berkshires with E. D. Lawton, except drink some more. "The thing is," Jase went on, "he can't back out of the contract, so the house is empty for three months. So I thought, with you finishing med school and all, maybe we could get together for at least a couple of weeks. Maybe talk Diane into joining us. Take in a concert. Walk in the woods. Be like old times. I'm headed there now, actually. What do you say, Tyler?"

I was about to turn him down. But I thought about Diane. I thought about the few letters and phone calls we had exchanged on the predictable occasions and all the unanswered questions that had stacked up between us. I knew the wise thing would be to beg off. But it was too late: my mouth had already said yes.

o o o

So I spent another night on Long Island; then I crammed the last of my worldly possessions into the trunk of the car and followed the Northern State Parkway to the Long Island Expressway.

Traffic was light and the weather was ridiculously pretty. It was a tall blue afternoon, just pleasantly warm. I wanted to sell tomorrow to the highest bidder and settle down forever in July second. I felt as stupidly, corporeally happy as I'd been in a long time.

Then I turned on the radio.

I was old enough to remember when a "radio station" was a building with a transmitter and a tower antenna, when radio reception flooded and ebbed from town to town. Plenty of those stations still existed, but the Hyundai's analog radio had died about a week out of warranty. Which left digital programming (relayed through one or more of E.D.'s high-atmosphere aerostats). Usually I listened to twentieth-century jazz downloads, a taste I'd picked up rummaging through my father's disc collection. This, I liked to pretend, was his real legacy to me: Duke Ellington, Billie Holiday, Miles Davis, music that had been old even when Marcus Dupree was young, passed down surreptitiously, like a family secret. What I wanted to hear right now was "Harlem Air Shaft," but the guy who serviced the car before the trip had dumped my presets and programmed a news channel I couldn't seem to lose. So I was stuck with natural disasters and celebrity misbehavior. There was even talk of the Spin.

We had begun calling it the Spin by then.

Even though most of the world didn't believe in it.

The polls were pretty clear about that. NASA had released data from their orbital probes the night Jason broke the news to Diane and me, and a flurry of European launches confirmed the American results. But still, eight years after the Spin had been made public, only a minority of Europeans and North Americans considered it "a threat to themselves or their families." In much of Asia, Africa, and the Middle East, sturdy majorities considered the whole thing a U.S. plot or accident, probably a failed attempt to create some kind of SDI defense system.

I had once asked Jason why this was. He said, "Consider what we're asking them to believe. We're talking about, globally, a population with an almost pre-Newtonian grasp of astronomy. How much do you really need to know about the moon and the stars when your life consists of scrounging enough biomass to feed yourself and your family? To say anything meaningful about the Spin to those people you have to start a long way back. The Earth, you have to tell them, is a few billion years old, to begin with. Let them wrestle with the concept of 'a billion years,' maybe for the first time. It's a lot to swallow, especially if you've been educated in a Moslem theocracy, an animist village, or a public school in the Bible Belt. Then tell them the Earth isn't changeless, that there was an era longer than our own when the oceans were steam and the air was poison. Tell them how living things arose spontaneously and evolved sporadically for three billion years before they produced the first arguably human being. Then talk about the sun, how the sun isn't permanent either but started out as a contracting cloud of gas and dust and will one day, some few more billion years from now, expand and swallow the Earth and eventually blow off its own outer layers and shrink to a nugget of superdense matter. Cosmology 101, right? You picked it up from all those paperbacks you used to read, it's second nature to you, but for most people it's a whole new worldview and probably offensive to a bunch of their core beliefs. So let that sink in. Let that sink in, then deliver the *real* bad news. *Time itself* is fluid and unpredictable. The world that looks so ruggedly normal—in spite of everything we just learned—has recently been locked up in a kind of cosmological cold storage. *Why* has this been done to us? We don't exactly know. We think it's caused by the deliberate action of entities so powerful and inaccessible they might as well be called gods. And if we anger the gods they might withdraw their protection, and pretty soon the mountains will melt and the oceans will boil. But don't take our word for it. Ignore the sunset and the snow that comes to the mountain every winter same as always. We have proof. We have calculations and logical inferences and photographs taken by machines. Forensic evidence of the highest caliber." Jason had smiled one of his quizzical, sad smiles. "Strangely, the jury is unconvinced."

And it wasn't only the ignorant who weren't convinced. On the radio, an insurance industry CEO began to complain about the economic impact of "all this relentless, uncritical discussion of the so-called Spin." People were starting to take it seriously, he said. And that was bad for business. It made people reckless. It encouraged immorality, crime, and deficit spending. Worse, it screwed up the actuary tables. "If the world doesn't come to an end in the next thirty or forty years," he said, "we may be facing disaster."

Clouds began to roll in from the west. An hour later that gorgeous blue sky was flatly overcast and raindrops began spattering the windshield. I put the headlights on.

The news on the radio progressed from actuary tables. There was much talk of something else from recent headlines: the silver boxes, big as cities, hovering outside the Spin barrier, hundreds of miles above both poles of the Earth. Hovering, not orbiting. An object can hang in a stable orbit over the equator—geosynchronous satellites used to do that—but nothing, by the most elementary laws of motion, can "orbit" in a fixed position above the planet's pole. And yet here these things were, detected by a radar probe and lately photographed from an unmanned fly-by mission: another layer of the mystery of the Spin, and just as incomprehensible to the untutored masses, in this case including me. I wanted to talk to Jason about it. I think I wanted him to make sense of it for me.

o o o

It was raining full-out, thunder rumbling through the hills, when I finally pulled up at E. D. Lawton's short-term rental outside Stockbridge.

The property was a four-bedroom English country–style cottage, the siding painted arsenic green, set into a hundred acres of preserved woodland. It glowed in the dusk like a storm lantern. Jason was already here, his white Ferrari parked under a dripping breezeway.

He must have heard me pull up: he opened the big front door before I knocked. "Tyler!" he said, grinning.

I came inside and set my single rain-dampened suitcase on the tiled floor of the foyer. "Been a while," I said.

We had kept in touch by e-mail and phone, but apart from a couple of brief holiday appearances at the Big House this was the first time we'd been in the same room in nearly eight years. I suppose the time showed on both of us, a subtle inventory of changes. I had forgotten how formidable he looked. He had always been tall, always at ease in his body; he still was, though he seemed skinnier, not delicate but delicately balanced, like a broomstick standing on end. His hair was a uniform layer of stubble about a quarter-inch long. And although he drove a Ferrari he remained unconscious of personal style: he wore tattered jeans, a baggy knit sweater pocked with balls of unraveling thread, discount sneakers.

"You ate on the way down?" he asked.

"Late lunch."

"Hungry?"

I wasn't, but I admitted I was craving a cup of coffee. Med school had made a caffeine addict of me. "You're in luck," Jason said. "I bought a pound of Guatemalan on the way here." The Guatemalans, indifferent to the end of the world, were still harvesting coffee. "I'll put on a pot. Show you around while it's brewing."

We trekked through the house. There was a twentieth-century fussiness about it, walls painted apple green or harvest orange, sturdy barn-sale antique furniture and brass bed frames, lace curtains over warped window glass down which the rain streamed relentlessly. Modern amenities in the kitchen and living room, big TV, music station, Internet link. Cozy in the rain. Downstairs again, Jason poured coffee. We sat at the kitchen table and tried to catch up.

Jase was vague about his work, out of modesty or for security reasons. In the eight years since the revelation of the true nature of the Spin he had earned himself a doctorate in astrophysics and then walked away from it to take a junior position in E.D.'s Perihelion Foundation. Perhaps not a bad move, now that E.D. was a ranking member of President Walker's Select Committee on Global and Environmental Crisis Planning. According to Jase, Perihelion was about to be transformed from an aerospace think tank into an official advisory body, with real authority to shape policy.

I said, "Is that legal?"

"Don't be naive, Tyler. E.D.'s already distanced himself from Lawton Industries. He resigned from the board and his shares are being administered by a blind trust. According to our lawyers he's conflict-free."

"So what do you at Perihelion?"

He smiled. "I listen attentively to my elders," he said, "and I make polite suggestions. Tell me about med school."

He asked whether I found it distasteful to see so much of human weakness and disease. So I told him about my second-year anatomy class. Along with a dozen other students I had dissected a human cadaver and sorted its contents by size, color, function, and weight. There was nothing pleasant about the experience. Its only consolation was its truth and its only virtue was its utility. But it was also a marker, a passage. Beyond this point there was nothing left of childhood.

"Jesus, Tyler. You want something stronger than coffee?"

"I'm not saying it was a big deal. That's what's shocking about it. It *wasn't* a big deal. You walk away from it and you go to a movie."

"Long way from the Big House, though."

"Long way. Both of us." I raised my cup.

Then we started reminiscing, and the tension drained out of the conversation. We talked about old times. We fell into what I recognized as a pattern. Jason would mention a place—the basement, the mall, the creek in the woods—and I would supply a story: the time we broke into the liquor cabinet; the time we saw a Rice girl named Kelley Weems shoplift a pack of Trojans from the Pharmasave; the summer Diane insisted on reading us breathless passages from Christina Rossetti, as if she had discovered something profound.

The big lawn, Jason offered. *The night the stars disappeared,* I said.

And then we were quiet for a while.

Finally I said, "So . . . is she coming or not?"

"She's making up her mind," Jase said neutrally. "She's juggling some commitments. She's supposed to call tomorrow and let me know."

"She's still down south?" This was the last I'd heard, the news relayed from my mother. Diane was at some southern college, studying something I couldn't quite remember: urban geography, oceanography, some other unlikely -ography.

"Yeah, still," Jason said, shifting in his chair. "You know, Ty, a lot of things have changed with Diane."

"I guess that's not surprising."

"She's semi-engaged. To be married."

I took this pretty gracefully. "Well, good for her," I said. How could I possibly be jealous? I had no relationship with Diane anymore—had never had one, in that sense of the word "relationship." And I had almost been engaged myself, back at Stony Brook, to a second-year student named Candice Boone. We had enjoyed saying "I love you" to each other, until we got tired of it. I think Candice got tired first.

And yet: *semi*-engaged? How did that work?

I was tempted to ask. But Jason was clearly uncomfortable with the whole drift of the conversation. It called up a memory: once, back at the Big House, Jason had brought a date home to meet his family. She was a plain but pleasant girl he'd met at the Rice chess club, too shy to say much. Carol had remained relatively sober that night, but E.D. had clearly disapproved of the girl, had been conspicuously rude to her, and when she was gone he had berated Jase for "dragging a specimen like that into the house." With great intellect, E.D. said, comes great responsibility. He didn't want Jason to be shanghaied into a conventional marriage. Didn't want to see him "hanging diapers on the line" when he could be "making a mark on the world."

A lot of people in Jason's position would have stopped bringing home their dates.

Jason had just stopped dating.

○ ○ ○

The house was empty when I woke up the next morning.

There was a note on the kitchen table: Jase had gone out to pick up provisions for a barbecue. *Back noon or later.* It was nine-thirty. I had slept luxuriously late, summer-vacation languor creeping over me.

The house seemed to generate it. Last night's storms had passed and a pleasant morning breeze came through the calico curtains. Sunlight picked out imperfections in the grain of the butcher-block kitchen counters. I ate a slow breakfast by the window and watched clouds like stately schooners sail the horizon.

A little after ten the doorbell rang, and for a second I was panicked by the thought that it might be Diane—had she decided to show up early? But it turned out to be "Mike, the landscape guy," in a bandanna and sleeveless T-shirt, warning me that he was going to do the lawn—he didn't want to wake anybody up but the mower was pretty loud. He could come back this afternoon if it was a problem. No problem at all, I said, and a few minutes later he was riding the contours of the property on an ancient green John Deere that smudged the air with burning oil. Still a little sleepy, I wondered how this yard work would look to what Jason was fond of calling the universe at large. To the universe at large, Earth was a planet in near-stasis. Those blades of grass had arisen over centuries, as stately in their motion as the evolution of stars. Mike, a force of nature born a couple of billion years ago, scythed them with a vast and irresistible patience. The severed blades fell as if lightly touched by gravity, many seasons between sun and loam, loam in which Methuselah worms slid while elsewhere in the galaxy, perhaps, empires rose and fell.

Jason was right, of course: it was a difficult thing to believe in. Or, no, not to "believe in"—people believe all kinds of implausible things—but to accept as a fundamental truth about the world. I sat on the porch of the house, on the side away from the roaring Deere, and the air was cool and the sun felt fine when I turned my face to it even though I knew it for what it was, radiation filtered from a star in full-out runaway Spin, in a world where centuries were squandered like seconds.

Can't be true. *Is* true.

I thought about med school again, the anatomy class I had told Jason about. Candice Boone, my one-time almost-fiancée, had shared that class with me. She had been stoic during the dissection but not afterward. A human body, she said, ought to contain love, hate, courage, cowardice, soul, spirit . . . not this slimy assortment of blue and red imponderables. Yes. And we ought not to be dragged unwilling into a harsh and deadly future.

But the world is what it is and won't be bargained with. I had said as much to Candice.

She told me I was "cold." But it was still the closest thing to wisdom I had ever been able to muster.

o o o

The morning rolled on. Mike finished the lawn and drove off, leaving the air full of humid silence. After a time I stirred myself and telephoned my mom in Virginia, where the weather, she said, was less inviting than in Massachusetts: still cloudy after a storm last night that had brought down a few trees and power lines. I told her I'd made it safely to E.D.'s summer rental. She asked me how Jason seemed, though she had probably seen him more recently than I had, during one of his visits to the Big House. "Older," I said. "But still Jase."

"Is he worried about this China thing?"

My mom had been a news junkie since the October Event, watching CNN not for pleasure or even information but mainly to reassure herself, the way a Mexican villager might keep an eye on a nearby volcano, hoping not to see smoke. The China thing was only a diplomatic crisis at this stage, she said, though sabers had been gently rattled. Something about a controversial proposed satellite launch. "You should ask Jason about it."

"Has E.D. been worrying you about this stuff?"

"Hardly. I do hear things from Carol every once in a while."

"I don't know how much of that you should trust."

"Come on, Ty. She drinks, but she's not stupid. Neither am I, particularly."

"I didn't mean that."

"Most of what I hear about Jason and Diane these days I get through Carol."

"Did she say whether Diane was coming up to the Berkshires? I can't get a straight answer out of Jase."

My mother hesitated. "Diane's been a little unpredictable the last couple of years. I guess that's what it's all about."

"What does 'unpredictable' mean, exactly?"

"Oh, you know. Not much success at school. A little trouble with the law—"

"With the *law*?"

"No, I mean, she didn't rob a bank or anything, but she's been picked up a couple of times when NK rallies got out of hand."

"What the hell was she doing at NK rallies?"

Another pause. "You should really ask Jason about that."

I intended to.

She coughed—I pictured her with her hand over the phone, her head turned delicately away—and I said, "How are you feeling?"

"Tired."

"Anything new with the doctor?" She was being treated for anemia. Bottles of iron tablets.

"No. I'm just getting old, Ty. Everybody gets old sooner or later." She added, "I'm thinking of retiring. If you call what I do work. Now that the twins are gone it's just Carol and E.D., and not much E.D. since this Washington business started up."

"Have you told them you're thinking of leaving?"

"Not yet."

"It wouldn't be the Big House without you."

She laughed, not happily. "I think I've had about enough of the Big House for one lifetime, thanks."

But she never mentioned the move again. It was Carol, I think, who convinced her to stay.

○ ○ ○

Jase came in the front door midafternoon. "Ty?" His overlarge jeans hung on his hips like the rigging of a becalmed ship, and his T-shirt was spackled with the ghosts of gravy stains. "Give me a hand with the barbecue, can you?"

I went out back with him. The barbecue was a standard propane grill. Jase had never used one. He opened the tank valve, pushed the lighter button and flinched when the flames blossomed up. Then he grinned at me. "We have steaks. We have three-bean salad from the deli in town."

"And hardly any mosquitos," I said.

"They sprayed for them this spring. Hungry?"

I was. Somehow, dozing through the afternoon, I had worked up an appetite. "Are we cooking for two or three?"

"I'm still waiting to hear from Diane. Probably won't know until this evening. Just us for dinner, I think."

"Assuming the Chinese don't nuke us first."

This was bait.

Jason rose to it. "Are you worried about the *Chinese,* Ty? That's not even a crisis anymore. It's been settled."

"That's a relief." I had heard about the crisis and the resolution all in the same day. "My mom mentioned it. Something on the news."

"The Chinese military want to nuke the polar artifacts. They have nuclear-tipped missiles sitting on pads in Jiuquan, ready to launch. The reasoning is, if they can damage the polar devices they might take down the entire October shield. Of course there's no reason to believe it would work. How likely is it that a technology capable of manipulating time and gravitation would be vulnerable to our weapons?"

"So we threatened the Chinese and they backed down?"

"A little of that. But we offered a carrot, too. We offered to take them onboard."

"I don't understand."

"To let them join us in our own little project to save the world."

"You're scaring me a little here, Jase."

"Hand me those tongs. I'm sorry. I know this sounds cryptic. I'm not supposed to be talking about these things at all. With anyone."

"You're making an exception in my case?"

"I always make an exception in your case." He smiled. "We'll discuss it over dinner, okay?"

I left him at the grill, shrouded in smoke and heat.

o o o

Two consecutive American administrations had been scolded by the press for "doing nothing" about the Spin. But it was a criticism without teeth. If there was anything practical that *could* be done, no one seemed to know what it was. And any clearly retaliatory action—like the one the Chinese had proposed—would have been prohibitively dangerous.

Perihelion was pushing a radically different approach.

"The governing metaphor," Jase said, "isn't combat. It's judo. Using a bigger opponent's weight and momentum against him. That's what we want to do with the Spin."

He told me this laconically while he cut up his grilled steak with surgical attention. We ate in the kitchen with the back door open. A huge bumblebee, so fat and yellow it looked like an airborne knot of woolen threads, bumped against the bug screen.

"Try to think about the Spin," he said, "as an opportunity rather than an assault."

"An opportunity to do what? Die prematurely?"

"An opportunity to use time for our own ends, in a way we never could before."

"Isn't time what they took away from us?"

"On the contrary. Outside our little terrestrial bubble we have millions of years to play with. And we have a tool that works extremely reliably over exactly those spans of time."

"Tool," I said, bewildered, while he speared another cube of beef. The meal was straight to the point. A steak on a plate, bottle of beer on the side. No frills, barring the three-bean salad, of which he took a modest helping.

"Yes, a tool, the obvious one: evolution."

"Evolution."

"We can't have this talk, Tyler, if you just repeat everything back to me."

"Okay, well, evolution as a tool . . . I still don't see how we can evolve sufficiently in thirty or forty years to make a difference."

"Not *us,* for god's sake, and certainly not in thirty or forty years. I'm talking about simple forms of life. I'm talking about eons. I'm talking about Mars."

"Mars." Oops.

"Don't be obtuse. Think about it."

Mars was a functionally dead planet, even if it may once have possessed the primitive precursors to life. Outside the Spin bubble, Mars had been "evolving" for millions of years since the October Event, warmed by the expanding sun. It was still, according to the latest orbital photographs, a dead, dry planet. If it had possessed simple life and a supportive climate it could have become, I guessed, a lush green jungle by now. But it didn't and it wasn't.

"People used to talk about terraforming," Jason said. "Remember those speculative novels you used to read?"

"I still read them, Jase."

"More power to you. How would you go about terraforming Mars?"

"Try to get enough greenhouse gases into the atmosphere to warm it up. Release its frozen water. Seed it with simple organisms. But even with the most optimistic assumptions, that would take—"

He smiled.

I said, "You're kidding me."

"No." The smile went away. "Not at all. No, this is quite serious."

"How would you even begin—?"

"We would begin with a series of synchronized launches containing payloads of engineered bacteria. Simple ion engines and a slow glide to Mars. Mostly controlled crashes, survivable for unicells, and a few larger payloads with bunker-buster warheads to deliver the same organisms below the surface of the planet where we suspect the presence of buried water. Hedge our bets with multiple launches and a whole spectrum of candidate organisms. The idea is to get enough organic action going to loosen up the carbon locked into the crust and respirate it into the atmosphere. Give it a few million years—months, our time—then survey the planet again. If it's a warmer place with a denser atmosphere and maybe a few ponds of semiliquid water we do the cycle again, this time with multicelled plants engineered for the environment. Which puts some oxygen into the air and maybe cranks up the atmospheric pressure another couple of millibars. Repeat as necessary. Add more millions of years and stir. In a reasonable time—the way our clocks measure time—you might be able to cook up a habitable planet."

It was a breathtaking idea. I felt like one of those sidekick

characters in a Victorian mystery novel—"It was an auda-
cious, even ludicrous, plan he had contrived, but try as I
might, I could find no flaw in it!"

Except one. One fundamental flaw.

"Jason," I said. "Even if this is possible. What *good* does it
do us?"

"If Mars is habitable, people can go there and live."

"All seven or eight billion of us?"

He snorted. "Hardly. No, just a few pioneers. Breeding
stock, if you want to be clinical about it."

"And what are they supposed to do?"

"Live, reproduce, and die. Millions of generations for each
of our years."

"To what end?"

"If nothing else, to give the human species a second
chance in the solar system. In the best case—they'll have all
the knowledge we can give them, plus a few million years to
improve on it. Inside the Spin bubble we don't have time
enough to figure out who the Hypotheticals are or why
they're doing this to us. Our Martian heirs might have a better chance. Maybe they can do our thinking for us."

Or our fighting for us?

(This was, incidentally, the first time I had heard them
called "Hypotheticals"—the hypothetical controlling intelli-
gences, the unseen and largely theoretical creatures who had
enclosed us in their time vault. The name didn't catch on with
the general public for a few more years. I was sorry when it
did. The word was too clinical, it suggested something abstract and coolly objective; the truth was likely to be more
complex.)

"There's a plan," I said, "to actually *do* these things?"

"Oh yes." Jason had finished three quarters of his steak. He
pushed his plate away. "It's not even prohibitively expensive.
Engineering extremely hardy unicells is the only problematic
part. The surface of Mars is cold, dry, virtually airless, and
bathed in sterilizing radiation every time the sun comes up.
Even so, we have whole rafts of extremophiles to work
with—bacteria living in Antarctic rocks, bacteria living in
the outflow from nuclear reactors. And everything else is

fully proven technology. We know rockets work. We know organic evolution works. The only really new thing is our perspective. To be able to get extremely long-term results literally days or months after we launch. It's . . . people are calling it 'teleological engineering.' "

"It's almost like," I said (testing the new word he had given me), "what the Hypotheticals are doing."

"Yes," Jason said, raising his eyebrows in a look I still found flattering after all these years: surprise, respect. "Yes, in a way I guess it is."

○ ○ ○

I had once read an interesting detail in a book about the first manned moon landing back in 1969. At that time, the book said, some of the very elderly—men and women born in the nineteenth century, old enough to remember a world before automobiles and television—had been reluctant to believe the news. Words that would have made only fairy-tale sense in their childhood ("two men walked on the moon tonight") were being offered as statements of fact. And they couldn't accept it. It confounded their sense of what was reasonable and what was absurd.

Now it was my turn.

We're going to terraform and colonize Mars, said my friend Jason, and he wasn't delusional . . . or at least no more delusional than the dozens of smart and powerful people who apparently shared his conviction. So the proposition was serious; it must already have been, at some bureaucratic level, a work in progress.

I took a walk around the grounds after dinner while there was still a little daylight.

Mike the yard guy had done a decent job. The lawn glowed like a mathematician's idea of a garden, the cultivation of a primary color. Beyond it, shadows had begun to rise in the wooded acreage. Diane would have appreciated the woods in this light, I thought. I thought again of those summer sessions by the creek, years ago now, when she would read to us from old books. Once, when we talked about the Spin, Diane had quoted a little rhyme by the English poet A. E. Housman:

The Grizzly Bear is huge and wild;
He has devoured the infant child.
The infant child is not aware
He has been eaten by the bear.

o o o

Jason was on the phone when I came back through the kitchen door. He looked at me, then turned away and lowered his voice.

"No," he said. "If it has to be that way, but—no, I understand. All right. I said all right, didn't I? All right means all right."

He pocketed the phone. I said, "Was that Diane?"

He nodded.

"She's coming?"

"She's coming. But there are a couple of things I want to mention before she gets here. You know what we talked about over dinner? We can't share that with her. Or, actually, anyone. It's not public information."

"You mean it's classified."

"Technically, I suppose so, yes."

"But you told *me* about it."

"Yes. That was a federal crime." He smiled. "Mine, not yours. And I trust you to be discreet about it. Be patient—it'll be all over CNN in a couple of months. Besides, I have plans for you, Ty. One of these days, Perihelion is going to vet candidates for some extremely rugged homesteading. We'll need all kinds of physicians on site. Wouldn't it be great if you could do that, if we could work together?"

I was startled. "I just graduated, Jase. I haven't interned."

"All things in time."

I said, "You don't trust Diane?"

His smile collapsed. "No, frankly. Not anymore. Not these days."

"When will she get here?"

"Before noon tomorrow."

"And what is it you don't want to tell me?"

"She's bringing her boyfriend."

"Is that a problem?"

"You'll see."

NO SINGLE THING ABIDES

I woke up knowing I wasn't ready to see her again.

Woke up in E. D. Lawton's plush summerhouse in the Berkshires with the sun shining through filigreed lace blinds thinking, *Enough bullshit.* I was tired of it. All the self-serving bullshit of the last eight years, up to and including my affair with Candice Boone, who had seen through my own wishful lies sooner than I had. "You're a little bit fixated on these Lawton people," Candice had once said. Tell me about it.

I couldn't honestly say I was still in love with Diane. The connection between us had never been as unambiguous as that. We had both grown in and out of it, like vines weaving through a latticework fence. But at its best it had been a real connection, an emotion almost frightening in its gravity and maturity. Which was why I had been so eager to disguise it. It would have frightened her, too.

I still found myself conducting imaginary conversations with her, usually late at night, offering asides to the starless sky. I was selfish enough to miss her but sane enough to know we had never really been together. I was fully prepared to forget about her.

I just wasn't prepared to see her again.

o o o

Downstairs, Jason sat in the kitchen while I fixed myself breakfast. He had propped open the door. Sweet breezes swept the house. I was thinking seriously of throwing my bag into the back of the Hyundai and just driving away. "Tell me about this NK thing," I said.

"Do you read the papers at all?" Jason asked. "Do they keep med students in isolation up at Stony Brook?"

Of course I knew a little bit about NK, mostly what I'd heard on the news or picked up from lunchroom conversation. I knew NK stood for "New Kingdom." I knew it was a Spin-inspired Christian movement—at least nominally Christian, though it had been denounced by mainstream and conservative churches alike. I knew it attracted mainly the young and disaffected. A couple of guys in my freshman class had dropped out of school and into the NK lifestyle, trading shaky academic careers for a less demanding enlightenment.

"It's really just a millenarian movement," Jase said. "Too late for the millennium but right on time for the end of the world."

"A cult, in other words."

"No, not exactly. 'NK' is a catchphrase for the whole Christian Hedonist spectrum, so it's not a cult in itself, though it does include some cultlike groups. There's no single leader. No holy writ, just a bunch of fringe theologians the movement is loosely identified with—C. R. Ratel, Laura Greengage, people like that." I'd seen their books on the drugstore racks. Spin theology with question-mark titles: *Have We Witnessed the Second Coming? Can We Survive the End of Time?* "And not much agenda, beyond a kind of weekend communalism. But what draws crowds isn't the theology. You ever see footage of those NK rallies, the kind they call an Ekstasis?"

I had, and unlike Jase, who had never been much at home with matters of the flesh, I could understand the appeal. What

I had seen was recorded video of a gathering in the Cascades, summer of last year. It had looked like a cross between a Baptist picnic and a Grateful Dead concert. A sunny meadow, wildflowers, ceremonial white robes, a guy with zero-percent body fat blowing a shofar. By nightfall a bonfire was burning briskly and a stage had been set up for musicians. Then the robes began to drop and the dancing started. And a few acts more intimate than dancing.

For all the disgust evinced by the mainstream media it had looked winsomely innocent to me. No preaching, just a few hundred pilgrims smiling into the teeth of extinction and loving their neighbors like they'd like to be loved. The footage had been burned onto hundreds of DVDs and passed from hand to hand in college dorms nationwide, including Stony Brook. There is no sexual act so Edenic that a lonely med student can't whack off to it.

"It's hard to picture Diane being attracted to NK."

"On the contrary. Diane's their target audience. She's scared to death of the Spin and everything it implies about the world. NK is an anodyne for people like her. It turns the thing they're most afraid of into an object of adoration, a door into the Kingdom of Heaven."

"How long has she been involved?"

"Most of a year now. Since she met Simon Townsend."

"Simon's NK?"

"Simon, I'm afraid, is *hard-core* NK."

"You met this guy?"

"She brought him to the Big House last Christmas. I think she wanted to watch the fireworks. E.D., of course, doesn't approve of Simon. In fact his hostility was pretty obvious." (Here Jason winced at the memory of what must have been one of E. D. Lawton's major tantrums.) "But Diane and Simon did the NK thing—they turned the other cheek. They practically smiled him to death. I mean that literally. He was one gentle, forgiving look away from the coronary ward."

Score one for Simon, I thought. "Is he good for her?"

"He's exactly what she wants. He's the last thing she needs."

○ ○ ○

They arrived that afternoon, sputtering up the driveway in a fifteen-year-old touring car that appeared to burn more oil than Mike-the-yard-guy's tractor. Diane was driving. She parked and climbed out on the far side of the car, obscured by the luggage rack, while Simon stepped into full view, smiling bashfully.

He was a good-looking guy. Six feet tall or a little over; skinny but not a weakling; a plain, slightly horsey face offset by his unruly golden-blond hair. His smile showed a cleft between his upper front teeth. He wore jeans and a plaid shirt and a blue bandanna tied around his left biceps like a tourniquet; that was an NK emblem, I learned later.

Diane circled the car and stood beside him, both of them grinning up the porch stairs at Jason and me. She was also decked out in high NK fashion: a cornflower-blue floor-sweeper skirt, blue blouse, and a ridiculous black wide-brimmed hat like the kind Amish men wear. But the clothes suited her, or rather they framed her in a pleasing way, suggested rude health and hayseed sensuality. Her face was as alive as an unplucked berry. She shaded her eyes in the sunlight and grinned—at me in particular, I wanted to believe. My god, that smile. Somehow both genuine and mischievous.

I began to feel lost.

Jason's phone trilled. He pulled it out of his pocket and checked the caller ID.

"Gotta take this one," he whispered.

"Don't leave me alone here, Jase."

"I'll be in the kitchen. Right back."

He ducked away just as Simon lofted his big duffel bag onto the wooden planking of the porch and said, "You must be Tyler Dupree!"

He stuck out his hand. I took it. He had a firm grip and a honeyed Southern accent, vowels like polished driftwood, consonants polite as calling cards. He made my name sound positively Cajun, though the family had never been south of Millinocket. Diane bounded up after him, yelled, "Tyler!" and grabbed me in a ferocious embrace. Suddenly her hair was in my face and all I could register was the sunny, salty smell of her.

We backed off to a comfortable arm's length. "Tyler, Tyler," she exclaimed, as if I had turned into something remarkable. "You're looking good after all these years."

"Eight," I said stupidly. "Eight years."

"Wow, is it really?"

I helped drag their luggage inside, showed them to the parlor off the porch, and hurried away to retrieve Jason, who was in the kitchen interacting with his cell. His back was turned when I came in.

"No," he said. His voice was tense. "No . . . not even the State Department?"

I stopped in my tracks. The State Department. Oh my.

"I can be back in a couple of hours if—oh. I see. Okay. No, it's all right. But keep me informed. Right. Thanks."

He pocketed the phone and caught sight of me.

"Talking to E.D.?" I asked.

"His assistant, actually."

"Everything okay?"

"Come on, Ty, you want me to let you in on *all* the secrets?" He attempted a smile, not too successfully. "I wish you hadn't overheard that."

"All I heard was you offering to go back to D.C. and leave me here with Simon and Diane."

"Well . . . I may have to. The Chinese are balking."

"What's that mean, *balking*?"

"They refuse to entirely abandon their planned launch. They want to keep that option open."

The nuclear attack on the Spin artifacts, he meant. "I assume somebody's trying to talk them out of it?"

"The diplomacy is ongoing. It's just not exactly *succeeding*. Negotiations seem to be deadlocked."

"So—well, *shit*, Jase! What's it mean if they *do* launch?"

"It means two high-yield fusion weapons would be detonated in close proximity to unknown devices associated with the Spin. As for the consequences . . . well, that's an interesting question. But it hasn't happened yet. Probably won't."

"You're talking about doomsday, or maybe the end of the Spin . . ."

"Keep your voice down. We have guests, remember? And you're overreacting. What the Chinese have in mind is rash and probably futile, but even if they go ahead with it it's not likely to be suicidal. Whatever the Hypotheticals are, they must know how to defend themselves without destroying us in the process. And the polar artifacts aren't necessarily the devices that enable the Spin. They could be passive observational platforms, communications devices, even decoys."

"If the Chinese do launch," I said, "how much warning do we get?"

"Depends what you mean by 'we.' The general public probably won't hear anything until it's over."

This was when I first began to understand that Jason wasn't just his father's apprentice, that he had already begun to forge his own connections in high places. Later I would learn a great deal more about the Perihelion Foundation and the work Jason did for it. For now it was still part of Jason's shadow life. Even when we were children Jase had had a shadow life: away from the Big House he'd been a math prodigy, breezing through an elite private school like a Masters titleist playing a mini-golf course; home, he was just Jase, and we had been careful to keep it that way.

It was still that way. But he was casting a bigger shadow now. He didn't spend his days impressing calculus instructors at Rice. He spent his days positioning himself to influence the course of human history.

He added, "If it happens, yes, I'll have some warning. *We'll* have some warning. But I don't want Diane worrying about it. Or Simon, of course."

"Great. I'll just put it out of my mind. The end of the world."

"It's no such thing. Nothing's happened yet. Calm down, Tyler. Pour drinks if you need something to do."

As nonchalant as he was trying to sound, his hand trembled as he took four tumblers out of the kitchen cupboard.

I could have left. I could have walked out the door, hustled into my Hyundai and been a long way down the road before I was missed. I thought about Diane and Simon in the front parlor practicing hippie Christianity and Jase in the kitchen taking doomsday bulletins on his cell phone:

did I really want to spend my last night on Earth with these people?

Thinking at the same time: but who else? Who else?

o o o

"We met in Atlanta," Diane said. "Georgia State hosted a seminar on alternative spirituality. Simon was there to hear C. R. Ratel's lecture. I just sort of found him in the campus cafeteria. He was sitting by himself reading a copy of *Second Coming*, and I was alone, so I put down my tray and we started talking."

Diane and Simon shared a plush yellow dust-scented sofa by the window. Diane slouched against the armrest. Simon sat alertly upright. His smile had begun to worry me. It never went away.

The four of us sipped drinks while the curtains wafted in the breeze and a horsefly mumbled at the window screen. It was hard to sustain a conversation when there was so much we weren't supposed to talk about. I made an effort to duplicate Simon's smile. "So you're a student?"

"Was a student," he said.

"What are you doing lately?"

"Traveling. Mostly."

"Simon can afford to travel," Jase said. "He's an heir."

"Don't be rude," Diane said, the edge in her voice signifying a real warning. "This once, please, Jase?"

But Simon shrugged it off. "No, it's true enough. I have some money set aside. Diane and I are taking the opportunity to see a little bit of the country."

"Simon's grandfather," Jason said, "was Augustus Townsend, the Georgia pipe cleaner king."

Diane rolled her eyes. Simon, still imperturbable—he was beginning to seem almost saintly—said, "That was in the old days. We aren't even supposed to call them pipe cleaners anymore. They're 'chenille stems.' " He laughed. "And here I sit, heir to a chenille stem fortune." Actually it was a gifts-and-notions fortune, Diane explained later. Augustus Townsend had started in pipe cleaners but made his money distributing tin-press toys, charm bracelets, and plastic combs to five-and-dime stores throughout the South. In the 1940s the family had been a big presence in Atlanta social circles.—

Jason pressed on: "Simon himself doesn't have what you'd call a career. He's a free spirit."

"I don't suppose any of us is truly a free spirit," Simon said, "but no, I don't have or want a career. I guess that makes me sound lazy. Well, I *am* lazy. It's my besetting vice. But I wonder how useful any career will be in the long run. Considering the state of things. No offense." He turned to me. "You're in medicine, Tyler?"

"Just out of school," I said. "As careers go—"

"No, I think that's wonderful. Probably the most valuable occupation on the planet."

Jason had accused Simon of being, in effect, useless. Simon had replied that careers in general were useless . . . except careers like mine. Thrust and parry. It was like watching a bar fight conducted in ballet shoes.

Still, I found myself wanting to apologize for Jase. Jason was offended not by Simon's philosophy but by his presence. This week in the Berkshires was supposed to be a reunion, Jason and Diane and me, back in the comfort zone, childhood revisited. Instead we were being treated to confinement at close quarters with Simon, whom Jason obviously regarded as an interloper, a sort of southern-fried Yoko Ono.

I asked Diane how long they'd been traveling.

"About a week," she said, "but we'll be on the road most of the summer. I'm sure Jason's told you about New Kingdom. But it's really pretty wonderful, Ty. We have Internet friends all across the country. People we can crash with a day or two. So we're doing conclaves and concerts from Maine to Oregon, July through October."

Jason said, "I guess that saves on accommodation *and* clothing expenses."

"Not every conclave is an Ekstasis," Diane shot back.

"We won't be doing much traveling at all," Simon said, "if that old car of ours falls apart. The engine misfires and we're getting lousy mileage. I'm not much of a mechanic, unfortunately. Tyler, do you know anything about automobile engines?"

"A thing or two," I said. I understood this was an invitation to step outside with Simon while Diane tried to negotiate a cease-fire with her brother. "Let's have a look."

The day was still clear, waves of warm air rippling up from the emerald lawn beyond the driveway. I listened with, I admit, partial attention, as Simon opened the hood of his old Ford and recited his problems. If he was as wealthy as Jase had implied, couldn't he buy himself a better car? But I guessed it was a dissipated fortune he had inherited, or maybe it was tied up in trust funds.

"I guess I seem pretty stupid," Simon said. "Especially in the company I'm keeping. I never much grasped scientific or mechanical things."

"I'm no expert either. Even if we get the motor running a little smoother you ought to have a real mechanic look at it before you start driving cross-country."

"Thank you, Tyler." He watched with a sort of goggle-eyed fascination as I inspected the engine. "I appreciate that advice."

The most likely culprit was the spark plugs. I asked Simon whether they had ever been replaced. "Not to my knowledge," he said. The car had 60,000-plus miles on it. I used the ratchet set from my own car to pull one of the plugs and showed it to him: "Here's most of your trouble."

"That thing?"

"And its friends. The good news is it's not an expensive part to replace. The bad news is, you're better off not driving until we replace it."

"Hmm," Simon said.

"We can go into town in my car and pick up replacements if you're willing to wait till morning."

"Well, surely. That's very kind. We weren't planning to leave right away. Ah, unless Jason insists."

"Jason will calm down. He's just—"

"You don't have to explain. Jason would rather I wasn't here. I understand that. It doesn't shock or surprise me. Diane just felt she couldn't accept an invitation that made a point of disincluding me."

"Well . . . good for her." I guess.

"But I could just as easily rent a room somewhere in town."

"No need for that," I said, wondering exactly how it had come to pass that I was pressing Simon Townsend to stay. I don't know what I had expected from a reunion with Diane, but Simon's presence had aborted any nascent hopes. For the best, probably.

"I suppose," Simon said, "Jason's talked to you about New Kingdom. It's been a point of contention."

"He told me you guys were involved in it."

"I'm not about to make a recruiting speech. But if you have any anxiety about the movement maybe I can put it to rest."

"All I know about NK is what I see on television, Simon."

"Some people call it Christian Hedonism. I prefer New Kingdom. That's the idea in a nutshell, really. Build the chiliasm by living it, right here and now. Make the last generation as idyllic as the very first."

"Uh-huh. Well . . . Jase doesn't have much patience with religion."

"No, he doesn't, but you know what, Tyler? I don't think it's the religion that upsets him."

"No?"

"No. In all honesty I admire Jason Lawton, and not just because he's famously smart. He's one of the cognoscenti, if you'll pardon a ten-dollar word. He takes the Spin seriously. There are, what, eight billion people on Earth? And pretty much each and every one of them knows, at the very least, that the stars and moon have disappeared out of the sky. But they go on living in denial. Only a few of us really believe in the Spin. NK takes it seriously. And so does Jason."

This was almost shockingly like what Jason himself had said. "Not in the same . . . *style,* though."

"That's the crux of the matter. Two visions competing for the public mind. Before long people will have to face up to reality whether they want to or not. And they'll have to choose between a scientific understanding and a spiritual one. That worries Jason. Because when it comes down to matters of life and death, faith always wins. Where would *you* rather spend eternity? In an earthly paradise or a sterile laboratory?"

The answer didn't seem as clear-cut to me as it evidently

did to Simon. I recalled Mark Twain's reply to a similar question:

Heaven, for the climate. Hell, for the company.

○ ○ ○

There was some audible arguing from inside the house—Diane's voice, scolding, and her brother's sullen, uninflected replies. Simon and I pulled a couple of folding chairs out of the garage and sat in the shade of the carport waiting for the twins to finish. We talked about the weather. The weather was very nice. We reached a consensus on that point.

The noise from the house eventually settled down. After a while a chastened-looking Jason came out and invited us to help him with the barbecue. We followed him around back and made more nice talk while the grill warmed up. Diane stepped out of the house looking flushed but triumphant. This was the way she used to look whenever she won an argument with Jase: a little haughty, a little surprised.

We sat down to chicken and iced tea and the remains of the three-bean salad. "Do y'all mind if I offer a blessing?" Simon asked.

Jason rolled his eyes but nodded.

Simon bent his head solemnly. I braced myself for a sermon. But all he said was, "Grant us the courage to accept the bounty You have placed before us this and every other day. Amen."

A prayer expressing not gratitude but the need for courage. Very contemporary. Diane smiled at me across the table. Then she squeezed Simon's arm, and we proceeded to dig in.

○ ○ ○

It was early when we finished, sunlight still lingering, the mosquitos not yet at their evening frenzy. The breeze had died and there was a softness in the cooling air.

Elsewhere, things were happening fast.

What we didn't know—what even Jason, for all his vaunted connections, hadn't yet been told—was that somewhere between that first bite of chicken and that last spoonful of three-bean salad the Chinese had pulled out of negotiations and ordered the immediate launch of a brace of modified Dong Feng missiles armed with thermonuclear warheads. The rockets might have been rising in their arcs even as we pulled Heinekens out of the cooler. Icy green rocket-shaped bottles dripping summer sweat.

We cleared the patio table. I mentioned the worn spark plugs and my plan to drive Simon into town in the morning. Diane whispered something to her brother, then (after a pause) nudged him with her elbow. Jase finally nodded and turned to Simon and said, "There's one of those automotive superstores outside Stockbridge that's open till nine. Why don't I drive you over there right now?"

It was a peace offering, however reluctant. Simon recovered from his initial surprise and said, "I'm not about to turn down a ride in that Ferrari, if that's what you're offering."

"I can put it through its paces for you." Mollified by the prospect of showing off his car, Jason went into the house to fetch his keys. Simon shot back a well-gosh expression before following him. I looked at Diane. She grinned, proud of this triumph of diplomacy.

Elsewhere, the Dong Feng missiles approached and then crossed the Spin barrier en route to their programmed targets. Strange to think of them streaking over a suddenly dark, cold, motionless Earth, operating solely on internal programming, aiming themselves at the featureless artifacts that drifted in suspension hundreds of miles over the poles.

Like a drama without an audience, too sudden to see.

○ ○ ○

The educated consensus—afterward—was that the detonation of the Chinese warheads had no effect on the differential flow of time. What was affected (profoundly) was the visual filter surrounding the Earth. Not to mention the human perception of the Spin.

As Jase had pointed out years ago, the temporal gradient meant that massive amounts of radically blue-shifted radiation would have bathed the surface of our planet had that radiation not been filtered and managed by the Hypotheticals. More than three years of sunlight for every second that passed: enough to kill every living thing on Earth, enough to sterilize the soil and boil the oceans. The Hypotheticals, who had engineered the temporal enclosure of the Earth, had also shielded us from its lethal side effects. Moreover, the Hypotheticals were regulating not only how much energy reached the static Earth but how much of the planet's own heat and light was radiated back into space. Which was perhaps why the weather these last few years had been so pleasantly . . . average.

The sky over the Berkshires, at least, was as cloudless as Waterford crystal when the Chinese payloads reached their targets, 7:55 Eastern time.

○ ○ ○

I was with Diane in the front room when the house phone rang.

Did we notice anything before Jason's call? A change in the light, something as insignificant as the feeling that a cloud might have passed in front of the sun? No. Nothing. All my attention was on Diane. We were drinking coolers and talking about trivia. Books we'd read, movies we'd seen. The conversation was mesmerizing, not for its content but for the cadences of the talk, the rhythm we fell into when we were alone, now as before. Every conversation between friends or lovers creates its own easy or awkward rhythms, hidden talk that runs like a subterranean river under even the most banal exchange. What we said was trite and conventional, but the undertalk was deep and occasionally treacherous.

And pretty soon we were flirting with each other, as if Simon Townsend and the last eight years signified nothing. Joking at first, then maybe not joking. I told her I'd missed her. She said, "There were times I wanted to talk to you. Needed to talk to you. But I didn't have your number, or I figured you were busy."

"You could have found my number. I wasn't busy."

"You're right. Actually it was more like . . . moral cowardice."

"Am I that frightening?"

"Not you. Our situation. I suppose I felt as if I ought to apologize to you. And I didn't know how to begin to do that." She smiled wanly. "I guess I still don't."

"There's nothing to apologize for, Diane."

"Thank you for saying so, but I happen to disagree. We're not kids anymore. It's possible to look back with a certain amount of insight. We were as close as two people can be without actually touching. But that was the one thing we couldn't do. Or even talk about. As if we had taken an oath of silence."

"Since the night the stars disappeared," I said, dry-mouthed, aghast at myself, terrified, aroused.

Diane waved her hand. "That night. That night—you know what I remember about that night? Jason's binoculars. I was looking at the Big House while you two stared off into the sky. I really don't remember the stars at all. What I remember is catching sight of Carol in one of the back bedrooms with somebody from the catering service. She was drunk and it looked like she was making a pass." She laughed bashfully. "That was my own little apocalypse. Everything I already hated about the Big House, about my family, it was all summed up in one night. I just wanted to pretend it didn't exist. No Carol, no E.D., no Jason—"

"No me?"

She moved across the sofa and, because it had become that kind of conversation, put a hand on my cheek. Her hand was cool, the temperature of the drink she'd been holding. "You were the exception. I was scared. You were incredibly patient. I appreciated that."

"But we couldn't—"

"Touch."

"Touch. E.D. would never have stood for it."

She took her hand away. "We could have hidden it from him if we'd wanted to. But you're right, E.D. was the problem. He infected everything. It was obscene, the way he made your mother live a kind of second-class existence. It was debasing. Can I confess this? I absolutely hated being his daughter. I especially hated the idea that if anything, you know, happened between us, it might be your way of taking revenge on E. D. Lawton."

She sat back, a little surprised at herself, I think.

"Of course," I said carefully, "it wouldn't have been."

"I was confused."

"Is that what NK is for you? Revenge on E.D.?"

"No," she said, still smiling, "I don't love Simon just because he makes my father angry. Life's not that simple, Ty."

"I didn't mean to suggest—"

"But you see how insidious it is? Certain suspicions come into your head and get stuck there. No, NK isn't about my father. It's about discovering the divinity in what's happened to the Earth and expressing that divinity in daily life."

"Maybe the Spin isn't that simple, either."

"We're either being murdered or transformed, Simon says."

"He told me you're building heaven on Earth."

"Isn't that what Christians are supposed to do? Make the Kingdom of God by expressing it in their lives?"

"Or at least dancing to it."

"Now you sound like Jason. Obviously I can't defend everything about the movement. Last week we were at a conclave in Philadelphia and we met this couple, our age, friendly, intelligent—'alive in the spirit,' Simon called them. We went out to dinner and talked about the Parousia. Then they invited us up to their hotel room, and suddenly they were laying out lines of coke and playing porn videos. All kinds of marginal people are attracted to NK. No question. And for most of them the theology barely exists, except as a fuzzy image of the Garden of Eden. But at its best the movement is everything it claims to be, a genuine living faith."

"Faith in what, Diane? Ekstasis? Promiscuity?"

I regretted the words as soon as I'd said them. She looked hurt. "Ekstasis isn't about promiscuity. Not when it succeeds, anyway. But in the body of God no act is prohibited as long as it isn't vengeful or angry, as long as it expresses divine as well as human love."

The phone rang then. I must have looked guilty. Diane saw my expression and laughed.

Jason's first words when I picked up: "I said we'd have some warning. I'm sorry. I was wrong."

"What?"

"Tyler . . . haven't you seen the sky?"

○ ○ ○

So we went upstairs to find a window facing the sunset.

The west bedroom was generously large, equipped with a mahogany chifferobe, a brass-railed bed, and big windows. I drew the curtains wide. Diane gasped.

There was no setting sun. Or, rather, there were several.

The entire western sky was alight. Instead of the single orb of the sun there was an arc of reddish glow that stretched across at least fifteen degrees of the horizon, containing what looked like a flickering multiple exposure of a dozen or more sunsets. The light was erratic; it brightened and faded like a distant fire.

We gaped at it for an endless time. Eventually Diane said, "What's happening, Tyler? What's going on?"

I told her what Jason had told me about the Chinese nuclear warheads.

"He knew this might happen?" she asked, then answered herself: "Of course he did." The strange light gave the room a roseate hue and fell on her cheeks like a fever. "Will it kill us?"

"Jason doesn't think so. It'll scare the hell out of people, though."

"But is it dangerous? Radiation or something?"

I doubted it. But it wasn't out of the question. "Try the TV," I said. There was a plasma panel in each bedroom, framed in walnut paneling opposite the bed. I figured any kind of remotely lethal radiation would also screw up broadcasting and reception.

But the TV worked well enough to show us news channel views of crowds gathering in cities across Europe, where it was already dark—or as dark as it was going to get that night. No lethal radiation but plenty of incipient panic. Diane sat motionless on the edge of the bed, hands folded in her lap, clearly frightened. I sat beside her and said, "If any of this was going to kill us we'd be dead by now."

Outside, the sunset stuttered toward darkness. The diffuse glow resolved into several distinct setting suns, each ghostly pale, then a coil of sunlight like a luminous spring that arced across the whole sky and vanished just as suddenly.

We sat hip to hip as the sky grew darker.

Then the stars came out.

○ ○ ○

I managed to get hold of Jase one more time before the bandwidth was overwhelmed. Simon had just finished paying for the plug set for his car, he said, when the sky erupted. The roads out of Stockbridge were already crowded and the radio reported scattered looting in Boston and stalled traffic on every major route, so Jase had pulled into a parking lot behind a motel and rented a room for the night for himself and Simon. In the morning, he said, he would probably have to head back to Washington, but he'd drop Simon at the house first.

Then he passed his phone to Simon and I passed mine to Diane and left the room while she talked to her fiancé. The summerhouse seemed ominously huge and empty. I walked around turning on lights until she called me back.

"Another drink?" I asked her.

"Oh yes," she said.

○ ○ ○

We went outside a little after midnight.

Diane was putting on a brave face. Simon had given her some kind of New Kingdom pep talk. In NK theology there was no conventional Second Coming, no Rapture or Armageddon; the Spin was all these things put together, all the ancient prophecies obliquely fulfilled. And if God wanted to use the canvas of the sky to paint us the naked geometry of time, Simon said, He would do so, and our awe and fear were entirely appropriate to the occasion. But we shouldn't be overwhelmed by these feelings because the Spin was ultimately an act of salvation, the last and best chapter in human history.

Or something like that.

So we went outside to watch the sky because Diane thought it was a brave and spiritual thing to do. The sky was cloudless and the air smelled of pine. The highway was a long way off, but we heard occasional faint sounds of car horns and sirens.

Our shadows danced around us as various fractions of the sky lit up, now north, now south. We sat on the grass a few yards from the steady glow of the porch light and Diane leaned into my shoulder and I put my arm around her, both of us a little drunk.

Despite years of emotional chill, despite our history at the Big House, despite her engagement to Simon Townsend, despite NK and Ekstasis and despite even the nuke-inspired derangement of the sky, I was exquisitely conscious of the pressure of her body next to mine. And the strange thing was that it felt absolutely familiar, the curve of her arm under my hand and the weight of her head against my shoulder: not discovered but remembered. She felt the way I had always known she would feel. Even the tang of her fear was familiar.

The sky sparked with strange light. Not the unadulterated light of the Spinning universe, which would have killed us on the spot. Instead it was a series of snapshots of the sky, consecutive midnights compressed into microseconds, afterimages fading like the pop of a flashbulb; then the same sky a century or a millennium later, like sequences in a surreal movie. Some of the frames were blurred long-exposures, starlight and moonlight become ghostly orbs or circles or scimitars. Some were crisp and quickly fading stills. Toward the north the lines and circles in the sky were narrower, their radii relatively small, while the equatorial stars were more restless, waltzing over huge ellipses. Full and half and waning moons blinked from horizon to horizon in pale orange transparencies. The Milky Way was a band of white fluorescence (now brighter, now darker) lit by flaring, dying stars. Stars were created and stars were demolished with every breath of summer air.

And it all moved.

Moved in vast shimmerings and intricate dances suggesting ever-greater, still-invisible cycles. The sky beat like a heart above us. "So alive," Diane said.

There is a prejudice imposed on us by our brief window of consciousness: things that move are alive; things that don't are dead. The living worm twines under the dead and static rock. Stars and planets move, but only according to the inert laws of gravitation: a stone may fall but is not alive, and orbital motion is only the same falling indefinitely prolonged.

But extend our mayfly existence, as the Hypotheticals had, and the distinction blurs. Stars are born, live, die, and bequeath their elementary ashes to newer stars. The sum of their various motions is not simple but unimaginably complex, a dance of attraction and velocity, beautiful but frightening. Frightening because, like an earthquake, the writhing stars made mutable what ought to be solid. Frightening because our deepest organic secrets, our couplings and our messy acts of reproduction, turn out not to be secrets after all: the stars are also bleeding and laboring. *No single thing abides, but all things flow.* I couldn't remember where I had read that.

"Heraclitus," Diane said.

I wasn't aware that I'd said it aloud.

"All those years," Diane said, "back at the Big House, all those fucking wasted years, I knew—"

I put my finger on her lips. I knew what she had known.

"I want to go back inside," she said. "I want to go back to the bedroom."

○ ○ ○

We didn't pull the blinds. The spinning, kinetic stars cast their light into the room and in the darkness the patterns played over my skin and Diane's in focusless images, the way city lights shine through a rain-streaked window, silently, sinuously. We said nothing because words would have been an impediment. Words would have been lies. We made love wordlessly, and only when it was over did I find myself thinking, *Let this abide. Just this.*

We were asleep when the sky once more darkened, when the celestial fireworks finally dimmed and disappeared. The Chinese attack had amounted to little more than a gesture. Thousands had died as a result of the global panic, but there had been no direct casualties on Earth—or, presumably, among the Hypotheticals.

The sun rose on schedule the next morning.

The buzz of the house phone woke me. I was alone in

bed. Diane took the call in another room and came in to tell
me it was Jase, he said the roads were clear and he was on
his way back.

She had showered and dressed and she smelled like soap
and starched cotton. "And that's it?" I said. "Simon shows up
and you drive away? Last night means nothing?"

She sat down on the bed next to me. "Last night never
meant that I wouldn't leave with Simon."

"I thought it meant more."

"It meant more than I can possibly say. But it doesn't erase
the past. I've made promises and I have a faith and those
things put certain boundaries on my life."

She sounded unconvinced. I said, "A faith. Tell me you
don't believe in this shit."

She stood up, frowning.

"Maybe I don't," she said. "But maybe I need to be around
someone who does."

○ ○ ○

I packed and loaded my luggage into the Hyundai before Jase
and Simon got back. Diane watched from the porch as I
closed the lid of the trunk.

"I'll call you," she said.

"You do that," I told her.

4×10^9 A.D.

I broke another lamp during one of my fits of fever.

This time Diane managed to conceal it from the concierge. She had bribed the housekeeping staff to exchange clean for dirty linen at the door every second morning rather than have a maid make up the room and risk finding me delirious. Cases of dengue, cholera, and human CVWS had cropped up at the local hospital within the last six months. I didn't want to wake up in an epidemiological ward next to a quarantine case.

"What worries me," Diane said, "is what might happen when I'm not here."

"I can take care of myself."

"Not if the fever spikes."

"Then it's a matter of luck and timing. Are you planning to go somewhere?"

"Only the usual. But I mean, in an emergency. Or if I can't get back to the room for some reason."

"What kind of emergency?"

She shrugged. "It's hypothetical," she said, in a tone that suggested it was anything but.

○ ○ ○

But I didn't press her about it. There was nothing I could do to improve the situation except cooperate.

I was beginning the second week of the treatment, approaching the crisis. The Martian drug had accumulated to some critical level in my blood and tissues. Even when the fevers subsided I felt disoriented, confused. The purely physical side effects were no fun either. Joint pain. Jaundice. Rash, if by "rash" you mean the sensation of having your skin slough off, layer by layer, exposing flesh almost as raw as an open wound. Some nights I slept for four or five hours—five was my record, I think—and woke in a slurry of dander, which Diane would clean from the blood-pocked bed while I shifted arthritically to a bedside chair.

I came to distrust even my most lucid moments. Just as often what I felt was a purely hallucinatory clarity, the world overbright and hyperdefined, words and memory cogged like gears in a runaway engine.

Bad for me. Maybe worse for Diane, who had to do bedpan duty during the times I was incontinent. In a way she was returning a favor. I had been with her when she endured this phase of the struggle herself. But that had been many years ago.

○ ○ ○

Most nights she slept beside me, though I don't know how she stood it. She kept a careful distance between us—at times just the pressure of the cotton sheet was painful enough to make me weep—but the almost subliminal sense of her presence was soothing.

On the really bad nights, when in my thrashing I might have thrown out an arm and hurt her, she curled up on the flower-print settee by the balcony doors.

She didn't say much about her trips into Padang. I knew approximately what she was doing there: making connections with pursers and cargo masters, pricing out options for a transit of the Arch. Dangerous work. If anything made me feel worse than the effects of the drug it was watching Diane walk out the door into a potentially violent Asian demimonde with no more protection than a pocket-sized can of Mace and her own considerable courage.

But even that intolerable risk was better than getting caught.

They—and by "they" I mean agents of the Chaykin administration or their allies in Jakarta—were interested in us for a number of reasons. Because of the drug, of course, and more important the several digital copies of the Martian archives we were carrying. And they would have loved to interrogate us about Jason's last hours: the monologue I had witnessed and recorded, everything he had told me about the nature of the Hypotheticals and the Spin, knowledge only Jason had possessed.

o o o

I slept and woke, and she was gone.

I spent an hour watching the balcony curtains move, watching sunlight angle up the visible leg of the Arch, daydreaming about the Seychelles.

Ever been to the Seychelles? Me neither. What was running in my head was an old PBS documentary I had once seen. The Seychelles are tropical islands, home to tortoises and *coco de mer* and a dozen varieties of rare birds. Geologically, they're all that remains of an ancient continent that once linked Asia and South America, long before the evolution of modern humans.

Dreams, Diane once said, are metaphors gone feral. The reason I dreamed about the Seychelles (I imagined her telling me) was because I felt submerged, ancient, almost extinct.

Like a drowning continent, awash in the prospect of my own transformation.

o o o

I slept again. Woke, and she still wasn't there.

o o o

Woke in the dark, still alone and knowing that by now too much time had passed. Bad sign. In the past, Diane had always come back by nightfall.

I'd been thrashing in my sleep. The cotton sheet lay pud-dled on the floor, barely visible in the light reflected by the plaster ceiling from the street outside. I was chilly but too sore to reach over and retrieve it.

The sky outside was exquisitely clear. If I gritted my teeth and inclined my head to the left I could see a few bright stars through the glass balcony doors. I entertained myself with the idea that in absolute terms some of those stars might be younger than I was.

I tried not to think about Diane and where she might be and what might be happening to her.

And eventually I fell asleep with the starlight burning through my eyelids, phosphorescent ghosts floating in the reddish dark.

○ ○ ○

Morning.

At least I thought it was morning. There was daylight be-yond the window now. Someone, most likely the maid, knocked twice and said something testy in Malay from the hall. And went away again.

Now I was genuinely worried, though in this particular phase of the treatment the anxiety came through as a mud-dled peevishness. What had possessed Diane to stay away so intolerably long, and why wasn't she here to hold my hand and sponge my forehead? The idea that she might have come to harm was unwelcome, unproven, inadmissible before the court.

Still, the plastic bottle of water by the bed had been empty since at least yesterday or longer, my lips were chapped to the point of cracking, and I couldn't remember the last time I had hobbled to the toilet. If I didn't want my kidneys to shut down altogether I'd have to fetch water from the bathroom tap.

But it was hard enough just sitting up without screaming. The act of levering my legs over the side of the mattress was nearly unendurable, as if my bones and cartilage had been re-placed with broken glass and rusty razors.

And although I tried to distract myself by thinking of something else (the Seychelles, the sky), even that feeble anodyne was distorted by the lens of the fever. I imagined I heard Jason's voice behind me, Jason asking me to get him something—a rag, a chamois; his hands were dirty. I came out of the bathroom with a washcloth instead of a glass of water and was halfway back to bed before I realized my mistake. Stupid. Start again. Take the empty water bottle this time. Fill it all the way up. Fill it to brimming. Follow the drinking gourd.

Handing him a chamois in the garden shed behind the Big House where the landscapers kept their tools.

He would have been about twelve years old. Early summer, a couple of years before the Spin.

Sip water and taste time. Here comes memory again.

○ ○ ○

I was surprised when Jason suggested we try to fix the gardener's gas mower. The gardener at the Big House was an irritable Belgian named De Meyer, who chain-smoked Gauloises and would only shrug sourly when we spoke to him. He had been cursing the mower because it coughed smoke and stalled every few minutes. Why do him a favor? But it was the intellectual challenge that fascinated Jase. He told me he'd been up past midnight researching gasoline engines on the Internet. His curiosity was piqued. He said he wanted to see what one looked like in vivo. The fact that I didn't know what in vivo meant made the prospect sound doubly interesting. I said I'd be happy to help.

In fact I did little more than watch while he positioned the mower over a dozen sheets of yesterday's *Washington Post* and began his examination. This was inside the musty but private tool shed at the back of the lawn, where the air reeked of oil and gasoline, fertilizer and herbicide. Bags of lawn seed and bark mulch spilled from raw pine shelves among the spavined blades and splintered handles of garden tools. We weren't supposed to play in the tool shed. Usually it was locked. Jason had taken the key from a rack inside the basement door.

It was a hot Friday afternoon outside and I didn't mind being in there watching him work; it was both instructive and oddly soothing. First he inspected the machine, stretching his body along the floor beside it. He patiently ran his fingers over the cowling, locating the screw heads, and when he was satisfied he removed the screws and set them aside, in order, and the housing next to them when he lifted it off.

And so into the deep workings of the machine. Somehow Jason had taught himself or intuited the use of a ratchet driver and a torque wrench. His moves were sometimes tentative but never uncertain. He worked like an artist or an athlete— nuanced, knowing, conscious of his own limitations. He had disassembled every part he could reach and laid them all out on the grease-blackened pages of the *Post* like an anatomical illustration when the shed door squealed open and we both jumped.

E. D. Lawton had come home early.

"Shit," I whispered, which won me a hard look from the senior Lawton. He stood in the doorway in an immaculately tailored gray suit, surveying the wreckage, while Jason and I stared at our feet, as instinctively guilty as if we'd been caught with a copy of *Penthouse*.

"Are you *fixing* that or *vandalizing* it?" he asked finally, his tone conveying the mixture of contempt and disdain that was E. D. Lawton's verbal signature, a trick he had mastered so long ago it was second nature to him now.

"Sir," Jason said meekly. "Fixing it."

"I see. Is it *your* lawn mower?"

"No, of course not, but I thought Mr. De Meyer might like it if I—"

"But it's not Mr. De Meyer's lawn mower, either, is it? Mr. De Meyer doesn't own his own tools. He'd be collecting welfare if I didn't hire him every summer. It happens to be *my* lawn mower." E.D. let the silence expand until it was almost painful. Then he said, "Have you found the problem?"

"Not yet."

"Not yet? Then you'd better get on with it."

Jason looked almost supernaturally relieved. "Yes, sir," he said. "I thought after dinner I'd—"

"No. Not after dinner. You took it apart, you fix it and put it back together. Then you can eat." E.D. turned his unwelcome attention my way. "Go home, Tyler. I don't want to find you in here again. You ought to know better."

I scurried out into the afternoon glare, blinking.

He didn't catch me in the shed again, but only because I was careful to avoid him. I was back later that night—after ten, when I looked out my bedroom window and saw light still leaking from the crevice under the shed door. I took a leftover chicken leg from the refrigerator, wrapped it in tinfoil, and hustled over under cover of darkness. Whispered to Jase, who doused the light long enough for me slip inside unseen.

He was covered in Maori tattoos of grease and oil, and the mower engine was still only halfway reassembled. After he'd wolfed down a few bites of chicken I asked him what was taking so long.

"I could put it back together in fifteen minutes," he said. "But it wouldn't work. The hard part is figuring out exactly what's wrong. Plus I keep making it worse. If I try to clean the fuel line I get air inside it. Or the rubber cracks. Nothing's in very good shape. There's a hairline fracture in the carburetor housing, but I don't know how to fix it. I don't have spare parts. Or the right tools. I'm not even sure what the right tools *are*." His face wrinkled, and for a moment I thought he might cry.

"So give up," I said. "Go tell E.D. you're sorry and let him take it out of your allowance or whatever."

He stared at me as if I had said something noble but ridiculously naive. "No, Tyler. Thanks, but I won't be doing that."

"Why not?"

But he didn't answer. Just set aside the chicken leg and returned to the scattered pieces of his folly.

I was about to leave when there was another ultraquiet knock at the door. Jason gestured at me to douse the light. He cracked the door and let his sister in.

She was obviously terrified E.D. would find her here. She wouldn't speak above a whisper. But, like me, she'd brought Jase something. Not a chicken leg. A wireless Internet browser the size of her palm.

Jason's face lit up when he saw it. "Diane!" he said.

She shushed him and gave me a nervous sideways smile.

"It's just a gadget," she whispered, and nodded at us both before she slipped out again.

"She knows better," Jason said after she left. "The gadget's trivial. It's the network that's useful. Not the gadget but the network."

Within the hour he was consulting a group of West Coast gearheads who modified small engines for remote-control robotics competitions. By midnight he had rigged temporary repairs for the mower's dozen infirmities. I left, snuck home, and watched from my bedroom window when he summoned his father. E.D. traipsed out of the Big House in pajamas and an open flannel shirt and stood with his arms crossed while Jason powered up the mower, the sound of it incongruous in the early-morning dark. E.D. listened a few moments, then shrugged and beckoned Jason back in the house.

Jase, hovering at the door, saw my light across the lawn and gave me a little covert wave of his hand.

Of course, the repairs were temporary. The Gauloises-smoking gardener showed up the following Wednesday and had trimmed about half the lawn when the mower seized and died for good and all. Listening from the shade of the treeline we learned at least a dozen useful Flemish curses. Jason, whose memory was very nearly eidetic, took a shine to *God-verdomme mijn kloten miljardedju!*—literally, "God damn my balls a million times Jesus!" according to what Jason pieced together from the Dutch/English dictionary in the Rice school library. For the next few months he used the expression whenever he broke a shoelace or crashed a computer.

Eventually E.D. had to ante up for a whole new machine. The shop told him the old one would cost too much to fix; it was a miracle it had worked as long as it did. I heard this through my mother, who heard it from Carol Lawton. And as far as I know E.D. never spoke to Jason about it again.

Jase and I laughed over it a few times, though—months later, when most of the sting had gone out of it.

○ ○ ○

I shuffled back to bed thinking about Diane, who had given her brother a gift that was not just conciliatory, like mine, but actually useful. So where was she now? What gift could she bring me that would lighten my burden? Her own presence would do.

Daylight flowed through the room like water, like a luminous river in which I was suspended, drowned in empty minutes.

Not all delirium is bright and frantic. Sometimes it's slow, reptilian, cold-blooded. I watched shadows crawl like lizards up the walls of the hotel room. Blink, and an hour was gone. Blink again and night was falling, no sunlight on the Archway when I inclined my head to look at it, dark skies instead, tropical stormclouds, lightning indistinguishable from the visual spikes induced by fever, but thunder unmistakable and a sudden wet mineral smell from outside and the sound of raindrops spitting on the concrete balcony.

And eventually another sound: a card in the doorlock, the squeal of hinges.

"Diane," I said. (Or whispered, or croaked.)

She hurried into the room. She was dressed for the street, in a leather-trimmed jumper and broad-brimmed hat dripping rainwater. She stood by the side of the bed.

"I'm sorry," she said.

"Don't have to apologize. Just—"

"I mean, I'm sorry, Tyler, but you have to get dressed. We have to leave. Right away. *Now*. There's a cab waiting."

It took me some time to process this information. Meanwhile Diane started throwing stuff into a hard shell suitcase: clothes, documents both forged and legitimate, memory cards, a padded rack of small bottles and syringes. "I can't stand up," I tried to say, but the words wouldn't come out right.

So a moment later she started dressing me, and I salvaged a little dignity by lifting my legs without being asked and gritting my teeth instead of screaming. Then I sat up and she made me take more water from the bottle by the bedside. She led me to the bathroom, where I emitted a sludgy trickle of canary-yellow urine. "Oh hell," she said, "you're all dried out." She gave me another mouthful of water and a shot of analgesic that burned in my arm like venom. "Tyler, I'm so sorry!" But not sorry enough to stop urging me into a raincoat and a heavy hat.

I was alert enough to hear the anxiety in her voice. "What are we running from?"

"Just say I had a close encounter with some unpleasant people."

"Where are we going?"

"Inland. Hurry."

So we hustled along the dim corridor of the hotel, down a flight of stairs to ground level, Diane dragging the suitcase with her left hand and supporting me with her right. It was a long trek. The stairs, especially. "Stop moaning," she whispered a couple of times. So I did. Or at least I think I did.

Then out into the night. Raindrops bouncing off muddy sidewalks and sizzling on the hood of an overheated twenty-year-old taxi. The driver looked at me suspiciously from the shelter of his cab. I stared back. "He's not sick," Diane told him, making a bottle-to-the-mouth gesture, and the driver scowled but accepted the bills she pressed into his hand.

The narcotics took effect while we drove. The night streets of Padang had a cavernous smell, of dank asphalt and rotting fish. Oil slicks parted like rainbows under the wheels of the cab. We left the neon-lit tourist district and entered the tangle of shops and housing that had grown around the city in the last thirty years, makeshift slums giving way to the new prosperity, bulldozers parked under tarps between tin-roofed shacks. High-rise tenements grew like mushrooms from a compost of squatters' fields. Then we passed through the factory zone, gray walled and razor wired, and I slept, I think, again.

Dreaming not of the Seychelles but of Jason. Of Jason and his fondness for networks ("not a gadget but a network"), of the networks he had created and inhabited and the places those networks had taken him.

UNQUIET NIGHTS

Seattle, September, five years after the failed Chinese missile attack: I drove home through a rainy Friday rush hour and as soon as I was inside the door of my apartment I switched on the audio interface and cued a playlist I had put together labeled "Therapy."

It had been a long day in the Harborview ER. I had attended two gunshot wounds and an attempted suicide. Hovering in back of my eyelids was an image of blood sluicing from the rails of a gurney cart. I changed out of my rain-dampened day clothes into jeans and a sweatshirt, poured a drink, and stood by a window watching the city simmer in the dark. Somewhere out there was the lightless gap of Puget Sound, obscured by rolling clouds. Traffic was almost static on I-5, a luminous red river.

My life, essentially, as I had made it. And it was all balanced on a word.

Pretty soon Astrud Gilberto was singing, wistfully and a little off-key, about guitar chords and Corcovado, but I was still too wired to think about what Jason had said on the phone last night. Too wired even to hear the music the way it deserved to be heard. "Corcovado," "Desafinado," some Gerry Mulligan tracks, some Charlie Byrd. Therapy. But it all blurred into the sound of the rain. I microwaved dinner and ate it without tasting it; then I abandoned all hope of karmic equanimity and decided to knock on Giselle's door, see if she was home.

Giselle Palmer rented the apartment three doors down the hall. She opened the door wearing ragged jeans and an old flannel shirt that announced an evening at home. I asked her if she was busy or if she felt like hanging out.

"I don't know, Tyler. You look pretty gloomy."

"More like conflicted. I'm thinking about leaving town."

"Really? Some kind of business trip?"

"For good."

"Oh?" Her smile faded. "When did you decide that?"

"I haven't decided. That's the point."

She opened the door wider and waved me in. "Seriously? Where are   you going?"

"Long story."

"Meaning you need a drink before you talk about it?"

"Something like that," I said.

○ ○ ○

Giselle had introduced herself to me at a tenants' meeting in the basement of the building last year. She was twenty-four years old and about as tall as my collarbone. She worked days at a chain restaurant in Renton, but when we started getting together for coffee Sunday afternoons she told me she was "a hooker, a prostitute, it's my part-time job."

What she meant was that she was part of a loose group of female friends who traded among themselves the names of older men (presentable, usually married) who were willing to pay generously for sex but were terrified of the street trade. As she told me this Giselle had squared her shoulders and looked at me defiantly, in case I was shocked or repelled. I hadn't been. These were, after all, the Spin years. People Giselle's age made their own rules, for better or worse, and people like me abstained from passing judgment.

We continued to share coffee or an occasional dinner, and I had written requisitions for blood work for her on a couple of occasions. As of her last test Giselle was HIV-free and the only major communicable disease for which she carried antibodies was West Nile virus. In other words, she had been both careful and lucky.

But the thing about the sex trade, Giselle had told me, was that even at the semi-amateur level it begins to define your life. You become, she said, the kind of person who carries condoms and Viagra in her purse. So why do it, when she could have taken, say, a night job at Wal-Mart? That was a question she didn't welcome and which she answered defensively: "Maybe it's a kink. Or maybe it's a hobby, you know, like model trains." But I knew she had run away from an abusive stepfather in Saskatoon at an early age, and the ensuing career arc wasn't difficult to imagine. And of course she had the same ironclad excuse for risky behavior all of us of a certain age shared: the near-certainty of our own mass extinction. Mortality, a writer of my generation once said, trumps morality.

She said, "So how drunk do you need to get? Tipsy or totally fucked? Actually we may not have a choice. Liquor cabinet's a little bare tonight."

She mixed me something that was mostly vodka and tasted like it had been drained from a fuel tank. I cleared the daily paper off a chair and sat down. Giselle's apartment was decently furnished but she kept house like a freshman in a dorm room. The newspaper was open to the editorial page. The cartoon was about the Spin: the Hypotheticals portrayed as a couple of black spiders gripping the Earth in their hairy legs. Caption: DO WE EAT THEM NOW OR WAIT FOR THE ELECTION?

"I don't get that at all," Giselle said, slumping onto the sofa and waving at the paper with her foot.

"The cartoon?"

"The whole thing. The Spin. 'No return.' Reading the papers, it's like . . . what? There's something on the other side of the sky, and it's not friendly. That's all I really know."

Probably the majority of the human race could have signed off on that declaration. But for some reason—maybe it was the rain, the blood that had been spilled in my presence today—what she said made me feel indignant. "It's not that hard to understand."

"No? So why's it happening?"

"Not the *why*. Nobody knows the *why*. As for the *what*—"

"No, I know, I don't need that lecture. We're in a sort of cosmic baggie and the universe is spinning out of control, yada yada yada."

Which irked me again. "You know your own address, don't you?"

She sipped her own drink. "Course I do."

"Because you like to know where you are. A couple of miles from the ocean, a hundred miles from the border, a few thousand miles west of New York City—right?"

"Right, but so what?"

"I'm making a point. People don't have any trouble distinguishing between Spokane and Paris, but when it comes to the sky all they see is a big amorphous mystery blob. How come?"

"I don't know. Because I learned all my astronomy from *Star Trek* reruns? I mean, how much do I really have to know about moons and stars? Things I haven't seen since I was a little kid. Even the scientists admit they don't know what they're talking about half the time."

"And that's okay with you?"

"The fuck difference does it make if it's okay with me? Listen, maybe I should turn on the TV. We can watch a movie and you can tell me why you're thinking about leaving town."

Stars were like people, I told her: they live and die in predictable spans of time. The sun was aging fast, and as it aged it burned its fuel faster. Its luminosity increased ten percent for every billion years. The solar system had already changed in ways that would render the raw Earth uninhabitable even if the Spin stopped today. Point of no return. That's what the newspapers were talking about. It would not have been news, except that President Clayton had made it official, admitted in a speech that according to the best scientific opinion there was no way back to the *status quo ante*.

And she gave me a long unhappy stare and said, "All this bullshit—"

"It's not bullshit."

"Maybe not, but it's not doing me any good."

"I'm just trying to explain—"

"Fuck, Tyler. Did I ask for an explanation? Take your nightmares and go home. Or else settle down and tell me why you want to leave Seattle. This is about those friends of yours, isn't it?"

I had told her about Jason and Diane. "Mostly Jason."

"The so-called genius."

"Not just so-called. He's in Florida . . ."

"Doing something for the satellite people, you said."

"Turning Mars into a garden."

"That was in the papers, too. Is it really possible?"

"I have no idea. Jason seems to think so."

"But wouldn't it take a long time?"

"The clocks run faster," I said, "past a certain altitude."

"Uh-huh. So what's he need you for?"

Well, yeah, what? Good question. Excellent question. "They're hiring a physician for the in-house clinic at Perihelion."

"I thought you were just an ordinary GP."

"I am."

"So what makes you qualified to be an astronaut doctor?"

"Absolutely nothing. But Jason—"

"He's doing a favor for an old buddy? Well, that figures. God bless the rich, huh? Keep it among friends."

I shrugged. Let her think so. No need to share this with Giselle, and Jase hadn't said anything specific. . . .

But when we talked I had formed the impression that Jason wanted me not just as a house doctor but as his personal physician. Because he was having a problem. Some kind of problem he didn't want to share with the Perihelion staff. A problem he wouldn't talk about over the phone.

Giselle had run out of vodka but she rummaged in her purse and came up with a joint concealed in a box of tampons. "The pay is good, I bet." She clicked a plastic lighter and applied the flame to the twist of the joint and inhaled deeply.

"We didn't get into details."

She exhaled. "*Such* a geek. Maybe that's why you can

stand thinking about the Spin all the time. Tyler Dupree, bor-
derline autistic. You *are*, you know. All the signs. I bet this Jason Lawton is exactly the same. I bet he gets a hard-on every
time he says the word 'billion.' "

"Don't underestimate him. He might actually help preserve the human race." If not any particular specimen of it.

"A geek ambition if I ever heard one. And this sister of his,
the one you slept with—"

"Once."

"Once. She got religion, right?"

"Right." Got it and still had it, as far as I knew. I hadn't
heard from Diane since that night in the Berkshires. Not entirely for lack of trying. A couple of e-mails had gone unanswered. Jase didn't hear much from her either, but according
to Carol she was living with Simon somewhere in Utah or
Arizona—some western state I'd never visited and couldn't
picture—where the dissolution of the New Kingdom movement had stranded them.

"That's not hard to figure out either." Giselle passed the
joint. I wasn't totally at ease with pot. But that "geek" remark
had stung. I toked deeply, and the effect was exactly what it
had been back in residence at Stony Brook: instant aphasia.
"It must have been awful for her. The Spin happening, and all
she wanted to do was forget about it, which was the last thing
you or her family would let her do. I'd get religion too, in her
place. I'd be singing in the fucking choir."

I said—belatedly, behind the buzz—"Is the world really so
hard to look at?"

Giselle reached out and took back the joint. "From where I
stand," she said, "yes. Mostly."

She turned her head, distracted. Thunder rattled the window as if it resented the dry warmth inside. Some serious
weather was coming in across the Sound. "Bet it's gonna be
one of those winters," she said. "The nasty kind. I wish I had
a fireplace in here. Music would help. But I'm too tired to
get up."

I went over to her audio rig and cued a download of a Stan
Getz album, the saxophone warming the room the way no
fireplace could have. She nodded at that: not what she would

have picked, but yeah, good. . . . "So he called you and offered you this job."

"Right."

"And you told him you'd take it?"

"I told him I'd think about it."

"Is that what you're doing? Thinking about it?"

She seemed to be implying something, but I didn't know what. "I guess I am."

"I guess you're not. I guess you already know what you're going to do. You know what I guess? I guess you're here to say good-bye."

I said I guessed that was possible.

"So at least come and sit next to me."

I moved to the sofa lethargically. Giselle stretched out and put her feet in my lap. She was wearing men's socks, a slightly ridiculous pair of fuzzy argyles. The cuffs of her jeans rode up her ankles. "For a guy who can look at a gunshot wound without flinching," she said, "you're pretty good at avoiding mirrors."

"What's that mean?"

"Means you're really obviously not finished with Jason and Diane. Her especially."

But it wasn't possible that Diane still mattered to me.

Maybe I wanted to prove that. Maybe that's why we ended up stumbling together into Giselle's messy bedroom, smoking another joint, falling down on the Barbie-pink bedspread, making love under the rain-blinded windows, holding each other until we fell asleep.

But it wasn't Giselle's face that floated into my mind in the dreamy aftermath, and I woke a couple of hours later thinking: My god, she's right, I'm going to Florida.

o o o

In the end it took weeks to arrange, both at Jason's end and at the hospital. During that time I saw Giselle again, but only briefly. She was in the market for a used car and I sold her mine; I didn't want to risk the drive cross-country. (Road robbery on the interstates was up by double digits.) But we didn't mention the intimacy that had come and gone with the

rainy weather, an act of slightly drunken kindness on someone's part, most likely hers.

Apart from Giselle there were few people in Seattle I
needed to say good-bye to and not much in my apartment I
needed to keep, nothing more substantial than some digital
files, eminently portable, and a few hundred old discs. The
day I left, Giselle helped me stack my luggage in the back of
the taxi. "SeaTac," I told the driver, and she waved good-
bye—not particularly sadly but at least wistfully—as the cab
pulled into traffic.

Giselle was good person and she was leading a perilous
life. I never saw her again, but I hope she survived the chaos
that came later.

○ ○ ○

The flight to Orlando was a creaking old Airbus. The cabin
upholstery was threadbare, the seatback video screens overdue for replacement. I took my place between a Russian businessman in the window seat and a middle-aged woman on the
aisle. The Russian was sullenly indifferent to conversation
but the woman wanted to talk: she was a professional medical
transcriptionist bound for Tampa for a two-week visit with
her daughter and son-in-law. Her name was Sarah, she said,
and we talked medical shop while the aircraft lumbered toward cruising altitude.

Vast amounts of federal money had been pumped into the
aerospace industry in the five years since the Chinese fireworks display. Very little of it had been devoted to commercial aviation, however, which was why these refurbished
Airbuses were still flying. Instead the money had gone into
the kind of projects E. D. Lawton was managing from his
Washington office and Jason was designing at Perihelion in
Florida: Spin investigations, including, lately, the Mars effort. The Clayton administration had shepherded all this
spending through a compliant Congress pleased to appear to
be doing something tangible about the Spin. It was good for
public morale. Better still, no one expected immediate tangible results.

Federal money had helped keep the domestic economy

afloat, at least in the Southwest, greater Seattle, coastal Florida. But it was a laggard and ice-thin prosperity, and Sarah was worried about her daughter: her son-in-law was a licensed pipe fitter, laid off indefinitely by a Tampa-area natural gas distributor. They were living in a trailer, collecting federal relief money and trying to raise a three-year-old boy, Sarah's grandson, Buster.

"Isn't that an odd name," she asked, "for a boy? I mean, *Buster?* Sounds like a silent-movie star. But the thing is, it kind of suits him."

I told her names were like clothes: either you wore them or they wore you. She said, "Is that right, Tyler Dupree?" and I smiled sheepishly.

"Of course," she said, "I don't know why young people want to have children at all these days. As awful as that sounds. Nothing against Buster, of course. I dearly love him and I hope he'll have a long and happy life. But I can't help wondering, what are the odds?"

"Sometimes people need a reason to hope," I said, wondering if this banal truth was what Giselle had been trying to tell me.

"But then," she said, "many young people *aren't* having children, I mean deliberately not having them, as an act of kindness. They say the best thing you can do for a child is to spare it the suffering we're all in store for."

"I'm not sure anybody knows what we're in store for."

"I mean, the point of no return and all . . ."

"Which we've passed. But here we are. For some reason."

She arched her eyebrows. "You believe there are *reasons,* Dr. Dupree?"

We chatted some more; then Sarah said, "I must try to sleep," wadding the airline's miniature pillow into the gap between her neck and the headrest. Outside the window, partially obscured by the indifferent Russian, the sun had set, the sky had gone sooty black; there was nothing to see but a reflection of the overhead light, which I dimmed and focused on my knees.

Idiotically, I had packed all my reading material in my checked luggage. But there was a tattered magazine in the pouch in front of Sarah, and I reached over and snagged it. The magazine, with a plain white cover, was called *Gateway*. A religious publication, probably left behind by a previous passenger.

I leafed through it, thinking, inevitably, of Diane. In the years since the failed attack on the Spin artifacts the New Kingdom movement had lost whatever coherence it had once possessed. Its founding figures had disavowed it and its happy sexual communism had burned out under the pressure of venereal disease and human cupidity. No one today, even on the *avant* fringe of trendy religiosity, would describe himself simply as "NK." You might be a Hectorian, a Preterist (Full or Partial), a Kingdom Reconstructionist—never just "New Kingdom." The Ekstasis circuit Diane and Simon had been traveling the summer we met in the Berkshires had ceased to exist.

None of the remaining NK factions carried much demographic clout. The Southern Baptists alone outnumbered all the Kingdom sects put together. But the millenarian focus of the movement had lent it disproportional weight in the religious anxiety surrounding the Spin. It was partly because of New Kingdom that so many roadside billboards proclaimed TRIBULATION IN PROGRESS and so many mainstream churches had been compelled to address the question of the apocalypse.

Gateway appeared to be the print organ of a West Coast Reconstructionist faction, aimed at the general public. It contained, along with an editorial denouncing Calvinists and Covenanters, three pages of recipes and a movie review column. But what caught my eye was an article called "Blood Sacrifice and the Red Heifer"—something about a pure red calf that would appear "in fulfillment of prophecy" and be sacrificed at the Temple Mount in Israel, ushering in the Rapture. Apparently the old NK faith in the Spin as an act of redemption had grown unfashionable. "For as a snare shall it come on all them that dwell on the face of the whole Earth," Luke 21:35. A snare, not a deliverance. Better find an animal to burn: the Tribulation was proving more troublesome than expected.

I tucked the magazine back into the seat pouch while the

aircraft bumped into a wave of turbulence. Sarah frowned in her sleep. The Russian businessman rang for the steward and ordered a whiskey sour.

∘ ∘ ∘

The car I rented at Orlando the next morning had two bullet holes in it, puttied and painted but still visible in the passenger-side door. I asked the clerk if there was anything else. "Last one on the lot," he said, "but if you don't mind waiting a couple of hours—"

No, I said, it would do.

I took the Bee Line Expressway east and then turned south on 95. I stopped for breakfast at a roadside Denny's outside Cocoa, where the waitress, maybe sensing my essential homelessness, was generous with the coffeepot. "Long haul?"

"Not more than an hour to go."

"Well, then, you're practically *there*. Home or away?" When she realized I didn't have a ready answer she smiled. "You'll sort it out, hon. We all do, sooner or later." And in exchange for this roadside blessing I left her a silly-generous tip.

The Perihelion campus—which Jason had called, alarmingly, "the compound"—was located well south of the Canaveral/Kennedy launch platforms where its strategies were transformed into physical acts. The Perihelion Foundation (now officially an agency of the government) wasn't part of NASA, although it "interfaced" with NASA, borrowing and lending engineers and staff. In a sense it was a layer of bureaucracy imposed on NASA by successive administrations since the beginning of the Spin, taking the moribund space agency in directions its old bosses couldn't have anticipated and might not have approved. E.D. ruled its steering committee, and Jason had taken effective control of program development.

The day had begun to heat up, a Florida heat that seemed to rise from the earth, the moist land sweating like a brisket in a barbecue. I drove past stands of ragged palmettos, fading surf shops, stagnant green roadside ditches, and at least one crime scene: police cars surrounding a black pickup truck, three men bent over the hot metal hood with their wrists slip-tied behind their backs. A cop directing traffic gave my rental's license plate a long look and then waved me past, eyes glittering with a blank, generic suspicion.

o o o

The Perihelion "compound," when I reached it, was nothing as grim as the word suggested. It was a salmon-colored industrial complex, modern and clean, set into an immaculate rolling green lawn, heavily gated but hardly intimidating. A guard at the gatehouse peered inside the car, asked me to open the trunk, pawed through my suitcases and boxes of disks, then gave me a temporary pass on a pocket clip and directed me to the visitor's lot ("behind the south wing, follow the road to your left, have a nice day"). His blue uniform was indigo with perspiration.

I had barely parked the car when Jason came through a pair of frosted-glass doors marked ALL VISITORS MUST REGISTER and crossed a patch of lawn into the blistering desert of the parking lot. "Tyler!" he said, stopping a yard short of me as if I might vanish, a mirage.

"Hey, Jase," I said, smiling.

"Dr. Dupree!" He grinned. "But that car. A rental? We'll have somebody drive it back to Orlando. Set you up with something nicer. You have a place to stay yet?"

I reminded him that he'd promised to take care of that, too.

"Oh, we did. Or rather, we *are*. Negotiating a lease on a little place not twenty minutes from here. Ocean view. Ready in a couple of days. In the meantime you'll need a hotel, but that's easily arranged. So why are we standing out here absorbing UV?"

I followed him into the south wing of the complex. I watched the way he walked. I noted the way he listed a little to the left, the way he favored his right hand.

Air conditioning assaulted us as soon as we were inside, an arctic chill that smelled as if it had been pumped out of sterile vaults deep in the earth. There was a great deal of polished tile and granite in the lobby. More guards, these trained to an impeccable politeness. "So glad you're here," Jase said. "I shouldn't take the time but I want to show you around. The quick tour. I've got Boeing people in the conference room. Guy from Torrance and a guy from the IDS group in St. Louis. Xenon-ion upgrades, they're very proud, squeezing out a little more throughput, as if that mattered much. We don't need finesse, I tell them, we need reliability, simplicity. . . ."

"Jason," I said.

"They—what?"

"Take a breath," I said.

He gave me a stiff, irritated look. Then he relented, laughed out loud. "I'm sorry," he said. "It's just, it's like—remember when we were kids? Any time one of us got a new toy we had to show it off?"

Usually it had been Jase who had the new toys, or at least the expensive ones. But yes, I told him, I remembered.

"Well, it would be flippant to describe it this way to anyone but you, but what we have here, Tyler, is the world's biggest toy chest. Let me show it off, okay? Then we'll get you settled. Give you time to adjust to the climate. If possible."

So I followed him through the ground floor of all three wings, duly admiring the conference rooms and offices, the huge laboratories and engineering bays where prototypes were devised or mission goals shuffled before plans and objectives were handed off to big-money contractors. All very interesting, all very bewildering. We ended up at the in-house infirmary, where I was introduced to Dr. Koenig, the outgoing physician, who shook my hand without enthusiasm and then shuffled off, saying "Good luck to you, Dr. Dupree" over his shoulder.

By this time Jason's pocket pager had buzzed so often he could no longer ignore it. "The Boeing people," he said. "Gotta admire their PPUs, or else they'll get sulky. Can you find your own way back to reception? I've got Shelly waiting there—my personal assistant—she'll set you up with a room. We can talk later. Tyler, it's really good to see you again!"

Another handshake, strangely weak, and then he was off, still listing to the left, leaving me to wonder not whether he was ill but how ill he was and how much worse it would get.

o o o

Jason was as good as his word. Within a week I had moved into a small furnished house, as apparently fragile as all these Florida houses seemed to my eyes, wood and lath, walls mostly windows, but it must have been expensive: the up-stairs porch looked down a long slope past a commercial strip to the sea. During this time I was briefed on three occa-sions by the taciturn Dr. Koenig, who had clearly been un-happy at Perihelion but handed over his practice with great *gravitas,* entrusting me with his case files and his support staff, and on Monday I saw my first patient, a junior metal-lurgist who had twisted his ankle during a game of intramu-ral football on the south lawn. Clearly, the clinic was "overengineered," as Jase might say, for the trivial work we did on a daily basis. But Jason claimed to be anticipating a time when medical care might be hard to come by in the world outside the gates.

I began to settle in. I wrote or extended prescriptions, I dis-pensed aspirin, I browsed the case files. I exchanged pleas-antries with Molly Seagram, my receptionist, who liked me (she said) a lot better than she had liked Dr. Koenig.

Nights, I went home and watched lightning flicker from clouds that parked themselves off the coast like vast electri-fied clipper ships.

And I waited for Jason to call: which he didn't, not for most of a month. Then, one Friday evening after sunset, he was suddenly at the door, unannounced, in off-duty garb (jeans, T-shirt) that subtracted a decade from his apparent age. "Thought I'd drop by," he said. "If that's okay?"

Of course it was. We went upstairs and I fetched two bot-tles of beer from the refrigerator and we sat awhile on the whitewashed balcony. Jase started saying things like "Great to see you" and "Good to have you on board," until I inter-rupted him: "I don't need the fuckin' welcome wagon any-more. It's just me, Jase."

He laughed sheepishly, and it was easier after that.

We reminisced. At one point I asked him, "You hear much from Diane?"

He shrugged. "Rarely."

I didn't pursue it. Then, when we had both killed a couple of beers and the air was cooler and the evening had grown quiet, I asked him how he was doing, personally speaking.

"Been busy," he said. "As you may have guessed. We're close to the first seed launches—closer than we've let on to the press. E.D. likes to stay ahead of the game. He's in Washington most of the time, Clayton himself is keeping a close eye on us, we're the administration's darlings, at least for now. But that leaves me doing managerial shit, which is endless, instead of the work I want and *need* to do, mission design. It's—" He waved his hands helplessly.

"Stressful," I supplied.

"Stressful. But we're making progress. Inch by inch."

"I notice I don't have a file on you," I said. "At the clinic. Every other employee or administrator has a medical jacket. Except you."

He looked away, then laughed, a barking, nervous laugh. "Well . . . I'd kind of like to keep it that way, Tyler. For the time being."

"Dr. Koenig had other ideas?"

"Dr. Koenig thinks we're all a little nuts. Which is, of course, true. Did I tell you he took a job running a cruise-ship clinic? Can you picture that? Koenig in a Hawaiian shirt, handing out Gravol to the tourists?"

"Just tell me what's wrong, Jase."

He looked into the darkening eastern sky. There was a faint light hanging a few degrees above the horizon, not a star, almost certainly one of his father's aerostats.

"The thing is," he said, almost whispering, "I'm a little bit afraid of being sidelined just when we're starting to get results." He gave me long look. "I want to be able to trust you, Ty."

"Nobody here but us," I said.

And then, at last, he recited his symptoms—quietly, almost schematically, as if the pain and weakness carried no more emotional weight than the misfires of a malfunctioning engine. I promised him some tests that wouldn't be entered on my charts. He nodded his acquiescence, and then we dropped the subject and cracked yet another beer, and eventually he thanked me and shook my hand, maybe more solemnly than necessary, and left this house he had rented on my behalf, my new and unfamiliar home.

I went to bed afraid for him.

UNDER THE SKIN

I learned a lot about Perihelion from my patients: the scientists, who loved to talk, more than the administrators, who were generally more taciturn; but also from the families of staff who had begun to abandon their crumbling HMOs in favor of the in-house clinic. Suddenly I was running a fully functional family practice, and most of my patients were people who had looked deeply into the reality of the Spin and confronted it with courage and resolve. "Cynicism stops at the front gate," a mission programmer told me. "We know what we're doing is important." That was admirable. It was also infectious. Before long I began to consider myself one of them, part of the work of extending human influence into the raging torrent of extraterrestrial time.

Some weekends I drove up the coast to Kennedy to watch the rockets lift off, modernized Atlases and Deltas roaring into the sky from a forest of newly constructed launch platforms; and occasionally, late that fall, early that winter, Jase would set aside his work and come with me. The payloads were simple ARVs, preprogrammed reconnaissance devices, clumsy windows on the stars. Their recovery modules would drift down (barring mission failure) into the Atlantic Ocean or onto the salt pans of the western desert, bearing news from the world beyond the world.

I liked the grandeur of the launches. What fascinated Jase, he admitted was the relativistic disconnect they represented. These small payload packages might spend weeks or even months beyond the Spin barrier, measuring the distance to the receding moon or the volume of the expanding sun, but would fall back to Earth (in our frame of reference) the same afternoon, enchanted bottles filled with more time than they could possibly contain.

And when this wine was decanted, inevitably, rumors would sweep the halls of Perihelion: gamma radiation up, indicating some violent event in the stellar neighborhood; new striations on Jupiter as the sun pumped more heat into its turbulent atmosphere; a vast, fresh crater on the moon, which no longer kept one face aligned with Earth but turned its dark side toward us in slow rotation.

One morning in December Jase took me across the campus to an engineering bay where a full-scale mockup of a Martian payload vessel had been installed. It occupied an aluminum platform in a corner of the huge sectored room where, around us, other prototypes were being assembled or rigged for testing by men and women in white Tyvek suits. The device was dismayingly small, I thought, a knobby black box the size of a doghouse with a nozzle fitted to one end, drab under the merciless high ceiling lights. But Jase showed it off with a parent's pride.

"Basically," he said, "it has three parts: the ion drive and reaction mass, the onboard navigational systems, and the payload. Most of the mass is engine. No communications: it can't talk to Earth and it doesn't need to. The nav programs are multiply redundant but the hardware itself is no bigger than a cell phone, powered by solar panels." The panels weren't attached but there was an artist's impression of the fully deployed vehicle pinned to the wall, the doghouse transformed into a Picasso dragonfly.

"It doesn't look powerful enough to get to Mars."

"Power isn't the problem. Ion engines are slow but stubborn. Which is exactly what we want—simple, rugged, durable technology. The tricky part is the nav system, which has to be smart and autonomous. When an object passes through the Spin barrier it picks up what some people are calling 'temporal velocity,' which is a dumb descriptor but gets the idea across. The launch vehicle is speeded up and heated up—not relative to itself but relative to us—and the differential is extremely large. Even a tiny change of velocity or trajectory during launch, something as small as a gust of wind or a sluggish fuel feed on the booster, makes it impossible to predict not how but *when* the vehicle will emerge into exterior space."

"Why does that matter?"

"It matters because Mars and Earth are both in elliptical orbits, circling the sun at different speeds. There's no reliable way to precalculate the relative positions of the planets at the time the vehicle achieves orbit. Essentially, the machine has to find Mars in a crowded sky and plot its own trajectory. So we need clever, flexible software and a rugged, durable drive. Fortunately we've got both. It's a sweet machine, Tyler. Plain on the outside but pretty under the skin. Sooner or later, left to its own devices and barring disaster, it'll do what it's designed to do, park itself in orbit around Mars."

"And then?"

Jase smiled. "Heart of the matter. Here." He pulled a series of dummy bolts from the mock-up and opened a panel at the front, revealing a shielded chamber divided into hexagonal spaces, a honeycomb. Nestled in each space was a blunt, black oval. A nest of ebony eggs. Jason drew one of these from its resting place. The object was small enough to hold in one hand.

"It looks like a pregnant lawn dart," I said.

"It's only a little more sophisticated than a lawn dart. We scatter these into the Martian atmosphere. When they reach a certain altitude they pop out vanes and spin the rest of the way down, bleeding off heat and velocity. Where you scatter them—the poles, the equator—depends on each vehicle's particular payload, whether we're looking for subsurface brine slurries or raw ice, but the basic process is the same. Think of them as hypodermic needles, inoculating the planet with life."

This "life," I understood, would consist of engineered microbes, their genetic material spliced together from bacteria discovered inside rocks in the dry valleys of Antarctica, from anaerobes capable of surviving in the outflow pipes of nuclear reactors, from unicells recovered from the icy sludge at the bottom of the Barents Sea. These organisms would function mainly as soil conditioners, meant to thrive as the aging sun warmed the Martian surface and released trapped water vapor and other gasses. Next would come hyper-engineered strains of blue-green algae, simple photosynthesizers, and eventually more complex forms of life capable of exploiting the environment the initial launches helped to create. Mars would always be, at best, a desert; all its liberated water might create no more than a few shallow, salty, unstable lakes . . . but that might be enough. Enough to create a marginally habitable place beyond the shrouded Earth, where human beings might go and live, a million centuries for each of our years. Where our Martian cousins might have time to solve puzzles we could only grope at.

Where we would build, or allow evolution to build on our behalf, a race of saviors.

"It's hard to believe we can actually do this—"

"*If* we can. It's hardly a foregone conclusion."

"And even so, as a way of solving a problem—"

"It's an act of teleological desperation. You're absolutely right. Just don't say it too loudly. But we do have one powerful force on our side."

"Time," I guessed.

"No. Time is a useful lever. But the active ingredient is life. Life in the abstract, I mean: replication, evolution, complexification. The way life has of filling up cracks and crevices, surviving by doing the unexpected. I believe in that process: it's robust, it's stubborn. Can it rescue us? I don't know. But the possibility is real." He smiled. "If you were chairing a congressional budget committee I'd be less equivocal."

He handed me the dart. It was surprisingly light, no

weightier than a Major League baseball. I tried to imagine hundreds of these raining out of a cloudless Martian sky, impregnating the sterile soil with human destiny. Whatever destiny was left us.

○ ○ ○

E. D. Lawton visited the Florida compound three months into the new year, the same time Jason's symptoms recurred. They had been in remission for months.

When Jase had come to me last year he described his condition reluctantly but methodically. Transient weakness and numbness in his arms and legs. Blurred vision. Episodic vertigo. Occasional incontinence. None of the symptoms were disabling but they had become too frequent to ignore.

Could be a lot of things, I told him, although he must have known as well as I did that we were probably looking at a neurological problem.

We had both been relieved when his blood tests came back positive for multiple sclerosis. MS had been a curable (or containable) disease since the introduction of chemical sclerostatins ten years ago. One of the small ironies of the Spin was that it had coincided with a number of medical breakthroughs coming out of proteinomic research. Our generation—Jason's and mine—might well be doomed, but we wouldn't be killed by MS, Parkinson's, diabetes, lung cancer, arteriosclerosis, or Alzheimer's. The industrialized world's last generation would probably be its healthiest.

Of course, it wasn't quite that simple. Nearly five percent of diagnosed cases of MS still failed to respond to sclerostatins or other therapy. Clinicians were starting to talk about these cases as "poly-drug-resistant MS," maybe even a separate disease with the same symptomology.

But Jason's initial treatment had proceeded as expected. I had prescribed a minimum daily dose of Tremex and he had been in full remission ever since. At least until the week E.D. arrived at Perihelion with all the subtlety of a tropical storm, scattering congressional aides and press attachés down the hallways like wind-blown debris.

E.D. was Washington, we were Florida; he was administration, we were science and engineering. Jase was poised a little precariously between the two. His job was essentially to see that the steering committee's dictates were enforced, but he had stood up to the bureaucracy often enough that the science guys had stopped talking about "nepotism" and started buying him drinks. The trouble was, Jase said, E.D. wasn't content to have set the Mars project into motion; he wanted to micromanage it, often for political reasons, occasionally handing off contracts to dubious bidders in order to buy congressional support. He was sneered at by the staff, though they were happy enough to shake his hand when he was in town. This year's junket culminated in an address to staff and guests in the compound auditorium. We all filed in, dutiful as schoolchildren but more plausibly enthusiastic, and as soon as the audience was settled Jason stood up to introduce his father. I watched him as he mounted the risers to the stage and took the podium. I watched the way he kept his left hand loose at thigh-level, the way he turned, pivoting awkwardly on his heel, when he shook his father's hand.

Jase introduced his father briefly but graciously and melted back into the crowd of dignitaries at the rear of the stage. E.D. stepped forward. E.D. had turned sixty the week before Christmas but could have passed for an athletic fifty, his stomach flat under a three-piece suit, his sparse hair cut to a brisk military stubble. He gave what might as well have been a campaign speech, praising the Clayton administration for its foresight, the assembled staff for their dedication to the "Perihelion vision," his son for an "inspired stewardship," the engineers and technicians for "bringing a dream to life and, if we're successful, bringing life to a sterile planet and fresh hope to this world we still call home." An ovation, a wave, a feral grin, and then he was gone, spirited away by his cabal of bodyguards.

I caught up with Jase an hour later in the executive lunchroom, where he sat at a small table pretending to read an offprint from *Astrophysics Review*.

I took the chair opposite him. "So how bad is it?"

He smiled weakly. "You don't mean my father's whirlwind visit?"

"You know what I mean."

He lowered his voice. "I've been taking the medication. Clockwork, every morning and evening. But it's back. Bad this morning. Left arm, left leg, pins and needles. And getting worse. Worse than it's ever been. Almost by the hour. It's like an electric current running through one side of my body."

"You have time to come to the infirmary?"

"I have time, but—" His eyes glittered. "I may not have the means. Don't want to alarm you. But I'm glad you showed up. Right now I'm not certain I can walk. I made it in here after E.D.'s speech. But I'm pretty sure if I try to stand up I'll fall over. I don't think I can walk. Ty—*I can't walk.*"

"I'll call for help."

He straightened in his chair. "You'll do no such thing. I can sit here until there's nobody around except the night guard, if necessary."

"That's absurd."

"Or you can *discreetly* help me stand up. We're what, twenty or thirty yards from the infirmary? If you grab my arm and look congenial we can probably get there without attracting too much attention."

In the end I agreed, not because I approved of the charade but because it seemed to be the only way to get him into my office. I took his left arm and he braced his right hand on the table edge and levered himself up. We managed to cross the cafeteria floor without weaving, though Jason's left foot dragged in a way that was hard to disguise—fortunately no one looked too closely. Once we reached the corridor we stayed close to the wall where his shuffling was less conspicuous. When a senior administrator appeared at the end of the hallway Jason whispered, "Stop," and we stood as if in casual conversation with Jason braced against a display case, his right hand gripping the steel shelf so fiercely that his knuckles turned bloodless and beads of sweat stood out on his forehead. The exec passed with a wordless nod.

By the time we made the clinic entrance I was bearing most of his weight. Molly Seagram, fortunately, was out of the office; once I closed the outer door we were alone. I helped Jase onto a table in one of the examination rooms, then went back to the reception desk and posted a note for Molly to make sure we wouldn't be disturbed.

When I returned to the consultation room Jason was crying. Not weeping, but tears had streaked his face and lingered on his chin. "This is so fucking awful." He wouldn't meet my eyes. "I couldn't help it," he said. "I'm sorry. I couldn't help it."

He had lost control of his bladder.

○ ○ ○

I helped him into a medical gown and rinsed his wet clothes in the consulting room sink and put them to dry next to a sunny window in the seldom-used storage room beyond the pharmaceutical cupboards. Business was slow today and I used that excuse to give Molly the afternoon off.

Jason recovered some of his composure, though he looked diminished in the paper gown. "You said this was a curable disease. Tell me what went wrong."

"It is treatable, Jase. For most patients, most of the time. But there are exceptions."

"And what, I'm one of them? I won the bad news lottery?"

"You're having a relapse. That's typical of the untreated disease, periods of disability followed by intervals of remission. You might just be a late responder. In some cases the drug needs to reach a certain level in the body for an extended length of time before it's fully effective."

"It's been six months since you wrote the prescription. And I'm worse, not better."

"We can switch you to one of the other sclerostatins, see if that helps. But they're all chemically very similar."

"So changing the prescription won't help."

"It might. It might not. We'll try it before we rule it out."

"And if that doesn't work?"

"Then we stop talking about eliminating the disease and start to talk about managing it. Even untreated, MS is hardly a death sentence. Lots of people experience full remission between attacks and manage to lead relatively normal lives." Although, I did not add, such cases were seldom as severe or as aggressive as Jason's seemed to be. "The usual fallback treatment is a cocktail of anti-inflammatory drugs, selective protein inhibitors, and targeted CNS stimulants. It can be very effective at suppressing symptoms and slowing the course of the disease."

"Good," Jason said. "Great. Write me a ticket."

"It's not that simple. You could be looking at side effects."

"Such as?"

"Maybe nothing. Maybe some psychological distress— mild depression or manic episodes. Some generalized physical weakness."

"But I'll pass for normal?"

"In all likelihood." For now and probably for another ten or fifteen years, maybe more. "But it's a control measure, not a cure—a brake, not a full stop. The disease will come back if you live long enough."

"You can give me a decade, though, for sure?"

"As sure as anything is in my business."

"A decade," he said thoughtfully. "Or a billion years. Depending on how you look at it. Maybe that's enough. Ought to be enough, don't you think?"

I didn't ask, Enough for what? "But in the meantime—"

"I don't want a 'meantime,' Tyler. I can't afford to be away from my work and I don't want anyone to know about this."

"It's nothing to be ashamed of."

"I'm not ashamed of it." He gestured at the paper gown with his right hand. "Fucking humiliated, but not ashamed. This isn't a psychological issue. It's about what I do here at Perihelion. What I'm *allowed* to do. E.D. hates illness, Tyler. He hates weakness of any kind. He hated Carol from the day her drinking became a problem."

"You don't think he'd understand?"

"I love my father, but I'm not blind to his faults. No, he would not understand. All the influence I have at Perihelion flows through E.D. And that's a little precarious at the moment. We've had some disagreements. If I became a liability to him he'd have me relegated to some expensive treatment facility in Switzerland or Bali before the week was out, and he'd tell himself he was doing it for my sake. Worse, he would believe it."

"What you choose to make public is your business. But you need to be seeing a neurologist, not a staff GP."

"No," he said.

"I can't in good conscious continue to treat you, Jase, if you won't talk to a specialist. It was dicey enough putting you on Tremex without consulting a brain guy."

"You have the MRI and the blood tests, right? What else do you need?"

"Ideally, a fully equipped hospital lab and degree in neurology."

"Bullshit. You said yourself, MS is no big deal nowadays."

"Unless it fails to respond to treatment."

"I can't—" He wanted to argue. But he was also obviously, brutally tired. Fatigue might be another symptom of his relapse, though; he had been pushing himself hard in the weeks before E.D.'s visit. "I'll make a deal with you. I'll see a specialist if you can arrange it discreetly and keep it off my Perihelion chart. But I need to be functional. I need to be functional *tomorrow*. Functional as in walking without assistance and not pissing myself. The drug cocktail you talked about, does it work fast?"

"Usually. But without a neurological workup—"

"Tyler, I have to tell you, I appreciate what you've done for me, but I can buy a more cooperative doctor if I need one. Treat me now and I'll see a specialist, I'll do whatever you think is right. But if you imagine I'm going to show up at work in a wheelchair with a catheter up my dick, you're dead wrong."

"Even if I write a script, Jase, you won't be better overnight. It takes a couple of days."

"I might be able to spare a couple of days." He thought about it. "Okay," he said finally. "I want the drugs and I want you to get me out of here inconspicuously. If you can do that, I'm in your hands. No arguments."

"Physicians don't bargain, Jase."

"Take it or leave it, Hippocrates."

○ ○ ○

I didn't start him on the whole cocktail—our pharmacy didn't stock all the drugs—but I gave him a CNS stimulant that would at least return his bladder control and the ability to walk unassisted for the next few days. The downside was an edgy, icy state of mind, like, or so I'm told, the tail end of a cocaine run. It raised his blood pressure and put dark baggage under his eyes.

We waited until most of the staff had gone home and there was only the night shift at the compound. Jase walked stiffly but plausibly past the front desk to the parking lot, waved amicably to a couple of late-departing colleagues, and sank into the passenger seat of my car. I drove him home.

He had visited my little rental house several times, but I hadn't been to his place before. I had expected something that reflected his status at Perihelion. In fact the apartment where he slept—clearly, he did little else there—was a modest condo unit with a sliver of an ocean view. He had furnished it with a sofa, a television, a desk, a couple of bookcases and a broadband media/Internet connection. The walls were bare except for the space above the desk, where he had taped a hand-drawn chart depicting the linear history of the solar system from the birth of the sun to its final collapse into a smoldering white dwarf, with human history diverging from the line at a spot marked THE SPIN. The bookcases were crowded with journals and academic texts and decorated with exactly three framed photographs: E. D. Lawton, Carol Lawton, and a demure image of Diane that must have been taken years ago.

Jase stretched out on the sofa. He looked like a study in paradox, his body in repose, his eyes bright with drug-induced hyperalertness. I went to the small adjoining kitchen and scrambled eggs (neither of us had eaten since breakfast) while Jason talked. And talked some more. And kept on talking. "Of course," he said at one point, "I know I'm being way too verbal, I'm conscious of that, but I can't even think about sleeping—does this wear off?"

"If we put you on the drug cocktail long-term, then yes, the obvious stimulant effect will go away." I carried a plate to the sofa for him.

"It's very speedy. Like one of those cramming-for-the-finals pills people take. But physically, it's calming. I feel like a neon sign on an empty building. All lit up but basically hollow. The eggs, the eggs are very good. Thank you." He put the plate aside. He had eaten maybe a spoonful.

I sat at his desk, glancing at the Spin chart on the opposite wall. Wondering what it was like to live with this stark depiction of human origins and human destiny, the human species rendered as a finite event in the life of an ordinary star. He had drawn it with a felt-tip pen on a scroll of ordinary brown wrapping paper.

Jason followed my look. "Obviously," he said, "they mean for us to do *something* . . ."

"Who does?"

"The Hypotheticals. If we must call them that. And I suppose we must. Everyone does. They expect something from us. I don't know what. A gift, a signal, an acceptable sacrifice."

"How do you know that?"

"It's hardly an original observation. Why is the Spin barrier permeable to human artifacts like satellites, but not to meteors or even Brownlee particles? Obviously it's *not* a barrier; that was never the right word." Under the influence of the stimulant Jase seemed particularly fond of the word *obviously*. "Obviously," he said, "it's a selective filter. We know it filters the energy reaching the surface of the Earth. So the Hypotheticals want to keep us, or at least the terrestrial ecology, intact and alive, but then why grant us access to space? Even after we attempted to nuke the only two Spin-related artifacts anyone has ever found? What are they *waiting* for, Ty? What's the prize?"

"Maybe it's not a prize. Maybe it's a ransom. Pay up and we'll leave you alone."

He shook his head. "It's too late for them to leave us alone. We need them now. And we still can't rule out the possibility that they're benevolent, or at least benign. I mean, suppose they hadn't arrived when they did. What were we looking forward to? A lot of people think we were facing our last century as a viable civilization, maybe even as a species. Global warming, overpopulation, the death of the seas, the loss of arable land, the proliferation of disease, the threat of nuclear or biological warfare . . ."

"We might have destroyed ourselves, but at least it would have been our own fault."

"Would it, though? *Whose* fault exactly? Yours? Mine? No, it would have been the result of several billion human beings making relatively innocuous choices: to have kids, drive a car to work, keep their job, solve the short-term problems first. When you reach the point at which even the most trivial acts are punishable by the death of the species, then obviously, obviously, you're at a critical juncture, a different kind of point of no return."

"Is it better, being consumed by the sun?"

"That hasn't happened yet. And we aren't the first star to burn out. The galaxy is littered with white dwarf stars that might once have hosted habitable planets. Do you ever wonder what happened to *them*?"

"Seldom," I said.

I walked across the bare parquet floor to the bookcase, to the family photos. Here was E.D., smiling into the camera—a man whose smiles were never entirely convincing. His physical resemblance to Jason was marked. (Was obvious, Jase might have said.) Similar machine, different ghost.

"How could life survive a stellar catastrophe? But obviously it depends on what 'life' is. Are we talking about organic life, or any kind of generalized autocatalytic feedback loop? Are the Hypotheticals organic? Which is an interesting question in itself . . ."

"You really ought to try to get some sleep." It was past midnight. He was using words I didn't understand. I picked up the photo of Carol. Here the resemblance was more subtle. The photographer had caught Carol on a good day: her eyes were open, not stuck at half-mast, and although her smile was grudging, a barely perceptible lift of her thin lips, it was not altogether inauthentic.

"They may be mining the sun," Jason said, still talking about the Hypotheticals. "We have some suggestive data on solar flares. Obviously, what they've done to the Earth requires vast amounts of usable energy. It's the equivalent of refrigerating a planet-sized mass to a temperature close to absolute zero. So where's the power supply? Most likely, the sun. And we've observed a marked reduction in large solar flares since the Spin. Something, some force or agency, may be tapping high-energy particles before they crest in the heliosphere. Mining the sun, Tyler! That's an act of technological hubris almost as startling as the Spin itself."

I picked up the framed photo of Diane. The photograph predated her marriage to Simon Townsend. It had captured a certain characteristic disquiet, as if she had just narrowed her eyes at a puzzling thought. She was beautiful without trying but not quite at ease, all grace but at the same time just slightly off balance.

I had so many memories of her. But those memories were years old now, vanishing into the past with an almost Spin-like momentum. Jason saw me holding the picture frame and was silent for a few blessed moments. Then he said, "Really, Tyler, this fixation is unworthy of you."

"Hardly a fixation, Jase."

"Why? Because you're *over* her or because you're *afraid* of her? But I could ask her the same question. If she ever called. Simon keeps her on a tight leash. I suspect she misses the old NK days, when the movement was full of naked Unitarians and Evangelical hippies. The price of piety is steeper now." He added, "She talks to Carol every now and then."

"Is she at least happy?"

"Diane is among zealots. She may be one herself. Happiness isn't an option."

"Do you think she's in danger?"

He shrugged. "I think she's living the life she chose for herself. She could have made other choices. She could, for instance, have married *you,* Ty, if not for this ridiculous fantasy of hers—"

"What fantasy?"

"That E.D. is your father. That she's your biological sister."

I backed away from the bookcase too hastily and knocked the photographs to the floor.

"That's ridiculous."

"Patently ridiculous. But I don't think she entirely gave up on the idea until she was in college."

"How could she even think—"

"It was a fantasy, not a theory. Think about it. There was never much affection between Diane and E.D. She felt ignored by him. And in a sense, she was right. E.D. never wanted a daughter, he wanted an heir, a male heir. He had high expectations, and I happened to live up to them. Diane was a distraction as far as E.D. was concerned. He expected Carol to raise her, and Carol—" He shrugged. "Carol wasn't up to the task."

"So she made up this—story?"

"She thought of it as a deduction. It explained the way E.D. kept your mother and you living on the property. It explained Carol's constant unhappiness. And, basically, it made her feel good about herself. Your mother was kinder and more attentive to her than Carol ever was. She liked the idea of being blood kin to the Dupree family."

I looked at Jason. His face was pale, his pupils dilated, his gaze distant and aimed at the window. I reminded myself that he was my patient, that he was exhibiting a predictable psychological response to a powerful drug; that this was the same man who, only a few hours ago, had wept at his own incontinence. I said, "I really have to leave now, Jason."

"Why, this is all so shocking? You thought growing up was supposed to be painless?" Then, abruptly, before I could answer, he turned his head and met my eyes for the first time that evening. "Oh dear. I begin to suspect I've been behaving badly."

I said, "The medication—"

"Behaving monstrously. Tyler, I'm sorry."

"You'll feel better after a night's sleep. But you shouldn't go back to Perihelion for a couple of days."

"I won't. Will you stop by tomorrow?"

"Yes."

"Thank you," he said.

I left without replying.

CELESTIAL GARDENING

That was the winter of the gantries.

New launch platforms had been erected not just at Canaveral but across the desert Southwest, in southern France and equatorial Africa, at Jiuquan and Xichang in China and at Baikonur and Svobodnyy in Russia: gantries for the Martian seed launches and larger gantries for the so-called Big Stacks, the enormous booster assemblies that would carry human volunteers to a marginally habitable Mars if the crude terraforming succeeded. The gantries grew that winter like iron and steel forests, exuberant, lush, rooted in concrete and watered with reservoirs of federal money.

The first seed rockets were in a way less spectacular than the launch facilities built to support them. They were assembly-line boosters mass-produced from old Titan and Delta templates, not an ounce or a microchip more complicated than they needed to be, and they populated their pads in startling numbers as winter advanced into spring, spaceships like cottonwood pods, poised to carry dormant life to a distant, sterile soil.

It was also, in a sense, spring in the solar system at large, or at least a prolonged Indian summer. The habitable zone of the solar system was expanding outward as the sun depleted its helium core, beginning to encompass Mars as it would eventually encompass the watery Jovian moon Ganymede, another potential target for late-stage terraforming. On Mars, vast tonnages of frozen CO_2 and water ice had begun to sublimate into the atmosphere over millions of warming summers. At the beginning of the Spin the Martian atmospheric pressure at ground level had been roughly eight millibars, as rarified as the air three miles above the peak of Mount Everest. Now, even without human intervention, the planet had achieved a climate equivalent to an arctic mountaintop bathed in gaseous carbon dioxide—balmy, by Martian standards.

But we meant to take the process further. We meant to lace the planet's air with oxygen, to green its lowlands, to create ponds where, now, the periodically melting subsurface ice erupted in geysers of vapor or slurries of toxic mud.

We were perilously optimistic during the winter of the gantries.

○ ○ ○

On March third, shortly before the first scheduled wave of seed launches, Carol Lawton called me at home and told me my mother had suffered a severe stroke and wasn't expected to live.

I made arrangements for a local medic to cover for me at Perihelion, then drove to Orlando and booked the first morning flight to D.C.

Carol met me at Reagan International, apparently sober. She opened her arms and I hugged her, this woman who had never displayed more than a puzzled indifference toward me during the years I had lived on her property. Then she stood back and put her tremorous hands on my shoulders. "I'm so sorry, Tyler."

"Is she still alive?"

"She's hanging on. I have a car waiting. We can talk while we drive."

I followed her out to a vehicle that must have been dispatched by E.D. himself, a black limo with federal stickers. The driver barely spoke as he put my luggage in the trunk, tipped his hat when I thanked him, and climbed into a driver's seat meticulously isolated from the plush passenger compartment. He headed for George Washington University Hospital without being asked.

Carol was skinnier than I remembered her, birdlike against the leather upholstery. She took a cotton handkerchief out of her tiny purse and dabbed her eyes. "All this ridiculous crying," she said. "I lost my contacts yesterday. Just sort of cried them away, if you can imagine that. There are some things a person takes for granted. For me it was having your mother in the house, keeping things in order, or just knowing she was nearby, there across the lawn. I used to wake up at night—I don't sleep soundly, which probably doesn't surprise you—I used to wake up feeling like the world was fragile and I might fall through it, fall right through the floor and keep on falling forever. Then I would think of her over there in the Little House, sound asleep. Sleeping soundly. It was like courtroom evidence. Exhibit A, Belinda Dupree, the possibility of peace of mind. She was the pillar of the household, Tyler, whether you knew it or not."

I supposed I had known it. Really it had all been one household, though as a child I had seen mainly the distance between the two estates: my house, modest but calm, and the Big House, where the toys were more expensive and the arguments more vicious.

I asked whether E.D. had been to the hospital.

"E.D.? No. He's busy. Sending spaceships to Mars seems to require a great many dinners downtown. I know that's what's keeping Jason in Florida, too, but I believe Jason deals with the practical side of the matter, if it *has* a practical side, while E.D. is more like a stage magician, pulling money out of various hats. But I'm sure you'll see E.D. at the funeral." I winced, and she gave me an apologetic look. "If and when. But the doctors say—"

"She's not expected to recover."

"She's dying. Yes. As one physician to another. Do you remember that, Tyler? I had a practice once. Back in the days when I was capable of such a thing. And now you're a doctor with a practice of your own. My God."

I appreciated her bluntness. Maybe it came with her sudden sobriety. Here she was back in the brightly lit world she had been avoiding for twenty years, and it was exactly as awful as she remembered it.

We arrived at George Washington University Hospital. Carol had already introduced herself to the nursing staff on the life-support floor, and we proceeded directly to my mother's room. When Carol hesitated at the door I said, "Are you coming in?"

"I—no, I don't think so. I've said good-bye several times already. I need to be where the air doesn't smell like disinfectant. I'll stand out in the parking lot and smoke a cigarette with the gurney-pushers. Meet me there?"

I said I would.

My mother was unconscious in her room, embedded in life support, her breathing regulated by a machine that wheezed as her rib cage expanded and relaxed. Her hair was whiter than I remembered it being. I stroked her cheek, but she didn't respond.

Out of some misbegotten doctorly instinct I raised one of her eyelids, meaning, I suppose, to check the dilation of her pupils. But she had hemorrhaged into the eye after her stroke. It was red as a cherry tomato, flushed with blood.

o o o

I rode away from the hospital with Carol but turned down her invitation to dinner, told her I'd fix myself something. She said, "I'm sure there's something in the kitchen at your mother's place. But you're more than welcome to stay in the Big House if you like. Even though it's a bit of a mess these days without your mother to boss the help. I'm sure we can scare up a passable guest bedroom."

I thanked her but said I'd prefer to stay across the lawn.

"Let me know if you change your mind." She gazed from the gravel drive across the lawn to the Little House as if she were seeing it clearly for the first time in years. "You still carry a key—?"

"Still do," I said.

"Well, then. I'll leave you to it. The hospital has both numbers if her condition changes." And Carol hugged me again and walked up the porch stairs with a resoluteness, not quite eagerness, that suggested she had postponed her drinking long enough.

I let myself into my mother's house. Hers more than mine, I thought, though my presence had not been expunged from it. When I left for university I had denuded my small bedroom and packed whatever was important to me, but my mother had kept the bed and filled the blank spaces (the pine shelving, the windowsill) with potted plants, rapidly drying in her absence; I watered them. The rest of the house was equally tidy. Diane had once described my mother's housekeeping as "linear," by which I think she meant orderly but not obsessive. I surveyed the living room, the kitchen, glanced into her bedroom. Not everything was in its place. But everything *had* a place.

Come nightfall I closed the curtains and turned on every light in every room, more lights than my mother had ever deemed appropriate at any given time, a declaration against death. I wondered if Carol had noticed the glare across the winter-brown divide, and if so whether she found it comforting or alarming.

E.D. came home around nine that night, and he was gracious enough to knock at the door and offer his sympathy. He looked uncomfortable under the porch light, his tailored suit disheveled. His breath smoked in the evening chill. He touched his pockets, breast and hip, unconsciously, as if he had forgotten something or simply didn't know what to do with his hands. "I'm sorry, Tyler," he said.

His condolences seemed grossly premature, as if my mother's death were not merely inevitable but an established fact. He had already written her off. But she was still drawing breath, I thought, or at least processing oxygen, miles away, alone in her room at George Washington. "Thank you for saying so, Mr. Lawton."

"Jesus, Tyler, call me E.D. Everybody else does. Jason tells me you're doing good work down there at Perihelion Florida."

"My patients seem satisfied."

"Great. Every contribution counts, no matter how small. Listen, did Carol put you out here? Because we have a guest bedroom ready if you want it."

"I'm fine right where I am."

"Okay. I understand that. Just knock if you need anything, all right?"

He ambled back across the winter-brown lawn. Much had been made, in the press and in the Lawton family, of Jason's genius, but I reminded myself that E.D. could claim that title, too. He had parlayed an engineering degree and a talent for business into a major corporate enterprise, and he had been selling aerostat-enabled telecom bandwidth when Americom and AT&T were still blinking at the Spin like startled deer. What he lacked was not Jason's intelligence but Jason's wit and Jason's deep curiosity about the physical universe. And maybe a dash of Jason's humanity.

Then I was alone again, at home and not at home, and I sat on the sofa and marveled for a while at how little this room had changed. Sooner or later it would fall to me to dispose of the contents of the house, a job I could barely envision, a job more difficult, more preposterous, than the work of cultivating life on another planet. But maybe it was because I was contemplating that act of deconstruction that I noticed a gap on the top shelf of the étagère next to the TV.

Noticed it because, to my knowledge, the high shelf had received no more than a cursory dusting in all the years I had lived here. The top shelf was the attic of my mother's life. I could have recited the order of the contents of that shelf by closing my eyes and picturing it: her high school yearbooks (Martell Secondary School in Bingham, Maine, 1975, '76, '77, '78); her Berkeley grad book, 1982; a jade Buddha bookend; her diploma in a stand-up plastic frame; the brown accordion file in which she kept her birth certificate, passport, and tax documents; and, braced by another green Buddha, three tattered New Balance shoeboxes labeled MEMENTOS (SCHOOL), MEMENTOS (MARCUS), and ODDS & ENDS.

But tonight the second jade Buddha stood askew and the box marked MEMENTOS (SCHOOL) was missing. I assumed she had taken it down herself, though I hadn't seen it elsewhere in the house. Of the three boxes, the only one she had regularly opened in my presence was ODDS & ENDS. It had been packed with concert playbills and ticket stubs, brittle newspaper clippings (including her own parents' obituaries), a souvenir lapel pin in the shape of the schooner *Bluenose* from her honeymoon in Nova Scotia, matchbooks culled from restaurants and hotels she had visited, costume jewelry, a baptismal certificate, even a lock of my own baby hair preserved in a slip of waxed paper closed with a pin.

I took down the other box, the one marked MEMENTOS (MARCUS). I had never been especially curious about my father, and my mother had seldom spoken about him apart from the basic thumbnail sketch (a handsome man, an engineer, a jazz collector, E.D.'s best friend in college, but a heavy drinker and a victim, one night on the road home from an electronics supplier in Milpitas, of his own fondness for speedy automobiles). Inside the shoebox was a stack of letters in vellum envelopes addressed in a curt, clean handwriting that must have been his. He had sent these letters to Belinda Sutton, my mother's maiden name, at an address in Berkeley I didn't recognize.

I removed one of those envelopes and opened it, pulled out the yellowing paper and unfolded it.

The paper was unlined but the handwriting cut across the page in small, neat parallels. *Dear Bel,* it began, and continued, *I thought I said everything on the phone last night but can't stop thinking about you. Writing this seems to bring you closer tho not as close as I'd like. Not as close as we were last August! I play that memory like videotape every night I can't lie down next to you.*

And more, which I did not read. I folded the letter and tucked it into its yellowed envelope and closed the box and put it back where it belonged.

o o o

In the morning there was a knock at the door. I answered it expecting Carol or some amanuensis from the Big House.

But it wasn't Carol. It was Diane. Diane in a midnight-blue

floor-sweeper skirt and high-collared blouse. Her hands were clasped under her breasts. She looked up at me, eyes sparkling. "I'm so sorry," she said. "I came as soon as I heard."

But too late. The hospital had called ten minutes earlier. Belinda Dupree had died without regaining consciousness.

○ ○ ○

At the memorial service E.D. spoke briefly and uncomfortably and said nothing of significance. I spoke, Diane spoke; Carol meant to speak but in the end was too tearful or inebriated to mount the pulpit.

Diane's eulogy was the most moving, cadenced and heartfelt, a catalogue of the kindnesses my mother had exported across the lawn like gifts from a wealthier, kinder nation. I was grateful for it. Everything else about the ceremony seemed mechanical by comparison: half-familiar faces bobbed out of the crowd to utter homilies and half-truths, and I thanked them and smiled, thanked them and smiled, until it was time for the walk to the graveside.

○ ○ ○

There was a function at the Big House that evening, a post-funeral reception at which I was offered condolences by E.D.'s business associates, none of whom I knew but some of whom had known my father, and by the household staff at the Big House, whose grief was more authentic and harder to bear.

Caterers slid through the crowd with wineglasses on silvered platters and I drank more than I should have, until Diane, who had also been gliding among the guests, tugged me away from yet another round of so-sorry-for-your-loss and said, "You need air."

"It's cold out."

"If you keep drinking you'll get surly. You're halfway there already. Come on, Ty. Just for a few minutes."

Out onto the lawn. The brown midwinter lawn. The same lawn where we had witnessed the opening moments of the Spin almost twenty years ago. We walked the circumference of the Big House—strolled, really, despite the stiff March breeze and the granular snow still inhabiting every sheltered or shaded space.

We had already said all the obvious things. We had compared notes: my career, the move to Florida, my work at Perihelion; her years with Simon, drifting out of NK toward a blander orthodoxy, welcoming the Rapture with piety and self-denial. ("We don't eat meat," she had confided. "We don't wear artificial fibers.") Walking next to her, light-headed, I wondered whether I had become gross or repugnant in her eyes, whether she was conscious of the ham-and-cheese aperitifs on my breath or the cotton-poly jacket I was wearing. She hadn't changed much, though she was thinner than she used to be, maybe thinner than she ought to be, the line of her jaw a little stark against the high, tight collar.

I was sober enough to thank her for trying to sober me up.

"I needed to get away, too," she said. "All those people E.D. invited. None of them knew your mother in any important way. Not one. They're in there talking about appropriations bills or payload tonnage. Making deals."

"Maybe it's E.D.'s way of paying tribute to her. Salting the wake with political celebrities."

"That's a generous way of interpreting it."

"He still makes you angry." So easily, I thought.

"E.D.? Of course he does. Though it would be more charitable to forgive him. Which you seem to have done."

"I have less to forgive him for," I said. "He's not my father."

I didn't mean anything by it. But I was still too aware of what Jason had told me a few weeks ago. I choked on the remark, reconsidered it even before the sentence was out of my mouth, blushed when I finished. Diane gave me a long uncomprehending look; then her eyes widened in an expression that mingled anger and embarrassment so plainly that I could parse it even by the dim glow of the porch light.

"You've been talking to Jason," she said coldly.

"I'm sorry—"

"How does that work exactly? Do the two of you sit around making fun of me?"

"Of course not. He—anything Jason said, it was because of the medication."

Another grotesque faux pas, and she pounced on it: "What medication?"

"I'm his GP. Sometimes I write him prescriptions. Does it matter?"

"What medication makes you break a promise, Tyler? He promised he would never tell you—" She drew another inference. "Is Jason *sick*? Is that why he didn't come to the funeral?"

"He's busy. We're just days away from the first launches."

"But you're treating him for something."

"I can't ethically discuss Jason's medical history," I said, knowing this would only inflame her suspicions, that I had essentially given away his secret in the act of keeping it.

"It would be just like him to get sick and not tell any of us. He's so, so *hermetically sealed*. . . ."

"Maybe you should take the initiative. Call him sometime."

"You think I don't? Did he tell you that, too? I used to call him every week. But he would just turn on that blank charm and refuse to say anything meaningful. How are you, I'm fine, what's new, nothing. He doesn't want to hear from me, Tyler. He's deep in E.D.'s camp. I'm an embarrassment to him." She paused. "Unless that's changed."

"I don't know what's changed. But maybe you should see him, talk to him face to face."

"How would I do that?"

I shrugged. "Take another week off. Fly back with me."

"You said he's busy."

"Once the launches begin it's all sit back and wait. You can come to Canaveral with us. See history being made."

"The launches are futile," she said, but it sounded like something she had been taught to say; she added, "I'd like to, but I can't afford it. Simon and I do all right. But we're not rich. We're not Lawtons."

"I'll spot you the plane fare."

"You're a generous drunk."

"I mean it."

"Thank you, but no," she said. "I couldn't."

"Think about it."

"Ask me when you're sober." She added, as we mounted the steps to the porch, yellow light hooding her eyes, "Whatever I might once have believed—whatever I might have told Jason—"

"You don't have to say this, Diane."

"I know E.D. isn't your father."

What was interesting about her disclaimer was the way she delivered it. Firmly, decisively. As if she knew better now. As if she had discovered a different truth, an alternative key to the Lawton mysteries.

○ ○ ○

Diane went back to the Big House. I decided I couldn't face more well-wishing. I let myself into my mother's house, which seemed airless and overheated.

Carol, the next day, told me I could take my time about cleaning out my mother's things, which she called "making arrangements." The Little House wasn't going anywhere, she said. Take a month. Take a year. I could "make arrangements" whenever I had the time and as soon as I felt comfortable with it.

Comfort wasn't even on the horizon, but I thanked her for her patience and spent the day packing for the flight back to Orlando. I was nagged by the idea that I ought to take something of my mother's with me, that she would have wanted me to keep a memento for some shoebox of my own. But what? One of her Hummel figurines, which she had loved but which had always struck me as expensive kitsch? The cross-stitched butterfly from the living room wall, the print of *Water Lilies* in a do-it-yourself frame?

Diane showed up at the door while I was debating. "Does that offer still stand? The trip to Florida? Were you serious about that?"

"Of course I was."

"Because I talked to Simon. He's not completely delighted with the idea, but he thinks he'll be okay on his own for a few more days."

Mighty considerate of him, I thought.

"So," she said, "unless—I mean, I know you'd been drinking—"

"Don't be silly. I'll call the airline."

I booked a seat in Diane's name on the next day's first D.C./Orlando junket.

Then I finished packing. Of my mother's things, I settled at last on the pair of chipped jade Buddha bookends.

I looked around the house, even checked under the beds, but the missing MEMENTOS (SCHOOL) seemed to have vanished permanently.

SNAPSHOTS OF THE ECOPOIESIS

Jason suggested we take rooms in Cocoa Beach and wait a day for him to join us there. He was doing a last round of media Q & A at Perihelion but had cleared his schedule prior to the launches, which he wanted to witness without a CNN crew dunning him with boneheaded questions.

"Great," Diane said when I relayed this information. "I can ask all the boneheaded questions myself."

I had managed to calm her fears about Jason's medical condition: no, he wasn't dying, and any temporary blips on his medical record were his own business. She accepted that, or seemed to, but still wanted to see him, if only to reassure herself, as if my mother's death had shaken her faith in the fixed stars of the Lawton universe.

So I used my Perihelion ID and my connection with Jase to rent us two neighboring suites in a Holiday Inn with a view toward Canaveral. Not long after the Mars project was conceived—once the EPA's objections had been noted and ignored—a dozen shallow-water launch platforms had been constructed and anchored off the coast of Merritt Island. It was these structures we could see most clearly from the hotel. The rest of the view was parking lots, winter beaches, blue water.

We stood on the balcony of her suite. She had showered and changed after the drive from Orlando and we were about to go down and brave the lobby restaurant. Every other balcony we could see bristled with cameras and lenses: the Holiday Inn was a designated media hotel. (Simon may have distrusted the secular press but Diane was suddenly knee-deep in it.) We couldn't see the setting sun but its light caught the distant gantries and rockets and rendered them more ethereal than real, a squadron of giant robots marching off to some battle in the Mid-Atlantic Trench. Diane stood back from the balcony railing as if she found the view frightening. "Why are there so many of them?"

"Shotgun ecopoiesis," I said.

She laughed, a little reproachfully. "Is that one of Jason's words?"

It wasn't, not entirely. "Ecopoiesis" was a word coined by a man named Robert Haynes in 1990, back when terraforming was a purely speculative science. Technically it meant the creation of a self-regulating anaerobic biosphere where none had existed before, but in modern usage it referred to any purely biological modification of Mars. The greening of Mars required two different kinds of planetary engineering: crude terraforming, to raise the surface temperature and atmospheric pressure to a plausible threshold for life, and ecopoiesis: using microbial and plant life to condition the soil and oxygenate the air.

The Spin had already done the heavy lifting for us. Every planet in the solar system—barring Earth—had been warmed significantly by the expanding sun. What remained was the subtler work of ecopoiesis. But there were many possible routes to ecopoiesis, many candidate organisms, from rock-dwelling bacteria to alpine mosses.

"So it's called shotgun," Diane surmised, "because you're sending all of them."

"All of them, and as many of them as we can afford, because no single organism is guaranteed to adapt and survive. But one of them might."

"More than one might."

"Which is fine. We want an ecology, not a monoculture." In fact the launches would be timed and staggered. The first wave would carry only anaerobic and photoautotrophic organisms, simple forms of life that required no oxygen and derived energy from sunlight. If they thrived and died in sufficient numbers they would create a layer of biomass to nurture more complex ecosystems. The next wave, a year from now, would introduce oxygenating organisms; the last unmanned launches would include primitive plants to fix the soil and regulate evaporation and rainfall cycles.

"It all seems so unlikely."

"We live in unlikely times. But no, it's not guaranteed to work."

"And if it doesn't?"

I shrugged. "What have we lost?"

"A lot of money. A lot of manpower."

"I can't think of a better use for it. Yes, this is a wager, and no, it's not a sure thing, but the potential payoff is more than worth the risk. And it's been good for everybody, at least so far. Good for morale at home and a good way of promoting international cooperation."

"But you'll have misled a lot of ordinary people. Convinced them the Spin is something we can manage, something we can find a technological fix for."

"Given them hope, you mean."

"The wrong kind of hope. And if you fail you leave them with no hope at all."

"What would you have us do, Diane? Retreat to our prayer mats?"

"It would hardly be an admission of defeat—prayer, I mean. And if you do succeed, the next step is to send people?"

"Yes. If we green the planet we send people." A much more difficult and ethically complex proposition. We'd be sending candidates in crews of ten. They would have to endure an unpredictably long passage in absurdly small quarters on limited rations. They would have to suffer atmospheric braking at a near-lethal delta-V after months of weightlessness, followed by a perilous descent to the planet's surface. If all this worked, and if their meager allotment of survival gear made its parallel descent and landed anywhere near them, they would then have to teach themselves subsistence skills in an environment only approximately fit for human habitation. Their mission brief was not to return to Earth but to live long enough to reproduce in sufficient numbers and pass on to their offspring a sustainable mode of existence.

"What sane person would agree to that?"

"You'd be surprised." I couldn't speak for the Chinese, the Russians, or any of the other international volunteers, but the North American flight candidates were a shockingly ordinary group of men and women. They had been selected for their youth, physical hardiness, and ability to tolerate and endure discomfort. Only a few had been Air Force test pilots but all possessed what Jason called "the test pilot mentality," a willingness to accept grave physical risk in the name of a spectacular achievement. And, of course, most of them were in all likelihood doomed, just as most of the bacteria mounted on these distant rockets were doomed. The best outcome we could reasonably expect was that some band of nomadic survivors wandering the mossy canyons of Valles Marineris might encounter a similar group of Russians or Danes or Canadians and engender a viable Martian humanity.

"And you *countenance* this?"

"Nobody asked my opinion. But I wish them well."

Diane gave me a that's-not-good-enough look but chose not to pursue the argument. We rode an elevator down to the lobby restaurant. As we lined up for table service behind a dozen network news technicians she must have felt the growing excitement.

After we ordered she turned her head, listening as fragments of conversation—words like "photodissociation" and "cryptoendelithic" and, yes, "ecopoiesis"—spilled over from crowded tables, journalists rehearsing the jargon for their next day's work or just struggling to understand it. There was also laughter and the reckless clash of cutlery, an air of giddy if uncertain expectation. This was the first time since the moon landing more than sixty years ago that the world's attention had been so completely focused on a space adventure, and the Spin gave this one what even the moon landing had lacked: real urgency and a global sense of risk.

"This is all Jason's work, isn't it?"

"Without Jason and E.D. this might still be happening. But it would be happening differently, probably less quickly and efficiently. Jase has always been at the center of it."

"And us at the periphery. Orbiting his genius. Tell you a secret. I'm a little afraid of him. Afraid of seeing him after so long. I know he disapproves of me."

"Not you. Your lifestyle, maybe."

"You mean my faith. It's okay to talk about it. I know Jase feels a little—I guess betrayed. As if Simon and I have repudiated everything he believes in. But that's not true. Jason and I were never on the same path."

"Basically, you know, he's just Jase. Same old Jase."

"But am I the same old Diane?"

For which I had no answer.

She ate with an obvious appetite, and after the main course we ordered dessert and coffee. I said, "It's lucky you could take the time for this."

"Lucky that Simon let me off my leash?"

"I didn't mean that."

"I know. But in a way it's true. Simon can be a little controlling. He likes to know where I am."

"Is that a problem for you?"

"You mean, is my marriage in trouble? No. It isn't, and I wouldn't let it be. That doesn't mean we don't occasionally disagree." She hesitated. "If I talk about this, I'm sharing it with *you*, right? Not Jason. Just you."

I nodded.

"Simon has changed some since you met him. We all have, everybody from the old NK days. NK was all about being young and making a community of belief, a kind of sacred space where we didn't have to be afraid of each other, where we could embrace each other not just figuratively but literally. Eden on Earth. But we were mistaken. We thought AIDS didn't matter, jealousy didn't matter—they couldn't matter, because we'd come to the end of the world. But it's a slow

Tribulation, Ty. The Tribulation is a lifetime's work, and we need to be strong and healthy for it."

"You and Simon—"

"Oh, we're healthy." She smiled. "And thank you for asking, Dr. Dupree. But we lost friends to AIDS and drugs. The movement was a roller-coaster ride, love all the way up and grief all the way down. Anyone who was part of it will tell you that."

Probably so, but the only NK veteran I knew was Diane herself. "The last few years haven't been easy for anyone."

"Simon had a hard time dealing with it. He really believed we were a blessed generation. He once told me God had come so close to humanity it was like sitting next to a furnace on a winter night, that he could practically warm his hands at the Kingdom of Heaven. We all felt that way, but it really did bring out the best in Simon. And when it started to go bad, when so many of our friends were sick or drifting into addictions of one kind or another, it hurt him pretty deeply. That was when the money started running out, too, and eventually Simon had to look for work—we both did. I did temp work for a few years. Simon couldn't find a secular job but he does janitorial work at our church in Tempe, Jordan Tabernacle, and they pay him when they can . . . he's studying for his pipe fitter's certificate."

"Not exactly the Promised Land."

"Yeah, but you know? I don't think it's supposed to be. That's what I tell him. Maybe we can feel the chiliasm coming, but it's not here yet—we still have to play out the last minutes of the game even if the outcome is a foregone conclusion. And maybe we're being judged on that. We have to play it like it matters."

We rode the elevator up to our rooms. Diane paused at her door and said, "What I'm remembering is how good it feels to talk to you. We used to be pretty good talkers, remember?"

Confiding our fears through the chaste medium of the telephone. Intimacy at a distance. She had always preferred it that way. I nodded.

"Maybe can do that again," she said. "Maybe I can call you from Arizona sometimes."

She, of course, would call me, because Simon might not like it if I called her. That was understood. As was the nature of the relationship she was proposing. I would be her platonic buddy. Someone harmless to confide in during troubled times, like the leading lady's gay male friend in a cineplex drama. We would chat. We would share. Nobody would get hurt.

It wasn't what I wanted or needed. But I couldn't say that to the eager, slightly lost look she was giving me. Instead I said, "Yeah, of course."

And she grinned and hugged me and left me in the hall.

I sat up later than I should have, nursing my wounded dignity, embedded in the noise and laughter from nearby rooms, thinking about all the scientists and engineers at Perihelion and JPL and Kennedy, all these newspaper people and video journalists watching klieg lights play over the distant rockets, all of us doing our jobs here at the tag end of human history, doing what was expected of us, playing it like it mattered.

○ ○ ○

Jason arrived at noon the next day, ten hours before the first wave of launches was scheduled to begin. The weather was bright and calm, a good omen. Of all the global launch sites the only obvious no-go was the European Space Agency's expanded Kourov complex in French New Guinea, shut down by a fierce March storm. (The ESA microorganisms would be delayed a day or two—or half a million years, Spin-time.)

Jase came directly to my suite, where Diane and I were waiting for him. He wore a cheap plastic windbreaker and a Marlins cap pulled low over his eyes to disguise him from the resident reporters. "Tyler," he said when I opened the door. "I'm sorry. If I could have been there I would have."

The funeral service. "I know."

"Belinda Dupree was the best thing about the Big House. I mean that."

"I appreciate it," I said, and stepped out of his way.

Diane came across the room with a wary expression. Jason closed the door behind him, not smiling. They stood a yard apart, eyeing each other. The silence was weighty. Jason broke it.

"That collar," he said, "makes you look like a Victorian banker. And you ought to put on a little weight. Is it so hard to scrounge a meal out there in cow country?"

Diane said, "More cactus than cows, Jase."

And they laughed and fell into each other's arms.

o o o

We staked out the balcony after dark, brought out comfortable chairs and ordered up a tray of crudités (Diane's choice) from room service. The night was as dark as every starless Spin-shrouded night, but the launch platforms were illuminated by gigantic spotlights and their reflections danced in the gently rolling swells.

Jason had been seeing a neurologist for some weeks now. The specialist's diagnosis had been the same as mine: Jason suffered from severe and nonresponsive multiple sclerosis for which the only useful treatment was a regimen of palliative drugs. In fact the neurologist had wanted to submit Jason's case to the Centers for Disease Control as part of their ongoing study of what some people were calling AMS— atypical multiple sclerosis. Jase had threatened or bribed him out of the idea. And for now, at least, the new drug cocktail was keeping him in remission. He was as functional and mobile as he had ever been. Any suspicions Diane might have harbored were quickly allayed.

He had brought along a bottle of expensive and authentically French champagne to celebrate the launches. "We could have had VIP seats," I told Diane. "Bleachers outside the Vehicle Assembly Building. Brushing elbows with President Garland."

"The view from here is as good," Jason said. "Better. Here, we're not props in a photo opportunity."

"I've never met a president," Diane said.

The sky, of course, was dark, but the TV in the hotel room (we had turned it up to hear the countdown) was talking about the Spin barrier, and Diane looked into the sky as if it might have become miraculously visible, the lid that enclosed the world. Jason saw the tilt of her head. "They shouldn't call it a barrier," he said. "None of the journals call it that anymore."

"Oh? What *do* they call it?"

He cleared his throat. "A 'strange membrane.' "

"Oh no." Diane laughed. "No, that's awful. That's not acceptable. It sounds like a gynecological disorder."

"Yeah, but 'barrier' is incorrect. It's more like a boundary layer. It's not a line you cross. It acquires objects selectively and accelerates them into the external universe. The process is more like osmosis than, say, crashing a fence. Ergo, membrane."

"I'd forgotten what it's like talking to you, Jase. It can be a little surreal."

"Hush," I told them both. "Listen."

Now the TV had cut to the NASA feed, a bland Mission Control voice talking the numbers down. Thirty seconds. There were twelve rockets fueled and nominal on their pads. Twelve simultaneous launches, an act that a less ambitious space agency would once have deemed impractical and radically unsafe. But we lived in more daring or desperate times.

"Why do they all have to go up at once?" Diane asked.

"Because," Jason began; then he said, "No. Wait. Watch."

Twenty seconds. Ten. Jase stood up and leaned into the balcony railing. The hotel balconies were mobbed. The beach was mobbed. A thousand heads and lenses swiveled in the same direction. Estimates later put the crowd in and around the Cape at nearly two million. According to police reports, more than a hundred wallets were lifted that night. There were two fatal stabbings, fifteen attempted assaults, and one premature labor. (The child, a four-pound girl, was delivered on a trestle table at the International House of Pancakes in Cocoa Beach.)

Five seconds. The TV in the hotel room went quiet. For a moment there was no sound but the buzz and whine of photographic gear.

Then the ocean was ablaze with firelight as far as the horizon.

No single one of these rockets would have impressed a local crowd even in darkness, but this wasn't one column of flame, it was five, seven, ten, twelve. The seaborne gantries were briefly silhouetted like skeletal skyscrapers, lost soon after in billows of vaporized ocean water. Twelve pillars of white fire, separated by miles but compressed by perspective, clawed into a sky turned indigo blue by their combined light. The beach crowd began to cheer, and the sound merged with the sound of the solid-fuel boosters hammering for altitude, a throb that compressed the heart like ecstasy or terror. But it wasn't only the brute spectacle we were cheering. Almost certainly every one of these two million people had seen a rocket launch before, at least on television, and although this multiple ascendancy was grand and loud it was remarkable mainly for its intent, its motivating idea. We weren't just planting the flag of terrestrial life on Mars, we were defying the Spin itself.

The rockets rose. (And on the rectangular screen of the TV, when I glanced at it through the balcony door, similar rockets bent into cloudy daylight in Jiuquan, Svobodnyy, Baikonur, Xichang.) The fierce horizontal light became oblique and began to dim as night rushed back from the sea. The sound spent itself in sand and concrete and superheated salt water. I imagined I could smell the reek of fireworks coming ashore with the tide, the pleasantly awful stench of Roman candles.

A thousand cameras clattered like dying crickets and went still.

The cheering lasted, in one form or another, until dawn.

o o o

We went inside and drew the drapes against the anticlimactic darkness and opened the champagne. We watched the news from overseas. Apart from the French rain delay, every launch had been successful. A bacterial armada was en route to Mars.

"So why *do* they all have to go up at once?" Diane asked again.

Jason gave her a long thoughtful look. "Because we want them to arrive at their destination at roughly the same time. Which is not as easy as it sounds. They have to enter the Spin membrane more or less simultaneously, or they'll exit separated by years or centuries. Not so critical with these anaerobic cargos, but we're practicing for when it really matters."

"Years or *centuries*? How is that possible?"

"Nature of the Spin, Diane."

"Right, but centuries?"

He turned his chair to face her, frowning. "I'm trying to grasp the extent of your ignorance here. . . ."

"Just a question, Jase."

"Count a second for me."

"What?"

"Look at your watch and count me one second. No, I'll do it. One—" He paused. "Second. Got that?"

"Jason—"

"Bear with me. You understand the Spin ratio?"

"Roughly."

"Roughly isn't good enough. One terrestrial second equals 3.17 years Spin time. Keep that in mind. If one of our rockets enters the Spin membrane a single second behind the rest, it reaches orbit more than three years late."

"Just because I can't quote numbers—"

"They're important numbers, Diane. Suppose our flotilla just emerged from the membrane, just now, *now*—" He ticked the air with his finger. "*One second,* here and gone. For the flotilla, that was three and a fraction years. One second ago they were in Earth orbit. Now they've delivered their cargo to the surface of Mars. I mean *now,* Diane, literally *now*. It's already happened, it's done. So let a minute pass on your watch. That's approximately a hundred and ninety years by an outside clock."

"That's a lot, of course, but you can't make over a planet in two hundred years, can you?"

"So now it's two hundred Spin years into the experiment. Right now, as we speak, any bacterial colonies that survived the trip will have been reproducing on Mars for two centuries. In an hour, they will have been there eleven thousand four hundred years. This time tomorrow they'll have been multiplying for almost two hundred seventy-four thousand years."

"Okay, Jase. I get the idea."

"This time next week, 1.9 million years."

"Okay."

"A month, 8.3 million years."

"Jason—"

"This time next year, one hundred million years."

"Yes, but—"

"On Earth, one hundred million years is roughly the span of time between the emergence of life from the sea and your last birthday. One hundred million years is time enough for those microorganisms to pump carbon dioxide out of carbonate deposits in the crust, leach nitrogen from nitrates, purge oxides from the regolith and enrich it by dying in large numbers. All that liberated CO_2 is a greenhouse gas. The atmosphere gets thicker and warmer. A year from now we send another armada of respirating organisms, and they begin to cycle CO_2 into free oxygen. Another year—or as soon as the spectroscopic signature from the planet looks right—we introduce grasses, plants, other complex organisms. And when all that stabilizes into some kind of crudely homeostatic planetary ecology, we send human beings. You know what that means?"

"Tell me," Diane said sullenly.

"It means that within five years there'll be a flourishing human civilization on Mars. Farms, factories, roads, cities . . ."

"There's a Greek word for this, Jase."

"Ecopoiesis."

"I was thinking of 'hubris.' "

He smiled. "I worry about a lot of things. But offending the gods isn't one of them."

"Or offending the Hypotheticals?"

That stopped him. He leaned back and sipped champagne, a little flat by now, from his hotel-room glass.

"I'm not afraid of offending them," he said finally. "On the contrary. I'm afraid we may be doing exactly what they want us to do."

But he wouldn't explain, and Diane was eager to change the subject.

○ ○ ○

I drove Diane to Orlando the next day for her flight back to Phoenix.

It had become obvious over the last few days that we

would not discuss, mention, or allude in any way to the physical intimacy we had shared that night in the Berkshires before her marriage to Simon. If we acknowledged it at all it was only in the cumbersome detours we took to avoid it. When we hugged (chastely) in the space in front of the airport security gate she said, "I'll call you," and I knew she would—Diane made few promises but was scrupulous about keeping them—but I was equally conscious of the time that had passed since I had last seen her and the time that would inevitably pass before I saw her again: not Spin time, but something just as erosive and just as hungry. There were creases at the corners of her eyes and mouth, not unlike the ones I saw in the mirror every morning.

Amazing, I thought, how busily we had turned ourselves into people who didn't know one another very well.

○ ○ ○

There were more launches during the spring and summer of that year, surveillance packages that spent months in high Earth orbit and returned with visual and spectrographic images of Mars—snapshots of the ecopoiesis.

The first results were equivocal: a modest increase in atmospheric CO_2 that might have been a side effect of solar warming. Mars remained a cold, inhospitable world by any plausible measure. Jason admitted that even the GEMOs— the genetically engineered Mars organisms that comprised the bulk of the initial seeding—might not have adjusted well to the planet's unfiltered daylight UV levels and oxidant-ridden regolith.

But by midsummer we were seeing strong spectrographic evidence of biological activity. There was more water vapor in a denser atmosphere, more methane and ethane and ozone, even a tiny but detectable increase in free nitrogen.

By Christmas these changes, while still subtle, had so dramatically outpaced what could be attributed to solar warming that no doubt remained. Mars had become a living planet.

The launch platforms were readied once more, new cargos of microbial life cultured and packaged. In the United States that year, fully two percent of the gross domestic product was devoted to Spin-related aerospace work—essentially, the Mars program—and the ratio was similar in other industrialized countries.

○ ○ ○

Jason suffered a relapse in February. He woke up unable to focus his eyes. His neurologist adjusted his medication and prescribed an eye patch as a temporary fix. Jase recovered rapidly but was away from work for most of a week.

Diane was as good as her word. She began to call me at least monthly, usually more often, often late at night when Simon was asleep at the other end of their small apartment. They lived in a few rooms over a secondhand book-store in Tempe, the best they could do on Diane's salary and the irregular income Simon took home from Jordan Tabernacle. In warm weather I could hear the drone of a swamp cooler in the background; in winter, a radio playing softly to disguise the sound of her voice.

I invited her to come back to Florida for the next series of launches, but of course she couldn't: she was busy with work, they were having church friends to dinner that weekend, Simon wouldn't understand. "Simon's going through a minor spiritual crisis. He's trying to deal with the Messiah issue. . . ."

"There's a Messiah issue?"

"You should read the newspapers," Diane said, possibly overestimating how often these religious debates made the mainstream press, at least in Florida; maybe it was different out west. "The old NK movement believed in a Christless Parousia. That was what made us distinctive." That, I thought, and their penchant for public nudity. "The early writers, Ratel and Greengage, saw the Spin as a direct fulfillment of scriptural prophecy—which meant the prophecy itself was redefined, reconfigured by historical events. There didn't have to be a literal Tribulation or even a physical Second Coming of Christ. All that stuff in Thessalonians and Corinthians and Revelation could be reinterpreted or ignored, because the Spin was a genuine intervention by God in human history—a tangible miracle, which supersedes scripture.

That was what freed us to make the Kingdom on Earth. Suddenly we were responsible for our own chiliasm."

"I'm not sure I follow." Actually she had lost me somewhere around the word "Parousia."

"It means—well, all that really matters is that Jordan Tabernacle, our little church, has officially renounced all NK doctrine, even though half the congregation is old NK people like me and Simon. So suddenly there are all these arguments about the Tribulation and how the Spin tallies against Biblical prophecy. People taking sides. Bereans versus Progressives, Covenanters versus Preterists. Is there an Antichrist, and if so, where is he? Does the Rapture happen before the Tribulation or during or after? Issues like that. Maybe it sounds picayune, but the spiritual stakes are very high, and the people having these arguments are people we care about, our friends."

"Where do you stand?"

"Me personally?" She was quiet, and there it was again, the sound of the radio murmuring behind her, some Valium-voiced announcer delivering late-night news to insomniacs. *Latest on the shooting in Mesa.* Parousia or no Parousia. "You could say I'm conflicted. I don't know what I believe. Sometimes I miss the old days. Making up paradise as we went along. It seems like—"

She paused. Now there was another voice doubling the staticky murmur of the radio: *Diane? Are you still up?*

"Sorry," she whispered. Simon on patrol. It was time to cut short our telephone tryst, her act of touchless infidelity. "Talk to you soon."

She was gone before I could say good-bye.

○ ○ ○

The second series of seed launches went off as flawlessly as the first. The media mobbed Canaveral again, but I watched this round on a big digital projection in the auditorium at Perihelion, a sunshine launch that scattered herons into the sky over Merritt Island like bright confetti.

Followed by another summer of waiting. ESA lofted a series of next-generation orbital telescopes and interferometers, and the stored data they retrieved was even sleeker and cleaner than last year's. By September every office at Perihelion was plastered with high-res images of our success. I framed one for the infirmary waiting room. It was a color-composite rendering of Mars showing Olympus Mons outlined in frost or ice and scarred with fresh drainage channels, fog flowing like water through Valles Marineris, green capillaries snaking over Solis Lacus. The southern highlands of the Terra Sirenum were still deserts, but the region's impact craters had eroded to near-invisibility under a wetter, windier climate.

The oxygen content of the atmosphere rose and fell for a few months as the population of aerobic organisms oscillated, but by December it had topped twenty millibars and stabilized. Out of a potentially chaotic mix of increasing greenhouse gases, an unstable hydrologic cycle, and novel biogeochemical feedback loops, Mars was discovering its own equilibrium.

The string of successes was good for Jason. He remained in remission and was happily, almost therapeutically, busy. If anything dismayed him it was his own emergence as the iconic genius of the Perihelion Foundation, or at least its scientific celebrity, poster child for the transformation of Mars. This was more E.D.'s doing than Jason's: E.D. knew the public wanted Perihelion to have a human face, preferably young, smart but not intimidating, and he had been pushing Jase in front of cameras since the days when Perihelion was an aerospace lobby group. Jase put up with it—he was a good and patient explainer, and reasonably photogenic—but he hated the process and would leave a room rather than see himself on television.

That was the year of the first unmanned NEP flights, which Jase watched with particular attention. These were the vehicles that would transport human beings to Mars, and unlike the comparatively simple seed carriers, the NEP vehicles were new technology. NEP stood for "nuclear electric propulsion": miniature nuclear reactors feeding ion engines vastly more powerful than the ones that drove the seed vessels, powerful enough to enable massive payloads. But getting these leviathans into orbit required boosters as large as anything NASA had ever launched, acts of what Jason called "heroic engineering," heroically expensive. The price tag had begun to raise red flags even in a largely supportive Congress, but the stream of notable successes kept a lid on dissent. Jason worried that even a single conspicuous failure would shift that equation.

Shortly after New Year's Day a NEP test vehicle failed to return its reentry package of test data and was presumed disabled in orbit. There were finger-pointing speeches on Capitol Hill led by a coterie of fiscal ultraconservatives representing states without significant aerospace investment, but E.D.'s friends in Congress overrode the objections and a successful test a week later buried the controversy. Still, Jason said, we had dodged a bullet.

Diane had followed the debate but considered it trivial. "What Jase *needs* to worry about," she said, "is what this Mars thing is doing to the world. So far it's all good press, right? Everybody's gung-ho, we all want something to reassure us about the—I'm not sure what to call it—the *potency* of the human race. But the euphoria will wear off sooner or later, and in the meantime people are getting extremely savvy about the nature of the Spin."

"Is that a bad thing?"

"If the Mars project fails or doesn't live up to expectations, yeah. Not just because people will be disappointed. They've watched the transformation of an entire planet—they have a yardstick to measure the Spin by. The sheer insane power of it, I mean. The Spin's not just some abstract phenomenon— you guys made them look the beast in the eye, and good for you, I guess, but if your project goes wrong you steal that courage away again, and now it's worse because they've *seen* the thing. And they will not love you for failing, Tyler, because it will leave them more frightened than they've ever been."

I quoted the Housman poem she had taught me long ago: *The infant child is not aware / He has been eaten by the bear.*

"The infant child is starting to figure it out," she said. "Maybe that's how you define the Tribulation."

Maybe so. Some nights, when I couldn't sleep, I thought about the Hypotheticals, whoever or whatever they were. There was really only one salient, obvious fact about them: not simply that they were capable of enclosing the Earth in this . . . strange membrane, but that they had been out there—owning us, regulating our planet and the passage of time—for almost two billion years.

Nothing even remotely human could be so patient.

○ ○ ○

Jason's neurologist tipped me off to a *JAMA* study published that winter. Researchers at Cornell had discovered a genetic marker for acute drug-resistant MS. The neurologist—a genial, fat Floridian named David Malmstein—had run Jason's DNA profile and found the suspect sequence in it. I asked him what that meant.

"It means we can tailor his medication a little more specifically. It also means we can never deliver the kind of permanent remission a typical MS patient expects."

"Seems like he's been in remission for most of a year now. Isn't that long-term?"

"His symptoms are under control, that's all. The AMS goes on burning, sort of like a fire in a coal seam. The time will come when we can't compensate for it."

"The point of no return."

"You could say."

"How long can he pass for normal?"

Malmstein paused. "You know," he said, "that's exactly what Jason asked me."

"What did you tell him?"

"That I'm not a fortune-teller. That AMS is a disease without a well-established etiology. That the human body has its own calendar."

"I'm guessing he didn't like the answer."

"He was vocal in his disapproval. But it's true. He could walk around for the next decade asymptomatic. Or he could be in a wheelchair by the end of the week."

"You told him *that*?"

"A kindler, gentler version. I don't want him to lose hope.

He has a fighting spirit, and that counts for a lot. My honest opinion is that he'll do all right over the short term—two years, five years, maybe more. Then all bets are off. I wish I had a better prognosis."

I didn't tell Jase I'd talked to Malmstein, but I saw the way, in the following weeks, he redoubled his work, counting his successes against time and mortality, not the world's but his own.

○ ○ ○

The pace of the launches, not to mention the cost of them, began to escalate. The last wave of seed launches (the only one to carry, in part, actual seeds) happened in March, two years after Jase and Diane and I had watched a dozen similar rockets depart Florida for what had been at the time a barren planet.

The Spin had given us the necessary leverage for a long ecopoiesis. Now that we had launched the seeds of complex plants, however, timing became crucial. If we waited too long Mars could evolve out of our grasp: a species of edible grain after a million years evolving in the wild might not resemble its ancestral form, might have grown unpalatable or even poisonous.

This meant the survey satellites had to be launched only weeks after the seed armada, and the manned NEP vessels, if the results looked promising, immediately after that.

I took another late-night call from Diane the night after the survey sats went up. (Their data packages had been retrieved within hours but were still en route to JPL in Pasadena to be analyzed.) She sounded stressed and admitted when I questioned her that she had been laid off at least until June. She and Simon had run into trouble with their back rent. She couldn't ask E.D. for money, and Carol was impossible to talk to. She was working up the nerve to speak to Jase, but she didn't relish the humiliation.

"What kind of money are we talking about, Diane?"

"Tyler, I didn't mean—"

"I know. You didn't ask. I'm offering."

"Well . . . this month, even five hundred dollars would make a real difference."

"I guess the pipe cleaner fortune ran dry."

"Simon's trust fund ran out. There's still family money, but his family's not talking to him."

"He won't catch on if I send you a check?"

"He wouldn't like it. I thought I'd tell him I found an old insurance policy and cashed it in. Something like that. The kind of lie that doesn't really count as a sin. I hope."

"You guys are still at the Collier Street address?" Where I mailed a politely neutral Christmas card every year and from which I received one in return, generic snow scenes signed *Simon and Diane Townsend, God Bless!*

"Yes," she said, then, "Thank you, Tyler. Thank you so much. You know this is incredibly mortifying."

"Hard times for a lot of folks."

"You're doing all right, though?"

"Yeah, I'm doing all right."

I sent her six checks each postdated for the fifteenth of the month, half a year's worth, not sure whether this would cement our friendship or poison it. Or whether it mattered.

○ ○ ○

The survey data revealed a world still drier than the Earth but marked with lakes like polished turquoise inlaid on a copper disk; a planet gently swirled with bands of cloud, storms dropping rainfall on the windward slopes of ancient volcanos and feeding river basins and silty lowland deltas green as suburban lawns.

The big boosters were fueled on their pads, and at launch facilities and cosmodromes around the world nearly eight hundred human beings climbed gantries to lock themselves into cupboard-sized chambers and confront a destiny that was anything but certain. The NEP arks enclosed atop these boosters contained (in addition to astronauts) embryonic sheep, cattle, horses, pigs, and goats, and the steel wombs from which they could, with luck, be decanted; the seeds of ten thousand plants; the larvae of bees and other useful insects; dozens of similar biological cargos which might or might not survive the journey and the rigors of regenesis; condensed archives of essential human knowledge both digital (including the means to read them) and densely printed; and parts and supplies for simple shelters, solar power generators, greenhouses, water purifiers, and elementary field hospitals. In a best-case scenario all these human expeditionary vessels would arrive at roughly the same equatorial lowlands within a span of several years depending on their transit of the Spin membrane. At worst, even a single ship, if it arrived reasonably intact, could support its crew through a period of acclimation.

Once more into the Perihelion auditorium, then, along with everyone who hadn't gone up the coast to see the event in person. I sat up front next to Jason and we craned our heads at the video feed from NASA, a spectacular long shot of the offshore launch platforms, steel islands linked by immense rail bridges, ten huge Prometheus boosters (called "Prometheus" when they were manufactured by Boeing or Lockheed-Martin; the Russians, the Chinese, and the EU used the same template but named and painted them differently) bathed in spotlights and ranked like whitewashed fenceposts far into the blue Atlantic. Much had been sacrificed for this moment: taxes and treasure, shorelines and coral reefs, careers and lives. (At the foot of each gantry off Canaveral was an engraved plaque bearing the names of the fifteen construction workers who had died during the assembly work.) Jason tapped his foot in a violent rhythm while the countdown drained into its last minute, and I wondered if this was symptomatic, but he caught me looking and leaned into my ear and said, "I'm just nervous. Aren't you?"

There had already been problems. Worldwide, eighty of these big boosters had been assembled and prepared for tonight's synchronized launch. But they were a new design, not entirely debugged. Four had been scrubbed before launch for technical problems. Three were currently holding in their counts—in a launch that was supposed to be synchronized worldwide—for the usual reasons: dicey fuel lines, software glitches. This was inevitable and had been accounted for in the planning, but it still seemed ominous.

So much had to happen so quickly. What we were transplanting this time was not biology but human history, and human history, Jase had said, burned like a fire compared to the slow rust of evolution. (When we were much younger, after the Spin but before he left the Big House, Jase used to have a parlor trick to demonstrate this idea. "Stick out your arms," he'd say, "straight out at your sides," and when he had you in the appropriate cruciform position he'd say, "Left index finger to right index finger straight across your heart, that's the history of the Earth. You know what *human* history is? Human history is the nail on your right-hand index finger. Not even the whole nail. Just that little white part. The part you clip off when it gets too long. That's the discovery of fire and the invention of writing and Galileo and Newton and the moon landing and 9/11 and last week and this morning. Compared to evolution we're newborns. Compared to geology, we barely exist.")

Then the NASA voice announced, "Ignition," and Jason sucked air between his teeth and turned his head half away as nine of ten boosters, hollow tubes of explosive liquid taller than the Empire State Building, detonated skyward against all logic of gravity and inertia, burning tons of fuel to achieve the first few inches of altitude and vaporizing seawater in order to mute a sonic event that would otherwise have shaken them to pieces. Then it was as if they had made ladders of steam and smoke and climbed them, their speed apparent now, plumes of fire outpacing the rolling clouds they had created. Up and gone, just like every successful launch: swift and vivid as a dream, then up and gone.

The last booster was delayed by a faulty sensor but launched ten minutes late. It would arrive on Mars nearly a thousand years after the rest of the fleet, but this had been taken into account in the planning and might prove to be a good thing, an injection of Terrestrial technology and know-how long after the paper books and digital readers of the original colonists had crumbled into dust.

○ ○ ○

Moments later the video broadcast cut to French Guyana, the old and much-expanded Centre National d'Études Spatiales at Kourou, where one of the big boosters from the

Aerospatiale factory had risen a hundred feet and then lost thrust and tumbled back onto its pad in a mushroom of flame.

Twelve people were killed, ten aboard the NEP ark and two on the ground, but it was the only conspicuous tragedy of the entire launch sequence, and that probably amounted to good luck, taken all in all.

○ ○ ○

But that wasn't the end of the exercise. By midnight—and this, it seemed to me, was the clearest indicator yet of the grotesque disparity between terrestrial time and Spin-time—human civilization on Mars had either failed entirely or had been in progress for most of a hundred thousand years.

That's roughly the amount of time between the emergence of *Homo sapiens* as a distinct species and yesterday afternoon.

It passed while I was driving home from Perihelion to my rental. It was entirely possible that Martian dynasties rose and fell while I waited for traffic lights to change. I thought about those lives—those fully real human lives, each one of them boxed into a span of less than a minute as my watch counted time—and felt a little dizzy. Spin vertigo. Or something deeper.

A half dozen survey satellites were launched that night, programmed to look for signs of human life on Mars. Their payload packages parachuted back to Earth and were retrieved before morning.

○ ○ ○

I saw the results before they were made public.

This was a full week after the Prometheus launches. Jason had booked a 10:30 appointment at the infirmary, subject to breaking news from JPL. He didn't cancel the appointment but showed up an hour late with a manila envelope in his hand, clearly anxious to discuss something not related to his medical regimen. I hurried him into a consultation room.

"I don't know what to tell the press," he said. "I just got off a conference call with the ESA director and a bunch of Chinese bureaucrats. We're trying to put together a draft of a joint statement for heads of state, but as soon as the Russians agree to a sentence the Chinese want to veto it, and vice versa."

"A statement about what, Jase?"

"The satellite data."

"You got the results?" In fact they were overdue. JPL was usually quicker about sharing its photos. But from what Jason had said I guessed someone had been sitting on the data. Which meant it wasn't what they'd expected. Bad news, perhaps.

"Look," Jason said.

He opened the manila folder and pulled out two composite telescopic photos, one atop the other. Both were images of Mars taken from Earth orbit after the Prometheus launches.

The first photograph was heart-stopping. It was not as distinct as the framed image I had put up in the waiting room, since in this one the planet was far from its closest approach to Earth; the clarity it did possess was a testament to modern imaging technology. Superficially it didn't seem much different from the framed photo: I could make out enough green to know that the transplanted ecology was still intact, still active.

"Look a little closer," Jason said.

He ran his finger down the sinuous line of a riverine lowland. There were green places here with sharp, regular borders. More of them, the more I looked.

"Agriculture," Jase said.

I held my breath and thought about what that meant. I thought: *Now there are two inhabited planets in the solar system.* Not hypothetically, but really. These were places where people lived, where people lived *on Mars*.

I wanted to stare. But Jase slid the printout back into its envelope, revealing the one beneath.

"The second photo," he said, "was taken twenty-four hours later."

"I don't understand."

"Taken from the same camera on the same satellite. We have parallel images to confirm the result. It looked like a flaw in the imaging system until we juiced the contrast enough to read a little starlight."

But there was nothing *in* the photograph. A few stars, a fat central nothingness in the shape of a disk. "What is it?"

"A Spin membrane," Jason said. "Seen from the outside. Mars has its own now."

4×10^9 A.D.

We were traveling inland from Padang—that much I understood—uphill, over roads that were sometimes silken-smooth and sometimes pitted and uneven, until the car pulled up in front of what in the darkness appeared to be a concrete bunker but must have been (by the painted red crescent under a glaring tungsten bulb) some kind of medical clinic. The driver was upset when he saw where he had taken us—this was further evidence that I was sick, not just drunk—but Diane pushed more bills into his hand and sent him away mollified if not happy.

I was having trouble standing. I leaned into Diane, who took my weight gamely, and we stood in the wet night, on an empty road, moonlight cutting through tattered clouds. There was the clinic in front of us and a gas station across the pavement and nothing else but forest and flat spaces that might have been cultivated fields. There was no visible human presence until the screened door of the clinic wheezed open and a short, rotund woman wearing a long skirt and small white hat hurried out to us.

"Ibu Diane!" the woman said, excitedly but softly, as if she were afraid of being overheard, even at this lonely hour. "Welcome!"

"Ibu Ina," Diane said respectfully.

"And this must be—?"

"Pak Tyler Dupree. The one I told you about."

"Too sick to speak?"

"Too sick to say anything sensible."

"Then by all means let's get him inside."

Diane supported me on one side and the woman she had called Ibu Ina grabbed my right arm by the shoulder. She wasn't a young woman but she was remarkably strong. The hair under her white cap was gray and thinning. She smelled like cinnamon. Judging by the way she wrinkled her nose, I smelled like something much worse.

Then we were inside, past an empty waiting room furnished with rattan and cheap metal chairs, into what looked like a fairly modern consultancy, where Diane dumped me onto a padded table and Ina said, "Well, then, let's see what we can do for him," and I felt safe enough to pass out.

o o o

I woke to the sound of a call to prayer from a distant mosque and the smell of fresh coffee.

I was lying naked on a pallet in a small concrete room with one window, which admitted the only light, a pale premonition of dawn. There was a doorway covered with a sort of bamboo lacework, and from beyond it the noise of someone doing something energetic with cups and bowls.

The clothes I had been wearing last night had been laundered and were folded next to the pallet. I was between fevers—I had learned to recognize these little oases of well-being—and strong enough to dress myself.

I was balancing on one leg and aiming the other into my trousers when Ibu Ina peeked in through the curtain. "So you're well enough to stand!" she said.

Briefly. I fell back onto the pallet, half dressed. Ina came into the room with a bowl of white rice, a spoon, an enameled tin cup. She knelt beside me and glanced at the wooden tray: did I want any of this?

I discovered I did. For the first time in many days I was hungry. Probably a good thing. My pants were ridiculously loose, my ribs obscenely prominent. "Thank you," I said.

"We were introduced last night," she said, handing me the bowl. "Do you remember? I apologize for the crude nature of the accommodations. This room serves concealment better than comfort."

She might have been fifty or sixty years old. Her face was round and wrinkled, her features concentrated in a moon of brown flesh, an apple-doll look that was accentuated by her long black dress and white cap. If the Amish had settled in West Sumatra they might have produced something like Ibu Ina.

Her accent was lilting Indonesian but her diction was primly correct. "You speak very well," I said, the only compliment I could come up with on short notice.

"Thank you. I studied at Cambridge."

"English?"

"Medicine."

The rice was bland but good. I made a show of finishing it.

"Perhaps more, later?" Ibu Ina said.

"Yes, thank you."

Ibu was a Minangkabau term of respect used in addressing women. (The male equivalent was *Pak*.) Which implied that Ina was a Minangkabau doctor and that we were in the Sumatran highlands, probably within sight of Mount Merapi. Everything I knew about Ina's people I had learned from the Sumatran guidebook I had read on the plane from Singapore: there were more than five million Minangkabau living in villages and cities in the highlands; many of Padang's finest restaurants were operated by Minangkabau; they were famous for their matrilineal culture, their business savvy, and their blend of Islam and traditional *adat* customs.

None of which explained what I was doing in the back room of a Minang doctor's office.

I said, "Is Diane still asleep? Because I don't understand—"

"Ibu Diane has taken the bus back to Padang, I'm afraid. But you'll be safe here."

"I was hoping she'd be safe, too."

"She would be safer here than in the city, certainly. But that wouldn't get either of you out of Indonesia."

"How did you come to know Diane?"

Ina grinned. "Sheerly by luck! Or mostly luck. She was negotiating a contract with my ex-husband, Jala, who is in the import-export business, among others, when it became obvious that the New Reformasi were much too interested in her. I work a few days a month at the state hospital in Padang and I was delighted when Jala introduced me to Diane, even if he was simply looking for a place to temporarily hide a prospective client. It was so exciting to meet the sister of Pak Jason Lawton!"

This was startling in almost too many ways. "You know about Jason?"

"I know *of* him—unlike you, I have never had the privilege of speaking to him. Oh, but I was a great follower of the news about Jason Lawton in the early days of the Spin. And you were his personal physician! And now here you are in the back room of my clinic!"

"I'm not sure Diane should have mentioned any of that." I was certain she shouldn't have. Our only protection was our anonymity, and now it was compromised.

Ibu Ina looked crestfallen. "Of course," she said, "it would have been better not to mention *that* name. But foreigners with legal problems are terribly commonplace in Padang. There is an expression: a dime a dozen. Foreigners with legal and medical troubles are even more problematic. Diane must have learned that Jala and I were both great admirers of Jason Lawton—it could only have been an act of desperation for her to invoke his name. Even then, I didn't quite believe her until I sought out photographs on the Internet. I suppose one of the drawbacks of celebrity must be this constant taking of pictures. At any rate, there was a photograph of the Lawton family, taken very early in the Spin, but I recognized her: it was true! And so it must be true what she told me about her sick friend. You were a physician to Jason Lawton, and of course the other, the more famous one—"

"Yes."

"The small black wrinkled man."

"Yes."

"Whose medicine is making you sick."

"Whose medicine, I hope, is also making me better."

"As it has already Diane, or so she said. This interests me. Is there really an adulthood beyond adulthood? How do you feel?"

"Could be better, frankly."

"But the process is not finished."

"No. The process is not finished."

"Then you should rest. Is there anything I can get for you?"

"I had notebooks—paper—"

"In a bundle with your other luggage. I'll bring them. Are you a writer as well as a physician?"

"Only temporarily. I need to put some thoughts down on paper."

"Perhaps when you're feeling better you can share some of those thoughts with me."

"Perhaps so. I would be honored."

She rose from her knees. "Especially about the little black wrinkled man. The man from Mars."

o o o

I slept erratically through the next couple of days, waking up surprised by the passage of time, the sudden nights and unexpected mornings, marking what I could of the hours by the call to prayer, the sound of traffic, by Ibu Ina's offerings of rice and curried eggs and periodic sponge baths. We talked, but the conversations washed through my memory like sand through a sieve, and I could tell by her expression that I occasionally repeated myself or had forgotten things she'd said. Light and dark, light and dark; then, suddenly, Diane was kneeling next to Ina beside the bed, both of them giving me somber looks.

"He's awake," Ibu Ina said. "Please excuse me. I'll leave the two of you alone."

Then it was just Diane beside me.

She wore a white blouse, a white scarf over her dark hair, billowy blue trousers. She could have passed for any secularized mall-dweller in downtown Padang, though she was too tall and too pale to really fool anyone.

"Tyler," she said. Her eyes were blue and wide. "Are you paying attention to your fluids?"

"Do I look that bad?"

She stroked my forehead. "It isn't easy, is it?"

"I didn't expect it to be painless."

"Another couple of weeks and it'll be over. Until then—"

She didn't have to tell me. The drug was beginning to work deep into muscle tissue, nervous tissue.

"But this is a good place to be," she added. "We have antispasmodics, decent analgesics. Ina understands what's going on." She smiled sadly. "Still . . . not exactly what we'd planned."

We had planned on anonymity. Any of the Arch Port cities should have been a safe place for a moneyed American to lose himself. We had settled on Padang not just for its convenience—Sumatra was the land mass closest to the Arch—but because its hyperfast economic growth and the recent troubles with the New Reformasi government in Jakarta had made the city a functioning anarchy. I would suffer through the drug regimen in some undistinguished hotel, and when it was finished—when I was effectively remade—we would buy ourselves passage to a place where nothing bad could touch us. That was how it was supposed to go.

What we had not counted on was the vindictiveness of the Chaykin administration and its determination to make examples of us—both for the secrets we had kept and the secrets we had already divulged.

"I guess I made myself a little too conspicuous in the wrong places," Diane said. "I had us booked with two different *rantau* collectives, but both deals fell apart, suddenly people weren't talking to me, and it was obvious we were drawing way too much attention. The consulate, the New Reformasi, and the local police all have our descriptions. Not entirely *accurate* descriptions, but close enough."

"That's why you told these people who we are."

"I told them because they already suspected. Not Ibu Ina, but certainly Jala, her ex. Jala's a very canny guy. He runs a relatively respectable shipping company. A lot of the bulk concrete and palm oil that transits the port of Teluk Bayur also passes through one or another of Jala's warehouses. The *rantau gadang* business nets less money but it's tax-free, and those ships full of emigrants don't come back empty. He does a brisk sideline in black-market cattle and goats."

"Sounds like a man who would be glad to sell us to the New Reformasi."

"But we pay better. And present fewer legal difficulties, as long as we're not caught."

"Does Ina approve of this?"

"Approve of what? The *rantau gadang*? She has two sons and a daughter in the new world. Of Jala? She thinks he's more or less trustworthy—if you pay him he stays bought. Of us? She thinks we're next door to sainthood."

"Because of Wun Ngo Wen?"

"Basically."

"You were lucky to find her."

"It's not entirely luck."

"Still, we should get away as soon as possible."

"Soon as you're better. Jala has a ship lined up. The *Capetown Maru*. That's why I've been back and forth between here and Padang. There are more people I have to pay."

We were rapidly being transformed from foreigners with money to foreigners who used to have money. "Still," I said, "I wish—"

"Wish what?" She ran a finger over my forehead, back and forth, langorously.

"Wish I didn't have to sleep alone."

She gave a little laugh and put her hand on my chest. On my emaciated rib cage, on my skin still alligator-textured and ugly. Not exactly an invitation to intimacy. "It's too hot to cuddle up."

"Too hot?"

I'd been shivering.

"Poor Tyler," she said.

I wanted to tell her to be careful. But I closed my eyes, and when I opened them she was gone again.

○ ○ ○

Inevitably there was worse to come, but in fact I felt much better over the next few days: the eye of the storm, Diane had called it. It was as if the Martian drug and my body had negotiated a temporary truce, both sides rallying for the ultimate battle. I tried to take advantage of the time.

I ate everything Ina offered, and I paced the room from time to time, trying to channel some strength into my scrawny legs. Had I felt stronger this concrete box (in which Ina had stored medical supplies before she built a more secure lock-and-alarm system adjoining the clinic) might have seemed like a prison cell. Under the circumstances it was almost cozy. I piled our hard-shell suitcases in one corner and used them as a sort of desk, sitting on a reed mat while I wrote. The high window allowed in a wedge of sunlight.

It also allowed in the face of a local schoolboy, whom I had caught on two occasions peering at me. When I mentioned this to Ibu Ina she nodded, disappeared for a few minutes, and came back with the boy in tow: "This is En," she said, practically throwing him through the curtain at me. "En is ten years old. He is very bright. He wants to be a doctor one day. He is also my nephew's son. Unfortunately he's cursed with curiosity at the expense of sensibility. He climbed on top of the trash bin to see what I was hiding in my back room. Unforgivable. Apologize to my guest, En."

En hung his head so drastically low that I was afraid his enormous eyeglasses would drop off the end of his nose. He mumbled something.

"In English," Ina said.

"Sorry!"

"Inelegant but to the point. Perhaps En can do something for you, Pak Tyler, to make up for his bad behavior?"

En was clearly on the hook. I tried to let him off. "Apart from respecting my privacy, nothing."

"He will certainly respect your privacy from this moment onward—*won't* you, En?" En cringed and nodded. "How-

ever, I have a job for him. En comes by the clinic almost
every day. If I'm not busy I show him a few things. The chart
of human anatomy. The litmus paper that turns color in vine-
gar. En claims to be grateful for these indulgences." En's
nodding became almost spastically vigorous. "So in return,
and as a way of compensating for his gross negligence of
common *budi,* En will now become the clinic's lookout. En,
do you know what that means?"

En stopped nodding and looked wary.

"It means," Ibu Ina said, "that from now on you will put
your vigilance and curiosity to good use. If anyone comes to
the village asking about the clinic—anyone from the city, I
mean, especially if they look or act like policemen—you will
immediately run here and tell me about it."

"Even if I'm in school?"

"I doubt the New Reformasi will trouble you at school.
When you're at school, pay attention to your lessons. Any
other time, in the street, at a *warung,* whatever, if you see
something or overhear something involving me or the clinic
or Pak Tyler (whom you must *not* mention), come to the
clinic at once. Understand?"

"Yes," En said, and he murmured something else I
couldn't hear.

"No," Ina said promptly, "there is no payment involved,
what a scandalous question! Although, if I'm pleased, favors
might follow. Right now I am not at all pleased."

En scooted away, his oversized white T-shirt billowing behind him.

By nightfall a rain had begun, a deep tropical rain that
lasted days, during which I wrote, slept, ate, paced, endured.

○ ○ ○

Ibu Ina sponged my body during the dark of a rainy night,
scrubbing away a slough of dead skin.

"Tell me something you remember about them," she said.
"Tell me what it was like growing up with Diane and Jason
Lawton."

I thought about that. Or rather, I dipped into the increasingly murky pond of memory for something to offer her,

something both true and emblematic. I couldn't fish out exactly what I wanted but something did float to the surface: a starlit sky, a tree. The tree was a silver poplar, darkly mysterious. "One time we went camping," I said. "This was before the Spin, but not by much."

It felt good to have the dead skin washed away, at least at first, but the revealed derma was sensitive, raw. The first stroke of the sponge was soothing, the second felt like iodine on a paper cut. Ina understood this.

"The three of you? Weren't you young for that, a camping trip, I mean, as they calculate such things where you come from? Or did you travel with your parents?"

"Not with our parents. E.D. and Carol vacationed once a year, resorts or cruise ships, preferably without children."

"And your mother?"

"Preferred to stay home. It was a couple from down the road who took us into the Adirondacks along with their own two boys, teenagers who didn't want anything to do with us."

"Then why—oh, I suppose the father wanted to ingratiate himself with E. D. Lawton? Beg a favor perhaps?"

"Something like that. I didn't ask. Nor did Jason. Diane might have known—she paid attention to those kind of things."

"It hardly matters. You went to a campground in the mountains? Roll on your side, please."

"The kind of campground with a parking lot. Not exactly pristine nature. But it was a weekend in September and we had the place almost to ourselves. We pitched tents and built a fire. The adults—" Their name came back to me. "The Fitches sang songs and made us come in on the choruses. They must have had fond memories of summer camp. It was pretty depressing, actually. The Fitch teenagers hated the whole thing and hid out in their tent with headphones. The older Fitches eventually gave up and went to bed."

"And left the three of you around the dying campfire. Was it a clear night or a rainy one, like this one?"

"A clear early autumn night." Hardly like this one, with its frog choruses and raindrops bulleting the thin roof. "No moon but plenty of stars. Not warm but not really cold, even though we were some ways up in the hills. Windy. Windy enough that you could hear the trees talking to themselves."

Ina's smile broadened. "The trees talking to themselves! Yes, I know what that sounds like. Now on your left side, please."

"The trip had been tedious but it started to feel good now that it was just the three of us. Jase fetched a flashlight and we walked a few yards away from the fire, to an open space in a poplar grove, away from the cars and tents and people, where the land sloped down to the west. Jason showed us the zodiacal light rising in the sky."

"What is the zodiacal light?"

"Sunlight reflecting on grains of ice in the asteroid belt. You can sometimes see it on a very clear, dark night." Or could, before the Spin. Was there still a zodiacal light or had solar pressure swept away the ice? "It came up from the horizon like breath in winter, far away, delicate. Diane was fascinated. She listened to Jase explain it, and this was back when Jason's explanations still fascinated her—she hadn't outgrown them yet. She loved his intelligence, loved him *for* his intelligence—"

"As did Jason's father, perhaps? On your stomach now, please."

"But not in that proprietary way. It was pure goggle-eyed enchantment."

"Excuse me, 'goggle-eyed'?"

"Wide-eyed. Then the wind started to pick up, and Jason turned on the flashlight and pointed it into the poplars so Diane could see the way the branches moved." With this came a vivid memory of young Diane in a sweater at least a size too big for her, hands lost in knitted wool, hugging herself, her face turned up into the cone of light and her eyes reflecting it back in solemn moons. "He showed her the way the biggest branches tossed in a kind of slow motion, and the smaller branches more quickly. That was because each branch and twig had what Jase called a resonant frequency. And you could think of those resonant frequencies as musical notes, he said. The tree's motion in the wind was really a kind of music pitched too low for human ears, the trunk of the tree singing a bass note and the branches singing tenor lines and the twigs playing piccolo. Or, he said, you could think of it as pure numbers, each resonance, from the wind itself to the tremor of a leaf, working out a calculation inside a calculation inside a calculation."

"You describe it very beautifully," Ina said.

"Not half as beautifully as Jason did. It was like he was in love with the world, or at least the patterns in it. The music in it. Ouch."

"I'm sorry. And Diane was in love with Jason?"

"In love with being his sister. Proud of him."

"And were you in love with being his friend?"

"I suppose I was."

"And in love with Diane."

"Yes."

"And she with you."

"Maybe. I hoped so."

"Then, if I may ask, what went wrong?"

"What makes you think anything went wrong?"

"You're obviously still in love. The two of you, I mean. But not like a man and woman who have been together for many years. Something must have kept you apart. Excuse me, this is terribly impertinent."

Yes, something had kept us apart. Many things. Most obviously, I supposed, it was the Spin. She had been especially, particularly frightened by it, for reasons I had never completely understood; as if the Spin were a challenge and a rebuke to everything that made her feel safe. What made her feel safe? The orderly progression of life; friends, family, work—a kind of fundamental *sensibility* of things, which in E.D. and Carol Lawton's Big House must already have seemed fragile, more wished-for than real.

The Big House had betrayed her, and eventually even Jason had betrayed her: the scientific ideas he presented to her like peculiar gifts, which had once seemed reassuring—the cozy major chords of Newton and Euclid—became stranger and more alienating: the Planck length (beneath which things no longer behaved like *things*); black holes, sealed by their own imponderable density into a realm beyond cause and effect; a universe not only expanding but accelerating toward its own decay. She told me once, while St. Augustine was still alive, that when she put her hand on the dog's coat she wanted to feel his heat and his liveliness—not count the beats of his heart or consider the vast spaces between the nuclei and the electrons that constituted his physical being. She wanted St. Dog to be himself and whole, not the sum of his terrifying parts, not a fleeting evolutionary epiphenomenon in the life of a dying star. There was little enough love and affection in her life and each instance of it had to be accounted and stored up in heaven, hoarded against the winter of the universe.

The Spin, when it came, must have seemed like a monstrous vindication of Jason's worldview—more so because of his obsession with it. Clearly, there was intelligent life elsewhere in the galaxy; and, just as obviously, it was nothing like our own. It was immensely powerful, terrifyingly patient, and blankly indifferent to the terror it had inflicted on the world. Imagining the Hypotheticals, one might picture hyperintelligent robots or inscrutable energy beings; but never the touch of a hand, a kiss, a warm bed, or a consoling word.

So she had hated the Spin in a deeply personal way, and I think it was that hatred that ultimately led her to Simon Townsend and the NK movement. In NK theology the Spin became a sacred event but also a subordinate one: large but not as large as the God of Abraham; shocking but less shocking than a crucified Savior, an empty tomb.

I said some of this to Ina. She said, "Of course, I'm not a Christian. I'm not even Islamic enough to satisfy the local authorities. Corrupted by the atheistic West, that's me. But even in Islam there were such movements. People babbling about Imam Mehdi and Ad-Dajjal, Yajuj and Majuj drinking up the Sea of Galilee. Because they thought this made a better kind of sense. There. I'm finished." She had scrubbed the soles of my feet. "Have you always known these things about Diane?"

Known in what sense? Felt, suspected, intuited; but *known*—no, I couldn't say so.

"Then perhaps the Martian drug is living up to your expectations," Ina said as she exited with her stainless steel pan of warm water and her assortment of sponges, leaving me something to think about in the dark of the night.

○ ○ ○

There were three doors leading into or out of Ibu Ina's medical clinic. She walked me through the building once, after her last scheduled patient had departed with a splinted finger.

"This is what I've built in my lifetime," she said. "Little enough, you might think. But the people of this village needed something between here and the hospital in Padang— quite a distance, especially if you have to travel by bus or the roads are undependable."

One door was the front door, where her patients came and went.

One door was the back door, metal-lined and sturdy. Ina parked her little power-cell car in the pressed-earth lot behind the clinic, and she used this door when she arrived in the morning and locked it when she left at night. It was adjacent to the room where I lived and I had learned to recognize the sound of her keys jingling in it not long after the first call to prayer from the village mosque a quarter mile away.

The third door was a side door, down a little corridor that also housed the toilet and a row of supply cupboards. This was where she accepted deliveries and this was the route by which En preferred to come and go.

En was just as Ina had described him: bashful but bright, smart enough to earn the medical degree on which he had set his heart's hopes. His parents weren't rich, Ina said, but if he landed a scholarship, studied premed at the new university in Padang, excelled, found a way to finance a graduate degree— "Then, who knows? The village might have another doctor. That's how I did it."

"You think he'd come back and practice here?"

"He might. We go out, we come back." She shrugged, as if this were the natural order of things. And for the Minang, it was: *rantau,* the tradition of sending young men abroad, was part of the system of *adat,* custom and obligation. *Adat,* like conservative Islam, had been eroded by the last thirty years of modernization, but it pulsed under the surface of Minang life like a heartbeat.

En had been warned not to bother me, but he gradually lost his fear of me. With Ibu Ina's express permission, when I was between bouts of fever, En would hone his English vocabulary by bringing me items of food and naming them for me: *silomak,* sticky rice; *singgang ayam,* curried chicken. When I said, "Thank you," En would call out "Welcome!" and grin, displaying a set of bright white but wildly irregular teeth: Ina was trying to convince his parents to have braces installed.

Ina herself shared a small house in the village with relatives, although lately she had been sleeping in a consulting room in the clinic, a space that couldn't have been any more comfortable than my own bleak cell. Some nights, however, family duties called her away; on those nights she would note my temperature and condition, provision me with food and water, and leave me a pager in case of emergencies. And I would be alone until her key rattled in the door the next morning.

But one night I woke out of a frantic, labyrinthine dream to the sound of the side door shuddering as someone turned the knob in an attempt to open it. Not Ina. Wrong door, wrong hour. It was midnight by my watch, only the beginning of the deepest part of the night; there would still be a few villagers haunting the local *warungs,* cars transiting the main road, trucks trying to reach some distant *desa* by morning. Maybe a patient hoping she was still here. Or maybe an addict looking for drugs.

The knob-turning stopped.

Quietly, I levered myself up and pulled on jeans and a T-shirt. The clinic was dark, my cell was dark, the only light was moonlight through the high window . . . which was suddenly eclipsed.

I looked up and saw the silhouette of En's head like a hovering planet. "Pak Tyler!" he whispered.

"En! You scared me." In fact the shock had drained the strength out of my legs. I had to lean on the wall to stay upright.

"Let me in!" En said.

So I padded barefoot to the side door and threw the latch.

The breeze that rushed in was warm and moist. En rushed in after it. "Let me talk to Ibu Ina!"

"She's not here. What's up, En?"

He was deeply disconcerted. He pushed his glasses up the bump of his nose. "But I need to talk to her!"

"She's at home tonight. You know where she lives?"

En nodded unhappily. "But she said to come *here* and tell her."

"What? I mean, when did she say this?"

"If a stranger asks about the clinic I have to come here and tell her."

"But she's not—" Then the significance of what he'd said pierced the fog of incipient fever. "En, is someone in town asking about Ibu Ina?"

I coaxed the story out of him. En lived with his family in a house behind a *warung* (a food stall) in the heart of the village, only three doors away from the office of the mayor, the *kepala desa*. En, on wakeful nights, was able to lie in his room and listen to the murmur of conversation from the *warung*'s customers. Thus he had acquired an encyclopedic if poorly understood store of village gossip. After dark it was usually the men who sat talking and drinking coffee, En's father and uncles and neighbors. But tonight there had been two strangers who arrived in a sleek black car and approached the lights of the *warung* bold as water buffalo and asked without introducing themselves how to find the local clinic. Neither was ill. They wore city clothes and behaved rudely and carried themselves like policemen, and so the directions they received from En's father were vague and incorrect and would send them in exactly the wrong direction.

But they were looking for Ina's clinic and, inevitably, they would find it; in a village this size the misdirection was at best only a delay. So En had dressed himself and scooted out of the house unseen and come here, as instructed, to complete his bargain with Ibu Ina and to warn her of the danger.

"Very good," I told him. "Good work, En. Now you need to go to the house where she lives and tell her these things." And in the meantime I'd gather my possessions and exit the clinic. I figured I could hide myself in the adjoining rice fields until the police had been and gone. I was strong enough to do that. Probably.

But En crossed his arms and backed away from me. "She said to wait *here* for her."

"Right. But she won't be back till morning."

"She sleeps here most nights." He craned his head, looking past me down the darkened clinic hallway as if she might step out of the consulting room to reassure him.

"Yeah, but not tonight. Honest. En, this could be dangerous. These people might be Ibu Ina's enemies, understand?"

But some fierce innate stubbornness had possessed him. As friendly as we had been, En still distrusted me. He trembled a moment, wide-eyed as a lemur, then darted around me and deeper into the moonlit clinic, calling, *"Ina! Ina!"*

I chased him, switching on lights as I went.

Trying at the same time to think coherently about this. The rude men looking for the clinic could be New Reformasi from Padang, or local cops, or they might be working for Interpol or the State Department or whatever other agency the Chaykin administration chose to swing like a hammer.

And if they were here looking for me, did that mean they had found and interrogated Jala, Ina's ex-husband? Did it mean they had already arrested Diane?

En blundered into a darkened consulting room. His forehead collided with the extended stirrups of an examination table and he fell back on his rump. When I reached him he was crying soundlessly, frightened, tears rolling down his cheeks. The welt above his left eyebrow was angry-looking but not dangerous.

I put my hands on his shoulders. "En, she's not here. Really. She's really, really not here. And I know for a fact she didn't mean for you to stay here in the dark when something bad might happen. She wouldn't do that, would she?"

"Uh," En said, conceding the point.

"So you run home, okay? You run home and stay there. I'll take care of this problem and we'll both see Ibu Ina tomorrow. Does that make sense?"

En attempted to exchange his fear for a judicial look. "I think so," he said, wincing.

I helped him to his feet.

But then there was the sound of gravel crunching under tires in front of the clinic, and we both crouched down again.

○ ○ ○

We hurried to the reception room, where I peered through the slatted bamboo blinds with En behind me, his small hands knotted into the fabric of my shirt.

The car idled in the moonlight. I didn't recognize the model but judging by the inky shine it looked relatively new. There was a brief flare from the interior darkness that might have been a cigarette lighter. Then a much brighter light, a high-beam spotlight sweeping out from the passenger-side window. It came through the blinds and cast rolling shadows over the hygiene posters on the opposite wall. We ducked our heads. En whimpered.

"Pak Tyler?" he said.

I closed my eyes and discovered it was hard to open them again. Behind my eyelids I saw pinwheels and starbursts. The fever again. A small chorus of interior voices repeated, *The fever again, the fever again.* Mocking me.

"Pak Tyler!"

This was very bad timing. (*Bad timing, bad timing . . .*) "Go to the door, En. The side door."

"Come with me!"

Good advice. I checked the window again. The spotlight had winked out. I stood and led En down the corridor and past the supply cupboards to the side door, which he had left open. The night was deceptively quiet, deceptively inviting; a span of pressed earth, a rice field; the forest, palm trees black in the moonlight and tossing their crowns softly.

The bulk of the clinic was between us and the car. "Run straight for the forest," I said.

"I know the way—"

"Stay away from the road. Hide if you have to."

"I know. Come with me!"

"I can't," I said, meaning it literally. In my present condition the idea of sprinting after a ten-year-old was absurd.

"But—" En said, and I gave him a little push and told him not to waste time.

He ran without looking back, disappearing with almost alarming speed into the shadows, silent, small, admirable. I envied him. In the ensuing quiet I heard a car door open and close.

The moon was three-quarters full, ruddier and more distant than it used to be, presenting a different face than the one I remembered from my childhood. No more Man in the Moon; and that dark ovoid scar across the lunar surface, that new but now ancient *mare,* was the result of a massive impact that had melted regolith from pole to equator and slowed the moon's gradual spiral away from the Earth.

Behind me, I heard the policemen (I guessed two of them) pounding at the front door, announcing themselves gruffly, rattling the lock.

I thought about running. I believed I could run—not as deftly as En, but successfully—at least as far as the rice field. And hide there, and hope for the best.

But then I thought of the luggage I had left in Ina's back room. Luggage containing not just clothing but notebooks and discs, small slivers of digital memory and incriminating vials of clear liquid.

I turned back. Inside, I latched the door behind me. I walked barefoot and alert, listening for the sound of the policemen. They might be circling the building or they might make another attempt at the front door. The fever was coming on fast, however, and I heard many things, only some of which were likely to be real sounds.

Back in Ina's hidden room the overhead light was still out. I worked by touch and moonlight. I opened one of the two hard-shell suitcases and shoved in a stack of handwritten pages; closed it, latched it, lifted it and staggered. Then I picked up the second case for starboard ballast and discovered I could barely walk.

I nearly tripped over a small plastic object which I recognized as Ina's pager. I stopped, put down the luggage, grabbed the pager and slid it into my shirt pocket. Then I drew a few deep breaths and lifted the cases again; mysteriously, they seemed to have grown even heavier. I tried to tell myself *You can do this,* but the words were trite and unconvincing and they echoed as if my skull had expanded to the size of a cathedral.

I heard noises from the back door, the one Ina kept closed with an exterior padlock: clinking metal and the groaning of the latch, maybe a crowbar inserted between the hasps of the lock and twisted. And pretty soon, inevitably, the lock would give way and the men from the car would come inside.

I staggered to the third door, En's door, the side door, unlatched it and eased it open in the blind hope that no one was standing outside. No one was. Both intruders (if there were only two of them) were at the back. They whispered as they worked the lock, their voices faintly audible over frogchoruses and the small sound of the wind.

I wasn't sure I could make it to the concealment of the rice field without being seen. Worse, I wasn't sure I could make it without falling down.

But then there was a loud percussive bang as the padlock parted company with the door. The starting gun, I thought. You can do this, I thought. I gathered up my luggage and staggered barefoot into the starry night.

HOSPITALITY

Have you seen this?"

Molly Seagram waved her hand at a magazine on the reception desk as I entered the Perihelion infirmary. Her expression said: *Bad juju, evil omens.* It was the glossy print edition of a major monthly news magazine, and Jason's picture was on the cover. Tag line: THE VERY PRIVATE PERSONALITY BEHIND THE PUBLIC FACE OF THE PERIHELION PROJECT.

"Not good news, I take it?"

She shrugged. "It's not exactly flattering. Take it. Read it. We can talk about it over dinner." I had already promised her dinner. "Oh, and Mrs. Tuckman is prepped and waiting in stall three."

I had asked Molly not to refer to the consulting rooms as "stalls," but it wasn't worth arguing about. I slid the magazine into my mail tray. It was a slow, rainy April morning and Mrs. Tuckman was my only scheduled patient before lunch.

She was the wife of a staff engineer and had been to see me three times in the last month, complaining of anxiety and fatigue. The source of her problem wasn't hard to divine.

Two years had passed since the enclosure of Mars, and rumors of layoffs abounded at Perihelion. Her husband's financial situation was uncertain and her own attempts to find work had foundered. She was going through Xanax at an alarming pace and she wanted more, immediately.

"Maybe we should consider a different medication," I said.

"I don't want an antidepressant, if that's what you mean." She was a small woman, her otherwise pleasant face crunched into a fierce frown. Her gaze flickered around the consulting room and alighted for a time on the rain-streaked window overlooking the landscaped south lawn. "Seriously. I was on Paraloft for six months and I couldn't stop running to the bathroom."

"When was this?"

"Before you came. Dr. Koenig prescribed it. Of course, things were different then. I hardly saw Carl at all, he was so busy. Lots of lonely nights. But at least it looked like good, steady employment in those days, something that would last. I guess I should have counted my blessings. Isn't that in my, um, chart or whatever you call it?"

Her patient history was open on the desk in front of me. Dr. Koenig's notes were often difficult to decipher, though he had kindly used a red pen to highlight matters of pressing urgency: allergies, chronic conditions. The entries in Mrs. Tuckman's folder were prim, terse, and ungenerous. Here was the note about Paraloft, discontinued (date indecipherable) at patient's request, "patient continues to complain of nervousness, fears for future." Didn't we all fear for the future?

"Now we can't even count on Carl's job. My heart was beating so hard last night—I mean, very rapidly, *unusually* rapidly. I thought it might be, you know."

"What?"

"You know. CVWS."

CVWS—cardiovascular wasting syndrome—had been in the news the last few months. It had killed thousands of people in Egypt and the Sudan and cases had been reported in Greece, Spain, and the southern U.S. It was a slow-burning bacterial infection, potential trouble for tropical third world economies but treatable with modern drugs. Mrs. Tuckman had nothing to fear from CVWS, and I told her so.

"People say they dropped it on us."

"Who dropped what, Mrs. Tuckman?"

"That disease. The Hypotheticals. They dropped it on us."

"Everything I've read suggests CVWS crossed over from cattle." It was still mainly an ungulate disease and it regularly decimated cattle herds in northern Africa.

"Cattle. Huh. But they wouldn't necessarily *tell* you, would they? I mean, they wouldn't come out and announce it on the news."

"CVWS is an acute illness. If you did have it you'd have been hospitalized by now. Your pulse is normal and your cardio is fine."

She looked unconvinced. In the end I wrote her a prescription for an alternative anxiolytic—essentially, Xanax with a different molecular side chain—hoping the new brand name, if not the drug itself, would have a useful effect. Mrs. Tuckman left the office mollified, clutching the script in her hand like a sacred scroll.

I felt useless and vaguely fraudulent.

But Mrs. Tuckman's condition was far from unique. The whole world was reeling with anxiety. What had once looked like our best shot at a survivable future, the terraforming and colonization of Mars, had ended in impotence and uncertainty. Which left us no future but the Spin. The global economy had begun to oscillate; consumers and nations accumulating debt loads they expected never to have to repay, while creditors hoarded funds and interest rates spiked. Extreme religiosity and brutal criminality had increased in tandem, at home and abroad. The effects were especially devastating in third world nations, where collapsing currencies and recurrent famine helped revive slumbering Marxist and militant Islamic movements.

The psychological tangent wasn't hard to understand. Neither was the violence. Lots of people harbor grievances, but only those who have lost faith in the future are likely to show up at work with an automatic rifle and a hit list. The Hypotheticals, whether they meant to or not, had incubated exactly that kind of terminal despair. The suicidally disgruntled were legion, and their enemies included any and all Americans, Brits, Canadians, Danes, et cetera; or, conversely, all Moslems, dark-skinned people, non-English-speakers, immigrants; all Catholics, fundamentalists, atheists; all liberals, all conservatives . . . For such people the consummate act of moral clarity was a lynching or a suicide bombing, a *fatwa* or a pogrom. And they were ascendant now, rising like dark stars over a terminal landscape.

We lived in dangerous times. Mrs. Tuckman knew that, and all the Xanax in the world wasn't going to convince her otherwise.

o o o

During lunch I secured a table at the back of the staff cafeteria, where I nursed a coffee, watched rain fall on the parking lot, and perused the magazine Molly had given me.

If there were a science of Spinology, the lead article began, *Jason Lawton would be its Newton, its Einstein, its Stephen Hawking.*

Which was what E.D. had always encouraged the press to say and what Jase had always dreaded hearing.

From radiological surveys to permeability studies, from hard-core science to philosophical debate, there is hardly an area of Spin study his ideas haven't touched and transformed. His published papers are numerous and oft-cited. His attendance turns sleepy academic conferences into instant media events. And as acting director of the Perihelion Foundation he has powerfully influenced American and global aerospace policy in the Spin era.

But amidst the real accomplishments—and occasional hype—surrounding Jason Lawton, it's easy to forget that Perihelion was founded by his father, Edward Dean (E. D.) Lawton, who still holds a preeminent place on the steering committee and in the presidential cabinet. And the public image of the son, some would argue, is also the creation of the more mysterious, equally influential, and far less public elder Lawton.

The article went on to detail E.D.'s early career: the massive success of aerostat telecommunications in the aftermath of the Spin, his virtual adoption by three successive presidential administrations, the creation of the Perihelion Foundation.

Originally conceived as a think tank and industry lobby, Perihelion was eventually reinvented as an agency of the federal government, designing Spin-related space missions and coordinating the work of dozens of universities, research institutions, and NASA centers. In effect, the decline of "the old NASA" was Perihelion's rise. A decade ago the relationship was formalized and a subtly reorganized Perihelion was officially annexed to NASA as an advisory body. In reality, insiders say, it was NASA that was annexed to Perihelion. And while young prodigy Jason Lawton was charming the press, his father continued to pull the strings.

The article went on to question E.D.'s long relationship with the Garland administration and hinted at a potential scandal: certain instrument packages had been manufactured for several million dollars apiece by a small Pasadena firm run by one of E.D.'s old cronies, even though Ball Aerospace had tendered a lower-cost proposal.

We were living through an election campaign in which both major parties had spun off radical factions. Garland, a Reform Republican of whom the magazine notoriously disapproved, had already served two terms, and Preston Lomax, Clayton's V.P. and anointed successor, was running ahead of his opponent in recent polls. The "scandal" really wasn't one. Ball's proposal had been lower but the package they designed was less effective; the Pasadena engineers had crammed more instrumentation into an equivalent payload weight.

I said as much to Molly over dinner at Champs, a mile down the road from Perihelion. There was nothing really new about the article. The insinuations were more political than substantial.

"Does it matter," Molly asked, "if they're right or wrong? The important thing is how they're playing us. Suddenly it's okay for a major media outlet to take shots at Perihelion."

Elsewhere in the issue an editorial had described the Mars project as "the single most expensive boondoggle in history, costly in human lives as well as cash, a monument to the human ability to squeeze profit from a global catastrophe." The author was a speechwriter for the Christian Conservative Party. "The CCP owns this rag, Moll. Everybody knows that."

"They want to shut us down."

"They won't shut us down. Even if Lomax loses the election. Even if they scale us back to surveillance missions, we're the only eye on the Spin the nation has."

"Which doesn't mean we won't all be fired and replaced."

"It's not that bad."

She looked unconvinced.

Molly was the nurse/receptionist I had inherited from Dr. Koenig when I first came to Perihelion. For most of five years she had been a polite, professional, and efficient piece of office furniture. We had exchanged little more than customary pleasantries, by which I had come to know that she was single, three years younger than I was, and living in a walk-up apartment away from the ocean. She had never seemed especially talkative and I had assumed she preferred it that way.

Then, less than a month ago, Molly had turned to me as she collected her purse for a Thursday-night drive home and asked me if I'd like to join her for dinner. Why? "Because I got tired of waiting for you to ask. So? Yes? No?"

Yes.

Molly turned out to be smart, sly, cynical, and better company than I had expected. We'd been sharing meals at Champs for three weeks now. We liked the menu (unpretentious) and the atmosphere (collegial). I often thought Molly looked her best in that vinyl booth at Champs, gracing it with her presence, lending it a certain dignity. Her blond hair was long and, tonight, limp in the massive humidity. The green in her eyes was a deliberate effect, colored contacts, but it looked good on her.

"Did you read the sidebar?" she asked.

"Glanced at it." The magazine's sidebar profile of Jason had contrasted his career success with a private life either impenetrably hidden or nonexistent. *Acquaintances say his home is as sparsely furnished as his romantic life. There has never been a rumor of a fiancé, girlfriend, or spouse of either gender. One comes away with an impression of a man not merely married to his ideas but almost pathologically devoted to them. And in many ways Jason Lawton, like Perihelion itself, remains under the stifling influence of his father. For all his accomplishments, he has yet to emerge himself as his own man.*

"At least that part sounds right," Molly said.

"Does it? Jason can be a little self-centered, but—"

"He comes through reception like I don't exist. I mean, that's trivial, but it's not exactly *warm*. How's his treatment going?"

"I'm not treating him for anything, Moll." Molly had seen Jason's charts, but I hadn't made any entries about his AMS. "He comes in to talk."

"Uh-huh. And sometimes when he comes in to talk he's practically limping. No, you don't have to tell me about it. But I'm not blind. For your information. Anyway, he's in Washington now, right?"

More often than he was in Florida. "Lot of talking going on. People are positioning themselves for the post-election."

"So something's in the works."

"Something's always in the works."

"I mean about Perihelion. The support staff gets clues. For instance, you want to know what's weird? We just acquired another hundred acres of property west of the fence. I heard this from Tim Chesley, the transcriptionist in human resources. Supposedly, we've got surveyors coming in next week."

"For what?"

"Nobody knows. Maybe we're expanding. Or maybe they're turning us into a mall."

It was the first I'd heard of it.

"You're out of the loop," Molly said, smiling. "You need contacts. Like me."

o o o

After dinner we adjourned to Molly's apartment, where I spent the night.

I won't describe here the gestures, looks, and touches by which we negotiated our intimacy. Not because I'm prudish but because I seem to have lost the memory. Lost it to time, lost it to the reconstruction. And yes, I register the irony in that. I can quote the magazine article we discussed and I can tell you what she had for dinner at Champs . . . but all that's left of our lovemaking is a faded mental snapshot: a dimly lit room, a damp breeze turning spindles of cloth in an open window, her green eyes close to mine.

○ ○ ○

Within a month Jase was back at Perihelion, stalking the hallways as if he had been infused with some strange new energy.

He brought with him an army of security personnel, black-clad and of uncertain origin but believed to represent the Department of the Treasury. These were followed in turn by small battalions of contractors and surveyors who cluttered the hallways and refused to speak to resident staff. Molly kept me posted on rumors: the compound was going to be leveled; the compound was going to be expanded; we would all be fired; we would all get raises. In short, something was afoot.

For most of a week I heard nothing from Jason himself. Then, a slow Thursday afternoon, he paged me in my office and asked me to come up to the second floor: "There's someone I want you to meet."

Before I reached the now heavily guarded stairwell I had picked up an escort of armed guards with all-pass badges who conducted me to an upstairs conference room. Not just a casual hello, obviously. This was deep Perihelion business, to which I should not have been privy. Once again, apparently, Jason had decided to share secrets. Never an unmixed blessing. I took a deep breath and pushed through the door.

The room contained a mahogany table, a half dozen plush chairs, and two men in addition to myself.

One of the men was Jason.

The second man could have been mistaken for a child. A horribly burned child in desperate need of a skin graft: that was my first impression. This individual, roughly five feet tall, stood in a corner of the room. He wore blue jeans and a plain white cotton T-shirt. His shoulders were broad, his eyes were wide and bloodshot, and his arms seemed a trifle too long for his abbreviated torso.

But what was most striking about him was his skin. His skin was glossless, ash black, and completely hairless. It wasn't wrinkled in the conventional sense—it wasn't *loose,* like a bloodhound's skin—but it was deeply textured, furrowed, like the rind of a cantaloupe.

The small man walked toward me and put out his hand. A small wrinkled hand at the end of a long wrinkled arm. I took it, hesitantly. Mummy fingers, I thought. But fleshy, plump, like the leaves of a desert plant, like grabbing a handful of aloe vera and feeling it grab back. The creature grinned.

"This is Wun," Jason said.

"One *what*?"

Wun laughed. His teeth were large, blunt, and immaculate. "I never tire of that splendid joke!"

His full name was Wun Ngo Wen, and he was from Mars.

○ ○ ○

The man from Mars.

It was a misleading description. Martians have a long literary history, from Wells to Heinlein. But in reality, of course, Mars was a dead planet. Until we fixed it. Until we birthed our own Martians.

And here, apparently, was a living specimen, 99.9 percent human if slightly oddly designed. A Martian *person,* descended through millennia of Spin-hinged time from the colonists we had dispatched only two years ago. He spoke punctilious English. His accent sounded half Oxford, half New Delhi. He paced the room. He took a bottle of spring water from the table, unscrewed the cap, and drank deeply. He wiped his mouth with his forearm. Small droplets beaded on his corrugated flesh.

I sat down and tried not to stare while Jase explained.

Here's what he said, a little simplified and fleshed out with details I learned later.

○ ○ ○

The Martian had left his planet shortly before the Spin membrane was imposed upon it.

Wun Ngo Wen was a historian and a linguist, relatively young by Martian standards—fifty-five terrestrial years—and physically fit. He was a scholar by trade, currently between assignments, donating labor to agricultural cooperatives, and he had just spent a Sparkmonth on the delta of the Kirioloj River, in what we called the Argyre Basin and Martians called the Baryal Plain (*Epu Baryal*) when his summons to duty came.

Like thousands of other men and women of his age and class, Wun had submitted his credentials to the committees who were designing and coordinating a proposed journey to Earth, without any real expectation that he would be selected. He was, in fact, relatively timid by nature and had never ventured far beyond his own prefecture, except for scholarly journeys and family reunions. He was deeply dismayed when his name was called, and if he had not recently entered his Fourth Age he might have refused the request. Surely someone else would be better suited to the task? But no, apparently not; his talents and life history were uniquely suited to the work, the authorities insisted; so he settled his affairs (such as they were) and boarded a train to the launch complex at Basalt Dry (on our maps, Tharsis), where he was trained to represent the Five Republics on a diplomatic mission to Earth.

Martian technology had only recently embraced the notion of manned space travel. In the past it had seemed to the governing councils a profoundly unwise adventure, liable to attract the attention of the Hypotheticals, wasteful of resources, requiring acts of large-scale manufacturing that would dump unbudgeted volatiles into a meticulously managed and highly vulnerable biosphere. The Martians were conservators by nature, hoarders by instinct. Their small-scale and biological technologies were ancient and sophisticated, but their industrial base was shallow and had already been strained by the unmanned exploration of the planet's tiny, useless moons.

But they had watched and speculated about the Spin-enshrouded Earth for centuries. They knew the dark planet was mankind's cradle, and they had learned from telescopic observation and data retained from a late-arriving NEP ark that the membrane surrounding it was penetrable. They understood the temporal nature of the Spin, though not the mechanisms that produced it. A journey from Mars to Earth, they reasoned, while physically possible, would be difficult and impractical. The Earth, after all, was effectively static; an explorer dropped into the terrestrial darkness would remain entrapped there for millennia, even if, by his own reckoning, he left for home the next day.

But vigilant astronomers had lately detected boxlike structures quietly constructing themselves hundreds of miles above the Martian poles—Hypothetical artifacts, nearly identical to the ones associated with the Earth. After a hundred thousand years of undisturbed solitude, Mars had finally come to the attention of the faceless and omnipotent creatures with whom it shared the solar system. The conclusion—that Mars would soon be placed under a Spin membrane of its own—was inescapable. Powerful factions argued for a consultation with the shrouded Earth. Scarce resources were mustered. A spacecraft was designed and assembled. And Wun Ngo Wen, a linguist and scholar deeply familiar with the extant fragments of terrestrial history and language, was conscripted to make the journey—much to his own dismay.

Wun Ngo Wen made peace with the likelihood of his own death even as he prepared his body for the confinement and debilitation of a long space voyage and the rigors of a high-gravity terrestrial environment. Wun had lost most of his immediate family in the Kirioloj flood of three summers ago—one reason he had volunteered for the flight, and one reason he had been accepted. For Wun, the risk of death was a lighter burden than it would have been for most of his peers. Still, it was not something he looked forward to; he hoped to avoid it altogether. He trained vigorously. He taught himself the intricacies and idiosyncrasies of his vehicle. And if the Hypotheticals did embrace Mars—not that he was hoping for such a thing—it would mean he might have a chance of returning, not to a planet rendered strange by millions of passing years but to his own familiar home, preserved with all its memories and losses against the erosion of time.

Although, of course, no return voyage was anticipated: Wun's vessel was a one-way device. If he ever did come back to Mars it would be at the pleasure of the terrestrials, who would have to be very generous indeed, Wun thought, to provide him with a ticket home.

And so Wun Ngo Wen had savored what would likely be his final look at Mars—the wind-gullied flatlands of Basalt Dry, *Odos on Epu-Epia*—before he was locked into the flight chamber of the crude iron-and-ceramic multistage rocket that carried him into space.

He spent much of the subsequent journey in a state of drug-induced metabolic lethargy, but it was still a bitter and debilitating test of endurance. The Martian Spin membrane was emplaced while he was in transit, and for the remainder of the flight Wun was isolated, cut off by temporal discontinuity from both human worlds: the one ahead and the one behind. Dreadful as death might be, he thought, could it be much different from this sedated silence, his brooding custodianship of a tiny machine falling endlessly through an inhuman vacuum?

His hours of true consciousness ebbed. He took refuge in reverie and forced sleep.

His vessel, primitive in many ways but equipped with subtle and semi-intelligent guidance and navigation devices, spent most of its fuel reserves braking into a high orbit around the Earth. The planet beneath him was a black nothingness, its moon a huge gyrating disk. Microscopic probes from Wun's vessel sampled the outer reaches of the Earth's atmosphere, generating increasingly red-shifted telemetry before they vanished into the Spin, just enough data to calculate an angle of entry. His spacecraft was equipped with an array of flight surfaces, aerodynamic brakes, and deployable parachutes, and with luck it would carry him through the dense and turbulent air to the surface of the enormous planet without baking or crushing him. But much still depended on luck. Far too much, in Wun's opinion. He immersed himself in a vat of protective gel and initiated the final descent, fully prepared to die.

He woke to find his only slightly charred vessel at rest in a canola field in southern Manitoba, surrounded by curiously pale and smooth-skinned men, some of them wearing what he recognized as biological isolation gear. Wun Ngo Wen emerged from his spacecraft, heart pounding, muscles leaden and aching in the terrible gravity, lungs insulted by the thick and insulating air, and was quickly taken into custody.

He spent the next month in a plastic bubble in a room at the Department of Agriculture's Animal Disease Center on Plum Island, off the coast of New York's Long Island. During that time he learned to speak a language he had known only from ancient written records, teaching his lips and tongue to accommodate the rich modalities of its vowels, refining his vocabulary as he struggled to explain himself to grim or intimidated strangers. This was a difficult time. Earthlings were pallid, lanky creatures, not at all what he had imagined when he deciphered the ancient documents. Many were pale as ghosts, reminding him of Embermonth stories that had terrified him as a child: he half expected one of them to rise up at his bedside like Huld of Phraya, demanding an arm or a leg for tribute. His dreams were restless and unpleasant.

He was, fortunately, still in possession of his skills as a linguist, and before long he was introduced to men and women of status and power who proved far more hospitable than his initial captors. Wun Ngo Wen cultivated these useful friendships, struggling to master the social protocols of an ancient and confusing culture and waiting patiently for the correct moment to convey the proposal he had carried at such personal and public expense between the two human worlds.

○ ○ ○

"Jason," I said when he had reached approximately this point in the narrative. "Stop. *Please*."

He paused. "You have a question, Tyler?"

"No question. It's just that it's . . . a lot to absorb."

"But you're okay with this? You follow me? Because I'm going to be telling this story more than once. I want it to flow. Does it flow?"

"Flows fine. Telling it to who?"

"Everybody. The media. We're going public."

"I don't want to be a secret anymore," Wun Ngo Wen said. "I didn't come here to hide. I have things to say." He uncapped his bottle of spring water. "Would you like some of this, Tyler Dupree? You look like you could use a drink."

I took the bottle from his plump, wrinkled fingers and drank deeply from it.

"So," I said, "does this make us water-brothers?"

Wun Ngo Wen looked puzzled. Jason laughed out loud.

FOUR PHOTOGRAPHS OF THE KIRIOLOJ DELTA

It's hard to capture the brute craziness of the times.

Some days it seemed almost liberating. Beyond our picayune illusion of the sky the sun went on expanding, stars burned out or were born, a dead planet had been infused with life and had evolved a civilization that rivaled or surpassed our own. Closer to home, governments were toppled and replaced and their replacements were overthrown; religions, philosophies, and ideologies morphed and merged and begat mutant offspring. The old, ordered world was crumbling. New things grew in the ruins. We picked love green and savored it for its tartness: Molly Seagram loved me, I assumed, mainly because I was available. And why not? The summer was waning and the harvest was uncertain.

The long-defunct New Kingdom movement had begun to seem both prescient and grossly old-fashioned, its timid rebellion against the old ecclesiastical consensus a shadow of newer, edgier devotions. Dionysian cults sprang up everywhere in the western world, stripped of the piety and hypocrisy of the old NK—fuck clubs with flags or sacred symbols. They did not disdain human jealousy but embraced or even reveled in it: scorned lovers favored .45 pistols at close range, a red rose on a victim's body. It was the Tribulation reconfigured as Elizabethan drama.

Simon Townsend, had he been born a decade later, might have stumbled into one of these brands of Quentin Tarantino spirituality. But the failure of NK had left him disillusioned and yearning for something simpler. Diane still called me from time to time—once a month or so, when the auspices were right and Simon was out of the house—to update me on her situation or simply to reminisce, stoking memories like embers and warming herself at the heat. Not much heat at home, apparently, though her financial situation had improved a little. Simon was doing full-time maintenance for Jordan Tabernacle, their little independent church; Diane was doing clerical temp jobs, off-and-on work that often left her fidgeting around the apartment or sneaking off to the local library to read books of which Simon disapproved: contemporary novels, current events. Jordan Tabernacle, she said, was a "disengagement" church; parishioners were encouraged to turn off the TV and avoid books, newspapers, and other cultural ephemera. Or risk meeting the Rapture in an impure condition.

Diane never advocated these ideas—she never preached to me—but she deferred to them, left them carefully unquestioned. Sometimes I got a little impatient with that. "Diane," I said one night, "do you really believe this stuff?"

"What 'stuff,' Tyler?"

"Take your pick. Not keeping books in the house. The Hypotheticals as agents of the Parousia. All that shit." (I'd had maybe a beer too many.)

"Simon believes in it."

"I didn't ask you about Simon."

"Simon's more devout than I am. I envy him that. I know how it must sound. *Put those books in the trash,* like he's being monstrous, arrogant. But he isn't. It's an act of humility, really—an act of submission. Simon can give himself to God in a way I can't."

"Lucky Simon."

"He *is* lucky. You can't see it, but he's very peaceful. He's found a kind of equanimity at Jordan. He can look the Spin in the face and smile at it, because he knows he's saved."

"What about you? Aren't you saved?"

She let a long silence ride down the phone line between us. "I wish that was a simple question. I really do. I keep thinking, maybe it isn't about my faith. Maybe Simon's faith is enough for both of us. Powerful enough that I can ride it a little way. He's been very patient with me, actually. The only thing we argue about is having kids. Simon would like to have children. The church encourages it. And I understand that, but with the money so tight, and—you know—the world being what it is—"

"It's not a decision you ought to be pressured into."

"I don't mean to imply he's pressuring me. 'Put it in God's hands,' he says. Put it in God's hands and it'll work out right."

"But you're too smart to believe that."

"Am I? Oh, Tyler, I hope not. I hope that isn't true."

○ ○ ○

Molly, on the other hand, had no use for what she called "all this God crap." Every woman for herself, that was Moll's philosophy. Especially, she said, if the world was coming unglued and none of us was going to live past fifty. "I don't intend to spend that time kneeling."

She was tough by nature. Molly's folks were dairy farmers. They had spent ten years in legal arguments over a tarsands oil-extraction project that bordered their property and was slowly poisoning it. In the end they traded their ranch for an out-of-court settlement large enough to buy a comfortable retirement for themselves and a decent education for their daughter. But it was the kind of experience, Molly said, that would grow calluses on an angel's ass.

Very little about the evolving social landscape surprised her. One night we sat in front of the TV watching coverage of the Stockholm riots. A mob of cod fishermen and religious radicals threw bricks through windows and burned cars; police helicopters peppered the crowd with tanglefoot gel until much of Gamla Stan looked like something a tubercular Godzilla might have coughed up. I made a fatuous remark about how badly people behave when they're frightened, and Molly said, "Come on, Tyler, you actually feel sympathy for these assholes?"

"I didn't say that, Moll."

"Because of the Spin, they get a free pass to trash their parliament building? Why, because they're *frightened*?"

"It's not an excuse. It's a motive. They don't have a future. They believe they're doomed."

"Doomed to die. Well, welcome to the human condition. They're gonna die, you're gonna die, I'm gonna die—and when was that ever *not* the case?"

"We're all mortal, but we used to have the consolation of knowing the human species would go on without us."

"But species are mortal, too. All that's changed is that suddenly it's not way off in the foggy future. It's possible we'll all die together in some spectacular way in a few years . . . but even that's still just a *possibility*. The Hypotheticals might keep us around longer than that. For whatever unfathomable reason."

"That doesn't frighten you?"

"Of course it does! All of it frightens me. But it's no reason to go out and kill people." She waved at the TV. Someone had launched a grenade into the Riksdag. "This is so overwhelmingly *stupid*. It accomplishes nothing. It's a hormonal exercise. It's simian."

"You can't pretend you're not affected by it."

She surprised me by laughing. "No . . . that's *your* style, not mine."

"Is it?"

She ducked her head away but came back staring, almost defiant. "The way you always pretend to be cool about the Spin. Same way you're cool about the Lawtons. They use you, they ignore you, and you smile like it's the natural order of things." She watched me for a reaction. I was too stubborn to give her one. "I just think there are better ways to live out the end of the world."

But she wouldn't say what those better ways were.

○ ○ ○

Everyone who worked at Perihelion had signed a nondisclosure agreement when we were hired, all of us had undergone background checks and Homeland Security vetting. We were discreet and we respected the need to keep high-echelon talk in-house. Leaks might spook congressional committees, embarrass powerful friends, scare away funding.

But now there was a Martian living on campus—most of the north wing had been converted into temporary quarters for Wun Ngo Wen and his handlers—and that was a secret difficult to keep.

It couldn't be kept much longer in any case. By the time Wun arrived in Florida much of the D.C. elite and several foreign heads of state had heard all about him. The State Department had granted him ad hoc legal status and planned to introduce him internationally when the time was right. His handlers were already coaching him for the inevitable media feeding frenzy.

His arrival could and perhaps should have been managed differently. He could have been processed through the U.N., his presence immediately made public. Garland's administration was bound to take some heat for hiding him. The Christian Conservative Party was already hinting that "the administration knows more than it's saying about the results of the terraforming project," hoping to draw out the president or open up Lomax, his would-be successor, for criticism. Criticism there would inevitably be; but Wun had expressed his wish not to become a campaign issue. He wanted to go public but he would wait until November, he said, to announce himself.

But the existence of Wun Ngo Wen was only the most conspicuous of the secrets surrounding his arrival. There were others. It made for a strange summer at Perihelion.

Jason called me over to the north wing that August. I met him in his office—his real office, not the tastefully furnished suite where he greeted official visitors and the press; a windowless cube with a desk and sofa. Perched on his chair between stacks of scientific journals, wearing Levi's and a greasy sweatshirt, he looked as if he'd grown out of the clutter like a hydroponic vegetable. He was sweating. Never a good sign with Jase.

"I'm losing my legs again," he said.

I cleared a space on the sofa and sat down and waited for him to elaborate.

"I've been having little episodes for a couple of weeks. The usual thing, pins and needles in the morning. Nothing I can't work around. But it isn't going away. In fact it's getting worse. I think we might need to adjust the medication."

Maybe so. But I really didn't like what the medication had been doing to him. Jase by this time was taking a daily handful of pills: myelin enhancers to slow the loss of nerve tissue, neurological boosters to help the brain rewire damaged areas, and secondary medication to treat the side effects of the primary medication. Could we boost his dosage? Possibly. But the process had a toxicity ceiling that was already alarmingly close. He had lost weight, and he had lost something perhaps more important: a certain emotional equilibrium. Jase talked faster than he used to and smiled less often. Where he had once seemed utterly at home in his body, he now moved like a marionette—when he reached for a cup his hand overshot the target and jogged back for a second intercept.

"In any case," I said, "we'll have to get Dr. Malmstein's opinion."

"There is absolutely no way I can leave here long enough to see him. Things have changed, if you haven't noticed. Can't we do a telephone consult?"

"Maybe. I'll ask."

"And in the meantime, can you do me another favor?"

"What would that be, Jase?"

"Explain my problem to Wun. Dig up a couple of textbooks on the subject for him."

"Medical texts? Why, is he a physician?"

"Not exactly, but he brought a lot of information with him. The Martian biological sciences are considerably in advance of ours." (He said this with a crooked grin I was unable to interpret.) "He thinks he might be able to help."

"Are you serious?"

"Quite serious. Stop looking shocked. Will you talk to him?"

A man from another planet. A man with a hundred thousand years of Martian history behind him. "Well, yeah," I said. "I'd be privileged to talk to him. But—"

"I'll set it up, then."

"But if he has the kind of medical knowledge that can effectively treat AMS, it needs to reach better doctors than me."

"Wun brought whole encyclopedias with him. There are already people going through the Martian archives—parts of them, anyway—looking for useful information, medical and otherwise. This is just a sideshow."

"I'm surprised he can spare the time for a sideshow."

"He's bored more often than you might think. He's also short of friends. I thought he might enjoy spending a little time with someone who doesn't believe he's either a savior or a threat. In the short term, though, I'd still like you to talk to Malmstein."

"Of course."

"And call him from your place, all right? I don't trust the phones here anymore."

He smiled as if he had said something amusing.

∘ ∘ ∘

Occasionally that summer I took myself for walks on the public beach across the highway from my apartment.

It wasn't much of a beach. A long undeveloped spit of land protected it from erosion and rendered it useless for surfers. On hot afternoons the old motels surveyed the sand with glassy eyes and a few subdued tourists washed their feet in the surf.

I came down and sat on a scalding wooden walkway suspended over scrub grass, watching clouds gather on the eastern horizon and thinking about what Molly had said, that I was pretending to be cool about the Spin (and about the Lawtons), faking an equanimity I couldn't possibly possess.

I wanted to give Molly her due. Maybe that was the way I looked to her.

"Spin" was a dumb but inevitable name for what had been done to the Earth. That is, it was bad physics—nothing was actually spinning any harder or faster than it used to—but it was an apt metaphor. In reality the Earth was more static than it had ever been. But did it *feel* like it was spinning out of control? In every important sense, yes. You had to cling to something or slide into oblivion.

So maybe I was clinging to the Lawtons—not just Jason and Diane but their whole world, the Big House and the Little House, lost childhood loyalties. Maybe that was the only handle I could grab. And maybe that wasn't necessarily a bad thing. If Moll was right, we all had to grab something or be lost. Diane had grabbed faith, Jason had grabbed science.

And I had grabbed Jason and Diane.

I left the beach when the clouds came up, one of those inevitable late-August afternoon squalls, the eastern sky restless with lightning, rain beginning to whip the sad pastel balconies of the motels. My clothes were wet by the time I got home. It took them hours to dry in the humid air. The storm passed by nightfall but left a fetid, steamy stillness behind it.

Molly came over after dinner and we downloaded a current movie, one of the Victorian drawing-room dramas she was fond of. After the film she went to the kitchen to fix us drinks while I called David Malmstein from the phone in the spare room. Malmstein said he'd like to see Jase "as soon as it's practical" but thought it would be all right to adjust the meds upward a few notches, as long as both Jase and I kept an eye out for any unpleasant reaction.

I hung up the phone and left the room and found Molly in the hall with a drink in each hand and a puzzled expression on her face: "Where'd you go?"

"Just making a call."

"Anything important?"

"No."

"Checking up on a patient?"

"Something like that," I said.

○ ○ ○

Within the next few days Jase arranged a meeting between me and Wun Ngo Wen in Wun's quarters at Perihelion.

The Martian ambassador lived in a room he had furnished to his own taste, from catalogs. The furniture was lightweight, wicker, low to the ground. A rag rug covered the linoleum floor. A computer sat on a simple raw pine desk. There were bookcases to match the desk. Apparently Martians decorated like newlywed college students.

I supplied Wun with the technical material he wanted: a couple of books on the etiology and treatment of multiple sclerosis, plus a series of *JAMA* offprints on AMS. AMS, in current thinking, wasn't really MS at all; it was a different disease entirely, a genetic disorder with MS-like symptoms and a similar degradation of the myelin sheaths that protect human nervous tissue. AMS was distinguishable by its severity, rapid progression, and resistance to standard therapies. Wun said he wasn't familiar with the condition but would search his archives for information.

I thanked him but raised the obvious objection: he wasn't a doctor, and Martian physiology was conspicuously unusual—even if he found a suitable therapy, would it work in Jason's case?

"We're not as different as you might think. One of the first things your people did was to sequence my genome. It's indistinguishable from your own."

"I didn't mean to give offense."

"I'm not offended. One hundred thousand years is a long separation, long enough for what biologists call a speciation event. As it happens, however, your people and mine are fully interfertile. The obvious differences between us are superficial adaptations to a cooler, drier environment."

He spoke with an authority that belied his size. His voice was pitched higher than an average adult's but there was nothing juvenile about it; it was lilting, almost feminine, but always statesmanlike.

"Even so," I said, "there are potential legal problems if we're talking about a therapy that hasn't gone through the FDA approval process."

"I'm sure Jason would be willing to wait for official approval. His disease might not be so patient." Here Wun raised his hand to forestall further objections. "Let me read what you brought me. Then we'll discuss it again."

Then, the immediate business discharged, he asked me to stay and talk. I was flattered. Despite his strangeness there was something comforting about Wun's presence, a communicable ease. He sat back in his oversized wicker chair, feet dangling, and listened with apparent fascination to a quick sketch of my life. He asked a couple of questions about Diane ("Jason doesn't speak much about his family") and more about med school (the concept of dissecting cadavers was new to him; he flinched when I described it . . . most people do).

And when I asked him about his own life he reached into the small gray satchel he carried with him and produced a series of printed images, photographs he had brought with him as digital files. Four pictures of Mars.

"Just four?"

He shrugged. "No number is large enough to substitute for memory. And of course there is much more visual material in the official archives. These are mine. Personal. Would you care to see them?"

"Yes, certainly."

He handed them to me.

Photo 1: A house. It was obviously a human dwelling place despite the odd techno/retro architecture, low and rounded, like a porcelain model of a sod hut. The sky behind it was a brilliant turquoise, or at least that's how the printer had rendered it. The horizon was strangely close but geometrically flat, divided into receding rectangles of cultivated green, a crop I couldn't identify but which was too fleshy to be wheat or corn and too tall to be lettuce or kale. In the foreground were two adult Martians, male and female, with comically stern expressions. Martian Gothic. All it needed was a pitchfork and a Grant Wood signature.

"My mother and father," Wun said simply.

Photo 2: "Myself as a child."

This one was startling. The prodigiously wrinkled Martian skin, Wun explained, develops at puberty. Wun at roughly seven terrestrial years was smooth-faced and smiling. He looked like any Earthly child, though you couldn't place the ethnicity—blond hair, coffee-colored skin, narrow nose and generous lips. He stood in what looked at first glance like an eccentric theme park but was, Wun said, a Martian city. A marketplace. Food stalls and shops, the buildings made of the same porcelainlike material as the farmhouse, in gaudy primary colors. The street behind him was crowded with light machinery and foot traffic. Only a patch of sky was visible between the tallest buildings, and even there some sort of vehicle had been caught in passing, whirligig blades blurred into a pale oval.

"You look happy," I said.

"The city is called Voy Voyud. We came from the countryside to shop on this day. Because it was springtime my parents let me buy *murkuds*. Small animals. Like frogs, for pets. In the bag I'm holding—see?"

Wun clutched a white cloth bag containing mysterious lumps. *Murkuds*.

"They only live a few weeks," he said. "But their eggs are delicious."

Photo 3: This one was a panoramic view. In the near ground: another Martian house, a woman in a multicolored kaftan (Wun's wife, he explained) and two smooth-skinned, pretty young girls in sacklike amber dresses (his daughters). The photograph had been taken from high ground. Beyond the house, an entire semirural landscape was visible. Green marshy fields basked under another turquoise sky. The agricultural land was divided by elevated roadways on which a few boxy vehicles traveled, and there were agricultural machines among the crops, graceful black harvesters. And on the horizon where the roads converged was a city, the same city, Wun said, where he had bought *murkuds* as a child, Voy Voyud, the capital of Kirioloj Province, its low-g towers tall and intricately terraced.

"You can see most of the delta of the Kirioloj in this picture." The river was a blue band feeding a lake the color of the sky. The city of Voy Voyud had been built on higher ground, the eroded rim of an ancient impact crater, Wun said, though it looked like an ordinary line of low hills to me. Black dots on the distant lake might have been boats or barges.

"It's a beautiful place," I said.

"Yes."

"The landscape, but your family, too."

"Yes." His eyes met mine. "They're dead."

"Ah—I'm sorry to hear that."

"They died in a massive flood several years ago. The last photograph, do you see? It's the same view, but taken just after the disaster."

A freakish storm had dumped record rainfall on the slopes of the Solitary Mountains at the end of a long dry season. Most of that rain had been funneled into the parched tributaries of the Kirioloj. The terraformed Mars was in some ways still a young world, still establishing its hydrological cycles, its landscapes evolving rapidly as ancient dust and regolith were rearranged by circulating water. The result of the sudden extreme rain was a slurry of oxide-red mud that had roared down the Kirioloj and into the agricultural delta like a fluid freight train.

Photo 4: The aftermath. Of Wun's house, only the foundation and a single wall remained, standing like shards of pottery in a chaotic plain of mud, rubble, and rocks. The distant city on the hill was untouched but the fertile farmland had been buried. Except for a glint of brown water from the lake this was Mars returned almost to its virgin condition, a lifeless regolith. Several aircraft hovered overhead, presumably searching for survivors.

"I had spent a day in the foothills with friends and came home to this. A great many lives were lost, not just my family. So I keep these four photographs to remind me of where I came from. And why I can't go back."

"It must have been unbearable."

"I've made peace with it. As much as one can. By the time I left Mars the delta had been restored. Not the way it used to be, of course. But fertile, alive, productive."

Which was as much as he seemed to want to say about it.

I looked back at the earlier images, reminded myself what I was seeing. Not some fanciful CGI effect but ordinary photographs. Photographs of another world. Of Mars, a planet long freighted with our own reckless imagination. "It's not Burroughs, certainly not Wells, maybe a little Bradbury. . . ."

Wun furrowed his already densely furrowed brow. "I'm sorry—I don't know those words."

"They're writers. Writers of fiction, who wrote about your planet."

Once I had communicated the idea—that certain authors had imagined a living Mars long before its actual terraforming—Wun was fascinated. "Would it be possible for me to read these books? And discuss them the next time you visit?"

"I'm flattered. Are you sure you can spare the time? There must be heads of state who would very much like to talk to you."

"I'm sure there are. But they can wait."

I told him I looked forward to it.

On my drive home I raided a secondhand bookshop and in the morning I delivered a bundle of paperbacks to Wun, or at least to the taciturn men guarding his quarters. *War of the Worlds, A Princess of Mars, The Martian Chronicles, Stranger in a Strange Land, Red Mars.*

I heard nothing more from him for a couple of weeks.

∘ ∘ ∘

Construction continued on the new facilities at Perihelion. By the end of September there was a massive concrete foundation where there used to be scrub pine and ratty palmettos, a great rigging of steel beams and aluminum piping.

Molly had heard there was military-grade lab and refrigeration equipment coming in next week. (Another dinner at Champs, most of the customers staring at a Marlins game on the billboard-sized plasma screen while we shared appetizers in a far, dark corner.) "Why do we need lab gear, Ty? Perihelion's all about space research and the Spin. I don't get it."

"I don't know. Nobody's talking."

"Maybe you could ask Jason, one of those afternoons you spend over at the north wing."

I had told her I was consulting with Jase, not that I had been adopted by the Martian ambassador. "I don't have that kind of security clearance." Nor, of course, did Molly.

"I'm starting to think you don't trust me."

"Just following the rules, Moll."

"Right," she said. "You're *such* a saint."

○ ○ ○

Jason stopped by my place unannounced, fortunately on an evening when Molly wasn't present, to talk about his meds. I told him what Malmstein had said, that it would likely be all right to bump up his dosage but that we'd have to watch out for side effects. The disease wasn't standing still and there was a practical limit to the degree to which we could suppress his symptoms. It didn't mean he was doomed, only that sooner or later he would have to conduct his business differently—to accommodate the disease rather than suppress it. (Beyond that was another threshold neither of us discussed: radical disability and dementia.)

"I understand that," Jason said. He sat in a chair by the window, glancing occasionally at his reflection in the glass, one long leg draped over the other. "All I need is another few months."

"A few months for what?"

"A few months to cut the legs out from under E. D. Lawton." I stared at him. I thought it was a joke. He wasn't smiling. "Do I have to explain this?"

"If you want me to make sense of it, yeah, you do."

"E.D. and I have divergent views about the future of Perihelion. As far as E.D.'s concerned, Perihelion exists to support the aerospace industry. That's the bottom line and always has been. He never believed we could do anything about the Spin." Jason shrugged. "He's almost certainly right, in the sense that we can't *fix* it. But that doesn't mean we can't understand it. We can't fight a war against the Hypotheticals in any meaningful way, but we can do a little guerilla science. That's what Wun's arrival is all about."

"I don't follow."

"Wun isn't just an interplanetary goodwill ambassador. He came here with a plan, a collaborative venture that might give us some clues about the Hypotheticals, where they come from, what they want, what they're doing to both planets. The idea's getting a mixed reception. E.D.'s trying to harpoon it— he doesn't think it's useful and he thinks it puts at risk whatever political capital we've got left after the terraforming."

"So you're undercutting him?"

Jason sighed. "This might sound cruel, but E.D. doesn't understand that his time has come and gone. My father is exactly what the world needed twenty years ago. I admire him for that. He's accomplished amazing, unbelievable things. Without E.D. to light fires under the politicians there would never have been a Perihelion. One of the ironies of the Spin is that the long-term consequences of E. D. Lawton's genius have come back to bite him—if E.D. had never existed, Wun Ngo Wen wouldn't exist. I'm not engaged in some Oedipal struggle here. I know exactly what my father is and what he's done. He's at home in the corridors of power, Garland is his golf buddy. Great. But he's a prisoner, too. A prisoner of his own shortsightedness. His days as a visionary are over. He dislikes Wun's plan because he distrusts the technology—he doesn't like anything he can't reverse-engineer; he doesn't like the fact that the Martians can wield technologies we're only beginning to guess at. And he hates the fact that Wun has me on his side. Me and, I might add, a new generation of D.C. power brokers, including Preston Lomax, who's likely to be the next president. Suddenly E.D.'s surrounded by people he can't manipulate. Younger people, people who've assimilated the Spin in a way E.D.'s generation never did. People like us, Ty."

I was a little flattered and a little alarmed to be included in that pronoun.

I said, "You're taking on a lot, aren't you?"

He looked at me sharply. "I'm doing exactly what E.D. trained me to do. From birth. He never wanted a son; he wanted an heir, an apprentice. He made that decision a long time before the Spin, Tyler. He knew exactly how smart I was and he knew what he wanted me to do with that intelligence. And I went along with it. Even when I was old enough to understand what he was up to, I cooperated. So here I am, an E. D. Lawton production: the handsome, savvy, sexless, media-friendly object you see before you. A marketable image, a certain intellectual acumen, and no loyalties that don't begin and end with Perihelion. But there was always a little rider on that contract, even if E.D. doesn't like to think about it.

'Heir' implies 'inheritance.' It implies that, at some point, my judgment supersedes his. Well, the time has come. The opportunity before us is simply too important to fuck up."

His hands, I noticed, were clenched into fists, and his legs were shaking, but was that intensity of emotion or a symptom of his disease? For that matter, how much of this monologue was genuine and how much was the product of the neurostimulants I was prescribing for him?

"You look scared," Jason said.

"Exactly what Martian technology are we talking about here?"

He grinned. "It's really very clever. Quasi-biological. Very small scale. Molecular autocatalytic feedback loops, basically, with contingent programming written into their reproductive protocols."

"In English, please, Jase."

"Little tiny artificial replicators."

"Living things?"

"In a certain sense, yes, living things. Artificial living things we can launch into space."

"So what do they *do*, Jase?"

His grin got bigger. "They eat ice," he said, "and they shit information."

4 X 10⁹ A.D.

I crossed a few yards of pressed earth to which weathered asphalt clung in scabrous patches, and came to an embankment and slid down it, noisily, with my hard shell suitcases full of modest clothing and handwritten notes and digital files and Martian pharmaceuticals. I landed in a drainage ditch, thigh-deep in water green as papaya leaves and warm as the tropical night. The water reflected the scarred moon and stank of manure.

I hid the luggage in a dry place halfway up the embankment and pulled myself the rest of the way up, lying at an angle that concealed my body but allowed a view of the road, Ibu Ina's concrete-box clinic, and the black car parked in front of it.

The men from the car had broken in through the back door. They switched on more lights as they moved through the building, making yellow squares of windows with drawn blinds, but I had no way of knowing what they were doing there. Searching the place, I guessed. I tried to estimate how long they spent inside, but I seemed to have lost the ability to calculate time or even to read the numbers on my watch. The numerals glowed like restless fireflies but wouldn't stand still long enough to make sense.

One of the men left by the front door, walked to the car, and started the engine. The second man emerged a few seconds later and ducked into the passenger seat. The midnight-colored car rolled close to me as it turned onto the road, headlights sweeping over the berm. I ducked and lay still until the motor noise faded.

Then I thought about what to do next. The question was difficult to answer, because I was tired—suddenly, massively tired; too weak to stand up. I wanted to go back to the clinic and find a phone and warn Ibu Ina about the men in the car. But maybe En would do that. I hoped so. Because I wasn't going to make it to the clinic. My legs wouldn't do anything but tremble when I willed them to move. This was more than fatigue. It felt like paralysis.

And when I looked at the clinic again there was smoke curling out of the roof vent and the light behind the blinds was flickery yellow. Fire.

The men from the car had set fire to Ibu Ina's clinic, and there was nothing I could do about it but close my eyes and hope I wouldn't die here before someone found me.

o o o

The stench of smoke and the sound of weeping woke me.

Still not yet daylight. But I found I could move, at least a little, with considerable effort and pain, and I seemed to be thinking more or less clearly. So I levered myself up the slope, inch after inch.

There were cars and people all over the open space between here and the clinic, headlights and flashlights cutting spastic arcs across the sky. The clinic was a smoldering ruin. Its concrete walls were still standing but the roof had collapsed and the building had been eviscerated by the fire. I managed to stand up. I walked toward the sound of weeping.

The sound came from Ibu Ina. She sat on an island of asphalt hugging her knees. She was surrounded by a group of women who gave me dark, suspicious looks as I approached her. But when Ina saw me she sprang to her feet, wiping her eyes with her sleeve. "Tyler Dupree!" She ran toward me. "I thought you were burned to death! Burned up along with everything else!"

She grabbed me, embraced me, held me up—my legs had turned rubbery again. "The clinic," I managed to say. "All your work. Ina, I'm so sorry. . . ."

"No," she said. "The clinic is a building. The medical paraphernalia can be replaced. You, on the other hand, are *unique*. En told us all how you sent him away when the arsonists came. You saved his life, Tyler!" She stood back. "Tyler? Are you all right?"

I wasn't all right. I looked past Ina's shoulder at the sky. It was almost dawn. The ancient sun was rising. Mount Merapi was outlined against the indigo blue sky. "Just tired," I said, and closed my eyes. I felt my legs fold under me and I heard Ina calling for help, and then I slept some more—for days, they told me later.

o o o

For obvious reasons, I couldn't stay in the village.

Ina wanted to nurse me through the last of the drug crisis, and she felt the village owed me protection. After all, I had saved En's life (or so she insisted), and En was not only her nephew but was related to virtually everyone else in town, one way or another. I was a hero. But I was also a magnet for the attention of evil men, and if not for Ina's pleading I suspect the *kepala desa* would have put me on the first bus to Padang and to hell with it. So I was taken, along with my luggage, to an uninhabited village house (the owners had gone *rantau* months ago) long enough for other arrangements to be made.

The Minangkabau of West Sumatra knew how to duck and weave in the face of oppression. They had survived the coming of Islam in the sixteenth century, the Padri War, Dutch colonialism, Suharto's New Order, the Negari Restoration and, post-Spin, the New Reformasi and their thuggish national police. Ina had told me some of these stories, both at the clinic and afterward, when I lay in a tiny room in a wooden house under the huge, slow blades of an electric fan. The strength of the Minang, she said, was their flexibility, their deep understanding that the rest of the world was not like home and never would be. (She quoted a Minang proverb: "In different fields, different grasshoppers; in different ponds, different fish.") The tradition of *rantau,* emigration—of young men going out into the world and coming back wealthier or wiser—had made them a sophisticated people. The simple wooden buffalo-horn houses of the village were adorned with aerostat antennas, and most families in the village, Ina said, regularly received letters or e-mail from family in Australia, Europe, Canada, the United States.

It was not surprising, then, that there were Minangkabau working at every level on the docks at Padang. Ina's ex-husband, Jala, was only one of many in the import/export trade who organized *rantau* expeditions to the Arch and beyond. It was no coincidence that Diane's inquiries had led her to Jala and thence to Ibu Ina and this highland village. "Jala is opportunistic and he can be mean in a petty way, but he's not unscrupulous," Ina said. "Diane was lucky to find him, or else she's a good judge of character—probably the latter. In any case Jala has no love for the New Reformasi, fortunately for all concerned."

(She had divorced Jala, she said, because he had formed the bad habit of sleeping with disreputable women in the city. He spent too much money on his girlfriends and had twice brought home curable but alarming venereal diseases. He was a bad husband, Ina said, but not an especially bad man. He wouldn't betray Diane to the authorities unless he was captured and physically tortured . . . and he was far too clever to let himself be captured.)

"The men who burned your clinic—"

"They must have followed Diane to the hotel in Padang and then interrogated the driver who brought you there."

"But why burn the building down?"

"I don't know, but I suspect it was an attempt to frighten you and drive you into the open. And a warning to anyone who might help you."

"If they found the clinic, they'll know your name."

"But they won't come into the village openly, guns blazing. Things have not quite deteriorated to that degree. I expect they'll watch the waterfront and hope we do something stupid."

"Even so, if your name is on a list, if you try to open another clinic—"

"But that was never my plan."

"No?"

"No. You've convinced me that the *rantau gadang* might be a good thing for a physician to undertake. If you don't mind the competition?"

"I don't understand."

"I mean that there is a simple solution for all our problems, one I've been contemplating a long time. The entire village has considered it, one way or another. Many have already left. We're not a big successful town like Belubus or Batusangkar. The land here isn't especially rich and every year we lose more people to the city or other clans in other towns or to the *rantau gadang,* and why not? There's room in the new world."

"You want to emigrate?"

"Me, Jala, my sister and her sister and my nephews and cousins—more than thirty of us, all told. Jala has several illegitimate children who would be happy to assume control of his business once he's on the other side. So you see?" She smiled. "You needn't be grateful. We're not your benefactors. Only fellow travelers."

I asked her several times whether Diane was safe. As safe as Jala could make her, Ina said. Jala had installed her in a living space above a customs house where she would be relatively comfortable and safely hidden until the final arrangements were made. "The difficult part will be getting you to the port undetected. The police suspect you're in the highlands and they'll be watching the roads for foreigners, especially *sick* foreigners, since the driver who brought you to the clinic will have told them you're not well."

"I'm finished being sick," I said.

The last crisis had begun outside the burning clinic and it

had passed while I was unconscious. Ibu Ina said it had been a difficult passage, that after the move to this small room in this empty house I had moaned until the neighbors complained, that she had needed her cousin Adek to hold me down during the worst of the convulsions—that was why my arms and shoulders were so badly bruised, hadn't I noticed? But I remembered none of it. All I knew was that I felt stronger as the days passed; my temperature was reliably normal; I could walk without trembling.

"And the other effects of the drug?" Ina asked. "Do you feel *different*?"

That was an interesting question. I answered honestly: "I don't know. Not yet, anyway."

"Well. For the moment it hardly matters. As I say, the trick will be to get you out of the highlands and back to Padang. Fortunately, I think we can arrange it."

"When do we leave?"

"Three or four days' time," Ina said. "In the meantime, rest."

o o o

Ina was busy most of those three days. I saw very little of her. The days were hot and sunny but breezes came through the wooden house in soothing gusts, and I spent the time cautiously exercising, writing, and reading—there were English-language paperbacks on a rattan shelf in the bedroom, including a popular biography of Jason Lawton called *A Life for the Stars*. (I looked for my name in the index and found it: *Dupree, Tyler,* with five page references. But I couldn't bring myself to read the book. The swaybacked Somerset Maugham novels were more tempting.)

En dropped in periodically to see that I was all right and to bring me sandwiches and bottled water from his uncle's *warung*. He adopted a proprietary manner and made a point of asking after my health. He said he was "proud to be making *rantau*" with me.

"You too, En? You're going to the new world?"

He nodded emphatically. "Also my father, my mother, my uncle," and a dozen other close relations for whom he used

Minang kinship words. His eyes glittered. "Perhaps you'll teach me medicine there."

Perhaps I would have to. Crossing the Arch would pretty much rule out a traditional education. This might not be the best thing for En, and I wondered if his parents had given their decision enough thought.

But that wasn't my business, and En was clearly excited about the journey. He could hardly control his voice when he talked about it. And I relished the eager, open expression on his face. En belonged to a generation capable of regarding the future with more hope than dread. No one in my generation of grotesques had ever smiled into the future like that. It was a good, deeply human look, and it made me happy, and it made me sad.

Ina came back the night before we were due to leave, bearing dinner and a plan.

"My cousin's son's brother-in-law," she said, "drives ambulances for the hospital in Batusangkar. He can borrow an ambulance from the motor pool to take you into Padang. There will be at least two cars ahead of us with wireless phones, so if there's a roadblock we ought to have some warning."

"I don't need an ambulance," I said.

"The ambulance is a disguise. You in the back, hidden, and me in my medical regalia, and a villager—En is pleading for the role—to play sick. Do you understand? If the police look in the back of the ambulance they see me and an ill child, and I say 'CVWS,' and the police become reluctant to search more thoroughly. Thus the ridiculously tall American doctor is smuggled past them."

"You think this will work?"

"I think it has a very good chance of working."

"But if you're caught with me—"

"As bad as things may be, the police can't arrest me unless I've committed a crime. Transporting a Westerner isn't a crime."

"Transporting a criminal might be."

"Are you criminal, Pak Tyler?"

"Depends how you interpret certain acts of Congress."

"I choose not to interpret them at all. Please don't worry about it. Did I tell you the trip has been delayed a day?"

"Why?"

"A wedding. Of course, weddings aren't what they once were. Wedding *adat* has eroded terribly since the Spin. As has everything else since money and roads and fast-food restaurants came to the highlands. I don't believe money is evil, but it can be terribly corrosive. Young people are in a hurry nowadays. At least we don't have Las Vegas–style ten-minute weddings. . . . Do those still exist in your country?"

I admitted they did.

"Well, we're headed in that direction as well. *Minang hilang, tinggal kerbau.* At least there will still be a *palaminan* and lots of sticky rice and *saluang* music. Are you well enough to attend? At least for the music?"

"I would be privileged."

"So tomorrow night we sing, and on the following morning we defy the American Congress. The wedding works in our favor, too. Lots of traveling, lots of vehicles on the road; we won't seem conspicuous, our little *rantau* group heading for Teluk Bayur."

I slept late and woke feeling better than I had for a long time, stronger and subtly more alert. The morning breeze was warm and rich with the smell of cooking and the complaints of roosters and hammering from the center of town where an outdoor stage was under construction. I spent the day at the window, reading and watching the public procession of the bride and groom on their way to the groom's house. Ina's village was small enough that the wedding had brought it to a standstill. Even the local *warungs* had closed for the day, though the franchise businesses on the main road were staffed for tourists. By late afternoon the smell of curried chicken and coconut milk was thick in the air, and En dropped by very briefly with a prepared meal for me.

Ibu Ina, in an embroidered gown and silk head scarf, came to the door a little after nightfall and said, "It's done, the wedding proper, I mean. Nothing left but the singing and dancing. Do you still want to come along, Tyler?"

I dressed in the best clothes I had with me, white cotton

pants and a white shirt. I was nervous about being seen in public, but Ina assured me there were no strangers in the wedding party and I would be welcome in the crowd.

Despite Ina's reassurances I felt painfully conspicuous as we walked together down the street toward the stage and the music, less because of my height than because I had been indoors too long. Leaving the house was like stepping out of water into air; suddenly I was surrounded by nothing substantial at all. Ina distracted me by talking about the newlyweds. The groom, a pharmacist's apprentice from Belubus, was a young cousin of hers. (Ina called any relative more distant than brother, sister, aunt or uncle her "cousin"; the Minang kinship system used precise words for which there were no simple English equivalents.) The bride was a local girl with a slightly disreputable past. Both would be going *rantau* after the wedding. The new world beckoned.

The music began at dusk and would continue, she said, until morning. It was broadcast village-wide through enormous pole-mounted loudspeakers, but the source was the raised stage and the group seated on reed mats there, two male instrumentalists and two female singers. The songs, Ina explained, were about love, marriage, disappointment, fate, sex. Lots of sex, couched in metaphors Chaucer would have appreciated. We sat on a bench at the periphery of the celebration. I drew more than a few long looks from people in the crowd, at least some of whom must have heard the story of the burned clinic and the fugitive American, but Ina was careful not to let me become a distraction. She kept me to herself, though she smiled indulgently at the young people mobbing the stage. "I'm past the age of lament. My field no longer requires ploughing, as the song has it. All this fuss. My goodness."

Bride and groom in their embroidered finery sat on mock thrones near the platform. I thought the groom, with his whip-thin mustache, looked shifty; but no, Ina insisted, it was the girl, so innocent in her blue and white brocaded costume, who was the one to watch. We drank coconut milk. We smiled. Coming on toward midnight many of the village's women drifted away, leaving a crowd of men, young men mobbing the stage, laughing; older men sitting at tables gambling studiously at cards, faces blank as aged leather.

I had shown Ina the pages I had written about my first meeting with Wun Ngo Wen. "But the account can't be entirely accurate," she said during a lull in the music. "You sounded much too calm."

"I wasn't calm at all. Just trying not to embarrass myself."

"Introduced, after all, to a man from Mars . . ." She looked up at the sky, at the post-Spin stars in their frail, scattered constellations, dim in the glare from the wedding party. "What must you have expected?"

"I suppose, someone less human."

"Ah, but he was *very* human."

"Yes," I said.

Wun Ngo Wen had become something of a revered figure in rural India, Indonesia, southeast Asia. In Padang, Ina said, one sometimes saw his picture in people's homes, in a gilded frame like a watercolor saint or famous mullah. "There was," she said, "something extraordinarily attractive in his manner. A familiar way of speaking, even though we only heard him in translation. And when we saw photographs of his planet—all those cultivated fields—it looked so much more rural than urban. More Eastern than Western. The Earth visited by an ambassador from another world, and he was one of *us*! Or so it seemed. And he chastised the Americans in an enjoyable way."

"The last thing Wun meant to do was scold anyone."

"No doubt the legend outpaces the reality. Didn't you have a thousand questions, the day you were introduced to him?"

"Of course. But I figured he'd been answering the obvious questions ever since he arrived. I thought he might be tired of it."

"Was he reluctant to talk about his home?"

"Not at all. He loved to talk about it. He just didn't like being interrogated."

"My manners aren't as polished as yours. I'm sure I would have offended him with countless questions. Suppose, Tyler, you had been able to ask him anything at all, that first day: what would it have been?"

That was easy. I knew exactly what question I had been suppressing the first time I met Wun Ngo Wen. "I would have asked him about the Spin. About the Hypotheticals. Whether his people had learned anything we didn't already know."

"And *did* you ever discuss that with him?"

"Yes."

"And did he have much to say?"

"Much."

I glanced at the stage. A new *saluang* group had come on. One of them was playing a *rabab,* a stringed instrument. The musician hammered his bow against the belly of the *rabab* and grinned. Another lewd wedding song.

"I'm afraid I may have been interrogating *you,*" Ina said.

"I'm sorry. I'm still a little tired."

"Then you should go home and sleep. Doctor's orders. With a little luck you'll see Ibu Diane again tomorrow."

She walked with me down the loud street, away from the festivities. The music went on until nearly five the next morning. I slept soundly in spite of it.

○ ○ ○

The ambulance driver was a skinny, taciturn man in Red Crescent whites. His name was Nijon, and he shook my hand with exaggerated deference and kept his large eyes on Ibu Ina when he spoke to me. I asked if he was nervous about the drive to Padang. Ina translated his answer: "He says he's done more dangerous things for less compelling reasons. He says he's pleased to meet a friend of Wun Ngo Wen. He adds that we should get underway as soon as possible."

So we climbed into the back end of the ambulance. Along one wall was a horizontal steel locker where equipment was usually stored. It doubled as a bench. Nijon had emptied the locker, and we established that it was possible for me to cram myself inside by bending my legs at hip and knee and tucking my head into my shoulder. The locker smelled of antiseptic and latex and was about as comfortable as a monkey coffin, but there I would lie, should we be stopped at a checkpoint, with Ina on the bench in her clinic gown and En laid out on a stretcher doing his best impression of a CVWS infectee. In the hot morning light the plan seemed more than slightly ridiculous.

Nijon had shimmed the lid of the locker to allow some air to circulate inside, so I probably wouldn't suffocate, but I didn't relish the prospect of spending time in what was essentially a hot, dark metal box. Fortunately—once we had established that I fit—I didn't have to, at least not yet. All the police activity, Ina said, had been on the new highway between Bukik Tinggi and Padang, and because we were traveling in a loose convoy with other villagers we ought to have plenty of warning before we were pulled over. So for the time being I sat next to Ina while she taped a saline drip (sealed, no needle, a prop) to the crook of En's elbow. En was enthusiastic about the role and began rehearsing his cough, a deep-lung hack that provoked an equally theatrical frown from Ina: "You've been stealing your brother's clove cigarettes?"

En blushed. It was for the sake of realism, he said.

"Oh? Well, be careful you don't act yourself into an early grave."

Nijon slammed the rear doors and climbed into the driver's seat and started the engine and we began the bumpy drive to Padang. Ina told En to close his eyes. "Pretend to be asleep. Apply your theatrical skills." Before long his breathing settled into gentle snorts.

"He was awake all night with the music," Ina explained.

"I'm amazed he can sleep, even so."

"One of the advantages of childhood. Or the First Age, as the Martians call it—is that correct?"

I nodded.

"They have four, I understand? Four Ages to our three?"

Yes, as Ina undoubtedly knew. Of all the folkways in Wun Ngo Wen's Five Republics, this was the one that had most fascinated the terrestrial public.

Human cultures generally recognize two or three stages of life—childhood and adulthood; or childhood, adolescence, adulthood. Some reserve special status for old age. But the Martian custom was unique and depended on their centuries-long mastery of biochemistry and genetics. The Martians counted human lives in four installments, marked by biochemically mediated events. Birth to puberty was childhood. Puberty to the end of physical growth and the beginning of metabolic equilibrium was adolescence. Equilibrium to decline, death, or radical change was adulthood.

And beyond adulthood, the elective age: the Fourth.

Centuries ago, Martian biochemists had devised a means to prolong human life by sixty or seventy years on average. But the discovery wasn't an unmixed blessing. Mars was a radically constrained ecosystem, ruled by the scarcity of water and nitrogen. The cultivated land that had looked so familiar to Ibu Ina was a triumph of subtle, sophisticated bioengineering. Human reproduction had been regulated for centuries, pegged to sustainability estimates. Another seventy years tacked onto the average life span was a population crisis in the making.

Nor was the longevity treatment itself simple or pleasant. It was a deep cellular reconstruction. A cocktail of highly engineered viral and bacterial entities was injected into the body. Tailored viruses performed a sort of systemic update, patching or revising DNA sequences, restoring telomeres, resetting the genetic clock, while lab-grown bacterial phages flushed out toxic metals and plaques and repaired obvious physical damage.

The immune system resisted. The treatment was, at best, equivalent to a six-week course of some debilitating influenza—fevers, joint and muscle pain, weakness. Certain organs went into a kind of reproductive overdrive. Skin cells died and were replaced in fierce succession; nervous tissue regenerated spontaneously and rapidly.

The process was debilitating, painful, and there were potential negative side effects. Most subjects reported at least some long-term memory loss. Rare cases suffered temporary dementia and nonrecoverable amnesia. The brain, restored and rewired, became a subtly different organ. And its owner became a subtly different human being.

"They conquered death."

"Not quite."

"You would think," Ina said, "with all their wisdom, they could have made it a less unpleasant experience."

Certainly they could have relieved the superficial discomfort of the transition to Fourth. But they had chosen not to. Martian culture had incorporated the Fourth Age into its folkways, pain and all: pain was one of the limiting conditions, a tutelary discomfort. Not everyone chose to become a Fourth. Not only was the transition difficult, stiff social penalties had been written into their longevity laws. Any Martian citizen was entitled to undergo the treatment, free of charge and without prejudice. But Fourths were forbidden to reproduce; reproduction was a privilege reserved for adults. (For the last two hundred years the longevity cocktail had included drugs that produced irreversible sterilization in both sexes.) Fourths weren't allowed to vote in council elections—no one wanted a planet run by venerable ancients for their own benefit. But each of the Five Republics had a sort of judicial review body, the equivalent of a Supreme Court, elected *solely* by Fourths. Fourths were both more and less than adults, as adults are both more and less than children. More powerful, less playful; freer and less free.

But I could not decipher, to Ina or to myself, all the codes and totems into which the Martians had folded their medical technology. Anthropologists had spent years in the attempt, working from Wun Ngo Wen's archival records. Until such research had been banned.

"And now we have the same technology," Ina said.

"Some of us do. I hope eventually all of us will."

"I wonder if we'll use it as wisely."

"We might. The Martians did, and the Martians are as human as we are."

"I know. It's possible, certainly. But what do you think, Tyler—*will* we?"

I looked at En. He was still asleep. Dreaming, perhaps, his eyes darting under closed lids like fish underwater. His nostrils flared as he breathed and the motion of the ambulance rocked him from side to side.

"Not on this planet," I said.

o o o

Ten miles down the road out of Bukik Tinggi, Nijon knocked hard at the partition between us and the driver's seat. That was our prearranged signal: roadblock ahead. The ambulance slowed. Ina stood up hastily, bracing herself. She strapped a neon-yellow oxygen mask over En's face—En, awake now, seemed to be reconsidering the merits of the adventure—and covered her own mouth with a paper mask. "Be quick," she whispered at me.

So I contorted myself into the equipment locker. The lid banged down on the shims that allowed a little air to flow inside, a quarter-inch between me and asphyxiation.

The ambulance stopped before I was ready and my head gonged hard against the narrow end of the locker.

"And be quiet now," Ina said—to me or to En, I wasn't sure which.

I waited in the dark.

Minutes passed. There was a distant rumble of talk, impossible to decipher even if I had understood the language. Two voices. Nijon and someone unfamiliar. A voice that was thin, querulous, harsh. A policeman's voice.

They conquered death, Ina had said.

No, I thought.

The locker was heating up fast. Sweat slicked my face, drenched my shirt, stung my eyes. I could hear myself breathing. I imagined the whole world could hear me breathing.

Nijon answered the policeman in deferential murmurs. The policeman barked back fresh questions.

"Be still now, just be still," Ina whispered urgently. En had been bouncing his feet against the thin mattress of the gurney, a nervous habit. Too much energy for a CVWS victim. I saw the tips of Ina's fingers splayed across the quarter-inch of light above my head, four knuckled shadows.

Now the rear doors of the ambulance rattled open and I smelled gasoline exhaust and rank noonday vegetation. If I craned my head—gently, gently—I could see a thin swath of exterior light and two shadows that might be Nijon and a policeman or maybe just trees and clouds.

The policeman demanded something from Ina. His voice was a guttural monotone, bored and threatening, and it made

me angry. I thought about Ina and En, cowering or pretending
to cower from this armed man and what he represented. Doing it for me. Ibu Ina said something stern but unprovocative
in her native language. *CVWS, something something something CVWS.* She was exercising her medical authority, testing the policeman's susceptibility, weighing fear for fear.

The policeman's answer was curt, a demand to search the
ambulance or see her papers. Ina said something more force-
ful or desperate. The word *CVWS* again.

I wanted to protect myself, but more than that, I wanted to
protect Ina and En. I would surrender myself before I saw
them hurt. Surrender or fight. Fight or flight. Give up, if necessary, all the years the Martian pharmaceuticals had pumped
back into my body. Maybe that was the courage of the
Fourth, the special courage Wun Ngo Wen had talked about.
They conquered death. But no: as a species, terrestrial,
Martian, in all our years on both our planets, we had only engineered reprieves. Nothing was certain.

Footsteps, boots on metal. The policeman began climbing
into the ambulance. I could tell he had come aboard by the
way the vehicle sank on its shocks, rolling like a ship in a
gentle swell. I braced myself against the lid of the locker. Ina
stood up, screeching refusals.

I took a breath and got ready to spring.

But there was fresh noise from the road. Another vehicle
roared past. By the dopplered whine of its straining engine, it
was traveling at high speed—a conspicuous, shocking, fuck-
the-law velocity.

The policeman emitted a snarl of outrage. The floor
bounced again.

Scuffling noises, silence for a beat, a slammed door, and
then the sound of the policeman's car (I guessed) revved to
vengeful life, gravel snapping away from tires in an angry hail.

Ina lifted the lid of my sarcophagus.

I sat up in the stink of my own sweat. "What happened?"

"That was Aji. From the village. A cousin of mine. Running the roadblock to distract the police." She was pale but
relieved. "He drives like a drunk, I'm afraid."

"He did that to take the heat off us?"

"Such a colorful expression. Yes. We're a convoy, remember. Other cars, wireless telephones, he would have known we had been stopped. He's risking a fine or a reprimand, nothing more serious."

I breathed the air, which was sweet and cool. I looked at En. En gave me a shaky grin.

"Please introduce me to Aji when we get to Padang," I said. "I want to thank him for pretending to be a drunk."

Ina rolled her eyes. "Unfortunately Aji wasn't pretending. He *is* a drunk. An offense in the eyes of the Prophet."

Nijon looked in at us, winked, closed the rear doors.

"Well, that was frightening," Ina said. She put her hand on my arm.

I apologized for letting her take the risk.

"Nonsense," she said. "We're friends now. And the risk is not as great as you might imagine. The police can be difficult, but at least they're local men and bound by certain rules—not like the men from Jakarta, the New Reformasi or whatever they call themselves, the men who burned my clinic. And I expect you would risk yourself on our behalf if necessary. Would you, Pak Tyler?"

"Yes, I would."

Her hand was trembling. She looked me in the eye. "My goodness, I believe that's true."

No, we had never conquered death, only engineered reprieves (the pill, the powder, the angioplasty, the Fourth Age)—enacted our conviction that more life, even a *little* more life, might yet yield the pleasure or wisdom we wanted or had missed in it. No one goes home from a triple bypass or a longevity treatment expecting to live forever. Even Lazarus left the grave knowing he'd die a second time.

But he came forth. He came forth gratefully. I was grateful.

THE COLD PLACES OF THE UNIVERSE

I drove home after a late Friday session at Perihelion, keyed open the door of the house, and found Molly sitting at the keyboard of my PC terminal.

The desk was in the southwest corner of the living room against a window, facing away from the door. Molly half-turned and gave me a startled look. At the same time, deftly, she clicked an icon and exited the program she'd been running.

"Molly?"

I wasn't surprised to find her here. Moll spent most week-ends with me; she carried a duplicate key. But she'd never shown any interest in my PC.

"You didn't call," she said.

I'd been in a meeting with the insurance reps who underwrote Perihelion's employee coverage. I'd been told to expect a two-hour session but it turned out to be a twenty-minute update on billing policy, and when it finished I thought it would be quicker to just drive on home, maybe even beat Molly to the door if she'd stopped to pick up wine. Such was the effect of Molly's long level gaze that I felt

obliged to explain all this before I asked her what she was doing in my files.

She laughed as I came across the room, one of those embarrassed, apologetic laughs: *Look at the funny thing you
caught me doing.* Her right hand hovered over the touchpad
of the PC. She turned back to the monitor. On screen, the cursor dived for the shut-down icon.

"Wait," I said.

"What, you want on here?"

The cursor homed in on its target. I put my hand over
Molly's hand. "Actually, I'd like to know what you were
doing."

She was tense. A vein throbbed in the pinkness just forward of her ear. "Making myself at home. Um, a little too
much at home? I didn't think you'd mind."

"Mind what, Moll?"

"Mind me using your terminal."

"Using it for what?"

"Really nothing. Just checking it out."

But it couldn't be the machine Moll was curious about. It
was five years old, nearly an antique. She used more sophisticated gear at work. And I had recognized the program she'd
been in such a hurry to close when I came through the door. It
was my household tracker, the program I used to pay bills
and balance my checkbook and Rolodex my contacts.

"Kind of looked like a spreadsheet," I said.

"I wandered in there. Your desktop confused me. You
know. People organize things different ways. I'm sorry,
Tyler. I guess I was being presumptuous." She jerked her
hand out from under mine and clicked the shut-down tag. The
desktop shrank and I heard the processor's fan noise whine
down to silence. Molly stood up, straightening her blouse.
Molly always gave herself a crisp little tuck when she stood
up. Putting things in order. "How about I start dinner." She
turned her back on me and walked toward the kitchen.

I watched her disappear through the swinging doors. After
a ten count I followed her in.

She was pulling pans off the wall rack. She glanced at me
and looked away.

"Molly," I said. "If there's anything you want to know, all you have to do is ask."

"Oh. Is that all I have to do? Okay."

"Molly—"

She put a pan on the burner of the stove with exaggerated care, as if it were fragile. "Do you need me to apologize again? Okay, Tyler. I'm sorry I played with your terminal without your permission."

"I'm not accusing you of anything, Moll."

"Then why are we talking about it? I mean, why does it look like we're going to spend the entire *rest of the evening* talking about it?" Her eyes grew moist. Her tinted lenses turned a deeper shade of emerald. "So I was a little curious about you."

"Curious about what, my utility bills?"

"About *you*." She dragged a chair away from the kitchen table. The chair leg caught against the leg of the table and Molly yanked it free. She sat down and crossed her arms. "Yes, maybe even the trivial stuff. Maybe *especially* the trivial stuff." She closed her eyes and shook her head. "I say this and it sounds like I'm some kind of stalker. But yes, your utility bills, your brand of toothpaste, your shoe size, yes. Yes, I want to feel like I'm something more than your weekend fuck. I confess."

"You don't have to go into my files for that."

"Maybe I wouldn't have, if—"

"If?"

She shook her head. "I don't want to argue."

"Sometimes it's better to finish what you start."

"Well, like *that,* for instance. Anytime you feel threatened, you do your *detached* thing. Get all cool and reserved and analytical, like I'm some nature documentary you're watching on TV. The glass screen comes down. But the glass screen's *always* there, isn't it? The whole world's on the other side of it. That's why you don't talk about yourself. That's why I spent a year waiting for you to notice I was more than a piece of office furniture. That big dumb endless cool stare, watching life like it's the evening news, like it's some sorry war on the other side of the planet where all the people have unpronounceable names."

"Molly—"

"I mean I'm aware that we're all fucked up, Tyler, every one of us born into the Spin. Pretraumatic stress disorder, or what was it you called us? A generation of grotesques. That's why we're all divorced or promiscuous or hyperreligious or depressed or manic or *dispassionate*. We all have a really good excuse for our bad behavior, including me, and if being this big pillar of carefully premeditated helpfulness is what gets you through the night, okay, I get it. But it's also okay for me to want more than that. It's okay, in fact, it's perfectly human, for me to want to touch you. Not just fuck you. Touch you."

She said all this and then, realizing she was done, unfolded her arms and waited for me to react.

I thought about making a speech back at her. I *was* passionate about her, I would say. It might not have been obvious, but I'd been aware of her ever since I came to work at Perihelion. Aware of the lines and dynamics of her body, how she stood or walked or stretched or yawned; aware of her pastel wardrobe and the costume-jewelry butterfly she wore on a skinny silver chain; aware of her moods and impulses and the catalog of her smiles and frowns and gestures. When I closed my eyes I saw her face and when I went to sleep that was what I looked at. I loved her surface and her substance: the salt taste of her throat and the cadence of her voice, the arch of her fingers and the words they wrote on my body.

I thought about all that but couldn't bring myself to say it to her.

It wasn't a lie exactly. But it wasn't exactly the truth.

In the end we made up with vaguer pleasantries and brief tears and conciliatory hugs, let the issue drop, and I played sous-chef while she composed a really very good pasta sauce, and the tension began to lift, and by midnight we had cuddled an hour in front of the news (unemployment up, an election debate, some sorry war on the other side of the planet) and we were ready for bed. Molly turned out the light before we made love, and the bedroom was dark and the window was open and the sky was blank and empty. She arched her back when she came and when she sighed her breath was sweet and milky. Parted but still touching, hand to thigh, we spoke in unfinished sentences. I said, "You know, *passion,*" and she said, "In the bedroom, God, yes."

She fell asleep fast. I was still awake an hour later.

I climbed out of bed gently, registering no change in the pulse of her breathing. I slipped into a pair of jeans and left the bedroom. Sleepless nights like this, a little Drambuie usually helped shut down the nagging interior monologue, the petitions presented by doubt to the weary forebrain. But before I went into the kitchen I sat down at the terminal and called up my household tracker.

There was no telling what Moll had been looking at. But nothing had changed, as far as I could tell. All the names and numbers seemed intact. Maybe she had found something here that made her feel closer to me. If that was really what she wanted.

Or maybe it had been a futile search. Maybe she hadn't found anything at all.

○ ○ ○

In the weeks leading up to the November election I saw more of Jason. His disease was becoming more active despite the escalating medication, possibly due to the stress caused by the ongoing conflict with his father. (E.D. had announced his intention to "take back" Perihelion from what he considered a cabal of upstart bureaucrats and scientists aligned with Wun Ngo Wen—an empty threat, in Jason's opinion, but potentially disruptive and embarrassing.)

Jase kept me close in case it was necessary to dose him with antispasmodics at some critical moment, which I was willing to do, within the limits of the law and professional ethics. Keeping Jase functional in the short term was the most that medical science could do for him, and staying functional long enough to outmaneuver E. D. Lawton was, for the moment, all that mattered to Jase.

So I spent a lot of time in the V.I.P. wing at Perihelion, usually with Jason but often with Wun Ngo Wen. This made me an object of suspicion to the rest of Wun's handlers, an assortment of government subauthorities (junior representatives from the State Department, the White House, Homeland Security, Space Command, et cetera) and academics who had been recruited to translate, study, and classify the so-called Martian archives. My access to Wun, in the eyes of these people, was irregular and unwelcome. I was a hireling. A nobody. But that was why Wun preferred my company: I had no agenda to promote or protect. And because he insisted, I was from time to time ushered by sullen toadies through the several doors that separated the Martian ambassador's air-conditioned quarters from the Florida heat and all the wide world beyond.

On one of these occasions I found Wun Ngo Wen seated on his wicker chair—someone had brought in a matching footstool so his feet wouldn't dangle—gazing thoughtfully at the contents of a test tube–sized glass vial. I asked him what was inside.

"Replicators," he said.

He was dressed in a suit and tie that might have been tailored for a stocky twelve-year-old: he'd been doing show-and-tell for a congressional delegation. Although Wun's existence had not been formally announced there had been a steady traffic of security-approved visitors both foreign and domestic over the last few weeks. The official announcement would be made by the White House shortly after the election, after which time Wun would be very busy indeed.

I looked at the glass tube from a safe vantage point across the room. *Replicators*. Ice-eaters. Seeds of an inorganic biology.

Wun smiled. "Are you afraid of it? Please don't be. I assure you the contents are completely inactive. I thought Jason had explained this to you."

He had. A little. I said, "They're microscopic devices. Semi-organic. They reproduce in conditions of extreme cold and vacuum."

"Yes, good, essentially correct. And did Jason explain the purpose of them?"

"To go out and populate the galaxy. To send us data."

Wun nodded slowly, as if this answer were also essentially correct but less than satisfactory. "This is the most sophisticated technological artifact the Five Republics have produced, Tyler. We could never have sustained the kind of industrial activity your people practice on such an alarming scale—ocean liners, men on the moon, vast cities—"

"From what I've seen, your cities are fairly impressive."

"Only because we build them in a gentler gravitational gradient. On Earth those towers would crumble under their own weight. But my point is that this, the contents of this tube, this is our equivalent of an engineering triumph, something so complex and so difficult to make that we take a certain perhaps justifiable pride in it."

"I'm sure you do."

"Then come and appreciate it. Don't be afraid." He beckoned me closer and I came across the room and sat on a chair opposite him. I guess we would have looked, from a distance, like any two friends discussing anything at all. But my eyes wouldn't leave the vial. He held it out, offered it to me. "Go on," he said.

I took the tube between thumb and forefinger and held it up to let the ceiling light shine through. The contents looked like ordinary water with a slightly oily sheen. That was all.

"To truly appreciate it," Wun said, "you have to understand what you're holding. In that tube, Tyler, are some thirty or forty thousand individual man-made cells in a glycerin suspension. Each cell is an acorn."

"You know about acorns?"

"I've been reading. It's a commonplace metaphor. Acorns and oaks, correct? When you hold an acorn you hold in your hand the possibility of an oak tree, and not just a single oak but all the progeny of that oak for centuries upon centuries. Enough oak wood to build whole cities . . . are cities made of oak?"

"No, but it doesn't matter."

"What you're holding is an acorn. Completely dormant, as I said, and in fact that *particular* sample is probably quite dead, considering the time it's spent at terrestrial ambient temperatures. Analyze it, and the most you might find would be some unusual trace chemicals."

"But?"

"But—put it in an icy, airless, cold environment, an environment like the Oort Cloud, and then, Tyler, it comes to life! It begins, very slowly but very patiently, to grow and reproduce."

The Oort Cloud. I knew about the Oort Cloud from conversations with Jason and from the speculative novels I still occasionally read. The Oort Cloud was a nebulous array of cometary bodies occupying a space beginning roughly at the orbit of Pluto and extending halfway to the nearest star. These small bodies were far from tightly packed—they occupied an almost unimaginably large volume of space—but their total mass equaled twenty to thirty times the mass of the Earth, mostly in the form of dirty ice.

Lots to eat, if ice and dust are what you eat.

Wun leaned forward in his chair. His eyes, couched in skin like crumpled leather, were bright. He smiled, which I had learned to interpret as a signal of earnestness: Martians smile when they speak from the heart.

"This was not uncontroversial for my people. What you hold in your hand has the power to substantially transform not only our own solar system but many others. And of course the outcome is uncertain. While the replicators are not organic in the conventional sense, they *are* alive. They're living autocatalytic feedback loops, subject to modification by environmental pressure. Just like human beings, or bacteria, or, or—"

"Or *murkuds*," I said.

He grinned. "Or *murkuds*."

"In other words, they might evolve."

"They *will* evolve, and unpredictably. But we've placed some limits on that. Or we believe we have. As I said, controversy abounds."

Whenever Wun talked about Martian politics, I envisioned wrinkly men and women in pastel togas debating abstractions from stainless steel podiums. In fact, Wun insisted, Martian parliamentarians behaved more like cash-strapped farmers bickering at a grain auction; and the clothing—well, I didn't even try to picture the clothing; on formal occasions Martians of both sexes tended to dress like the queen of hearts in a Bicycle deck.

But while the debates had been long and heartfelt, the plan itself was relatively simple. The replicators would be delivered scattershot into the far, cold extremities of the solar system. Some infinitesimally small fraction of those replicators would alight on two or three of the cometary nuclei that constitute the Oort Cloud. There they would begin to reproduce.

Their genetic information, Wun said, was encoded into molecules that were thermally unstable anywhere warmer than the moons of Neptune. But in the hypercold environment for which they had been designed, submicroscopic filaments in the replicators would begin a slow, painstaking metabolism. They grew at speeds that would make a bristle-cone pine look rushed, but grow they would, assimilating trace volatiles and organic molecules and shaping ice into cellular walls, ribs, spars, and joiners.

By the time the replicators had consumed a few hundred cubic feet of cometary nucleus, give or take, their interconnections would begin to complexify and their behavior would become more purposeful. They would grow highly sophisticated appendages, eyes of ice and carbon to sweep the starry darkness.

In a decade or so the replicator colony would have made of itself a sophisticated communal entity capable of recording and broadcasting rudimentary data about its environment. It would look at the sky and ask: *Is there a planet-sized dark body circling the nearest star?*

Posing and answering the question would consume more decades of time, and at least initially the answer was a foregone conclusion: yes, two worlds circling this star were dark bodies, Earth and Mars.

Nevertheless—patiently, doggedly, slowly—the replicators would collate this data and broadcast it back to their point of origin: to us, or at least to our listening satellites.

Then, in its senescence as a complex machine, the replicator colony would break down into individual clusters of simple cells, identify another bright or nearby star, and use accumulated volatiles mined from the host cometary nucleus to propel its seeds out of the solar system. (They would leave behind a tiny fragment of themselves to act as a radio repeater, a passive node in a growing network.)

These second-generation seeds would drift in interstellar space for years, decades, millennia. Most would eventually perish, lost on fruitless trajectories or drawn into gravitational eddies. Some, unable to escape the faint but distant pull of the sun, would fall back into the solar Oort Cloud and repeat the process, stupidly but patiently eating ice and recording redundant information. If two strains encountered each other they would exchange cellular material, average out copying errors induced by time or radiation, and produce offspring nearly but not exactly like themselves.

Some few would reach the icy halo of a nearby star and begin the cycle anew, this time gathering fresh information, which they would eventually send home in bursts of data, brief digital orgasms. *Binary star,* they might say, *no dark planetary bodies;* or they might say, *White dwarf star, one dark planetary body.*

And the cycle would repeat again.

And again.

And again, one star to the next, stepwise, centuries by millennia, agonizingly slowly, but speedily enough as the galaxy measures time—as we clocked the external universe from our entombment. Our days would encompass their years by the hundreds of thousands and a decade of our slow time would see them infest most of the galaxy.

Information passed at light-speed node-to-node would be forwarded, would modify behavior, would direct new replicators toward unexplored territory, would suppress redundant information so that core nodes were not overwhelmed. In effect we would be wiring the galaxy for a kind of rudimentary thought. The replicators would build a neural network as big as the night sky, and it would talk to us.

Were there risks? Of course there were risks.

Absent the Spin, Wun said, the Martians would never have approved such an arrogant appropriation of the galaxy's resources. This wasn't just an act of exploration; it was an *intervention,* an imperial reordering of the galactic ecology. If there were other sentient species out there—and the existence of the Hypotheticals had pretty much answered that question in the affirmative—the dispersal of the replicators might be misunderstood as aggression. Which might invite retaliation.

The Martians had only reconsidered this risk when they detected Spin structures under construction above their own northern and southern poles.

"The Spin renders objections moot," Wun said, "or nearly so. With luck the replicators will tell us something important about the Hypotheticals, or at least the extent of their work in the galaxy. We might be able to discern the purpose of the Spin. Failing that, the replicators will serve as a sort of warning beacon to other intelligent species facing the same problem. Close analysis would suggest to a thoughtful observer the purpose for which the network was constructed. Other civilizations might choose to tap into it. The knowledge could help them protect themselves. To succeed where we failed."

"You think we'll fail?"

Wun shrugged. "Haven't we failed already? The sun is very old now. You know that, Tyler. Nothing lasts indefinitely. And under the circumstances, for us, even 'indefinitely' isn't a very long time."

Maybe it was the way he said it, smiling his sad little Martian sincerity-smile and leaning forward in his wicker chair, but the weight of the pronouncement was quietly shocking.

Not that it surprised me. We all knew we were doomed. Doomed, at the very least, to live out our lives under a shell that was the only thing protecting us from a hostile solar system. The sunlight that had made Mars habitable would cook the Earth if the Spin membrane was stripped away. And even Mars (in its own dark envelope) was rapidly slipping out of the so-called habitable zone. The mortal star that was the mother of all life had passed into bloody senescence and would kill us without conscience.

Life had been born on the fringe of an unstable nuclear reaction. That was true and it had always been true; it had been true before the Spin, even when the sky was clear and summer nights twinkled with distant, irrelevant stars. It had been true but it hadn't mattered because human life was short; countless generations would live and die in the span of a solar heartbeat. But now, God help us, we were outliving the sun. Either we would end up as cinders circling its corpse or we would be preserved into eternal night, encapsulated novelties with no real home in the universe.

"Tyler? Are you all right?"

"Yes," I said. Thinking, for some reason, of Diane. "Maybe the best we can hope for is a little understanding before the curtain comes down."

"Curtain?"

"Before the end."

"It's not much consolation," Wun admitted. "But yes, it may be the best we can hope for."

"Your people have known about the Spin for millennia. And in all that time you haven't been able to learn anything about the Hypotheticals?"

"No. I'm sorry. I don't have that to offer. About the physical nature of the Spin we have only a few speculations." (Which Jason had recently attempted to explain to me: something about temporal quanta, mostly mathematics and far beyond the reach of practical engineering, Martian or terrestrial.) "About the Hypotheticals themselves, nothing at all. As for what they want from us—" He shrugged. "Only more speculation. The question we asked ourselves was, what was special about the Earth when it was encapsulated? Why did the Hypotheticals wait to spin Mars, and what made them choose this particular moment in our history?"

"You have answers to that?"

One of his handlers knocked at the door and opened it. A balding guy in a tailored black suit. He spoke to Wun but he looked at me: "Just a reminder. We have the EU rep coming in. Five minutes." He held the door wide, expectantly. I stood up.

"Next time," Wun said.

"Soon, I hope."

"As soon as I can arrange it."

It was late and I was done for the day. I left through the north door. On my way to the parking lot I stopped at the wooden hoarding where the new addition to Perihelion was under construction. Between gaps in the security wall I could see a plain cinder-block building, huge external pressure tanks, pipes as thick as barrels plumbed through concrete embrasures. The ground was littered with yellow PTFE insulation and coiled copper tubing. A foreman in a white hard hat barked orders at men pushing wheelbarrows, men with safety goggles and steel-toed boots.

Men building an incubator for a new kind of life. This was where the replicators would be grown in cradles of liquid helium and prepped for their launch into the cold places of the universe: our heirs, in a sense, bound to live longer and travel farther than human beings ever would. Our final dialogue with the universe. Unless E.D. had his way and canceled the project entirely.

○ ○ ○

Molly and I took a beach walk that weekend.

It was a cloudless late-October Saturday. We had hiked a quarter mile of cigarette-stub-littered sand before the day got uncomfortably warm and the sun grew insistent, the ocean giving back the light in dazzling pinpoints, as if shoals of diamonds were swimming far offshore. Molly wore shorts and sandals and a white cotton T-shirt that had begun to stick to her body in alluring ways, a visor cap with the bill pulled down to shade her eyes.

"I never did understand this," she said, swiping her wrist across her forehead, turning back to face her own tracks in the sand.

"What's that, Moll?"

"The sun. I mean the sunlight. This light. It's fake, everybody says, but God, the heat: the *heat* is real."

"The sun's not fake exactly. The sun we see isn't the real sun, but this light would have originated there. It's managed by the Hypotheticals, the wavelengths stepped down and filtered—"

"I know, but I mean the way it rides the sky. Sunrise, sunset. If it's only a projection, how come it looks the same from Canada and South America? If the Spin barrier is only a few hundred miles up?"

I told her what Jason had once told me: the fake sun wasn't an illusion projected on a screen, it was a managed replica of sunlight passing *through* the screen from a source ninety million miles away, like a ray-trace program rendered on a colossal scale.

"Pretty fucking elaborate stage trick," Molly said.

"If they did it differently we'd all have died years ago. The planetary ecology needs a twenty-four-hour day." We had already lost a number of species that depended on moonlight to feed or mate.

"But it's a lie."

"If you want to call it that."

"A lie, I call it a lie. I'm standing here with the light of a lie on my face. A lie you can get skin cancer from. But I still don't understand it. I guess we won't, until we understand the Hypotheticals. If we ever do. Which I doubt."

You don't understand a lie, Molly said as we paralleled an ancient boardwalk gone white with salt, until you understand the motivation behind it. She said this glancing sidelong at me, eyes shadowed under her cap, sending me messages I couldn't decipher.

We spent the rest of the afternoon in my air-conditioned rental, reading, playing music, but Moll was restless and I hadn't quite come to terms with her raid on my computer, another indecipherable event. I loved Molly. Or at least I told myself I did. Or, if what I felt for her was not love, it was at least a plausible imitation, a convincing substitute.

What worried me was that she remained deeply unpredictable, as Spin-bent as the rest of us. I couldn't buy her gifts: there were things she wanted, but unless she had vocally admired something in a shop window I couldn't guess what they were. She kept her deepest needs deeply obscure. Maybe, like most secretive people, she assumed I was keeping important secrets of my own.

We had just finished dinner and started cleaning up when the phone rang. Molly picked it up while I dried my hands. "Uh-huh," she said. "No, he's here. Just wait a second." She muted the phone and said, "It's Jason. Do you want to talk to him? He sounds all freaked out."

"Of course I'll talk to him."

I took the receiver and waited. Molly gave me a long look, then rolled her eyes and left the kitchen. Privacy. "Jase? What's up?"

"I need you here, Tyler." His voice was tense, constricted. "Now."

"Got a problem?"

"Yes, I have a fucking problem. And I need you to come fix it."

"It's that urgent?"

"Would I be calling you if it wasn't?"

"Where are you?"

"Home."

"Okay, listen, it'll take some time if the traffic's bad—"

"Just get here," he said.

So I told Molly I had some urgent work to catch up on. She smiled, or maybe sneered, and said, "What work is that? Somebody missed an appointment? Delivering a baby? What?"

"I'm a doctor, Moll. Professional privilege."

"Being a doctor doesn't mean you're Jason Lawton's lapdog. You don't have to fetch every time he throws a stick."

"I'm sorry about cutting the evening short. Do you want me to give you a lift somewhere, or—?"

"No," she said. "I'll stay here until you're back." Staring at me defiantly, belligerently, almost wanting me to object.

But I couldn't argue. That would mean I didn't trust her. And I did trust her. Mostly. "I'm not sure how long I'll be."

"Doesn't matter. I'll curl up on the sofa and watch the tube. If that's okay with you?"

"As long as you're not bored."

"I promise I won't be bored."

o o o

Jason's barely furnished apartment was twenty miles up the highway, and on the way there I had to detour around a crime scene, a failed roadside attack on a bank truck that had killed a carful of Canadian tourists. Jase buzzed me into his building and when I knocked at his door he called out, "It's open."

The big front room was as spare as it ever had been, a parquet desert in which Jase had set up his Bedouin camp. He was lying on the sofa. The floor lamp next to the sofa put him in a hard, unflattering light. He was pale and his forehead was dotted with sweat. His eyes glittered.

"I thought you might not come," he said. "Thought maybe your hick girlfriend wouldn't let you out of the house."

I told him about the police detour. Then I said, "Do me a favor. Please don't talk about Molly that way."

"Please don't refer to her as an Idaho shitkicker with trailer-park sensibilities? Sure enough. Anything to oblige."

"What's the matter with you?"

"Interesting question. Many possible answers. Look."

He stood up.

It was a poor, feeble, ratcheting process. Jase was still tall, still slender, but the physical grace that had once seemed so effortless had deserted him. His arms flailed. His legs, when he managed to bring himself upright, jittered under him like jointed stilts. He blinked convulsively. "This is what's wrong with me," he said. Then, the anger coming on in another convulsive movement, his emotional state as volatile as his limbs: "Look at me! F-fuck, Tyler, *look at me!*"

"Sit back down, Jase. Let me examine you." I had brought my medical kit. I rolled up his sleeve and wrapped a BP cuff around his skinny arm. I could feel the muscle contracting under it, barely controlled.

His blood pressure was high and his pulse was fast. "You've been taking your anticonvulsants?"

"Of course I've been taking the fucking anticonvulsants."

"On schedule? No double-dosing? Because if you take too many, Jase, you're doing yourself more harm than good."

Jason sighed impatiently. Then he did something surprising. He reached behind my head and grabbed a handful of my hair, painfully, and tugged it down until my face was close to his. Words came out of him, a raging river of them.

"Don't get pedantic on me, Tyler. Don't do that, because I can't afford it right now. Maybe you have issues about my treatment. I'm sorry, but this is no time to take your fucking principles out for a walk. Too much is at stake. E.D. is flying in to Perihelion in the morning. E.D. thinks he has a trump card to play. E.D. would rather shut us down than let me ascend to his fucking throne. I can't let that happen, and look at me: do I look like I'm in any condition to commit an act of patricide?" His grip tightened until it hurt—he was still that strong—then he let go and with his other hand pushed me away. "So FIX ME! That's what you're *for,* isn't it?"

I pulled up a chair and sat silently until he lapsed back into the sofa, exhausted by his own outburst. He watched me take a syringe out of my kit and load it from a small brown bottle.

"What's that?"

"Temporary relief." In fact it was a harmless B-complex vitamin shot laced with a minor tranquilizer. Jason looked at it suspiciously but let me deliver it into his arm. A tiny bead of blood followed the needle out.

"You already know what I have to tell you," I said. "There's no cure for this problem."

"No *earthly* cure."

"What's that supposed to mean?"

"You know what it means."

He was talking about Wun Ngo Wen's longevity process.

The reconstruction, Wun had said, was also a cure for a long list of genetic disabilities. It would edit the AMS loop out of Jason's DNA, inhibiting the rogue proteins that were eroding his nervous system. "But that would take weeks," I said, "and anyway, I can't condone the idea of making you a guinea pig for an untested procedure."

"It's hardly untested. The Martians have been doing it for centuries, and the Martians are as human as we are. And I'm sorry, Tyler, but I'm not really interested in your professional scruples. They simply don't enter the equation."

"They do, though. As far as I'm concerned."

"Then the question is, how far are you concerned? If you don't want to be a part of it, step aside."

"The risk—"

"It's my risk, not yours." He closed his eyes. "Don't mistake this for arrogance or vanity, but it matters whether I live or die or even whether I can walk straight or pronounce my f-fucking consonants. It matters to the world, I mean. Because I'm in a uniquely important position. Not by accident. Not because I'm smart or virtuous. I was appointed. Basically, Tyler, I'm an artifact, a constructed object, engineered by E. D. Lawton the same way he and your father used to engineer airfoils. I'm doing the job he built me to do—running Perihelion, running the human response to the Spin."

"The president might disagree. Not to mention Congress. Or the U.N., for that matter."

"Please. I'm not delusional. That's the point. Running Perihelion means playing to the interested parties. All of them. E.D. knows that; he's perfectly cynical about it. He turned Perihelion into a dollar windfall for the aerospace industry and he did it by making friends and forging political alliances in high places. By cajoling and pleading and lobbying and funding friendly campaigns. He had a vision and he had contacts and he was in the right place at the right time; he stepped forward with the aerostat program and rescued the telecom industry from the Spin, and that dropped him into the company of powerful people—and he knows how to exploit an opportunity. Without E.D., there wouldn't be human beings on Mars. Without E. D. Lawton, Wun Ngo Wen wouldn't even exist. Give the old fucker credit. He's a great man."

"But?"

"But he's a man of his time. He's pre-Spin. His motives are archaic. The torch has been passed. Or will be, if I have anything to do with it."

"I don't know what that means, Jase."

"E.D. still thinks there's some personal advantage he can wring out of all this. He resents Wun Ngo Wen and he hates the idea of seeding the galaxy with replicators, not because it's too ambitious but because it's bad for business. The Mars project pumped trillions of dollars into aerospace. It made E.D. wealthier and more powerful than he ever dreamed of being. It made him a household name. And E.D. still thinks that matters. He thinks it matters the way it used to matter before the Spin, when you could play politics like a game, gamble for prizes. But Wun's proposal doesn't have that kind of payoff. Launching replicators is a trivial investment compared to terraforming Mars. We can do it with a couple of

Delta sevens and a cheap ion drive. A slingshot and a test tube is all it really takes."

"How is that bad for E.D.?"

"It doesn't do much to protect a collapsing industry. It hollows out his financial base. Worse, it takes him out of the spotlight. Suddenly everyone's going to be looking at Wun Ngo Wen—we're a couple of weeks away from a media shit-storm of unprecedented proportions—and Wun picked me as frontman for this project. The last thing E.D. wants is his ungrateful son and a wrinkly Martian dismantling his life's work and launching an armada that costs less to produce than a single commercial airliner."

"What would he prefer to do?"

"He's got a big-scale agenda worked out. Whole-system surveillance, he calls it. Looking for fresh evidence of activity by the Hypotheticals. Planetary surveyors from Mercury to Pluto, sophisticated listening posts in interplanetary space, fly-by missions to scout out the Spin artifacts here and at the Martian poles."

"Is that a bad idea?"

"It might yield a little trivial information. Eke out a little data and funnel cash into the industry. That's what it's designed to do. But what E.D. doesn't understand, what his *generation* doesn't truly understand—"

"What's that, Jase?"

"Is that the window is closing. The human window. Our time on Earth. The Earth's time in the universe. It's just about over. We have, I think, just one more realistic opportunity to understand what it means—what it *meant*—to have built a human civilization." His eyelids shuttered once, twice, slowly. Much of the wild tension had drained out of him. "What it means to have been singled out for this peculiar form of extinction. More than that, though. What it means . . . what it means . . ." He looked up. "What the fuck did you give me, Tyler?"

"Nothing serious. A mild anxiolytic."

"Quick fix?"

"Isn't that what you want?"

"I suppose so. I want to be presentable by morning, that's what I want."

"The medication isn't a cure. What you want me to do is like trying to repair a loose electrical connection by pushing more voltage through it. Might work, in the short term. But it's undependable and it puts unacceptable stress on other parts of the system. I would love to give you a good clean symptom-free day. I just don't want to kill you."

"If you *don't* give me a symptom-free day, you *might as well* kill me."

"All I have to offer you," I said, "is my professional judgment."

"And what can I expect from your professional judgment?"

"I can help. I think. A little. This time. *This time,* Jase. But there's not much room to maneuver. You have to face up to that."

"None of us has much room to maneuver. We all have to face up to that."

But he sighed and smiled when I opened the med kit again.

○ ○ ○

Molly was perched on the sofa when I got home, facing the TV square-on, watching a recently popular movie about elves, or maybe they were angels. The screen was full of fuzzy blue light. She switched it off when I came in. I asked her if anything had happened while I was gone.

"Not much. You got a phone call."

"Oh? Who was it?"

"Jason's sister. What's her name. Diane. The one in Arizona."

"Did she say what she wanted?"

"Just to talk. So we talked a little."

"Uh-huh. What did you talk about?"

Molly half turned, showing me her profile against the dim light from the bedroom. "You."

"Anything in particular?"

"Yeah. I told her to stop calling you because you have a new girlfriend. I told her I'd be handling your calls from now on."

I stared.

Molly bared her teeth in what I registered was meant to be

a smile. "Come on, Tyler, learn to take a joke. I told her you were out. Is that all right?"

"You told her I was out?"

"Yes, I told her you were out. I didn't say where. Because you didn't actually tell me."

"Did she say whether it was urgent?"

"Didn't sound urgent. Call her back if you want. Go ahead—I don't care."

But this, too, was a test. "It can wait," I said.

"Good." Her cheeks dimpled. "Because I have other plans."

SACRIFICIAL RITES

Jason, obsessed with E. D. Lawton's pending arrival, had neglected to mention that another guest was also expected at Perihelion: Preston Lomax, the current vice president of the United States and front-runner in the upcoming election.

Security was tight at the gates and there was a helicopter on the pad atop the hub of the Perihelion building. I recognized all these Code Red protocols from a series of visits by President Garland over the last month. The guard at the main entrance, the one who called me "Doc" and whose cholesterol levels I monitored once a month, tipped me off that it was Lomax this time.

I was just past the clinic door (Molly absent, a temp named Lucinda manning reception) when I got a paged message redirecting me to Jason's office in the executive wing. Four security perimeters later I was alone with him. I was afraid he'd ask for more medication. But last night's treatment had put him into a convincing if purely temporary remission. He stood up and came across the room with his tremorless hand extended, showing off: "Want to thank you for this, Ty."

"You're welcome, but I have to say it again—no guarantees."

"Noted. As long as I'm good for the day. E.D.'s due at noon."

"Not to mention the vice president."

"Lomax has been here since seven this morning. The man's an early riser. He spent a couple of hours conferencing with our Martian guest and I'm conducting the goodwill tour shortly. Speaking of which, Wun would like to see you if you have a few minutes free."

"Assuming national affairs aren't keeping him busy." Lomax was the man most likely to win the national vote next week—in a walkover, if the polls were to be trusted. Jase had been cultivating Lomax long before Wun's arrival, and Lomax was fascinated with Wun. "Is your father joining the tour?"

"Only because there's no polite way to keep him out."

"Do you foresee a problem?"

"I foresee many problems."

"Physically, though, you're all right?"

"I feel fine. But you're the doctor. All I need is a couple more hours, Tyler. I assume I'm good for that?"

His pulse was a little elevated—not surprisingly—but his AMS symptoms were effectively suppressed. And if the drugs had left him agitated or confused it didn't show. In fact he seemed almost radiantly calm, locked in some cool, lucid room at the back of his head.

So I went to see Wun Ngo Wen. Wun wasn't in his quarters; he had decamped to the small executive cafeteria, which had been cordoned off and encircled by tall men with coils of wire tucked behind their ears. He looked up when I came past the steam table and waved away the security clones who moved in to intercept me.

I sat down across a glass-topped table from him. He picked at a pallid salmon steak with a cafeteria fork and smiled serenely. I slouched in my chair to match his height. He could have used a booster seat.

But the food agreed with him. He had gained a little weight in his time at Perihelion, I thought. His suit, tailored a couple of months ago, was tight across his belly. He had neglected to button the matching vest. His cheeks were fuller, too, though they were as wrinkled as ever, the dark skin softly gullied.

"I hear you had a visitor," I said.

Wun nodded. "But not for the first time. I met with President Garland in Washington on several occasions and I've met with Vice President Lomax twice. The election is expected to bring him to power, people say."

"Not because he's especially well loved."

"I'm not in a position to judge him as a candidate," Wun said. "But he does ask interesting questions."

The endorsement made me feel a little protective. "I'm sure he's amiable when he wants to be. And he's done a decent job in office. But he spent a lot of his career as the most hated man on Capitol Hill. Party whip for three different administrations. Not much gets past him."

Wun grinned. "Do you think I'm naive, Tyler? Are you afraid Vice President Lomax will take advantage of me?"

"Not naive, exactly—"

"I'm a newcomer, admittedly. The finer political nuances are lost on me. But I'm several years older than Preston Lomax, and I've held public office myself."

"You have?"

"For three years," he said with detectable pride, "I was Agricultural Administrator for Ice Winds Canton."

"Ah."

"The governing body for most of the Kirioloj Delta. It wasn't the Presidency of the United States of America. There are no nuclear weapons at the disposal of the Agricultural Administration. But I did expose a corrupt local official who was falsifying crop reports by weight and selling his margin into the surplus market."

"A rake-off scheme?"

"If that's the term for it."

"So the Five Republics aren't free of corruption?"

Wun blinked, an event that rippled out along the convolute geography of his face. "No, how could they be? And why do so many terrestrials make that assumption? Had I come here from some other Earthly country—France, China, Texas—no one would be startled to hear about bribery or duplicity or theft."

"I guess not. But it's not the same."

"Isn't it? But you work here at Perihelion. You must have met some of the founding generation, as strange as that idea still seems to me—the men and women whose remote descendants we Martians are. Were they such ideal persons that you expect their progeny to be free of sin?"

"No, but—"

"And yet the misconception is almost universal. Even those books you gave me, written before the Spin—"

"You read them?"

"Yes, eagerly. I enjoyed them. Thank you. But even in those novels, the Martians . . ." He struggled after a thought.

"I guess some of them are a little saintly. . . ."

"Remote," he said. "Wise. Seemingly frail. Actually very powerful. The Old Ones. But to us, Tyler, *you're* the Old Ones. The elder species, the ancient planet. I would have thought the irony was inescapable."

I pondered that. "Even the H. G. Wells novel—"

"His Martians are barely seen. They're abstractly, indifferently evil. Not wise but clever. But devils and angels are brother and sister, if I understand the folklore correctly."

"But the more contemporary stories—"

"Those were deeply interesting, and the protagonists were at least human. But the truest pleasure of those stories is in the landscapes, don't you agree? And even so, they're *transformative* landscapes. A destiny behind every dune."

"And of course the Bradbury—"

"His Mars isn't Mars. But his Ohio makes me think of it."

"I understand what you're saying. You're just people. Mars isn't heaven. Agreed, but that doesn't mean Lomax won't try to use you for his own political purposes."

"And I mean to tell you that I'm fully aware of the possibility. The *certainty* would be more correct. Obviously I'll be used for political advantage, but that's the power I have: to bestow or withhold my approval. To cooperate or to be stubborn. The power to say the right word." He smiled again. His teeth were uniformly perfect, radiantly white. "Or not."

"So what *do* you want out of all this?"

He showed me his palms, a gesture both Martian and ter-

restrial. "Nothing. I'm a Martian saint. But it would be grati-
fying to see the replicators launched."

"Purely in the pursuit of knowledge?"

"That I *will* confess to, even if it is a saintly motive. To
learn at least something about the Spin—"

"And challenge the Hypotheticals?"

He blinked again. "I very much hope the Hypotheticals,
whoever or whatever they are, won't perceive what we're doing as a *challenge*."

"But if they do—"

"Why would they?"

"But if they do, they'll believe the challenge came from
Earth, not Mars."

Wun Ngo Wen blinked several more times. Then the smile
crept back: indulgent, approving. "You're surprisingly cynical yourself, Dr. Dupree."

"How un-Martian of me."

"Quite."

"And does Preston Lomax believe you're an angel?"

"Only he can answer that question. The last thing he said
to me—" Here Wun dropped his Oxford diction for a note-
perfect Preston Lomax impression, brusque and chilly as a
winter seashore: *"It's a privilege to talk to you, Ambassador
Wen. You speak your mind directly. Very refreshing for an old
D.C. hand like myself."*

The impression was startling, coming from someone who
had been speaking English for only a little over a year. I told
him so.

"I'm a scholar," he said. "I've been reading English since I
was a child. Speaking it is another matter. But I do have a talent for languages. It's one of the reasons I'm here. Tyler, may
I ask another favor of you? Would you be willing to bring me
more novels?"

"I'm all out of Martian stories, I'm afraid."

"Not Mars. Any sort of novel. Anything, anything you
consider important, anything that matters to you or gave you
a little pleasure."

"There must be plenty of English professors who'd be
happy to work up a reading list."

"I'm sure there are. But I'm asking *you*."

"I'm not a scholar. I like to read, but it's pretty random and mostly contemporary."

"All the better. I'm alone more often than you might think. My quarters are comfortable but I can't leave them without elaborate planning. I can't go out for a meal, I can't see a motion picture or join a social club. I could ask my minders for books, but the last thing I want is a work of fiction that's been approved by a committee. But an honest book is almost as good as a friend."

This was as close as Wun had come to complaining about his position at Perihelion, his position on Earth. He was happy enough during his waking hours, he said, too busy for nostalgia and still excited by the strangeness of what for him would always be an alien world. But at night, on the verge of sleep, he sometimes imagined he was walking the shore of a Martian lake, watching shore birds flock and wheel over the waves, and in his mind it was always a hazy afternoon, the light tinted by streamers of the ancient dust that still rose from the deserts of Noachis to color the sky. In this dream or vision he was alone, he said, but he knew there were others waiting for him around the next curve of the rocky shore. They might be friends or strangers, they might even be his lost family; he knew only that he would be welcomed by them, touched, drawn close, embraced. But it was only a dream.

"When I read," he said to me, "I hear the echo of those voices."

I promised to bring him books. But now we had business. There was a flurry of activity in the security cordon by the door of the cafeteria. One of the suits came across the floor and said, "They're asking for you upstairs."

Wun abandoned his meal and began clambering out of his chair. I told him I'd see him later.

The suit turned to me. "You too," he said. "They're asking for both of you."

o o o

Security hustled us to a boardroom adjoining Jason's office, where Jase and a handful of Perihelion division heads were facing a delegation that included E. D. Lawton and the likely next president, Preston Lomax. No one looked happy.

I faced E. D. Lawton, whom I hadn't seen since my mother's funeral. His gauntness had begun to look almost pathological, as if something vital had leaked out of him. Starched white cuffs, bony brown wrists. His hair was sparse, limp, and randomly combed. But his eyes were still quick. E.D.'s eyes were always lively when he was angry.

Preston Lomax, on the other hand, just looked impatient. Lomax had come to Perihelion to be photographed with Wun (photos for release after the official White House announcement) and to confer about the replicator strategy, which he was planning to endorse. E.D. was here on the weight of his reputation. He had talked himself into the vice president's pre-election tour and apparently hadn't stopped talking since.

During the hour-long Perihelion tour E.D. had questioned, doubted, derided, or viewed with alarm virtually every statement Jason's division heads made, especially when the junket wound past the new incubator labs. But (according to Jenna Wylie, the cryonics team leader, who explained this to me later) Jason had answered each of his father's outbursts with a patient and probably well-rehearsed rebuttal of his own. Which had driven E.D. to fresh heights of indignation, which in turn made him sound, according to Jenna, "like some crazed Lear raving about perfidious Martians."

The battle was still under way when Wun and I entered. E.D. leaned into the conference table, saying, "Bottom line, it's unprecedented, it's untested, and it embraces a technology we don't understand or control."

And Jason smiled in the manner of a man far too polite to embarrass a respected but cranky elder. "Obviously, nothing we do is risk-free. But—"

But here we were. A few of those present hadn't seen Wun before, and they self-identified, staring like startled sheep when they noticed him. Lomax cleared his throat. "Excuse me, but what I need right now is a word with Jason and our new arrivals—privately, if possible? Just a moment or two."

So the crowd dutifully filed out, including E.D., who looked, however, not dismissed but triumphant.

Doors closed. The upholstered silence of the boardroom settled around us like fresh snow. Lomax, who still hadn't acknowledged us, addressed Jason. "I know you told me we'd take some flak. Still—"

"It's a lot to deal with. I understand."

"I don't like having E.D. outside the tent pissing in. It's unseemly. But he can't do us any real harm, assuming . . ."

"Assuming there's no substance to what he says. I assure you, there's not."

"You think he's senile."

"I wouldn't go that far. Do I think his judgment has become questionable? Yes, I do."

"You know those accusations are flying both ways."

This was as close as I had been or would ever be to a sitting president. Lomax hadn't been elected yet, but only the formalities stood between him and the office. As V.P. Lomax had always seemed a little dour, a little brooding, rocky Maine to Garland's ebullient Texas, the ideal presence at a state funeral. During the campaign he had learned to smile more often but the effort was never quite convincing; political cartoonists inevitably accentuated the frown, the lower lip tucked in as if he were biting back a malediction, eyes as chilly as a Cape Cod winter.

"Both ways. You're talking about E.D.'s insinuations about my health."

Lomax sighed. "Frankly, your father's opinion on the practicality of the replicator project doesn't carry much weight. It's a minority point of view and likely to remain that way. But yes, I have to admit, the charges he made today are a little troubling." He turned to face me. "That's why you're here, Dr. Dupree."

Now Jason aimed his attention at me, and his voice was cautious, carefully neutral. "It seems E.D.'s been making some fairly wild claims. He says I'm suffering from, what was it, an aggressive brain disease—?"

"An untreatable neurological deterioration," Lomax said, "which is interfering with Jason's ability to oversee operations here at Perihelion. What do you say to that, Dr. Dupree?"

"I guess I would say Jason can speak for himself."

"I already have," Jase said. "I told Vice President Lomax all about my MS."

From which he did not actually suffer. It was a cue. I cleared my throat. "Multiple sclerosis isn't entirely curable, but it's more than just controllable. An MS patient today can expect a life span as long and productive as anyone else's. Maybe Jase has been reluctant to talk about it, and that's his privilege, but MS is nothing to be embarrassed about."

Jase gave me a hard look I couldn't interpret. Lomax said, "Thank you," a little dryly. "I appreciate the information. By the way, do you happen to know a Dr. Malmstein? David Malmstein?"

Followed by a silence that gaped like the jaws of a steel trap.

"Yes," I said, maybe a tick too late.

"This Dr. Malmstein is a neurologist, is he not?"

"Yes, he is."

"Have you consulted him in the past?"

"I consult with lots of specialists. It's part of what I do as a physician."

"Because, according to E.D., you called in this Malmstein regarding Jason's, uh, grave neurological disorder."

Which explained the frigid look Jase was shooting me. Someone had talked to E.D. about this. Someone close. But it hadn't been me.

I tried not to think about who it might have been. "I'd do the same for any patient with a possible MS diagnosis. I run a good clinic here at Perihelion, but we don't have the kind of diagnostic equipment Malmstein can access at a working hospital."

Lomax, I think, recognized this as a nonanswer, but he tossed the ball back to Jase: "Is Dr. Dupree telling the truth?"

"Of course he is."

"You trust him?"

"He's my personal physician. Of course I trust him."

"Because, no offense, I wish you well but I don't really give a shit about your medical problems. What concerns me is whether you can give us the support we need and see this project through to the end. Can you do that?"

"As long as we're funded, yes sir, I'll be here."

"And how about you, Ambassador Wen? Does this raise any alarms with you? Any concerns or questions about the future of Perihelion?"

Wun pursed his lips, three quarters of a Martian smile. "No concerns whatsoever. I trust Jason Lawton implicitly. I also trust Dr. Dupree. He's my personal physician as well."

Which caused both Jason and me to stifle our astonishment, but it closed the deal with Lomax. He shrugged. "All right. I apologize for bringing it up. Jason, I hope your health remains good and I hope you weren't offended by the tone of the questions, but given E.D.'s status I felt I had to ask."

"I understand," Jase said. "As for E.D.—"

"Don't worry about your father."

"I'd hate to see him humiliated."

"He'll be quietly sidelined. I think that's a given. If he insists on going public—" Lomax shrugged. "In that case I'm afraid it's his own mental capacity people will challenge."

"Of course," Jason said, "we all hope that's not necessary."

o o o

I spent the next hour in the clinic. Molly hadn't shown up this morning and Lucinda had been doing all the bookings. I thanked her and told her to take the rest of the day off. I thought about making a couple of phone calls, but I didn't want them routed through the Perihelion system.

I waited until I had seen Lomax's helicopter lift off and his imperial cavalcade depart by the front gates; then I cleared my desk and tried to think about what I wanted to do. I found my hands were a little shaky. Not MS. Anger, maybe. Outrage. Pain. I wanted to diagnose it, not experience it. I wanted to banish it to the index pages of the *Diagnostic and Statistical Manual.*

I was on my way past reception when Jason came through the door.

He said, "I want to thank you for backing me up. I assume that means you aren't the one who told E.D. about Malmstein."

"I wouldn't do that, Jase."

"I accept that. But someone did. And that presents a problem. Because how many people are aware I've been seeing a neurologist?"

"You, me, Malmstein, whoever works in Malmstein's office—"

"Malmstein didn't know E.D. was looking for dirt and neither did his staff. E.D. must have found out about Malmstein from a closer source. If not you or me—"

Molly. He didn't have to say it.

"We can't blame her without any kind of evidence."

"Speak for yourself. You're the one who's sleeping with her. Did you keep records on my meetings with Malmstein?"

"Not here in the office."

"At home?"

"Yes."

"You showed these to her?"

"Of course not."

"But she might have gained access to them when you weren't aware of it."

"I suppose so." Yes.

"And she's not here to answer questions. Did she call in sick?"

I shrugged. "She didn't call in at all. Lucinda tried to get hold of her, but her phone isn't answering."

He sighed. "I don't exactly blame you for this. But you have to admit, Tyler, you've made a lot of questionable choices here."

"I'll deal with it," I said.

"I know you're angry. Hurt and angry. I don't want you to walk out of here and do something that will make things worse. But I do want you to consider where you stand on this project. Where your loyalties lie."

"I know where they lie," I said.

○ ○ ○

I tried to reach Molly from my car but she still wasn't answering. I drove to her apartment. It was a warm day. The low-rise stucco complex where she lived was enshrouded in lawn-sprinkler haze. The fungal smell of wet garden soil infiltrated the car.

I was circling toward visitor parking when I caught sight of Moll stacking boxes in the back of a battered white U-Haul trailer hitched to the rear bumper of her three-year-old Ford. I pulled over in front of her. She spotted me and said something I couldn't hear but which looked a lot like "Oh, shit!" But she stood her ground when I got out of my car.

"You can't park there," she said. "You're blocking the exit."

"Are you going somewhere?"

Molly placed a cardboard box labeled DISHES on the corrugated floor of the U-Haul. "What does it look like?"

She was wearing tan slacks, a denim shirt, and a handkerchief tied over her hair. I came closer and she took an equivalent three steps back, clearly frightened.

"I'm not going to hurt you," I said.

"So what do you want?"

"I want to know who hired you."

"I don't know what you're talking about."

"Did you deal with E.D. himself or did he use an intermediary?"

"Shit," she said, gauging the distance between herself and the car door. "Just let me go, Tyler. What do you want from me? What's the point of this?"

"Did you go to him and make an offer or did he call you first? And when did all this start, Moll? Did you fuck me for information or did you sell me out at some point after the first date?"

"Go to hell."

"How much were you paid? I'd like to know how much I'm worth."

"Go to hell. What does it matter, anyway? It's not—"

"Don't tell me it's not about money. I mean, is some *principle* involved here?"

"Money *is* the principle." She dusted her hands on her slacks, a little less frightened now, a little more defiant.

"What is it you want to buy, Moll?"

"What do I want to *buy*? The only important thing any-body *can* buy. A better death. A cleaner, better death. One of these mornings the sun's going to come up and it won't *stop* coming up until the whole fucking sky is on fire. And I'm sorry, but I want to live somewhere nice until that happens. Somewhere by myself. Some place as comfortable as I can make it. And when that last morning arrives I want some ex-pensive pharmaceuticals to take me over the line. I want to go to sleep before the screaming starts. Really, Tyler. That's all I want, that's the only thing in this world I really really want, and thank you, thank you for making it possible." She was frowning angrily, but a tear dislodged and slid down her cheek. "Please move your car."

I said, "A nice house and a bottle of pills? That's your price?"

"There's no one looking out for me but me."

"This sounds pathetic, but I thought we could look out for each other."

"That would mean trusting you. And no offense, but—look at you. Skating through life like you're waiting for an answer or waiting for a savior or just permanently on hold."

"I'm trying to be reasonable here, Moll."

"Oh, I don't doubt it. If reasonability was a knife I'd be losing blood. Poor reasonable Tyler. But I figured that out, too. It's revenge, isn't it? All that sweet saintliness you wear like your own suit of clothes. It's your revenge on the world for disappointing you. The world didn't give you what you want, and you're not giving anything back but sympathy and aspirin."

"Molly—"

"And don't you dare say you love me, because I know that's not true. You don't know the difference between *being* in love and *conducting yourself* like you're in love. It's nice you picked me, but it could have been anybody, and believe me, Tyler, it would have been just as disappointing, one way or another."

I turned and walked back to my own car, a little unsteadily, shocked less by the betrayal than by the finality of it, intima-cies wiped out like penny stocks in a market crash. Then I turned back. "How about you, Moll? I know you were paid for information, but is that why you fucked me in the first place?"

"I *fucked* you," she said, "because I was *lonely*."

"Are you lonely now?"

"I never stopped," she said.

I drove away.

THE TICKING OF EXPENSIVE CLOCKS

The federal election was coming up fast. Jason intended to
use it for cover.

"Fix me," he had said. And, he insisted, there was a way to
do that. It was unorthodox. It wasn't FDA-approved. But it
was a therapy with a long and well-documented history. And
he made it clear he meant to take advantage of it, whether I
cooperated in the effort or not.

And because Molly had almost stripped him of everything
that was important to him—and left me among the
wreckage—I agreed to help. (Thinking, ironically, of what
E.D. had said to me years ago: *I expect you to look out for
him. I expect you to exercise your judgment.* Was that what I
was doing?)

In the days before the November election Wun Ngo Wen
briefed us on the procedure and its attendant risks.

Conferring with Wun wasn't easy. The problem wasn't so
much the web of security surrounding him, though that was
difficult enough to negotiate, but the crowd of analysts and
specialists who had been feeding at his archives like hum-

mingbirds at nectar. These were reputable scholars, vetted by the FBI and Homeland Security, sworn to secrecy at least *pro tem,* mesmerized by the vast data banks of Martian wisdom Wun had carried with him to Earth. The digital data amounted to more than five hundred volumes of astronomy, biology, math, physics, medicine, history, and technology at a thousand pages per volume, much of it considerably in advance of terrestrial knowledge. Had the entire contents of the Library of Alexandria been recovered by time machine it could hardly have produced a greater scholarly feeding frenzy.

These people were under pressure to complete their work before the official announcement of Wun's presence. The federal government wanted at least a rough index to the archives (much of which was in approximate English but some of which was written in Martian scientific script) before foreign governments began to demand equal access to it. The State Department planned to produce and distribute sanitized copies from which certain potentially valuable or dangerous technologies had been excised or "presented in summary form," the originals to remain highly classified.

Thus whole tribes of scholars battled for and jealously guarded their access to Wun, who could interpret or explain lacunae in the Martian text. On several occasions I was chased out of Wun's quarters by frantically polite men and women from "the high-energy physics group" or "the molecular biology group" demanding their negotiated quarter hour. Wun occasionally introduced me to these people but none of them was ever happy to see me, and the medical sciences team leader was alarmed almost to the point of tachycardia when Wun announced he'd chosen me as his personal physician.

Jase reassured the scholars by hinting that I was part of the "socialization process" by which Wun was polishing his terrestrial manners outside the context of politics or science, and I promised the med team leader I wouldn't provide medical treatment to Wun without her direct involvement. A rumor spread among the research people that I was a civilian opportunist who had charmed his way into Wun's inner circle and that my payoff would be a fat book contract after Wun went public. The rumor arose spontaneously but we did nothing to discourage it; it served our purposes.

Access to pharmaceuticals was easier than I'd expected. Wun had arrived on Earth with an entire pharmacopoeia of Martian drugs, none of which had terrestrial counterparts and any of which, he claimed, he might one day need in order to treat himself. The medical supplies had been confiscated from his landing craft but had been returned once his ambassadorial status was established. (Samples having no doubt been collected by the government; but Wun doubted that crude analysis would reveal the purpose of any of these highly engineered materials.) Wun simply supplied a few vials of raw drug to Jason, who carried them out of Perihelion in an obscuring cloud of executive privilege.

Wun briefed me on dosage, timing, contraindications, and potential problems. I was dismayed by the long list of attendant dangers. Even on Mars, Wun said, the mortality rate from the transition to Fourth was a nontrivial 0.1 percent, and Jason's case was complicated by his AMS.

But without treatment Jason's prognosis was even worse. And he would go ahead with this whether I approved of it or not—in a sense, the prescribing physician was Wun Ngo Wen, not me. My role was simply to oversee the procedure and treat any unexpected side effects. Which soothed my conscience, although the argument would have been hard to defend in court—Wun might have "prescribed" the drugs, but it wasn't his hand that would put them into Jason's body.

It would be mine.

Wun Ngo Wen wouldn't even be with us. Jase had booked a three-week leave of absence for the end of November, early December, by which time Wun would have become a global celebrity, a name (however unusual) everyone recognized. Wun would be busy addressing the United Nations and accepting the hospitality of our planet's somewhat bloodstained collection of monarchs, mullahs, presidents, and prime ministers, while Jason sweated and vomited his way toward better health.

We needed a place to go. A place where he could be inconspicuously sick, a place where I could attend him without attracting unwanted attention, but civilized enough that I could call an ambulance if things went wrong. Somewhere comfortable. Somewhere quiet.

"I know the perfect place," Jason said.

"Where's that?"

"The Big House," he said.

I laughed, until I realized he was serious.

○ ○ ○

Diane didn't call back until a week after Lomax's visit to Perihelion, a week after Molly left town to claim whatever reward E. D. Lawton or his hired detectives had promised her.

Sunday afternoon. I was alone in my rental. A sunny day, but the blinds were pulled. All week, balancing time between patients at the Perihelion clinic and secretive tutorials with Wun and Jase, I'd been staring down the barrel of this empty weekend. It was good to be busy, I reasoned, because when you were busy you were awash in the countless but comprehensible daily problems that crowd out pain and stifle remorse. That was healthy. That was a coping process. Or at least a delaying tactic. Useful but, alas, temporary. Because sooner or later the noise fades, the crowds disperse, and you go home to the burned-out lightbulb, the empty room, the unmade bed.

It was pretty bad. I wasn't even sure how to feel—or rather, which of the several conflicting and incompatible modes of pain I ought to acknowledge first. "You're better off without her," Jase had said a couple of times, and that was at least as true as it was banal: better off without her, but better still if I could make sense of her, if I could decide whether Molly had used me or had punished me for using her, whether my chilly and perhaps slightly counterfeit love equaled her cold and profitable repudiation of it.

Then the phone rang, which was embarrassing because I was busy stripping the sheets from my bed, balling them up for a trip to the laundry room, lots of detergent and scalding hot water to bleach out Molly's aura. You don't want to be interrupted at a task like that. Makes you feel the tiniest bit self-conscious. But I'd always been a slave to a ringing phone. I picked up.

"Tyler?" Diane said. "Is that you, Ty? Are you alone?"

I admitted that I was alone.

"Good, I'm glad I finally got hold of you. I wanted to tell you, we're changing our phone number. Unlisting it. But in case you need to get in touch with me—"

She recited the private number, which I scribbled on a handy napkin. "Why are you unlisting your phone?" She and Simon had only a single static land line between them, but I guessed that was a devotional penance, like wearing wool or eating whole grains.

"For one thing we've been getting these odd calls from E.D. A couple of times he called late at night and started haranguing Simon. He sounded a little drunk, frankly. E.D. hates Simon, E.D. hated Simon from the get-go, but after we moved to Phoenix we never heard from him. Until now. The silence was hurtful. But this is worse."

Diane's telephone number might have been something else Molly filched from my household tracker and passed on to E.D. I couldn't explain that to Diane without violating my security oath, for the same reason I couldn't mention Wun Ngo Wen or ice-eating replicators. But I did tell her that Jason had been engaged in a struggle with his father over control of Perihelion, and Jason had come out on top, and maybe that's what was bothering E.D.

"Could be," Diane said. "Coming so soon after the divorce."

"What divorce? Are you talking about E.D. and Carol?"

"Jason didn't tell you? E.D.'s been living in a rental in Georgetown since May. The negotiations are still going on, but it looks like Carol gets the Big House and maintenance payments and E.D. gets everything else. The divorce was his idea, not hers. Which is maybe understandable. Carol's been just this side of an alcoholic coma for decades. She wasn't much of a mother and she can't have been much of a wife for E.D."

"You're saying you approve?"

"Hardly. I haven't changed my mind about him. He was an awful, indifferent parent—at least to me. I didn't like him and he didn't care whether I liked him. But I wasn't in awe of him, either, not the way Jason was. Jason saw him as this monumental king of industry, this towering Washington mover and shaker—"

"Isn't he?"

"He's successful and he's got some leverage, but this stuff is all relative, Ty. There are ten thousand E. D. Lawtons in this country. E.D. would never have gotten anywhere if his father and his uncle hadn't bankrolled his first business—which I'm sure they expected to function as a tax write-off, nothing more. E.D. was good at what he did, and when the Spin opened up an opportunity he took advantage of it, and that brought him to the attention of genuinely powerful people. But he was still basically nouveau riche as far as the big boys were concerned. He never had that Yale-Harvard-Skull-and-Bones thing going for him. No cotillion balls for me. We were the poor kids on the block. I mean, it was a nice block, but there's old money and there's new money, and we were definitely new money."

"I guess it looked different," I said, "from across the lawn. How's Carol holding up?"

"Carol's medicine comes out of the same bottle it ever did. What about you? How are things with you and Molly?"

"Molly's gone," I said.

"Gone as in 'gone to the store,' or—"

"Plain gone. We broke up. I don't have a cute euphemism for it."

"I'm sorry, Tyler."

"Thank you, but it's for the best. Everybody says so."

"Simon and I are doing all right," she said, though I hadn't asked. "The church thing is hard on him."

"More church politics?"

"Jordan Tabernacle's in some kind of legal trouble. I don't know all the details. We're not directly involved, but Simon's taking it pretty hard. You sure you're okay, though? You sound a little hoarse."

"I'll survive," I said.

o o o

The morning before the election I packed a couple of suit-cases (fresh clothes, a brace of paperback books, my medical kit), drove to Jason's place, and picked him up for the drive to Virginia. Jase was still fond of quality cars, but we needed to travel inconspicuously. My Honda, therefore, not his Porsche. The interstates weren't safe for Porsches these days.

The Garland presidency had been good times for anybody with an income over half a million dollars, hard times for everybody else. That was pretty obvious from the look of the road, a rolling tableau of warehouse retailers bookended by boarded-over malls, parking lots where squatters lived in tireless automobiles, highway towns subsisting on the in-come from a Stuckey's and a radar trap. Warning signs posted by the state police announced NO STOPPING AFTER DARK or VERIFIED 911 CALL REQUIRED FOR PROMPT EMER-GENCY RESPONSE. Highway piracy had cut the volume of small-vehicle traffic by half. We spent much of the drive bracketed between eighteen-wheel rigs, some of them in con-spicuously poor repair, and camo-green troop trucks servic-ing various military bases.

But we didn't talk about any of that. And we didn't talk about the election, which was in any case a foregone conclusion, Lo-max outpolling any of the two major and three minor rival can-didates. We didn't talk about ice-eating replicators or Wun Ngo Wen and we surely didn't talk about E. D. Lawton. Instead we talked about old times and good books, and much of the time we didn't talk at all. I had loaded the dashboard memory with the kind of angular, contrarian jazz I knew Jason liked: Charlie Parker, Thelonious Monk, Sonny Rollins—people who had long ago fathomed the distance between the street and the stars.

We pulled up in front of the Big House at dusk.

The house was brightly lit, big windows butter yellow un-der a sky the color of iridescent ink. Election weather was chilly this year. Carol Lawton came down from the porch to meet the car, her small body shrouded in paisley scarves and a knitted sweater. She was nearly sober, judging by her steady if slightly overcalculated gait.

Jason unfolded himself slowly, cautiously from the passen-ger seat.

Jase was in remission, or as close as he came to remission these days. With a little effort he could pass for normal. What surprised me was that he stopped making the effort as soon as we arrived at the Big House. He careened through the entrance hall to the dining room. No servants were present—Carol had arranged for us to have the house to ourselves for a couple of weeks—but the cook had left a platter of cold meats and vegetables in case we arrived hungry. Jason slumped into a chair.

Carol and I joined him. Carol had aged visibly since my mother's death. Her hair was so fine now that the contours of her skull showed through it, pink and simian, and when I took her arm it felt like kindling under silk. Her cheeks were sunken. Her eyes had the brittle, nervous alacrity of a drinker at least temporarily on the wagon. When I said it was good to see her she smiled ruefully: "Thank you, Tyler. I know how awful I look. Gloria Swanson in *Sunset Boulevard*. Not quite ready for my close-up, thank you very effing much." I didn't know what she was talking about. "But I endure. How is Jason?"

"Same as always," I said.

"You're sweet for prevaricating. But I know—well, I won't say I know all about it. But I know he's ill. He told me that much. And I know he's expecting you to treat him for it. Some unorthodox but effective treatment." She took her arm away and looked into my eyes. "It is *effective,* isn't it, this medication you propose to give him?"

I was too startled to say anything but, "Yes."

"Because he made me promise not to ask questions. I suppose that's all right. Jason trusts you. Therefore I trust you. Even though when I look at you I can't help seeing the child who lives in the house across the lawn. But I see a child when I look at Jason, too. Vanished children—I can't think where I lost them."

○ ○ ○

That night I slept in a guest room at the Big House, a room I had only glimpsed from the hallway during the years I lived on the property.

I slept some of the night, anyway. Some of it I spent lying awake, trying to gauge the legal risk I had assumed by coming here. I didn't know exactly which laws or protocols Jase might have violated by smuggling prepared Martian pharmaceuticals off the Perihelion campus, but I had already made myself an accessory to the act.

Come the next morning Jason wondered where we ought to store the several vials of clear liquid Wun had passed on to him—enough to treat four or five people. ("In case we drop a suitcase," he had explained at the beginning of the trip. "Redundancy.")

"Are you expecting a search?"

I pictured federal functionaries in biohazard suits swarming up the steps of the Big House.

"Of course not. But it's never a bad idea to hedge a risk." He gave me a closer look, though his eyes jerked to the left every few seconds, another symptom of his disease. "Feeling a little apprehensive?"

I said we could conceal the spares in the house across the lawn, unless they needed refrigeration.

"According to Wun they're chemically stable under any condition short of thermonuclear warfare. But a warrant for the Big House would cover the entire property."

"I don't know about warrants. I do know where the hiding places are."

"Show me," Jason said.

So we trooped across the lawn, Jason following a little unsteadily behind me. It was early afternoon, election day, but in the grassy space between the two houses it might have been any autumn, any year. Somewhere off in the wooded patch straddling the creek a bird announced itself, a single note that began boldly but faded like a reconsidered thought. Then we reached my mother's house and I turned the key and opened the door into a deeper stillness.

The house had been periodically cleaned and dusted but essentially closed since my mother's death. I hadn't been back to organize her effects, no other family existed, and Carol had preferred to maintain the building rather than change it. But it wasn't timeless. Far from it. Time had nested here. Time had made itself at home. The front room smelled of enclosure, of the essences that seep out of undisturbed upholstery, yellow paper, settled fabric. In winter, Carol told me later, the house was kept just warm enough to prevent the pipes from freezing; in summer the curtains were drawn against the heat. It was cool today, inside and out.

Jason came across the threshold trembling. His gait had been ragged all morning, which was why he had let me carry the pharmaceuticals (apart from what I had already set aside for his treatment), a half pound or so of glass and biochemicals in a foam-padded leather overnight bag.

"This is the first time I've been here," he said shyly, "since before she died. Is it stupid to say I miss her?"

"No, not stupid."

"She was the first person I ever noticed being kind to me. All the kindness in the Big House came in the door with Belinda Dupree."

I led him through the kitchen to the half-size door that opened into the basement. The small house on the Lawton property had been designed to resemble a New England cottage, or someone's notion of one, down to the rude concrete-slab cellar with a ceiling low enough that Jason had to stoop to follow me. The space was just big enough to contain a furnace, water heater, washing machine and dryer. The air was even colder here and it had a moist, mineral scent.

I crouched into the nook behind the sheet-metal body of the furnace, one of those dusty cul-de-sacs even professional cleaners habitually ignore. I explained to Jase that there was a cracked slab of drywall here, and with a little dexterity you could pry it out to reveal the small uninsulated gap between the pine studs and the foundation wall.

"Interesting," Jason said from where he stood a yard behind me and around the angle of the quiescent furnace. "What did you keep in there, Tyler? Back issues of *Gent*?"

When I was ten I had kept certain toys here, not because I was afraid anyone would steal them but because it was fun knowing they were hidden and that only I could find them. Later on I stashed less innocent things: several brief attempts at a diary, letters to Diane never delivered or even finished, and, yes, though I wouldn't admit it to Jason, printouts of some relatively tame Internet porn. All these guilty secrets had been disposed of long ago.

"Should have brought a flashlight," Jase said. The single overhead bulb cast negligible light into this cobwebbed corner.

"There used to be one on the table by the fuse box." There still was. I backed out of the gap long enough to take it from Jason's hand. It emitted the watery, pale glow of a dying battery pack, but it worked well enough that I could find the loose chunk of drywall without groping. I lifted it away and slid the overnight bag into the space behind it, then fitted the drywall in place and brushed chalky dust over the visible seams.

But before I could back out I dropped the flashlight and it rolled even farther into the spidery shadows behind the furnace. I grimaced and reached for it, following the flickery glow. Touched the barrel of it. Touched something else. Something hollow but substantial. A box.

I pulled it closer.

"You almost finished in there, Ty?"

"One second," I said.

I trained the light on the box. It was a shoe box. A shoe box with a dusty New Balance logo printed on it and a different legend written over that in fat black ink: MEMENTOS (SCHOOL).

It was the box missing from my mother's étagère upstairs, the one I hadn't been able to find after her funeral.

"Having trouble?" Jason asked.

"No," I said.

I could investigate later. I pushed the box back where I'd found it and crawled out of the dusty space. Stood up and brushed my hands. "I guess we're done here."

"Remember this for me," Jason said. "In case I forget."

○ ○ ○

That night we watched the election returns on the Lawtons' impressively large but outdated video rig. Carol had misplaced her corrective lenses and sat close to the screen, blinking at it. She had spent most of her adult life ignoring politics—"That was always E.D.'s department"—and we had to explain who some of the major players were. But she seemed to enjoy the sense of occasion. Jason made gentle jokes and Carol obliged him by laughing, and when she laughed I could see a little of Diane in her face.

She tired easily, though, and she had gone to her room by the time the networks began calling states. No surprises there. In the end Lomax collected all the Northeast and most of the Midwest and West. He did less well in the South, but even there the dissenting vote was split almost evenly between old-line Democrats and the Christian Conservatives.

We started clearing away our coffee cups about the time the last opposing candidate delivered a grimly polite concession.

"So the good guys win," I said.

Jase smiled. "I'm not sure any of those were running."

"I thought Lomax was good for us."

"Maybe. But don't make the mistake of thinking Lomax cares about Perihelion or the replicator program, except as a convenient way to lowball the space budget and make it look like a great leap forward. The federal money he frees up will be dumped into the military budget. That's why E.D. couldn't put together any real anti-Lomax sentiment from his old aerospace cronies. Lomax won't let Boeing or Lockheed Martin starve. He just wants them to retool."

"For defense," I supplied. The lull in global conflict that had followed the initial confusion of the Spin was long past. Maybe a military refit wasn't such a bad idea.

"If you believe what Lomax says."

"Don't you?"

"I'm afraid I can't afford to."

On that note I retired to bed.

In the morning I administered the first injection. Jason stretched out on a sofa in the Lawtons' big front room, facing the window. He wore jeans and a cotton shirt and looked casually patrician, frail but at ease. If he was frightened he wasn't showing it. He rolled up his right sleeve to expose the crook of his elbow.

I took a syringe from my kit, attached a sterile needle, and filled it from one of the vials of clear liquid we had held back from the hiding place. Wun had rehearsed this with me. The protocols of the Fourth Age. On Mars there would have been a quiet ceremony and a soothing environment. Here we made do with November sunlight and the ticking of expensive clocks.

I swabbed his skin prior to the injection. "You don't have to watch," I said.

"But I want to," he said. "Show me how it's done."

He always did like to know how things worked.

○ ○ ○

The injection produced no immediate effects, but by noon the next day Jason was running a degree of fever.

Subjectively, he said, it was no worse than a mild cold, and by midafternoon he was begging me to take my thermometer and my pressure cuff and—well, take them elsewhere, was the gist of it.

So I turned up my collar against the rain (a blank, dumbly persistent rain that had started during the night and persisted through the afternoon) and crossed the lawn once more to my mother's house, where I rescued MEMENTOS (SCHOOL) from the basement and carried it up to the front room.

Rain-dim light came through the curtains. I switched on a lamp.

My mother had died at the age of fifty-six. For eighteen years I had shared this house with her. That was a little over one third of her life. Of the remaining two thirds I had seen only what she had chosen to show me. She had talked about Bingham, her home town, from time to time. I knew, for instance, that she had lived with her father (a realtor) and stepmother (a daycare worker) in a house at the top of a steep, tree-lined street; that she had had a childhood friend named Monica Lee; that there had been a covered bridge, a river called the Little Wyecliffe, and a Presbyterian church she had stopped attending when she turned sixteen and to which she had not returned until her parents' funerals. But she had never mentioned Berkeley or what she had hoped to achieve with her M.B.A. or why she had married my father.

She had, once or twice, taken down these boxes to show

me their contents, to impress on me that she had lived through the impossible years before I existed. This was her evidence, Exhibits A, B, and C, three boxes of MEMENTOS and ODDS & ENDS. Somewhere folded into these boxes were fragments of real, verifiable history: the toffee-brown front pages of newspapers announcing terrorist attacks, wars waged, presidents elected or impeached. Here too were the trinkets I had liked to hold in my hand as a child. A tarnished fifty-cent piece issued in the year of her father's birth (1951); four tan and pink seashells from the beach at Cobscook Bay.

MEMENTOS (SCHOOL) had been my least favorite box. It contained a campaign button for some evidently unsuccessful Democratic candidate for high office, which I had liked for its bright colors, but the rest of the space was taken up with her diploma, a few pages torn from her graduate yearbook, and a bundle of small envelopes none of which I had ever wanted (or been allowed) to touch.

I opened one of the envelopes now and sampled enough of the contents to register that it was: a) a love letter and b) in a handwriting not at all like my father's neat script from the missives in MEMENTOS: MARCUS.

So my mother had had a college sweetheart. This was news that might have discomfited Marcus Dupree (she had married him a week after graduation) but would hardly have shocked anyone else. Certainly it was no reason to conceal the box in the basement, not when it had been sitting in plain sight for years on end.

Had it even been my mother who had hidden it? I didn't know who might have been in the house between the time of her stroke and the time I arrived a day later. It was Carol who had found her collapsed on the sofa, and probably some of the Big House staff had helped clean up afterward, and there must have been EMS people in here prepping her for transport. But none of them would have had any remotely plausible reason to carry MEMENTOS (SCHOOL) downstairs and slide it into the dark gap between the furnace and the basement wall.

And maybe it didn't matter. No crime had been committed, after all, only a peculiar displacement. Could have been the local poltergeist. In all likelihood I would never know, and there was no point dwelling on the question. Everything in this room, every object in the house including these boxes, would sooner or later have to be salvaged, sold, or discarded. I had been putting it off, Carol had been putting it off, but the work was overdue.

But until then—

Until then, I put MEMENTOS (SCHOOL) back on the top shelf of the étagère between MEMENTOS (MARCUS) and ODDS & ENDS. And made the empty room complete.

o o o

The most troubling medical question I had raised with Wun Ngo Wen about Jason's treatment was the issue of drug-drug interactions. I couldn't discontinue Jason's conventional medications without throwing him into a disastrous relapse. But I was equally uneasy about combining his daily drug regimen with Wun's biochemical overhaul.

Wun promised me there wouldn't be a problem. The longevity treatment wasn't a "drug" in the conventional sense. What I was injecting into Jason's bloodstream was more like a biologically enabled computer program. Conventional drugs generally interact with proteins and cell surfaces. Wun's potion interacted with DNA itself.

But it still had to enter a cell to do its work, and it still had to negotiate Jason's blood chemistry and immune system on its way there—didn't it? Wun had said emphatically that none of this mattered. The longevity cocktail was flexible enough to operate through any kind of physiological condition short of death itself.

But the gene for AMS had never migrated to the red planet and the drugs Jase was taking were unknown there. And although Wun had insisted my concerns were unwarranted, I noticed he seldom smiled when he did so. So we hedged our bets. I had been backing off Jason's AMS meds for a week before the first injection. Not stopping them, just cutting back.

The strategy had seemed to work. By the time we arrived at the Big House Jason was exhibiting only minor symptomology while carrying a lighter drug load, and we began his treatment optimistically.

Three days later he was spiking fevers I couldn't knock down. A day after that he was semiconscious much of the time. Another day and his skin turned red and began to blister. That evening he began screaming.

He continued to scream despite the morphine I administered.

It was not a full-throated scream but a moan that periodically rose to high volume, a sound you might expect from a sick dog, not a human being. It was purely involuntary. When he was lucid he neither made the sound nor remembered having made it, even though it left his larynx inflamed and painful.

Carol made a brave show of putting up with it. There were parts of the house where Jason's keening was almost inaudible—the back bedrooms, the kitchen—and she spent most of her time there, reading or listening to local radio. But the strain was obvious and before long she started drinking again.

Maybe I shouldn't say "started." She had never stopped. What she had done was cut back to the minimum that allowed her to function, balancing between the very real terrors of sudden withdrawal and the lure of full-blown intoxication. And I hope that doesn't sound glib. Carol was walking a difficult path. She had stayed on it this long because of her love for her son, dormant as that love might have been these many years. The sound of his pain was what derailed her.

By the second week of the process Jase was hooked up to intravenous fluids and I was keeping an eye on his rising BP. He'd had a relatively good day despite his horrifying appearance, scabbed where he wasn't raw, eyes almost buried in the swollen flesh that surrounded them. He had been alert enough to ask whether Wun Ngo Wen had made his first television appearance. (Not yet. It was scheduled for the following week.) But by nightfall he had lapsed back into unconsciousness and the moaning, absent for a couple of days, started again, full-throated and painful to hear.

Painful for Carol, who showed up at the door of the bedroom with tear tracks down her cheeks and an expression of fierce, glassy anger. "Tyler," she said, "you have to stop this!"

"I'm doing what I can. He's not responding to the opiates. It might be better to talk about this in the morning."

"Can't you *hear* him?"

"Of course I can hear him."

"Does that mean nothing? Does that sound mean *nothing* to you? My god!" she said. "He would have been better off in Mexico with some quack. He would have been better off with a faith healer. Do you actually have *any* idea what you've been injecting into him? Fucking quack! My god."

Unfortunately she was echoing questions I had already begun to ask myself. No, I *didn't* know what I was injecting into him, not in any rigorous scientific sense. I had believed the promises of the man from Mars, but that was hardly a defense I could lay at Carol's feet. The process itself was more difficult, more obviously agonizing, than I had allowed myself to expect. Maybe it was working incorrectly. Maybe it wasn't working at all.

Jase emitted a mournful howl that ended in a sigh. Carol put her hands over her ears. "He's *suffering,* you fucking quack! *Look at him!*"

"Carol—"

"Don't Carol me, you butcher! I'm calling an ambulance. I'm calling the police!"

I came across the room and took her by the shoulders. She felt frail but dangerously alive under my hands, a cornered animal. "Carol, listen to me."

"Why, why should I listen to *you*?"

"Because your son put his life in my hands. Listen. Carol, listen. I'm going to need someone to help me here. I've been running on no sleep for days. Before too long I'm going to need someone to sit with him, someone with real medical savvy who can make informed judgments."

"You should have brought a nurse."

I should have, but it hadn't been possible, and that was beside the point. "I don't have a nurse. I need you to do this."

That took a moment to sink in. Then she gasped and stepped back. "Me!"

"You still have a medical license. Last I heard."

"I haven't practiced for—is it decades? Decades . . ."

"I'm not asking you to perform heart surgery. I just want you to keep an eye on his blood pressure and his temperature. Can you do that?"

Her anger dissipated. She was flattered. She was frightened. She thought about it. Then she gave me a steely look. "Why should I help you? Why should I make myself an accomplice to this, this *torture*?"

I was still composing an answer when a voice behind me said, "Oh, please."

Jason's voice. One of the trademarks of this Martian drug regimen was the lucidity that came at random and left at will. Apparently it had just arrived. I turned around.

He grimaced and made an attempt, not quite successful, to sit up. But his eyes were clear.

He addressed his mother: "Really," he said, "isn't this a little unseemly? Please do what Tyler wants. He knows what he's doing and so do I."

Carol stared at him. "But I don't. I haven't. I mean I can't—"

Then she turned and walked unsteadily out of the room, one hand braced against the wall.

I sat up with Jase. In the morning Carol came to the bedroom looking chastened but sober and offered to relieve me. Jason was peaceful and didn't really need tending, but I put her in charge and went off to catch up on my sleep.

I slept for twelve hours. When I came back to the bedroom Carol was still there, holding her unconscious son's hand, stroking his forehead with a tenderness I had never seen in her before.

o o o

The recovery phase began a week and a half into the course of Jason's treatment. There was no sudden transition, no magic moment. But his lucid periods began to lengthen and his blood pressure stabilized somewhere near the nominal range.

On the night of Wun's speech to the United Nations I located a portable TV in the servants' part of the house and lugged it up to Jason's bedroom. Carol joined us just before the broadcast.

I don't think Carol believed in Wun Ngo Wen.

His presence on Earth had been officially announced last Wednesday. His picture had been on front pages for days now, plus live footage of him striding across the White House lawn under the avuncular arm of the sitting president. The White House had made it clear that Wun was here to help but that he had no instant solution to the problem of the Spin and not much new knowledge about the Hypotheticals. Public reaction had been cautious.

Tonight he mounted the dais in the Security Council chamber and stepped up to the podium, which had been adjusted to suit his height. "Why, he's just a tiny thing," Carol said.

Jason said, "Show some respect. He represents a single continuous culture that's lasted longer than any of ours."

"Looks more like he represents the Lollipop Guild," Carol said.

His dignity was restored in the close-ups. The camera liked his eyes and his elusive smile. And when he spoke to the microphone he spoke softly, which took the effective pitch of his voice down to a more terrestrial level.

Wun knew (or had been coached to understand) how unlikely this event seemed to the average Earthling. ("Truly," the secretary general had said in his introduction, "we live in an age of miracles.") So he thanked us all for our hospitality in his best mid-Atlantic accent and talked wistfully about his home and why he had left it to come here. He painted Mars as a foreign but entirely human place, the kind of place you might like to visit, where the people were friendly and the scenery was interesting, although the winters, he admitted, were often harsh.

("Sounds like Canada," Carol said.)

Then to the heart of the matter. Everyone wanted to know about the Hypotheticals. Unfortunately Wun's people knew little more about them than we did—the Hypotheticals had encapsulated Mars while he was in transit to Earth, and the Martians were as helpless before it as we had been.

He couldn't guess the Hypotheticals' motives. That question had been debated for centuries, but even the greatest Martian thinkers had never resolved it. It was interesting,

Wun said, that both Earth and Mars had been sealed off when they were on the brink of global catastrophes: "Our population, like yours, is approaching the limit of sustainability. On Earth your industry and agriculture both run on oil, supplies of which are rapidly being depleted. On Mars we have no oil at all, but we depend on another scarce commodity, elemental nitrogen: it drives our agricultural cycle and imposes absolute limits on the number of human lives the planet can sustain. We've coped a little better than has the Earth, but only because we were forced to recognize the problem from the very beginning of our civilization. Both planets were and are facing the possibility of economic and agricultural collapse and a catastrophic human die-off. Both planets were encapsulated before that end point was reached.

"Perhaps the Hypotheticals understand that truth about us and perhaps it influenced their action. But we don't know that with any certainty. Nor do we know what they expect from us, if anything, or when or even whether the Spin will come to an end. We *can't* know, until we gather more direct information about the Hypotheticals.

"Fortunately," Wun said, the camera going close on him, "there is a way to gather that information. I've come here with a proposal, which I've discussed with both President Garland and President-elect Lomax as well as other heads of state," and he went on to sketch out the basics of the replicator plan. "With luck this will tell us whether the Hypotheticals have overtaken other worlds, how those worlds have reacted, and what the ultimate fate of the Earth might be."

But when he started talking about the Oort Cloud and "autocatalytic feedback technology" I saw Carol's eyes glaze over.

"This can't be happening," she said after Wun departed the podium to dazed applause and the network pundits began to chew and regurgitate his speech. She looked genuinely frightened. "Is any of this true, Jason?"

"Most all of it," Jason said calmly. "I can't speak for the weather on Mars."

"Are we really on the brink of disaster?"

"We've been on the brink of disaster since the stars went out."

"I mean about oil and all that. If the Spin hadn't happened, we'd all be starving?"

"People *are* starving. They're starving because we can't support seven billion people in North American–style prosperity without strip-mining the planet. The numbers are hard to argue with. Yes, it's true. If the Spin doesn't kill us, sooner or later we'll be looking at a global human die-back."

"And that has something to do with the Spin itself?"

"Perhaps, but neither I nor the Martian on television know for sure."

"You're making fun of me."

"No."

"Yes you are. But that's all right. I know I'm ignorant. It's been years since I looked at a newspaper. There was always the risk of seeing your father's face, for one thing. And the only television I watch is afternoon drama. In afternoon drama there aren't any Martians. I guess I'm Rip van Winkle. I slept too long. And I don't much like the world I woke up to. The parts of it that aren't terrifying are—" She gestured at the TV. "Are ludicrous."

"We're all Rip van Winkle," Jason said gently. "We're all waiting to wake up."

○ ○ ○

Carol's mood improved in tandem with Jason's health and she began to take a livelier interest in his prognosis. I briefed her about his AMS, a disease that had not been formally diagnosed when Carol graduated from medical school, as a way to dodge questions about the treatment itself, an unspoken bargain which she seemed to understand and accept. The important thing was that Jason's ravaged skin was healing and the blood samples I sent to a lab in D.C. for testing showed drastically reduced neural plaque proteins.

She was still reluctant to talk about the Spin, however, and she looked unhappy when Jase and I discussed it in her presence. I thought again of the Housman poem Diane had taught me so many years ago: *The infant child is not aware / He has been eaten by the bear.*

Carol had been beset by several bears, some as large as the

Spin and some as small as a molecule of ethanol. I think she might have envied the infant child.

o o o

Diane called (on my personal phone, not Carol's house phone) a few nights after Wun's U.N. appearance. I had retreated to my room and Carol was keeping the night watch. Rain had come and gone all November, and it was raining now, the bedroom window a fluid mirror of yellow light.

"You're at the Big House," Diane said.

"You talked to Carol?"

"I call her once a month. I'm a dutiful daughter. Sometimes she's sober enough to talk. What's wrong with Jason?"

"It's a long story," I said. "He's getting better. It's nothing to worry about."

"I hate it when people say that."

"I know. But it's true. There was a problem, but we fixed it."

"And that's all you can tell me."

"All for now. How are things with you and Simon?" Last time we talked she had mentioned legal trouble.

"Not too good," she said. "We're moving."

"Moving where?"

"Out of Phoenix, anyway. Away from the city. Jordan Tabernacle's been temporarily closed down—I thought maybe you'd heard about it."

"No," I said—why would I have heard about the financial troubles of a little southwest Tribulation church?—and we went on to discuss other matters, and Diane promised to update me once she and Simon had a new address. Sure, why not, what the hell.

But I did hear about Jordan Tabernacle the following night.

Uncharacteristically, Carol insisted on watching the late news. Jason was tired but alert and willing, so the three of us sat through forty minutes of international saber rattling and celebrity court cases. Some of this was interesting: there was an update on Wun Ngo Wen, who was in Belgium meeting with officials of the E.U., and good news from Uzbekistan, where the forward marine base had finally been relieved. Then there was a feature about CVWS and the Israeli dairy industry.

We watched dramatic pictures of culled cattle being bull-dozed into mass graves and salted with lime. Five years ago the Japanese beef industry had been similarly devastated. Bovine or ungulate CVWS had broken out and been suppressed in a dozen countries from Brazil to Ethiopia. The human equivalent was treatable with modern antibiotics but remained a smoldering problem in third-world economies.

But Israeli dairy farmers ran strict protocols of sepsis and testing, so the outbreak there had been unexpected. Worse, the index case—the first infection—had been tracked to an unauthorized shipment of fertilized ova from the United States.

The shipment was back-traced to a Tribulationist charity called Word for the World, headquartered in an industrial park outside of Cincinnati, Ohio. Why was WftW smuggling cattle ova into Israel? Not, it turned out, for particularly charitable reasons. Investigators followed WftW's sponsors through a dozen blind holding companies to a consortium of Tribulationist and Dispensationalist churches and fringe political groups both large and small. One item of Biblical doctrine shared by these groups was drawn from Numbers (chapter nineteen) and inferred from other texts in Matthew and Timothy—namely, that the birth in Israel of a pure red heifer would signal the second coming of Jesus Christ and the beginning of His reign on Earth.

It was an old idea. Allied Jewish extremists believed the sacrifice of a red calf on the Temple Mount would mark the coming of the Messiah. There had been several "red calf" attacks on the Dome of the Rock in prior years, one of which had damaged the Al-Aqsa Mosque and nearly precipitated a regional war. The Israeli government had been doing its best to quash the movement but had only succeeded in driving it underground.

According to the news there were several WftW-sponsored dairy farms across the American Midwest and Southwest all quietly devoted to the business of hastening Armageddon. They had been attempting to breed a pure blood-red calf, presumably superior to the numerous disappointing heifers that had been presented as candidates over the last forty years.

These farms had systematically evaded federal inspections and feed protocols, to the point of concealing an outbreak of bovine CVWS that had crossed the border from Nogales. The infected ova produced breeding stock with plentiful genes for red-tinged coats, but when the calves themselves were born (at a WftW-linked dairy farm in the Negev) most died of respiratory distress at an early age. The corpses were quietly buried, but too late. The infection had spread to mature stock and a number of human farmhands.

It was an embarrassment for the U.S. administration. The FDA had already announced a policy review and Homeland Security was freezing WftW bank accounts and serving warrants on Tribulationist fund-raisers. On the news there were pictures of federal agents carrying boxed documents out of anonymous buildings and applying padlocks to the doors of obscure churches.

The news reader cited a few examples by name.

One of them was Jordan Tabernacle.

4×10^9 A.D.

Outside Padang we transferred from Nijon's ambulance to a private car with a Minang driver, who dropped us off—me, Ibu Ina, En—at a cartage compound on the coast highway. Five huge tin-roofed warehouses sat in a black gravel plain between conical piles of bulk cement under tarps and a corroded rail tanker idle on a siding. The main office was a low wooden building under a sign that read BAYUR FORWARDING in English.

Bayur Forwarding, Ina said, was one of her ex-husband Jala's businesses, and it was Jala who met us in the reception room. He was a beefy, apple-cheeked man in a canary yellow business suit—he looked like a Toby jug dressed for the tropics. He and Ina embraced in the manner of the comfortably divorced, then Jala shook my hand and stooped to shake En's. Jala introduced me to his receptionists as "a palm oil importer from Suffolk," presumably in case she was quizzed by the New Reformasi. Then he escorted us to his seven-year-old fuel-cell BMW and we drove south toward Teluk Bayur, Jala and Ina up front, me and En in back.

Teluk Bayur—the big deepwater harbor south of the city of Padang—was where Jala had made all his money. Thirty years ago, he said, Teluk Bayur had been a sleepy Sumatran sand-mud basin with modest port services and a predictable trade in coal, crude palm oil, and fertilizer. Today, thanks to the economic boom of the *nagari* restoration and the population explosion of the Archway era, Teluk Bayur was a fully improved port basin with world-class quays and mooring, a huge storage complex, and so many modern conveniences that even Jala eventually lost interest in tallying up all the tugs, sheds, cranes and loaders by tonnage. "Jala is proud of Teluk Bayur," Ina said. "There's hardly a high official there he hasn't bribed."

"Nobody higher than General Affairs," Jala corrected her.

"You're too modest."

"Is there something wrong with making money? Am I too successful? Is it a crime to make something of myself?"

Ina inclined her head and said, "These are of course rhetorical questions."

I asked whether we were going directly to a ship at Teluk Bayur.

"Not directly," Jala said. "I'm taking you to a safe place on the docks. It isn't as simple as walking onto some vessel and making ourselves comfortable."

"There's no ship?"

"Certainly there's a ship. The *Capetown Maru,* a nice little freighter. She's loading coffee and spices just now. When the holds are full and the debts are paid and the permits are signed, then the human cargo goes aboard. Discreetly, I hope."

"What about Diane? Is Diane at Teluk Bayur?"

"Soon," Ina said, giving Jala a meaningful look.

"Yes, soon," he said.

o o o

Teluk Bayur might once have been a sleepy commercial harbor, but like any modern port it had become a city in itself, a city made not for people but for cargo. The port proper was enclosed and fenced, but ancillary businesses had grown up around it like whorehouses outside a military base: secondary shippers and expediters, gypsy truck collectives running rebuilt eighteen-wheelers, leaky fuel depots. We breezed past them all. Jala wanted to get us settled before the sun went down.

Bayur Bay itself was a horseshoe of oily saltwater. Wharfs and jetties lapped at it like concrete tongues. Abutting the shore was the ordered chaos of large-scale commerce, the first- and second-line godowns and stacking yards, the cranes like giant mantises feasting on the holds of tethered container ships. We stopped at a manned guardpost along the line of a steel fence and Jala passed something to the security guard through the window of the car—a permit, a bribe, or both. The guard nodded him through and Jala waved amiably and drove inside, following a line of CPO and Avigas tanks at what seemed like reckless speed. He said, "I've arranged for you to stay here overnight. I have an office in one of the E-dock warehouses. Nothing in there but bulk concrete, nobody to bother you. In the morning I'll bring Diane Lawton."

"And then we leave?"

"Patience. You're not the only ones making *rantau*—just the most conspicuous. There might be complications."

"Such as?"

"Obviously, the New Reformasi. The police sweep the docklands every now and then, looking for illegals and archrunners. Usually they find a few. Or more than a few, depending on who's been paid off. At the moment there is a great deal of pressure from Jakarta, so who knows? Also there's talk of a labor action. The stevedores' union is extremely militant. We'll cast off before any conflict begins, with luck. So you sleep a night on the floor in the dark, I'm afraid, and I'll take Ina and En to stay with the other villagers for now."

"No," Ina said firmly. "I'll stay with Tyler."

Jala paused. Then he looked at her and said something in Minang.

"Not funny," she said. "And not true."

"What, then? You don't trust me to keep him safe?"

"What have I ever gained by trusting you?"

Jala grinned. His teeth were tobacco brown. "Adventure," he said.

"Yes, quite," Ina said.

○ ○ ○

So we ended up in the north end of a warehousing complex off the docks, Ibu Ina and I in a grimly rectangular room that had been a surveyor's office, Ina said, until the building was temporarily closed pending repairs to its porous roof.

One wall of the room was a window of wire-reinforced glass. I looked down into a cavernous storage space pale with concrete dust. Steel support beams rose from a muddy, ponded floor like rusted ribs.

The only light came from security lamps placed at sparse intervals along the walls. Flying insects had penetrated the building's gaps and they hovered in clouds around the caged bulbs or died mounded beneath them. Ina managed to get a desk lamp working. Empty cardboard boxes had been piled in one corner, and I unfolded the driest of them and stacked them to make a pair of crude mattresses. No blankets. But it was a hot night. Close to monsoon season.

"You think you can sleep?" Ina asked.

"It's not the Hilton, but it's the best I can do."

"Oh, not that. I mean the noise. Can you sleep through the noise?"

Teluk Bayur didn't close down at night. The loading and unloading went on twenty-four hours a day. We couldn't see it but we could hear it, the sound of heavy motors and stressed metal and the periodic thunder of multiton cargo containers in transit. "I've slept through worse," I said.

"I doubt that," Ina said, "but it's kind of you to say."

Neither of us slept for hours. Instead we sat close to the glow of the desk lamp and talked sporadically. Ina asked about Jason.

I had let her read some of the long passages I'd written during my illness. Jason's transition to Fourth, she said, sounded as if it had been less difficult than mine. No, I said. I had simply neglected to include the bedpan details.

"But about his memory? There was no loss? He was unconcerned?"

"He didn't talk much about it. I'm sure he was concerned." In fact he had come swimming out of one of his recurrent fevers to demand that I document his life for him: *"Write it down for me, Ty,"* he had said. *"Write it down in case I forget."*

"But no graphomania of his own."

"No. Graphomania happens when the brain starts to rewire its own verbal faculties. It's only one possible symptom. The sounds he made were probably his own manifestation of it."

"You learned that from Wun Ngo Wen."

Yes, or from his medical archives, which I had studied later.

Ina was still fascinated with Wun Ngo Wen. "That warning to the United Nations, about overpopulation and resource depletion, did Wun ever discuss that with you? I mean, in the time before—"

"I know. Yes, he did, a little."

"What did he tell you?"

This was during one of our conversations about the ultimate aim of the Hypotheticals. Wun had drawn me a diagram, which I reproduced for Ina on the dusty parquet floor: a horizontal and vertical line defining a graph. The vertical line was population, the horizontal line was time. A jaggedy trend line crossed the graph space more or less horizontally.

"Population by time," Ina said. "I understand that much, but what exactly are we measuring?"

"Any animal population in a relatively stable ecosystem. Could be foxes in Alaska or howler monkeys in Belize. The population fluctuates with external factors, like a cold winter or an increase in predators, but it's stable at least over the short term."

But then, Wun had said, what happens if we look at an intelligent, tool-using species over a longer term? I drew Ina the same graph as before, except this time the trend line curved steadily toward the vertical.

"What's happening here," I said, "is that the population—we can just say 'people'—people are learning to pool their skills. Not just how to knap a flint but how to teach other people to knap flints and how to divide labor economically. Collaboration makes more food. Population grows. More people collaborate more efficiently and generate new skills. Agriculture. Animal husbandry. Reading and writing, which means skills can be shared more efficiently among living people and even inherited from generations long dead."

"So the curve rises ever more steeply," Ina said, "until we are all drowning in ourselves."

"Ah, but it doesn't. There are other forces that work to pull the curve to the right. Increasing prosperity and technological savvy actually work in our favor. Well-fed, secure people tend to want to limit their own reproduction. Technology and a flexible culture give them the means. Ultimately, or so Wun said, the curve will tend back toward flat."

Ibu Ina looked confused. "So there *is* no problem? No starvation, no overpopulation?"

"Unfortunately, the line for the population of Earth is still a long way from horizontal. And we're running into limiting conditions."

"Limiting conditions?"

One more diagram. This one showed a trend line like an italic letter *S,* level at the top. Over this I marked two parallel horizontal lines: one well above the trend line, marked "A," and one crossing it at the upcurve, marked "B."

"What are these lines?" Ina asked.

"They're both planetary sustainability. The amount of arable land available for agriculture, fuel and raw materials to sustain technology, clean air and water. The diagram shows the difference between a successful intelligent species and an unsuccessful one. A species that peaks under the limit has the potential for long-term survival. A successful species can go on to do all those things futurists used to dream about—expand into the solar system or even the galaxy, manipulate time and space."

"How grand," Ina said.

"Don't knock it. The alternative is worse. A species that runs into sustainability limits before it stabilizes its population is probably doomed. Massive starvation, failed technology, and a planet so depleted from the first bloom of civilization that it lacks the means to rebuild."

"I see." She shivered. "So which are we? Case A or Case B? Did Wun tell you that?"

"All he could say for sure was that both planets, Earth and Mars, were starting to run into the limits. And that the Hypotheticals intervened before it could happen."

"But *why* did they intervene? What do they expect from us?"

It was a question for which Wun's people didn't have an answer. Nor did we.

No, that wasn't quite true. Jason Lawton had found a sort of an answer.

But I wasn't ready to talk about that yet.

○ ○ ○

Ina yawned, and I brushed away the marks on the dusty floor. She switched off the desk light. The scattered maintenance lamps cast an exhausted glow. Outside the warehouse there was a sound like the striking of an enormous, muted bell every five or so seconds.

"Tick tock," Ina said, arranging herself on her mattress of mildewy cardboard. "I remember when clocks ticked, Tyler. Do you? The old-fashioned clocks?"

"There was one in my mother's kitchen."

"There are so many kinds of time. The time by which we measure our lives. Months and years. Or the *big* time, the time that raises mountains and makes stars. Or all the things that happen between one heartbeat and the next. It's hard to live in all those kinds of time. Easy to *forget* that you live in all of them."

The metronomic clanging went on.

"You sound like a Fourth," I said.

In the dim light I could just make out her weary smile.

"I think one lifetime is enough for me," she said.

○ ○ ○

In the morning we woke to the sound of an accordion door rolled back to its stops, a burst of light, Jala calling for us.

I hurried down the stairs. Jala was already halfway across the warehouse floor and Diane was behind him, walking slowly.

I came closer and said her name.

She tried to smile, but her teeth were clenched and her face was unnaturally pale. By then I had seen that she was holding a wadded cloth against her body above her hip, and that both the cloth and her cotton blouse were vivid red with the blood that had leaked through.

DESPERATE EUPHORIA

Eight months after Wun Ngo Wen's address to the General Assembly of the United Nations, the hypercold cultivation tanks at Perihelion began to yield payload quantities of Martian replicators, and at Canaveral and Vandenberg fleets of Delta sevens were prepped to deliver them into orbit. It was about this time that Wun developed an urge to see the Grand Canyon. What sparked his interest was a year-old copy of *Arizona Highways* one of the biology wonks happened to leave in his quarters.

He showed it to me a couple of days later. "Look at this," he said, almost trembling with eagerness, folding back the pages of a photo feature on the restoration of Bright Angel trail. The Colorado River cutting pre-Cambrian sandstone into green pools. A tourist from Dubai riding a mule. "Have you heard of this, Tyler?"

"Have I heard of the Grand Canyon? Yes. I think most people have."

"It's astonishing. Very beautiful."

"Spectacular. So they say. But isn't Mars famous for its canyons?"

He smiled. "You're talking about the Fallen Lands. Your people called it Valles Marineris when they discovered it from orbit sixty years ago—or a hundred thousand years ago. Parts of it do look a lot like these photographs from Arizona. But I've never been there. And I don't suppose I ever *will* be there. I think I'd like to see the Grand Canyon instead."

"Then see it. It's a free country."

Wun blinked at the expression—maybe the first time he'd heard it—and nodded. "Very well, I will. I'll talk to Jason about arranging transportation. Would you like to come?"

"What, to Arizona?"

"Yes! Tyler! To Arizona, to the Grand Canyon!" He might have been a Fourth, but at that moment he sounded like a ten-year-old. "Will you go there with me?"

"I'll have to think about that."

I was still thinking about it when I got a call from E. D. Lawton.

o o o

Since the election of Preston Lomax, E. D. Lawton had become politically invisible. His industry contacts were still in place—he could throw a party and expect powerful people to show up—but he would never again wield the kind of cabinet-level influence he had enjoyed under Garland's presidency. In fact there were rumors that he was in a state of psychological decline, holed up in his Georgetown residence making unwelcome phone calls to former political allies. Maybe so, but neither Jase nor Diane had heard from him recently; and when I picked up my home phone I was stunned when I heard his voice.

"I'd like to talk to you," he said.

Which was interesting, coming from the man who had conceived and financed Molly Seagram's acts of sexual espionage. My first and probably best instinct was to hang up. But as a gesture it seemed inadequate.

He added, "It's about Jason."

"So talk to Jason."

"I can't, Tyler. He won't listen to me."

"Does that surprise you?"

He sighed. "Okay, I understand, you're on his side, that's a given. But I'm not trying to hurt him. I want to help him. In fact it's urgent. Regarding his welfare."

"I don't know what that means."

"And I can't tell you over the goddamn phone. I'm in Florida now, I'm twenty minutes down the highway. Come to the hotel and I'll buy you a drink and then you can tell me to fuck off face-to-face. Please, Tyler. Eight o'clock, the lobby bar, the Hilton on ninety-five. Maybe you'll save somebody's life."

He hung up before I could answer.

I called Jason and told him what had happened.

"Wow," he said, then, "If the rumors are true, E.D.'s even less pleasant to spend time with than he used to be. Be careful."

"I wasn't planning to keep the appointment."

"You certainly don't have to. But . . . maybe you should."

"I've had enough of E.D.'s gamesmanship, thanks."

"It's just that it might be better if we know what's on his mind."

"You're saying you *want* me to see him?"

"Only if you're comfortable with it."

"Comfortable?"

"It's up to you, of course."

So I got in my car and drove dutifully up the highway, past Independence Day bunting (the fourth was tomorrow) and street-corner flag merchants (unlicensed, ready to bolt in their weathered pickups), rehearsing in my mind all the go-to-hell speeches I had ever imagined myself delivering to E. D. Lawton. By the time I reached the Hilton the sun was lost behind the rooftops and the lobby clock said 8:35.

E.D. was at a booth in the bar, drinking determinedly. He looked surprised to see me. Then he stood up, grabbed my arm, and steered me to the vinyl bench across the table from him.

"Drink?"

"I won't be here that long."

"Have a drink, Tyler. It'll improve your attitude."

"Has it improved yours? Just tell me what you want, E.D."

"I know a man's angry when he makes my name sound like an insult. What are you so pissed about? That thing with your girlfriend and the doctor, what's his name, Malmstein? Look, I want you to know I didn't arrange that. I didn't even sign off on it. I had a zealous staff working for me. Things were done in my name. Just so you know."

"That's a poor excuse for shitty behavior."

"I guess it is. Guilty as charged. I apologize. Can we move on to other things?"

I might have walked out then. I suppose the reason I stayed was the aura of desperate anxiety seeping out of him. E.D. was still capable of that brand of thoughtless condescension that had so endeared him to his family. But he was no longer confident. In the silence between vocal outbursts his hands were restless. He stroked his chin, folded and unfolded a cocktail napkin, smoothed his hair. This particular silence expanded until he was halfway through a second drink. Which was probably more than his second. The waitress had cycled past with a breezy familiarity.

"You have some influence with Jason," he said finally.

"If you want to talk to Jason, why not do it directly?"

"Because I can't. For obvious reasons."

"Then what do you want me to tell him?"

E.D. stared at me. Then he looked at his drink. "I want you to tell him to pull the plug on the replicator project. I mean literally. Turn off the refrigeration. Kill it."

Now it was my turn to be incredulous.

"You must know how unlikely that is."

"I'm not stupid, Tyler."

"Then why—"

"He's my son."

"You figured that out?"

"Because we had political arguments he's suddenly not my son? You think I'm so shallow I can't make that distinction? That because I don't agree with him I don't love him?"

"All I know about you is what I've seen."

"You've seen nothing." He started to say something else, then reconsidered. "Jason is a pawn for Wun Ngo Wen," he said. "I want him to wake up and understand what's happening."

"You raised him to be a pawn. Your pawn. You just don't like seeing someone else with that kind of influence over him."

"Bullshit. Bullshit. I mean, no, all right, we're confessing here, maybe it's true, I don't know, maybe we all need some family therapy, but that's not the point. The point is that every powerful person in this country happens to be in love with Wun Ngo Wen and his fucking replicator project. For the obvious reason that it's cheap and it looks plausible to the voting public. And who cares if it doesn't work because nothing *else* works and if *nothing* works then the end is nigh and everybody's problems will look different when the red sun rises. Right? Isn't that right? They dress it up, they call it a wager or gamble, but it's really just sleight-of-hand for the purpose of distracting the rubes."

"Interesting analysis," I said, "but—"

"Would I be here talking to you if I thought this was an interesting *analysis*? Ask the appropriate questions, if you want to argue with me."

"Such as?"

"Such as, who exactly is Wun Ngo Wen? Who does he represent, and what does he really want? Because despite what they say on television he's not Mahatma Gandhi in a Munchkin package. He's here because he wants something from us. He's wanted it from day one."

"The replicator launch."

"Obviously."

"Is that a crime?"

"A better question would be, why don't the Martians do this launch themselves?"

"Because they can't presume to speak on behalf of the entire solar system. Because a work like this can't be undertaken unilaterally."

He rolled his eyes. "Those are things people *say,* Tyler. Talking about multilateralism and diplomacy is like saying 'I love you'—it serves to facilitate the fucking. Unless, of course, the Martians really are angelic spirits descended from heaven to deliver us from evil. Which I presume you don't believe."

Wun had denied it so often that I could hardly object.

"I mean look at their technology. These guys have been doing high-end biotech for something like a thousand years. If they wanted to populate the galaxy with nanobots they could have done it a long time ago. So why didn't they? Ruling out explanations that depend on their better nature, *why?* Obviously, because they're afraid of a reprisal."

"Reprisal from the Hypotheticals? They don't know anything about the Hypotheticals we don't know."

"So they claim. Doesn't mean they're not afraid of them. As for us—we're the assholes who launched a nuclear strike on the polar artifacts not that long ago. Yeah, we'll take the responsibility, why not? Jesus, look at it, Tyler. It's a classic setup. It could hardly be more slick."

"Or maybe you're paranoid."

"Am I? Who defines paranoia this far into the Spin? We're all paranoid. We all know there are malevolent, powerful forces controlling our lives, which is pretty much the *definition* of paranoia."

"I'm just a GP," I said. "But intelligent people tell me—"

"You're talking about Jason, of course. Jason tells you it'll all be okay."

"Not just Jason. The whole Lomax administration. Most of Congress."

"But they depend on the wonks for advice. And the wonks are as hypnotized by all this as Jason is. You want to know what motivates your friend Jason? Fear. He's afraid of dying ignorant. The situation we're in, if he dies ignorant, it means the human race dies ignorant. And that scares the living shit out of him, the idea that a whole arguably intelligent species can be erased from the universe without ever understanding why or what for. Maybe instead of diagnosing my paranoia you ought to think about Jason's delusions of grandeur. He's made it his mission to figure out the Spin before he dies. Wun shows up and hands him a tool he can use to that end and of course he buys it: it's like handing a matchbook to a pyromaniac."

"Do you really want me to tell him this?"

"I don't—" E.D. looked suddenly morose, or maybe it was

just his blood alcohol peaking. "I thought, because he listens to you—"

"You know better than that."

He closed his eyes. "Maybe I do. I don't know. But I have to try. Do you see that? For the sake of my conscience." I was startled that he had confessed to having one. "Let me be frank with you. I feel like I'm watching a train wreck in slow motion. The wheels are off the track and the driver hasn't noticed. So what do I do? Is it too late to pull the alarm? Too late to yell 'duck'? Probably so. But he's my son, Tyler. The man driving the train is my son."

"He's in no more danger than the rest of us."

"I think that's wrong. Even if this thing succeeds, all we stand to get out of it is abstract information. That's good enough for Jason. But it's not good enough for the rest of the world. You don't know Preston Lomax. I do. Lomax would be more than happy to tag Jason with a failure and hang him for it. A lot of people in his administration want Perihelion closed down or turned over to the military. And those are *best*-case outcomes. Worst case, the Hypotheticals get annoyed and turn off the Spin."

"You're worried Lomax will shut down Perihelion?"

"I built Perihelion. Yes, I care about it. But that's not why I'm here."

"I can tell Jason what you said, but you think he'll change his mind?"

"I—" Now E.D. inspected the tabletop. His eyes went a little vague and watery. "No. Obviously not. But if he wants to talk . . . I want him to know he can reach me. If he wants to talk. I wouldn't make it an ordeal for him. Honestly. I mean, if he wants that."

It was as if he had opened a door and his essential loneliness had come spilling out.

Jason assumed E.D. had come to Florida as part of some Machiavellian plan. The old E.D. might have. But the new E.D. struck me as an aging, remorseful, newly powerless man who found his strategies at the bottom of a glass and who had drifted into town on a guilty whim.

I said, more gently, "Have you tried talking to Diane?"

"Diane?" He waved his hand dismissively. "Diane changed her number. I can't get through to her. Anyway, she's involved with that fucking end-of-the-world cult."

"It's not a cult, E.D. Just a little church with some odd ideas. Simon's more involved with it than she is."

"She's Spin-paralyzed. Just like the rest of your fucking generation. She took a nosedive into this religious bullshit when she was barely out of puberty. I remember that. She was so depressed by the Spin. Then suddenly she was quoting Thomas Aquinas at the dinner table. I wanted Carol to speak to her about it. But Carol was useless, typically. So you know what I did? I organized a debate. Her and Jason. For six months they'd been arguing about God. So I made it formal, like, you know, a college debate, and the trick was, they each had to take the side they *didn't* support—Jason had to argue for the existence of God, and Diane had to take the atheist's point of view."

They had never mentioned this to me. But I could imagine with what dismay they had approached E.D.'s educational assignment.

"I wanted her to know how gullible she was. She did her best. I think she wanted to impress me. She repeated back what Jason had been saying to her, basically. But Jason—" His pride was obvious. His eyes shone and some of the color crept back into his face. "Jason was absolutely brilliant. Just stunningly, beautifully brilliant. Jason gave back every argument she had ever offered him and then some. And he didn't just parrot this stuff. He'd read the theology, he'd read biblical scholarship. And he smiled through the whole thing, as if he was saying, Look, I know these arguments backward, I know them as intimately as you do, I can make them in my sleep, and I still think they're contemptible. He was absolutely fucking relentless. And by the end of it she was crying. She held out until the end, but the tears were streaming down her face."

I stared.

He registered my expression and winced. "Go to hell with your moral superiority. I was trying to teach her a lesson. I wanted her to be a realist, not one of these fucking Spin-driven navel gazers. Your whole fucking generation—"

"Do you care whether she's alive?"

"Of course I do."

"No one's heard from her lately. It's not just you, E.D. She's out of touch. I thought I might try to track her down. Do you think that's a good idea?"

But the waitress had come with another drink and E.D. was rapidly losing interest in the subject, in me, in the world around him. "Yeah, I'd like to know if she's all right." He took off his glasses and cleaned them with a cocktail napkin. "Yeah, you do that, Tyler."

Which is how I decided to accompany Wun Ngo Wen to the state of Arizona.

o o o

Traveling with Wun Ngo Wen was like traveling with a pop star or a head of state—heavy on security and light on spontaneity, but briskly efficient. A neatly timed succession of airport corridors, chartered planes, and highway convoys eventually deposited us at the head of Bright Angel trail, three weeks before the scheduled replicator launches, on a July day hot as fireworks and clear as creek water.

Wun stood where the guardrail followed the canyon's rim. The Park Service had closed the trail and visitor center to tourists, and three of their best and most photogenic rangers were poised to conduct Wun (and a contingent of federal security guys with shoulder holsters under their hiking whites) on an expedition to the canyon floor, where they would camp overnight.

Wun had been promised privacy once the hike began, but right now it was a circus. Media vans filled the parking area; journalists and paparazzi leaned into the cordon ropes like eager supplicants; a helicopter swooped along the canyon rim shooting video. Nevertheless Wun was happy. He grinned. He sucked in huge gulps of piney air. The heat was appalling, especially, I would have thought, for a Martian, but he showed no signs of distress despite the sweat glistening on his wrinkled skin. He wore a light khaki shirt, matching pants, and a pair of children's-size high-top hiking boots he'd been breaking in for the last couple of weeks.

He took a long drink from an aluminum canteen, then offered it to me.

"Water brother," he said.

I laughed. "Keep it. You'll need it."

"Tyler, I wish you could make the descent with me. This
is—" He said something in his own language. "Too much
stew for one pot. Too much beauty for one human being."

"You can always share it with the G-men."

He gave the security people a baleful glance. "Unfortunately I can't. They look but they do not see."

"Is that a Martian expression, too?"

"Might as well be," he said.

○ ○ ○

Wun gave the press pool and the newly arrived governor of
Arizona a few genial last words while I borrowed one of the
several Perihelion vehicles and headed for Phoenix.

Nobody interfered, nobody followed me; the press wasn't
interested. I may have been Wun Ngo Wen's personal
physician—a few of the press regulars might even have recognized me—but in the absence of Wun himself I wasn't
newsworthy. Not even remotely. It was a good feeling. I
turned up the air-conditioning until the interior of the car felt
like a Canadian autumn. Maybe this was what the media was
calling "desperate euphoria"—the we're-all-doomed-but-
anything-can-happen feeling that had begun to peak around
the time Wun went public. The end of the world, plus Martians: given that, what was impossible? What was even *unlikely*? And where did that leave the standard arguments in
favor of propriety, patience, virtue, and not rocking the boat?

E.D. had accused my generation of Spin paralysis, and
maybe that was true. We'd been caught in the headlights for
thirty-odd years now. None of us had ever shaken that feeling
of essential vulnerability, that deep personal awareness of the
sword suspended over our heads. It tainted every pleasure
and it made even our best and bravest gestures seem tentative
and timid.

But even paralysis erodes. Beyond anxiety lies recklessness. Beyond immobility, action.

Not necessarily good or wise action, however. I passed three sets of highway signs warning against the possibility of roadside piracy. The traffic reporter on local radio listed roads closed for "police purposes" as indifferently as if she'd been talking about maintenance work.

But I made it without incident to the parking lot in back of Jordan Tabernacle.

The current pastor of Jordan Tabernacle was a crew-cut young man named Bob Kobel who had agreed by phone to meet me. He came to the car as I was locking it and escorted me into the rectory for coffee and doughnuts and some hard talk. He looked like a high-school athlete gone slightly paunchy, but still full of that old team spirit.

"I've thought about what you said," he told me. "I understand why you want to get in touch with Diane Lawton. Do you understand why that's an awkward issue for this church?"

"Not exactly, no."

"Thank you for your honesty. Let me explain, then. I became pastor of this congregation after the red heifer crisis, but I was a member for many years before that. I know the people you're curious about—Diane and Simon. I once called them friends."

"Not anymore?"

"I'd like to say we're still friends. But you'd have to ask them about that. See, Dr. Dupree, Jordan Tabernacle has had a contentious history for a relatively small congregation. Mostly it's because we started out as a mongrel church, a bunch of old-fashioned Dispensationalists who came together with some disillusioned New Kingdom hippies. What we had in common was a fierce belief in the imminence of the end times and a sincere desire for Christian fellowship. Not an easy alliance, as you might imagine. We've been through our share of controversies. Schisms. People veering off into little corners of Christianity, doctrinal disputes that, frankly, were almost incomprehensible to much of the congregation. But what happened with Simon and Diane was, they aligned themselves with a crowd of hard-core post-Tribulationists who wanted to claim Jordan Tabernacle for themselves. That made for some difficult politics, what the secular world might even call a power struggle."

"Which they lost?"

"Oh no. They were firmly in control. At least for a while. They radicalized Jordan Tabernacle in a way that made a whole lot of us uncomfortable. Dan Condon was one of them, and he's the one who got us involved with that network of loose cannons trying to bring about the Second Coming with a red cow. Which still strikes me as grotesquely presumptuous. As if the Lord of Hosts would wait on a cattle-breeding program before gathering up the faithful."

Pastor Kobel sipped his coffee.

I said, "I can't speak for their faith."

"You said on the phone Diane's been out of touch with her family."

"Yes."

"That may be her choice. I used to see her father on television. He looks like an intimidating man."

"I'm not here to kidnap her. I just want to make sure she's all right."

Another sip of coffee. Another thoughtful look.

"I'd like to tell you she's fine. And probably she is. But after the scandals, that whole group moved out to the boonies. And some of 'em still have open invitations to speak to federal investigators. So visiting is discouraged."

"But not impossible?"

"Not impossible if you're known to them. I'm not sure you qualify, Dr. Dupree. I could give you directions, but I doubt they'd let you in."

"Even if you vouched for me?"

Pastor Kobel blinked. He appeared to think about it.

Then he smiled. He took a scrap of paper from the desk behind him and wrote an address and a few lines of directions on it. "That's a good idea, Dr. Dupree. You tell 'em Pastor Bob sent you. But be careful all the same."

o o o

Pastor Bob Kobel had given me directions to Dan Condon's ranch, which turned out to be a clean two-story farmhouse in a scrubby valley many hours from town. Not much of a ranch, though, at least to my untutored eyes. There was a big barn, in poor repair compared to the house, and a few cattle grazing on weedy patches of grama grass.

As soon as I braked a big man in overalls bounded down the porch steps, about two hundred fifty pounds of him, with a full beard and an unhappy expression. I rolled down my window.

"Private property, chief," he said.

"I'm here to see Simon and Diane."

He stared and said nothing.

"They're not expecting me. But they know who I am."

"Did they invite you? Because we're not big on visitors out here."

"Pastor Bob Kobel said you wouldn't mind me coming by."

"He did, huh."

"He said to tell you I was essentially harmless."

"Pastor Bob, huh. You got any identification?"

I took out my ID card, which he closed in his hand and carried into the house.

I waited. I rolled down the windows and let a dry wind whisper through the car. The sun was low enough to cast sundial shadows from the pillars of the porch, and those shadows lengthened more than a little before the man came back and returned my card and said, "Simon and Diane will see you. And I'm sorry if I sounded a little short. My name's Sorley." I climbed out of the car and shook his hand. He had a fierce grip. "Aaron Sorley. Brother Aaron to most people."

He escorted me through the wheezing screen door into the farmhouse. Inside, the house was summer-hot but lively. A child in a cotton T-shirt ran past us at knee-level, laughing. We passed a kitchen in which two women were collaborating on what looked like a meal for many people—gallon pots on the stove, mounds of cabbage on the chopping board.

"Simon and Diane share the back bedroom, top of the stairs, last door down on your right—you can go on up."

But I didn't need a guide. Simon was waiting at the top of the stairs.

The former chenille-stem heir looked a little haggard.

Which was not surprising given that I hadn't seen him since the night of the Chinese attack on the polar artifacts twenty years ago. He could have been thinking the same about me. His smile was still remarkable, big and generous, a smile Hollywood might have exploited if Simon had loved Mammon more than God. He wouldn't settle for a handshake. He put his arms around me.

"Welcome!" he said. "Tyler! Tyler Dupree! I apologize if Brother Aaron was a little brusque just now. We don't get many visitors, but you'll find our hospitality is on the generous side, at least once you're in the door. We would've invited you before this if we'd known there was a shadow of a chance you could make the trip."

"Happy coincidence," I said. "I'm in Arizona because—"

"Oh, I know. We do hear the news now and then. You came along with the wrinkled man. You're his doctor."

He led me down the hall to a cream-painted door—their door, Simon's and Diane's—and opened it.

The room inside was furnished in a comfortable if slightly time-warped style, a big bed in one corner with a quilted comforter over a billowing mattress, a window curtain of yellow gingham, a cotton throw rug on a plain plank floor. And a chair by the window. And Diane sitting in the chair.

o o o

"It's good to see you," she said. "Thank you for making time for us. I hope we haven't taken you away from your work."

"No more than I wanted to be taken away from it. How are you?"

Simon walked across the room and stood beside her. He put his hand on her shoulder and left it there.

"We're both fine," she said. "Maybe not prosperous, but we get by. I guess that's as much as anyone can expect in these times. I'm sorry we haven't been in touch, Tyler. After the troubles at Jordan Tabernacle it's harder to trust the world outside the church. I suppose you heard about all that?"

"A royal mess," Simon put in. "Homeland Security took the computer and the photocopy machine out of the rectory, took them away and never gave them back. Of course we didn't have anything to do with any of that red heifer nonsense. All we did was pass on some brochures to the congregation. For them to decide, you know, if this was the kind of thing they wanted to get involved with. That's what got us interviewed by the federal government, if you can imagine such a thing. Apparently that's a crime in Preston Lomax's America."

"Nobody arrested, I hope."

"Nobody close to us," Simon said.

"But it made everyone nervous," Diane said. "You start to think about things you took for granted. Phone calls. Letters."

I said, "I suppose you have to be careful."

"Oh, yes," Diane said.

"Really careful," Simon said.

Diane wore a plain cotton shift tied at the waist and a checkered red-and-white head scarf that looked like a down-home hijab. No makeup, but she didn't need it. Putting Diane in dowdy clothing was as futile as hiding a searchlight under a straw hat.

I realized how hungry I'd been for the simple sight of her. How unreasonably hungry. I was ashamed of the pleasure I took in her presence. For two decades we had been little more than acquaintances. Two people who had once known each other. I wasn't entitled to this speeding pulse, the sense of weightless acceleration she provoked just by sitting in that wooden chair glancing at me and glancing away, blushing faintly when our eyes met.

It was unrealistic and it was unfair—unfair to someone; maybe me, probably her. I should never have come here.

She said, "And how are *you*? Still working with Jason, I gather. I hope he's all right."

"He's fine. He sends his love."

She smiled. "I doubt that. It doesn't sound like Jase."

"He's changed."

"Has he?"

"There's been a lot of talk about Jason," Simon said, still gripping her shoulder, his hand calloused and dark against the pale cotton. "About Jason and the wrinkled man, the so-called Martian."

"Not just so-called," I said. "He was born and bred there."

Simon blinked. "If you say so then it must be true. But as I said, there's been talk. People know the Antichrist is walking among us, that's a given, and he may already be a famous man, biding his time, plotting his futile war. So public figures receive a lot of scrutiny around here. I'm not saying Wun Ngo Wen is the Antichrist, but I wouldn't be alone if I did make that assertion. Are you close to him, Tyler?"

"I talk to him from time to time. I don't think he's ambitious enough to be the Antichrist." Though E. D. Lawton might have disagreed with that statement.

"This is the kind of thing that makes us cautious, though," Simon said. "This is why it's been a problem for Diane to stay in touch with her family."

"Because Wun Ngo Wen might be the Antichrist?"

"Because we don't want to attract attention from powerful people, this close to the end of days."

I didn't know what to say to that.

"Tyler's been on the road a long time," Diane said. "He's probably thirsty."

Simon's smile flashed back. "Would you like a drink before dinner? We have plenty of soda pop. Do you like Mountain Dew?"

"That would be fine," I said.

He left the room. Diane waited until we heard his footsteps on the stairs. Then she cocked her head and looked at me more directly. "You traveled a long distance."

"There was no other way to get in touch."

"But you didn't have to go to all this trouble. I'm healthy and happy. You can tell that to Jase. And Carol, for that matter. And E.D., if he cares. I don't need a surveillance visit."

"That's not what this is."

"Just stopped by to say hello?"

"Actually, yes, something like that."

"We haven't joined a cult. I'm not under duress."

"I didn't say you were, Diane."

"But you thought about it, didn't you?"

"I'm glad you're all right."

She turned her head and the light of the setting sun caught

her eyes. "I'm sorry. I'm just a little startled. Seeing you like this. And I'm glad you're doing well back east. You are doing well, aren't you?"

I felt reckless. "No," I said. "I'm paralyzed. At least that's what your father thinks. He says our whole generation is Spin-paralyzed. We're all still caught in the moment when the stars went out. We never made peace with it."

"And do you think that's true?"

"Maybe truer than any of us want to admit." I was saying things I hadn't planned on saying. But Simon would be back any minute with his can of Mountain Dew and his adamantine smile and the opportunity would be lost, probably forever. "I look at you," I said, "and I still see the girl on the lawn outside the Big House. So yeah, maybe E.D. was right. Twenty-five stolen years. They went by pretty fast."

Diane accepted this in silence. Warm air turned the gingham curtains and the room grew darker. Then she said, "Close the door."

"Won't that look unusual?"

"Close the door, Tyler, I don't want to be overheard."

So I shut the door, gently, and she stood up and came to me and took my hands in her hands. Her hands were cool. "We're too close to the end of the world to lie to each other. I'm sorry I stopped calling, but there are four families sharing this house and one telephone and it gets to be pretty obvious who's talking to who."

"Simon wouldn't allow it."

"On the contrary. Simon would have accepted it. Simon accepts most of my habits and idiosyncrasies. But I don't want to lie to him. I don't want to carry that burden. But I admit I miss those calls, Tyler. Those calls were lifelines. When I had no money, when the church was splitting up, when I was lonely for no good reason . . . the sound of your voice was like a transfusion."

"Then why stop?"

"Because it was an act of disloyalty. Then. *Now.*" She shook her head as if she were trying to communicate a difficult but important idea. "I know what you mean about the Spin. I think about it, too. Sometimes I pretend there's a world where the Spin didn't happen and our lives were different. *Our* lives, yours and mine." She took a tremorous breath, blushing deeply. "And if I couldn't live in that world I thought I could at least visit it every couple of weeks, call you up and be old friends and talk about something besides the end of the world."

"You consider this disloyal?"

"It *is* disloyal. I gave myself to Simon. Simon is my husband in the eyes of God and the law. If that wasn't a wise choice it was still *my* choice, and I may not be the kind of Christian I ought to be but I do understand about duty and about perseverance and about standing by someone even if—"

"Even if *what,* Diane?"

"Even if it hurts. I don't think either one of us needs to look any harder at the lives we might have had."

"I didn't come here to make you unhappy."

"No, but you're having that effect."

"Then I won't stay."

"You'll stay for supper. It's only polite." She put her hands at her side and looked at the floor. "Let me tell you something while we still have a little privacy. For what it's worth. I don't share all of Simon's convictions. I can't honestly say I believe the world will end with the faithful ascending into heaven. God forgive me, but it just doesn't seem plausible to me. But I do believe the world *will end. Is* ending. It's been ending all our lives. And—"

I said, "Diane—"

"No, let me finish. Let me confess. I do believe the world will end. I believe what Jason told me years and years ago, that one morning the sun will rise swollen and hellish and in a few hours or days, our time on Earth will be finished. I don't want to be alone on that morning—"

"No one does." Except maybe Molly Seagram, I thought. Molly playing *On the Beach* with her bottle of suicide pills. Molly and all the people like her.

"And I *won't* be alone. I'll be with Simon. What I'm confessing to you, Tyler—what I want to be forgiven for—is that when I picture that day it isn't necessarily Simon I see myself with."

The door banged open. Simon. Empty-handed. "Turns out dinner's already on the table," he said. "Along with a big pitcher of iced tea for thirsty travelers. Come down and join us. There's plenty to go around."

"Thank you," I said. "That sounds nice."

o o o

The eight adults sharing the farmhouse were the Sorleys, Dan Condon and his wife, the McIsaacs, and Simon and Diane. The Sorleys had three children and the McIsaacs had five, so that made seventeen of us at a big trestle table in the room adjoining the kitchen. The result was a pleasant din that lasted until "Uncle Dan" announced the blessing, at which point all hands promptly folded and all heads promptly bowed.

Dan Condon was the alpha male of the group. He was tall and almost sepulchral, black-bearded, ugly in a Lincolnesque way, and by way of blessing the meal he reminded us that feeding a stranger was a virtuous act even if the stranger happened to arrive without an invitation, amen.

By the way conversation flowed I deduced that Brother Aaron Sorley was second in command and probably the enforcer when it came to disputes. Both Teddy McIsaac and Simon deferred to Sorley but looked to Condon for ultimate verdicts. Was the soup too salty? "Just about right," Condon said. The weather warm lately? "Hardly unusual in this part of the world," Condon declared.

The women spoke seldom and for the most part kept their eyes fixed on their plates. Condon's wife was a small, portly woman with a pinched expression. Sorley's wife was almost as big as he was and smiled prominently when the food drew compliments. McIsaac's wife looked barely eighteen to his morose over-forty. None of the women spoke directly to me nor were they introduced to me by their given names. Diane was a diamond among these zircons, conspicuously so, and maybe that explained her careful demeanor.

The families were all refugees from Jordan Tabernacle. They were not the most radical parishioners, Uncle Dan explained, like those wild-eyed Dispensationalists who had fled to Saskatchewan last year, but nor were they tepid in their

faith, like Pastor Bob Kobel and his crew of easy compromis-
ers. The families had moved to the ranch (Condon's ranch) in
order to separate themselves by a few miles from the tempta-
tions of the city and await the final call in monastic peace. So
far, he said, the plan had been successful.

The rest of the table talk concerned a truck with a bad
power cell, a roof-repair job still in progress, and a looming
septic-tank crisis. I was as relieved when the meal ended as
the children evidently were—Condon directed a fierce look
at one of the Sorley girls when she sighed too audibly.

Once the dishes had been cleared (women's work at the
Condon ranch), Simon announced that I had to leave.

Condon said, "Will you be all right on the road, Dr.
Dupree? There are robberies almost every night now."

"I'll keep the windows up and the gas pedal down."

"That's probably wise."

Simon said, "If you don't mind, Tyler, I'll ride with you as
far as the fence. I like the walk back, warm nights like this.
Even by lantern-light."

I agreed.

Then everyone lined up for a cordial good-bye. The children squirmed until I shook their hands and they were dismissed. When her turn came Diane nodded at me but lowered
her eyes, and when I offered my hand she took it without
looking at me.

o o o

Simon rode about a quarter mile uphill from the ranch with
me, fidgeting like a man with something to say but keeping
his mouth shut. I didn't prompt him. The night air was fra-
grant and relatively cool. I pulled over where he told me to, at
the peak of a ridge by a broken fence and a hedge of ocotillo.
"Thank you for the ride," he said.

When he got out he lingered a moment over the open door.

"Something you wanted to say?" I asked.

He cleared his throat. "You know," he said finally, his
voice barely louder than the wind, "I love Diane as much as I
love God. I admit that sounds blasphemous. It sounded that
way to me for a long time. But I believe God put her on Earth

to be my wife, that this is her entire purpose. So lately I think it's two sides of the same coin. Loving her is my way of loving God. Do you think that's possible, Tyler Dupree?"

He didn't wait for an answer but closed the door and switched on his flashlight, and I watched in the mirror as he ambled down the hill into darkness and the clatter of crickets.

○ ○ ○

I didn't run into bandits or road pirates that night.

The absence of stars or moon had made the night a darker and more dangerous place since the early years of the Spin. Criminals had worked out elaborate strategies for rural ambuscades. Traveling at night dramatically increased my chances of being robbed or murdered.

Traffic was therefore sparse during the drive back to Phoenix, mostly interstate truckers in well-defended eighteen-wheelers. Much of the time I was alone on the road, carving a bright wedge out of the night and listening to the grit of the wheels and the rush of the wind. If there's a lonelier sound I don't know what it is. I guess that's why they put radios in cars.

But there were no thieves or murderers on the road.

Not that night.

○ ○ ○

So I stayed in a motel outside Flagstaff and caught up with Wun Ngo Wen and his security crew in the executive lounge at the airport the following morning.

Wun was in a talkative mood on the flight to Orlando. He'd been studying the geology of the desert southwest and was particularly delighted by a rock he'd bought at a souvenir shack on the way back to Phoenix—forcing the entire cavalcade to pull over and wait while he picked through a bin of fossils. He showed me his prize, a chalky spiral concavity in a chunk of Bright Angel shale an inch on a side. The imprint of a trilobite, he said, dead some ten million years, recovered from these rocky, sandy wastes below us, which had once been the bed of an ancient sea.

He'd never seen a fossil before. There were no fossils on

Mars, he said. No fossils anywhere in the solar system except here, here on the ancient Earth.

○ ○ ○

At Orlando we were ushered into the backseat of another car in another convoy, this one bound for the Perihelion compound.

We rolled out at dusk after a perimeter sweep held us up for an hour or so. Once we reached the highway Wun apologized for yawning: "I'm not accustomed to so much physical exercise."

"I've seen you on the treadmill at Perihelion. You do all right."

"A treadmill is hardly a canyon."

"No, I suppose it isn't."

"I'm sore but not sorry. It was a wonderful expedition. I hope you spent your time as happily."

I told him I'd located Diane and that she was healthy.

"That's good. I'm sorry I couldn't meet her. If she's anything like her brother she must be a remarkable individual."

"She is."

"But the visit wasn't all you'd hoped?"

"Maybe I was hoping for the wrong thing." Maybe I'd been hoping for the wrong thing for a long time.

"Well," Wun said, yawning, eyes half-closed, "the question . . . as always, the question is how to look at the sun without being blinded."

I wanted to ask him what he meant, but his head had lolled against the upholstery and it seemed kinder to let him sleep.

○ ○ ○

There were five cars in our convoy plus a personnel carrier with a small detachment of infantrymen in case of trouble.

The APC was a boxy vehicle about the size of the armored cars used to ship cash to and from regional banks and easily mistaken for one.

In fact a Brink's convoy happened to be about ten minutes ahead of us until it turned off the highway toward Palm Bay. Gang spotters—placed on the road past major intersections and linked by phone—confused us with the Brink's shipment and marked us as a target for a band of strikers waiting up ahead.

The strikers were sophisticated criminals who had already emplaced surface mines at a stretch of the road skirting a swampy wilderness preserve. They also carried automatic rifles and a couple of rocket-propelled-grenade launchers, and a Brink's convoy would have been no match for them: five minutes after the first concussion the strikers would have been deep in bog country, dividing the spoils. But their spotters had made a critical mistake. Taking on a bank delivery is one thing; taking on five security-modified vehicles and an APC full of highly trained military and security personnel is a different matter entirely.

I was gazing out the tinted window of the car, watching low green water and bald cypress slide past, when the highway lights went out.

A pirate had cut the buried power cables. Suddenly the dark was truly dark, a wall beyond the window, nothing looking back at me but my own startled reflection. I said, "Wun—"

But he was still asleep, his wrinkled face blank as a thumbprint.

Then the lead car hit the mine.

The concussion beat at our hardened vehicle like a steel fist. The convoy was prudently spaced, but we were close enough to see the point car rise on a gout of yellow flame and drop back to the tarmac burning, wheels splayed.

Our driver swerved and, despite what he had probably been taught, slowed down. The road was blocked ahead. And now there was a second concussion at the back of the convoy, another mine, blasting chunks of pavement into the wetlands and boxing us in with ruthless efficiency.

Wun was awake now, baffled and terrified. His eyes were as big as moons and almost as bright.

Small-arms fire rattled in the near distance. I ducked and pulled Wun down next to me, both of us folded double around our seat belts and prying frantically at the clasps. The driver stopped, pulled a weapon from somewhere under the dash, and rolled out the door.

At the same time a dozen men spilled out of the APC behind us and began to fire into the darkness, trying to establish a perimeter. Plainclothes security men from other vehicles began to converge on our car, looking to protect Wun, but gunfire pinned them before they reached us.

The quick response must have rattled the road pirates. They opened up with heavy weapons. One of them fired what I was later told was a rocket-propelled grenade. All I knew was that I was suddenly deaf and the car was rotating around a complicated axis and the air was full of smoke and pebbled glass.

o o o

Then, mysteriously, I was halfway out the rear door, face pressed into the gritty pavement, tasting blood, and Wun was next to me, a few feet ahead, lying on his side. One of his shoes—one of the child-size hiking boots he'd bought for the Canyon—was on fire.

I called his name. He stirred, feebly. Bullets battered the ruin of the car behind us, punching craters in steel. My left leg was numb. I pulled myself closer and used a torn hank of upholstery to smother the burning shoe. Wun groaned and lifted his head.

Our guys returned fire, tracers streaking into the wetlands on each side of the road.

Wun arched his back and rose to his knees. He didn't seem to know where he was. He was bleeding from his nose. His forehead was gashed and raw.

"Don't stand up," I croaked.

But he went on trying to gather his feet under him, the burned boot flopping and stinking.

"For god's sake," I said. I reached out but he scuttled away. "For god's sake, *don't stand up!*"

But he managed it at last, levered himself up and stood trembling, profiled by the burning wreckage. He looked down and seemed to recognize me.

"Tyler," he said. "What happened?"

Then the bullets found him.

o o o

There were plenty of people who had hated Wun Ngo Wen. They distrusted his motives, like E. D. Lawton, or despised him for more complex and less defensible reasons: because they believed he was an enemy of God; because his skin happened to be black; because he espoused the theory of evolution; because he embodied physical evidence of the Spin and disturbing truths about the age of the external universe.

Many of those people had whispered about killing him. Dozens of intercepted threats were recorded in the files of Homeland Security.

But he wasn't killed by a conspiracy. What killed him was a combination of greed, mistaken identity, and Spin-engendered recklessness.

It was an embarrassingly terrestrial death.

Wun's body was cremated (after an autopsy and massive sample-extraction) and he was given a full state funeral. His memorial service in Washington's National Cathedral was attended by dignitaries from all over the planet. President Lomax delivered a lengthy eulogy.

There was talk of sending his ashes into orbit, but nothing ever came of it. According to Jason, the urn was stored in the basement of the Smithsonian Institution pending final disposition.

It's probably still there.

So I spent a few days in a Miami-area hospital, recovering from minor injuries, describing events to federal investigators, and coming to grips with the fact of Wun's death. It was during this time I resolved to leave Perihelion and open a private practice of my own.

But I decided not to announce my intention until after the replicator launch. I didn't want to trouble Jason with it at a critical time.

o o o

By comparison with the terraforming effort of previous years, the replicator launch was anticlimactic. Its results would be, if anything, greater and more subtle; but its very efficiency—a mere handful of rockets, no clever timing required—failed as drama.

President Lomax was keeping this one close to home. In a move that had infuriated the E.U., the Chinese, the Russians, and the Indians, Lomax had declined to share replicator technology beyond the must-know circles at NASA and Perihelion, and he had deleted all relevant passages in the publicly released editions of the Martian archives. "Artificial microbes" (in Lomax-speak) were a "high risk" technology. They could be "weaponized." (This was true, as even Wun had admitted.) The U.S. was thus obliged to take "custodial control" of the information in order to prevent "nanotech proliferation and a new and deadly arms race."

The European Union had cried foul and the U.N. was convening an investigatory panel, but in a world with brushfire wars burning on four continents Lomax's argument carried considerable weight. (Even though, as Wun might have countered, the Martians had successfully lived with the same technology for hundreds of years—and the Martians were no more or less human than their terrestrial ancestors.)

For all these reasons, the late-summer launch date at Canaveral drew minimal crowds and almost desultory media attention. Wun Ngo Wen was dead, after all, and the news services had exhausted themselves covering his murder. Now the four heavy Delta rockets set in their offshore gantries looked like little more than a footnote to the memorial service, or worse, a rerun: the seed launches retooled for an age of diminished expectations.

But even if it was a sideshow, it was still a show. Lomax flew in for the occasion. E. D. Lawton had accepted a courtesy invitation and by this time was willing to pledge good behavior. And so, on the morning of the appointed day, I rode with Jason to the V.I.P. bleachers at the eastern shore of Cape Canaveral.

We faced seaward. The old offshore gantries, still functional but gone a little ruddy with saltwater rust, had been built to hold the heaviest lifters of the seed-launch era. The brand-new Deltas were dwarfed by them. Not that we could see much detail from this distance, only four white pillars out at the misty limits of the summer ocean, plus the fretwork of other unused launch platforms, the rail connectors, the tenders and support vessels anchored at a safe perimeter. It was a clear, hot summer morning. The wind was gusty—not strong enough to scrub the launch but more than enough to snap the flag crisply and tousle the coifed hair of President

Lomax as he climbed the podium to address the assembled dignitaries and press.

He delivered a speech, mercifully brief. He cited the legacy of Wun Ngo Wen and his faith that the replicator network about to be planted in the icy fringes of the solar system would soon enlighten us about the nature and purpose of the Spin. He said brave things about humanity leaving its mark on the cosmos. ("He means the galaxy," Jason whispered, "not the cosmos. And—*leaving our mark?* Like a dog peeing on a hydrant? Someone really ought to edit these speeches.") Then Lomax quoted a poem by a nineteenth-century Russian poet named F. I. Tiutchev, who couldn't have imagined the Spin but wrote as if he had:

> *Gone like a vision is the external world*
> *and Man, a homeless orphan, has to face*
> *helpless, naked and alone,*
> *the blackness of immeasurable space.*
> *All life and brightness seem an ancient dream,*
> *while in the substance of the night,*
> *unraveled, alien, he now perceives*
> *a fateful something that is his by right.*

Then Lomax departed the stage, and after the prosaic business of backward counting, the first of the rockets rode its column of fire into the unraveling cosmos behind the sky. A fateful something. Ours by right.

While everyone else looked up, Jason closed his eyes and folded his hands in his lap.

o o o

We adjourned to a reception room along with the rest of the invited guests, pending a round of press interviews. (Jason was scheduled for twenty minutes with a cable news network, I was scheduled for ten. I was "the physician who attempted to save the life of Wun Ngo Wen," though all I had done was extinguish his burning shoe and pull his body out of the line of fire after he fell. A quick ABC check—airway, breathing, circulation—made it abundantly clear that I couldn't help him and that it would be wiser simply to keep my head down until help arrived. Which is what I told reporters, until they learned to stop asking.)

President Lomax came through the room shaking hands before he was hustled away once more by his handlers. Then E.D. cornered Jason and me at the buffet table.

"I guess you got what you wanted," he said, meaning the comment for Jason but looking at me. "It can't be undone now."

"In that case," Jason said, "perhaps it's not worth arguing about."

Wun and I had made a point of keeping Jase under observation in the months after his treatment. He had submitted to a battery of neurological tests including another series of clandestine MRIs. None of the tests had revealed any deficiency, and the only obvious physiological changes were the ones connected with his recovery from AMS. A clean bill of health, in other words. Cleaner than I once would have imagined possible.

But he did seem subtly different. I had asked Wun whether all Fourths underwent psychological changes. "In a certain sense," he had answered, "yes." Martian Fourths were expected to behave differently after their treatment, but there was a subtlety embedded in the word "expectation"—yes, Wun said, it was "expected" (i.e., considered likely) that a Fourth would change, but change was also "expected of him" (required of him) by his community and peers.

How had Jason changed? He moved differently, for one thing. Jase had disguised his AMS very cleverly, but there was a perceptible new freedom in his walk and his gestures. He was the Tin Man, post-oilcan. He was still occasionally moody, but his moods were less violent. He swore less often—that is, he was less likely to stumble into one of those emotional sinkholes in which the only useful adjective is "fucking." He joked more than he used to.

All these things sound good. And they were, but they were also superficial. Other changes were more troubling. He had withdrawn from the daily management of Perihelion to such a degree that his staff briefed him once a week and otherwise ignored him. He had begun reading Martian astrophysics from the raw translations, skirting security protocols if not absolutely violating them. The only event that had penetrated his newfound calm was the death of Wun, and that had left him haunted and hurt in ways I still didn't quite understand.

"You realize," E.D. said, "what we just saw was the end of Perihelion."

And in a real sense it was. Apart from interpreting whatever feedback we received from the replicators, Perihelion as a civilian space agency was finished. The downsizing had already begun in earnest. Half the support staff had been laid off. The tech people were draining away more slowly, lured by universities or big-money contractors.

"Then so be it," Jason said, displaying what was either the innate equanimity of a Fourth or a long-suppressed hostility to his father. "We've done the work we needed to do."

"You can stand here and deliver that verdict? To me?"

"I believe it's true."

"Does it matter that I spent my life building what you just tore down?"

"Does it matter?" Jason pondered this as if E.D. had asked a real question. "Ultimately, no, I don't suppose it does."

"Jesus, what happened to you? You make a mistake of this magnitude—"

"I don't think it's a mistake."

"—you ought to assume the responsibility for it."

"I think I have."

"Because if it fails, you'll be the one they'll blame."

"I understand that."

"The one they'll burn."

"If it comes to that."

"I can't protect you," E.D. said.

"You never could," Jason said.

o o o

I rode back to Perihelion with him. Jase was driving a German fuel-cell car these days—a niche car, since most of us still owned gas-burners designed by people who didn't believe there was a future worth worrying about. Commuters burned past us in the speed lanes, hurrying home before dark.

I told him I meant to leave Perihelion and establish a practice of my own.

Jase was silent for a little while, watching the road, warm air boiling off the pavement as if the edges of the world had softened in the heat. Then he said, "But you don't have to, Tyler. Perihelion ought to struggle along for a few years yet, and I have enough clout to keep you on payroll. I can hire you privately, if need be."

"That's the point, though, Jase. There *is* no need. I was always a little underutilized at Perihelion."

"Bored, you mean?"

"It might be nice to feel useful for a change."

"You don't feel useful? If not for you I'd be in a wheelchair."

"That wasn't me. That was Wun. All I did was push the plunger."

"Hardly. You saw me through the ordeal. I appreciate that. Besides . . . I need someone to talk to, someone who isn't trying to buy or sell me."

"When was the last time we had a real conversation?"

"Just because I weathered one medical crisis doesn't mean there won't be another."

"You're a Fourth, Jase. You won't need to see a doctor for another fifty years."

"And the only people who know that about me are you and Carol. Which is another reason I don't want you to leave." He hesitated. "Why not take the treatment yourself? Give yourself another fifty years, minimum."

I supposed I could. But fifty years would carry us deep into the heliosphere of the expanding sun. It would be a futile gesture. "I'd rather be useful now."

"You're absolutely determined to leave?"

E.D. would have said, *Stay.* E.D. would have said, *It's your job to take care of him.*

E.D. would have said a lot of things.

"Absolutely."

Jason gripped the wheel and stared down the road as if he had seen something infinitely sad there. "Well," he said. "Then all I can do is wish you luck."

○ ○ ○

The day I left Perihelion the support staff summoned me into one of the now seldom-used boardrooms for a farewell party, where I was given the kind of gifts appropriate to yet another departure from a dwindling workforce: a miniature cactus in a terra-cotta pot, a coffee mug with my name on it, a pewter tie pin in the shape of a caduceus.

Jase showed up at my door that evening with a more problematic gift.

It was a cardboard box tied with string. It contained, when I opened it, about a pound of densely printed paper documents and six unlabelled optical memory disks.

"Jase?"

"Medical information," he said. "You can think of it as a textbook."

"What kind of medical information?"

He smiled. "From the archives."

"The Martian archives?"

He nodded.

"But that's classified information."

"Yes, technically, it is. But Lomax would classify the phone number for 911 if he thought he could get away with it. There may be information here that would put Pfizer and Eli Lilly out of business. But I don't see that as a legitimate concern. Do you?"

"No, but—"

"Nor do I think Wun would have wanted it kept secret. So I've been quietly doling out little pieces of the archives, here and there, to people I trust. You don't have to actually do anything with it, Tyler. Look at it or ignore it, file it away—fine."

"Great. Thanks, Jase. A gift I could be arrested for possessing."

His smile widened. "I know you'll do the right thing."

"Whatever that is."

"You'll figure it out. I have faith in you, Tyler. Ever since the treatment—"

"What?"

"I seem to see things a little more clearly," he said.

He didn't explain, and in the end I tucked the box into my luggage as a kind of souvenir. I was tempted to write the word MEMENTOS on it.

○ ○ ○

Replicator technology was slow even by comparison with the terraforming of a dead planet. Two years passed before we had anything like a detectable response from the payloads we had scattered among the planetesimals at the edge of the solar system.

The replicators were busy out there, though, barely touched by the gravity of the sun, doing what they were designed to do: reproducing by the inch and the century, following instructions written into their superconductive equivalent of DNA. Given time and an adequate supply of ice and carbonaceous trace elements, they would eventually phone home. But the first few detector satellites placed in orbit beyond the Spin membrane dropped back to Earth without recording a signal.

During those two years I managed to find a partner (Herbert Hakkim, a soft-spoken Bengali-born physician who had finished his internship the year Wun visited the Grand Canyon), and we took over a San Diego practice from a retiring GP. Hakkim was frank and friendly with patients but he had no real social life and seemed to prefer it that way: we seldom got together outside office hours, and I think the most intimate question he ever asked me was why I carried two cell phones.

(One for the customary reasons; the other because the number assigned to it was the last one I'd given Diane. Not that it ever rang. Nor did I attempt to contact her again. But if I had let the number lapse she would have had no way of reaching me, and that still seemed . . . well, wrong.)

I liked my work, and by and large I liked my patients. I saw more gunshot wounds than I might once have expected, but these were the hard years of the Spin; the domestic trendlines for murder and suicide had begun to arc toward vertical. Years when it seemed like everyone under thirty was wearing some kind of uniform: armed forces, National Guard, Homeland Security, private security; even Home Scouts and Home Guides for the intimidated products of a dwindling birth rate. Years when Hollywood began to churn out ultraviolent or ultrapious films in which, however, the Spin was never explicitly mentioned; the Spin, like sex and the words describing it, having been banned from "entertainment discourse" by Lomax's Cultural Council and the FCC.

These were also the years when the administration enacted a raft of new laws aimed at sanitizing the Martian archives. Wun's archives, according to the president and his congressional allies, contained intrinsically dangerous knowledge that had to be redacted and secured. Opening them to the public would have been "like posting plans for a suitcase nuke on the Internet." Even the anthropological material was vetted: in the published version, a Fourth was defined as "a respected elder." No mention of medically mediated longevity.

But who needed or wanted longevity? The end of the world was closer every day.

The flickers were evidence of that, if anyone needed proof.

○ ○ ○

The first positive results from the replicator project had been in for half a year when the flickers began.

I heard most of the replicator news from Jase a couple of days before it broke in the media. In itself, it was nothing spectacular. A NASA/Perihelion survey satellite had recorded a faint signal from a known Oort Cloud body well beyond the orbit of Pluto—a periodic uncoded blip that was the sound of a replicator colony nearing completion. (Nearing maturity, you might say.)

Which appears trivial unless you consider what it means:

The dormant cells of an utterly novel, man-made biology had alighted on a chunk of dusty ice in deepest space. Those cells had then begun an agonizingly slow form of metabolism, in which they absorbed the scant heat of the distant sun, used it to separate a few nearby molecules of water and carbon, and duplicated themselves with the resulting raw materials.

Over the course of many years the same colony grew to, perhaps, the size of a ball bearing. An astronaut who had made the impossibly long journey and knew precisely where to look would have seen it as a black dimple on the rocky/icy regolith of the host planetesimal. But the colony was fractionally more efficient than its single-celled ancestor. It began to grow more quickly and generate more heat. The temperature differential between the colony and its surroundings was only a fraction of a degree Kelvin (except when brief reproductive bursts pumped latent energy into the local environment), but it was persistent.

More millennia (or terrestrial months) passed. Subroutines in the replicators' genetic substrate, activated by local heat gradients, modified the colony's growth. Cells began to differentiate. Like a human embryo, the colony produced not merely more cells but specialized cells, the equivalent of heart and lungs, arms and legs. Tendrils of it forced themselves into the loose material of the planetesimal, mining it for carbonaceous molecules.

Eventually, microscopic but carefully calculated vapor bursts began to slow the host object's rotation (patiently, over centuries), until the colony's face was turned perpetually to the sun. Now differentiation began in earnest. The colony extruded carbon/carbon and carbon/silicon junctions; it grew monomolecular whiskers to join these junctions together, bootstrapping itself up the ladder of complexity; from these junctions it generated light-sensitive dots—eyes—and the capacity to generate and process microbursts of radio-frequency noise.

And as more centuries passed the colony elaborated and refined these capabilities until it announced itself with a simple periodic chirp, the equivalent of the sound a newborn sparrow might make. Which was what our satellite had detected.

The news media ran the story for a couple of days (with stock footage of Wun Ngo Wen, his funeral, the launch) and then forgot about it. After all, this was only the first stage of what the replicators were designed to do.

Merely that. Uninspiring. Unless you thought about it for more than thirty seconds.

This was technology with, literally, a life of its own. A genie out of the bottle for good and all.

○ ○ ○

The flicker happened a few months later.

The flicker was the first sign of a change or disturbance in the Spin membrane—first, that is, unless you count the event that followed the Chinese missile attack on the polar artifacts, back in the earliest years of the Spin. Both events were visible from every point on the globe. But beyond that key resemblance they were not much alike.

After the missile attack the Spin membrane had seemed to stutter and recover, generating strobed images of the evolving sky, multiple moons and gyrating stars.

The flicker was different.

I watched it from the balcony of my suburban apartment. A warm September night. Some of the neighbors had already been outside when the flicker started. Now all of us were. We perched on our ledges like starlings, chattering.

The sky was bright.

Not with stars but with infinitesimally narrow threads of golden fire, crackling like heatless lightning from horizon to horizon. The threads moved and shifted erratically; some flickered or faded altogether; occasionally new ones flared into existence. It was as mesmerizing as it was frightening.

The event was global, not local. On the daylight side of the planet the phenomenon was only slightly visible, lost in sunlight or obscured by cloud; in North and South America and western Europe the dark-sky displays caused sporadic outbreaks of panic. After all, we'd been expecting the end of the world for more years than most of us cared to count. This looked like an overture, at least, to the real thing.

There were hundreds of successful or attempted suicides that night, plus scores of murders or mercy killings, in the city where I lived. Worldwide, the numbers were incalculably larger. Apparently there were plenty of people like Molly Seagram, people who chose to dodge the much-predicted boiling of the seas with a few lethal tablets of this or that. And spares for family and friends. Many of them opted for the final exit as soon as the sky lit up. Prematurely, as it turned out.

The display lasted eight hours. By morning I was at the local hospital lending a hand in the emergency ward. By noon I had seen seven separate cases of carbon monoxide poisoning, folks who had intentionally locked themselves in the garage with an idling car. Most were dead well before I pronounced them and the survivors were hardly better off. Otherwise healthy people, people I might have passed at the grocery store, would be spending the rest of their lives hooked up to ventilators, irreparably brain damaged, victims of a botched exit strategy. Not pleasant. But the gunshot wounds to the head were worse. I couldn't treat them without thinking of Wun Ngo Wen lying on that Florida highway, blood gouting from what remained of his skull.

Eight hours. Then the sky was blank again, the sun beaming out of it like the punchline to a bad joke.

It happened again a year and a half later.

o o o

"You look like a man who lost his faith," Hakkim once told me.

"Or never had one," I said.

"I don't mean faith in God. Of that you seem to be genuinely innocent. Faith in something else. I don't know what."

Which seemed cryptic. But I understood it a little more clearly the next time I talked to Jason.

He called me at home. (On my regular cell, not the orphan phone I carried with me like a luckless charm.) I said, "Hello?" and he said, "You must be watching this on television."

"Watching what?"

"Turn on one of the news networks. Are you alone?"

The answer was yes. By choice. No Molly Seagram to complicate the end of days. The TV remote was on the coffee table where I'd left it. Where I always left it.

The news channel showed a graph of many colors accompanied by a droning voice-over. I muted it. "What am I looking at, Jase?"

"A JPL press conference. The data set retrieved from the last orbital receiver."

Replicator data, in other words. "And?"

"We're in business," he said. I could practically hear his smile.

The satellite had detected multiple radio sources narrow-casting from the outer solar system. Which meant that more than one replicator colony had grown to maturity. And the data were complex, Jason said, not simple. As the replicator colonies aged, their growth rate slowed but their functions became more refined and purposeful. They weren't just leaning sunward for free energy anymore. They were analyzing starlight, calculating planetary orbits on neural networks made of silicon and carbon fibers, comparing them to templates etched into their genetic code. No less than a dozen fully adult colonies had sent back precisely the data they were designed to collect, four streams of binary data declaring:

1. This was a planetary system of a star with a solar mass of 1.0;
2. The system possessed eight large planetary bodies (Pluto falling under the detectable mass limit);
3. Two of those planets were optically blank, surrounded by Spin membranes; and
4. The reporting replicator colonies had shifted into reproductive mode, shedding nonspecific seed cells and launching them on bursts of cometary vapor toward neighboring stars.

The same message, Jase said, had been beamed at local, less mature colonies, which would respond by bypassing redundant functions and directing their energy into purely reproductive behavior.

In other words, we had successfully infected the outer system with Wun's quasi-biological systems.

Which were now sporulating.

I said, "This tells us nothing about the Spin."

"Of course not. Not yet. But this little trickle of information will be a torrent before long. In time we'll be able to put together a Spin map of all the nearby stars—maybe eventually the entire galaxy. From that we ought to be able to deduce where the Hypotheticals come from, where they've been Spinning, and what ultimately happens to Spin worlds when their stars expand and burn out."

"That won't fix anything, though, will it?"

He sighed as if I'd disappointed him by asking a stupid question. "Probably not. But isn't it better to know than to speculate? We might find out we're doomed, but we might find out we have more time left than we expected. Remember, Tyler, we're working on other fronts, too. We've been delving into the theoretical physics in Wun's archives. If you model the Spin membrane as a wormhole enclosing an object accelerating at near-light-speed—"

"But we're not accelerating. We're not going anywhere." Except headlong into the future.

"No, but if you do the calculation it yields results that match our observation of the Spin. Which might give us a clue as to which *forces* the Hypotheticals are manipulating."

"To what end, though, Jase?"

"Too soon to say. But I don't believe in the futility of knowledge."

"Even if we're dying?"

"Everyone dies."

"I mean, as a species."

"That remains to be seen. Whatever the Spin is, it has to be more than a sort of elaborate global euthanasia. The Hypotheticals must be acting with a purpose."

Maybe so. But this, I realized, was the faith that had deserted me. The faith in Big Salvation.

All the brands and flavors of Big Salvation. At the last minute we would devise a technological fix and save ourselves. Or: the Hypotheticals were benevolent beings who would turn the planet into a peaceable kingdom. Or: God would rescue us all, or at least the true believers among us. Or. Or. Or.

Big Salvation. It was a honeyed lie. A paper lifeboat, even if we were killing ourselves trying to cling to it. It wasn't the Spin that had mutilated my generation. It was the lure and price of Big Salvation.

o o o

The flicker came back the following winter, persisted for forty-four hours, then vanished again. Many of us began to think of it as a kind of celestial weather, unpredictable but generally harmless.

Pessimists pointed out that the intervals between episodes were growing shorter, the duration of the episodes growing longer.

In April there was a flicker that lasted three days and interfered with the transmission of aerostat signals. This one provoked another (smaller) wave of successful and attempted suicides—people driven to panic less by what they saw in the sky than by the failure of their telephones and TV sets.

I had stopped paying attention to the news, but certain events were impossible to ignore: the military setbacks in North Africa and eastern Europe, the cult coup in Zimbabwe, the mass suicides in Korea. Exponents of apocalyptic Islam scored big numbers in the Algerian and Egyptian elections that year. A Filipino cult that worshipped the memory of Wun Ngo Wen—whom they had reconceived as a pastoralist saint, an agrarian Gandhi—had successfully engineered a general strike in Manila.

And I got a few more calls from Jason. He mailed me a phone with some kind of built-in encryption pad, which he claimed would give us "pretty good protection against keyword hunters," whatever that meant.

"Sounds a little paranoid," I said.

"Usefully paranoid, I think."

Perhaps, if we wanted to discuss matters of national security. We didn't, though, at least not at first. Instead Jason asked me about my work, my life, the music I'd been listening to. I understood that he was trying to generate the kind of conversation we might have had twenty or thirty years ago—before Perihelion, if not before the Spin. He had been to see his mother, he told me. Carol was still counting out her days by clock and bottle. Nothing had changed. Carol had insisted on that. The house staff kept everything clean, everything in its place. The Big House was like a time capsule, he said, as if it had been hermetically sealed on the first night of the Spin. It was a little spooky that way.

I asked whether Diane ever called.

"Diane stopped talking to Carol back before Wun was killed. No, not a word from her."

Then I asked him about the replicator project. There hadn't been anything in the papers lately.

"Don't bother looking. JPL is sitting on the results."

I heard the unhappiness in his voice. "That bad?"

"It's not entirely bad news. At least not until recently. The replicators did everything Wun hoped they would. Amazing things, Tyler. I mean absolutely amazing. I wish I could show you the maps we generated. Big navigable software maps. Almost two hundred thousand stars, in a halo of space hundreds of light-years in diameter. We know more about stellar and planetary evolution now than an astronomer of E.D.'s generation could have imagined."

"But nothing about the Spin?"

"I didn't say that."

"So what did you learn?"

"For one thing, we're not alone. In that volume of space we've found three optically blank planets roughly the size of the Earth, in orbits that are habitable by terrestrial standards or would have been in the past. The nearest is circling the star Ursa Majoris 47. The farthest—"

"I don't need the details."

"If we look at the age of the stars involved and make some plausible assumptions, the Hypotheticals appear to emanate from somewhere in the direction of the galactic core. There are other indicators, too. The replicators found a couple of white dwarf stars—burned-out stars, essentially, but stars that would have looked like the sun a few billion years ago—with rocky planets in orbits that should never have outlasted the solar expansion."

"Spin survivors?"

"Maybe."

"Are these *living* planets, Jase?"

"We have no real way of knowing. But they don't have Spin membranes to protect them, and their current stellar environment is absolutely hostile by our standards."

"Meaning what?"

"I don't know. Nobody knows. We thought we'd be able to make more meaningful comparisons as the replicator network expanded. What we created with the replicators is really a neural network on an unimaginably large scale. They talk to themselves the way neurons talk to themselves, except they do it across centuries and light-years. It's absolutely, stunningly beautiful, what they do. A network larger than anything humanity has ever built. Gathering information, culling it, storing it, feeding it back to us—"

"So what went wrong?"

He sounded as if it hurt him to say it. "Maybe age. Everything ages, even highly protected genetic codes. They might be evolving beyond our instructions. Or—"

"Yeah, but what *happened,* Jase?"

"The data are diminishing. We're getting fragmentary, contradictory information from the replicators that are farthest from Earth. That could mean a lot of things. If they're dying, it might reflect some emerging flaw in the design code. But some of the long-established relay nodes are starting to shut down, too."

"Something's targeting them?"

"That's too hasty an assumption. Here's another idea. When we launched these things into the Oort Cloud we created a simple interstellar ecology—ice, dust, and artificial life. But what if we weren't the first? What if the interstellar ecology isn't simple?"

"You mean there might be other kinds of replicators out there?"

"Could be. If so, they'd be competing for resources. Maybe even using *each other* for resources. We thought we were sending our devices into a sterile void. But there might be competitor species, there might even be predator species."

"Jason . . . you think something's *eating* them?"

"It's possible," he said.

o o o

The flicker came back in June and clocked nearly forty-eight hours before it dissipated.

In August, fifty-six hours of flicker plus intermittent tele-com problems.

When it started again in late September no one was sur-prised. I spent most of the first evening with the blinds closed, ignoring the sky, watching a movie I'd downloaded a week before. An old movie, pre-Spin. Watching it not for the plot but for the faces, the faces of people the way they used to look, people who hadn't spent their lives afraid of the future. People who, every once in a while, talked about the moon and the stars without irony or nostalgia.

Then the phone rang.

Not my personal phone, and not the encrypting phone Jase had sent me. I recognized the three-tone ring instantly even though I hadn't heard it for years. It was audible but faint—faint because I'd left the phone in the pocket of a jacket that was hanging in the hallway closet.

It rang twice more before I fumbled it out and said, "Hello?"

Expecting a wrong number. Wanting Diane's voice. Want-ing it and dreading it.

But it was a man's voice on the other end. Simon, I recog-nized belatedly.

He said, "Tyler? Tyler Dupree? Is that you?"

I had taken enough emergency calls to recognize the anxi-ety in his voice. I said, "It's me, Simon. What's wrong?"

"I shouldn't be talking to you. But I don't know who else to call. I don't know any local doctors. And she's so sick. She's just so sick, Tyler! I don't think she's getting better. I think she needs—"

And then the flicker cut us off and there was nothing but noise on the line.

Behind Diane came En and two dozen of his cousins and an equal number of strangers, all bound for the new world. Jala herded them inside, then slid shut the corrugated steel door of the warehouse. The light dimmed. Diane put her arm around me and I walked her to a relatively clean space under one of the high halide lamps. Ibu Ina unrolled an empty jute bag for her to lie on.

"The noise," Ina said.

Diane closed her eyes as soon as she was horizontal, awake but obviously exhausted. I unbuttoned her blouse and began, gently, to peel it away from the wound.

I said, "My medical case—"

"Yes, of course." Ina summoned En and sent him up the warehouse stairs to bring both bags, mine and hers. "The noise—"

Diane winced when I began to pull the matted cloth from the caked blood of the wound, but I didn't want to medicate her until I'd seen the extent of the injury. "What noise?"

"Exactly!" Ina said. "The docks should be noisy this time of the morning. But it's quiet. There *is* no noise."

I raised my head. She was right. No noise, except the nervous talk of the Minang villagers and a distant drumming that was the sound of rain on the high metal roof.

But this wasn't the time to worry about it. "Go ask Jala," I said. "Find out what's happening."

Then I turned back to Diane.

o o o

"It's superficial," Diane said. She took a deep breath. Her eyes were clenched shut against the pain. "At least I think it's superficial."

"It looks like a bullet wound."

"Yes. The Reformasi found Jala's safe house in Padang. Fortunately we were just leaving. *Uh!*"

She was right. The wound itself was superficial, though it would need suturing. The bullet had passed through fatty tissue just above the hipbone. But the impact had bruised her badly where the skin wasn't torn and I worried that the bruising might be deep, that the concussion might have torn something inside her. But there had been no blood in her urine, she said, and her blood pressure and pulse were at reasonable numbers under the circumstances.

"I want to give you something for the pain, and we need to stitch this up."

"Stitch it if you have to, but I don't want any drugs. We have to get out of here."

"You don't want me suturing you without an anesthetic."

"Something local, then."

"This isn't a hospital. I don't have anything local."

"Then just sew it, Tyler. I can deal with the pain."

Yes, but could I? I looked at my hands. Clean—there was running water in the warehouse washroom, and Ina had helped me wrestle into latex gloves before I attended Diane. Clean and skilled. But not steady.

I had never been squeamish about my work. Even as a med student, even doing dissections, I'd always been able to switch off the loop of sympathy that makes us feel another's pain as if it were our own. To pretend that the torn artery demanding my attention was unconnected with a living human being. To pretend and for the necessary few minutes to really believe it.

But now my hand was shaking, and the idea of passing a needle through these bloody lips of flesh seemed brutal, cruel beyond countenance.

Diane put her hand on my wrist to steady it. "It's a Fourth thing," she said.

"What?"

"You feel like the bullet went through you instead of me. Right?"

I nodded, astonished.

"It's a Fourth thing. I think it's supposed to make us better people. But you're still a doctor. You just have to work through it."

"If I can't," I said, "I'll turn it over to Ina."

But I could. Somehow. I did.

o o o

Ina came back from her conference with Jala. "Today there was to be a labor action," she said. "The police and the Reformasi are at the gates and they mean to take control of the port. Conflict is anticipated." She looked at Diane. "How are you, my dear?"

"In good hands," Diane whispered. Her voice was ragged.

Ina inspected my work. "Competent," she pronounced.

"Thank you," I said.

"Under the circumstances. But listen to me, listen. We need very urgently to leave. Right now the only thing between us and prison is a labor riot. We have to board the *Capetown Maru* immediately."

"The police are looking for us?"

"I think not you, not specifically. Jakarta has entered into some sort of agreement with the Americans to suppress the emigration trade in general. The docks are being swept here and elsewhere, very publicly, in order to impress the people at the U.S. consulate. Of course it won't last. Too much money changes hands for the trade to be truly eliminated. But for cosmetic effect there's nothing like uniformed police dragging people out of the holds of cargo ships."

"They came to Jala's safe house," Diane said.

"Yes, they're aware of you and Dr. Dupree, ideally they would like to take you into custody, but that isn't why the police are forming ranks at the gates. Ships are still leaving the harbor but that won't last long. The union movement is powerful at Teluk Bayur. They mean to fight."

Jala shouted from the doorway, words I didn't understand.

"Now we really must leave," Ina said.

"Help me make a litter for Diane."

Diane tried to sit up. "I can walk."

"No," Ina said. "In this I believe Tyler is correct. Try not to move."

We doubled up more lengths of stitched jute and made a sort of hammock for her. I took one end and Ina called over one of the huskier Minang men to grab the other.

"Hurry now!" Jala shouted, waving us out into the rain.

○ ○ ○

Monsoon season. Was this a monsoon? The morning looked like dusk. Clouds like sodden bolts of wool came across the gray water of Teluk Bayur, clipping the towers and radars of the big double-hulled tankers. The air was hot and rank. Rain soaked us even as we loaded Diane into a waiting car. Jala had arranged a little convoy for his group of émigrés: three cars and a couple of little open-top cargo-haulers with hard rubber wheels.

The *Capetown Maru* was docked at the end of a high concrete pier a quarter mile away. Along the wharves in the opposite direction, past rows of warehouses and industrial godowns and fat red-and-white Avigas holding tanks, a dense crowd of dockworkers had gathered by the gates. Under the drumming of the rain I could hear someone shouting through a bullhorn. Then a sound that might or might not have been shots fired.

"Get in," Jala said, urging me into the backseat of the car where Diane bent over her wounds as if she were praying. "Hurry, hurry." He climbed into the driver's seat.

I took a final look back at the rain-obscured mob. Something the size of a football lofted high over the crowd, trailing spirals of white smoke behind it. A tear gas canister.

The car jolted forward.

o o o

"This is more than police," Jala said as we wheeled out along the finger of the quay. "Police would not be so foolish. This is New Reformasi. Street thugs hired out of the slums of Jakarta and dressed in government uniforms."

Uniforms and guns. And more tear gas now, roiling clouds of it that blurred into the rainy mist. The crowd began to unravel at its edges.

There was a distant *whoomp,* and a ball of flame rose a few yards into the sky.

Jala saw it in his mirror. "Dear God! How idiotic! Someone must have fired on a barrel of oil. The docks—"

Sirens bellowed over the water as we followed the quay. Now the crowd was genuinely panicked. For the first time I was able to see a line of police pushing through the gated entrance to the port. Those in the vanguard carried heavy weapons and wore black-snouted masks.

A fire truck rolled out of a shed and screamed toward the gate.

We rolled up a series of ramps and stopped where the pier was level with the main deck of the *Capetown Maru.* *Capetown Maru* was an old flag-of-convenience freighter painted white and rust orange. A short steel gangway had been emplaced between the main deck and the pier, and the first few Minang were already scurrying across it.

Jala leaped out of the car. By the time I had Diane on the quay—on foot, leaning hard into me, the jute litter abandoned—Jala was already conducting a heated argument in English with the man at the head of the gangway: if not the ship's captain or pilot then someone with similar authority, a squat man with Sikh headgear and a grimly clenched jaw.

"It was agreed months ago," Jala was saying.

"—but this weather—"

"—in *any* weather—"

"—but without approval from the Port Authority—"

"—yes but there *is* no Port Authority—look!"

Jala meant the gesture to be rhetorical. But he was waving his hand at the fuel and gas bunkers near the main gate when one of the tanks exploded.

I didn't see it. The concussion pushed me into the concrete and I felt the heat of it on the back of my neck. The sound was huge but arrived like an afterthought. I rolled onto my back as soon as I could move, ears ringing. The Avigas, I thought. Or whatever else they stored here. Benzene. Kerosene. Fuel oil, even crude palm oil. The fire must have spread, or the unschooled police had fired their weapons in an unwise direction. I turned my head to look for Diane and found her beside me, looking back, more puzzled than frightened. I thought: *I can't hear the rain.* But there was another, distinctly audible, more frightening sound: the *ping* of falling debris. Shards of metal, some burning. *Ping,* as they struck the concrete quay or the steel deck of the *Capetown Maru.*

"Heads down," Jala was shouting, his voice watery, submerged: "Heads down, everybody heads down!"

I tried to cover Diane's body with mine. Burning metal fell around us like hail or splashed into the dark water beyond the ship for a few interminable seconds. Then it simply stopped. Nothing fell except the rain, soft as the whisper of brushed cymbals.

We lifted ourselves up. Jala was already pushing bodies across the gangway, casting fearful glances back at the flames. "That might not be the last! Get on board, all of you, go on, go on!" He steered the villagers past the *Capetown*'s crew, who were extinguishing deck fires and casting off lines.

Smoke blew toward us, obscuring the violence ashore. I helped Diane aboard. She winced at every step, and her wound had started leaking into her bandages. We were last up the gangway. A couple of sailors began to draw the aluminum structure in behind us, hands on the winches but eyes darting toward the pillar of fire back ashore.

Capetown Maru's engines thrummed under the deck. Jala saw me and came to take Diane's other arm. Diane registered his presence and said, "Are we safe?"

"Not until we clear the harbor."

Across the green-gray water horns and whistles sounded. Every mobile ship was making for open ocean. Jala looked back at the quay and stiffened. "Your luggage," he said.

It had been loaded onto one of the small cargo-haulers. Two battered hard shell cases full of paper and pharmaceuticals and digital memory. Still sitting there, abandoned.

"Run that gangway back," Jala said to the deck hands.

They blinked at him, uncertain of his authority. The first mate had left for the bridge. Jala puffed up his chest and said something fierce in a language I didn't recognize. The sailors shrugged and reeled the extendable walk back to the quay.

The ship's engines sounded a deeper note.

I ran across the gangway, corrugated aluminum ringing underfoot. Grabbed the cases. Took a last look back. Down at the landward end of the quay a detachment of a dozen or so uniformed New Reformasi began to run toward the *Capetown Maru*. "Cast off," Jala was shouting as if he owned the ship, "cast off, quickly now, quickly!"

The scaffolding began to retreat. I threw the luggage onboard and scrambled after it.

Made the deck before the ship began to move.

Then another Avigas tank erupted, and we were all thrown down by the concussion.

BY DREAMS SURROUNDED

The nightly battles between road pirates and the CHP made for difficult traveling at the best of times. The flicker made it worse. During a flicker episode any kind of unnecessary travel was officially discouraged, but that didn't stop people from trying to reach family and friends or in some cases simply getting in their cars to drive until they ran out of gas or time. I quick-packed a couple of suitcases with anything I didn't want to leave behind, including the archival records Jase had given me.

Tonight the Alvarado Freeway was clotted with traffic and I-8 wasn't moving much faster. I had plenty of time to reflect on the absurdity of what I was attempting to do.

Running to the rescue of another man's wife, a woman I had once cared about more than was really good for me. When I closed my eyes and tried to picture Diane Lawton there was no coherent image anymore, only a blurred montage of moments and gestures. Diane brushing back her hair with one hand and leaning into the coat of St. Augustine, her dog. Diane smuggling an Internet link to her brother in the

tool shed where a lawn mower lay deconstructed on the floor.
Diane reading Victorian poetry in a patch of willow shade,
smiling at something in the text I hadn't understood: *Summer
ripens at all hours,* or, *The infant child is not aware . . .*

Diane, whose subtlest looks and gestures had always implied that she loved me, at least tentatively, but who had always been restrained by forces I didn't understand: her
father, Jason, the Spin. It was the Spin, I thought, that had
bound us and separated us, locked us in adjoining but door-
less rooms.

I was past El Centro when the radio reported "significant"
police activity west of Yuma and traffic backed up for at least
three miles at the state line. I decided not to risk the long delay and turned onto a local connector—it looked promising
on the map—through empty desert north, meaning to pick up
I-10 where it crossed the state border near Blythe.

The road was less crowded but still busy. The flicker made
the world seem inverted, brighter above than below. Every so
often an especially thick vein of light writhed from the northern to the southern horizon as if a fracture had opened in the
Spin membrane, fragments of the hurried universe burning
through.

I thought about the phone in my pocket, Diane's phone, the
number Simon had called. I couldn't call back: I didn't have
a return number for Diane and the ranch—if they were still
on the ranch—was unlisted. I just wanted it to ring again.
Wanted it and dreaded it.

The traffic was bad again where the road approached the
state highway near Palo Verde. It was after midnight now and
I was making maybe thirty miles per hour at best. I thought
about sleeping. I needed sleep. Decided it might be better to
sleep, to give up for the night and give the traffic time to
clear. But I didn't want to sleep in the car. The only stationary
cars I'd seen had been abandoned and looted, trunks agape
like startled mouths.

South of a little town called Ripley I spotted a sun-faded
and sand-blasted LODGING sign, briefly visible in the headlights, and a two-lane, barely paved road exiting the highway.
I took the turn. Five minutes later I was at a gated compound

that was or once had been a motel, a strip of rooms two stories tall horseshoed around a swimming pool that looked empty under the flickering sky. I stepped out of the car and pushed the buzzer.

The gate was remote controlled, the kind you could roll back from a control panel safely distant, and it was equipped with a palm-sized video camera on a high pole. The camera swiveled to examine me as a speaker mounted at car-window height crackled to life. From somewhere, from the motel's bunker or lobby, I was able to hear a few bars of music. Not programmed music, just something playing in the background. Then a voice. Brusque, metallic, and unfriendly. "We're not taking guests tonight."

After a few moments I reached out and pushed the buzzer again.

The voice returned. "What part of that didn't you understand?"

I said, "I can pay cash if it makes a difference. I won't quibble about the price."

"No sale. Sorry, partner."

"Okay, hang on . . . look, I can sleep in the car, but would it be all right if I pulled in just to get a little protection? Maybe park around back where I can't be seen from the road?"

Longer pause. I listened to a trumpet chase a snare drum. The song was naggingly familiar.

"Sorry. Not tonight. Please move along."

More silence. More minutes passed. A cricket sawed away in the little palm and pea-gravel oasis in front of the motel. I pushed the buzzer again.

The proprietor came back quickly. "I gotta tell you, we're armed and slightly pissed off in here. It would be better if you just hit the road."

" 'Harlem Air Shaft,' " I said.

"Excuse me?"

"The song you're playing. Ellington, right? 'Harlem Air Shaft.' Sounds like his fifties band."

Another long pause, though the speaker was still live. I was almost certain I was right, though I hadn't heard the Duke Ellington tune for years.

Then the music stopped, the thin thread of it cut off in mid-beat. "Anybody else in that car with you?"

I rolled the window down and switched on the overhead light. The camera panned, then swiveled back to me.

"All right," he said. "Okay. Tell me who plays trumpet on that cut and I'll spring the gate."

Trumpet? When I thought of Duke Ellington's midfifties band I thought of Paul Gonsalvez, but Gonsalvez played sax. There had been a handful of trumpeters. Cat Anderson? Willie Cook? It had been too long.

"Ray Nance," I said.

"Nope. Clark Terry. But I guess you can come in anyway."

○ ○ ○

The owner came out to meet me when I pulled up in front of the lobby. He was a tall man, maybe forty, in jeans and a loose plaid shirt. He looked me over carefully.

"No offense," he said, "but the first time this happened—" He gestured at the sky, the flicker that turned his skin yellow and the stucco walls a sickly ocher. "Well, when they closed the border at Blythe I had people fighting for rooms. I mean literally fighting. Couple guys pulled weapons on me, right there where you're standing. Any money I made that night I paid for twice over in maintenance. People drinking in the rooms, puking, tearing the shit out of things. It was even worse up on ten. Night clerk at the Days Inn out toward Ehrenberg was stabbed to death. That's when I installed the security fence, right after that. Now, soon as the flicker starts, I just turn off the VACANCY light and lock up until it's over."

"And play Duke," I said.

He smiled. We went inside so I could register. "Duke," he said, "or Pops, or Diz. Miles if I'm in the mood for it." The true fan's first-name intimacy with the dead. "Nothing after about 1965." The lobby was a bleakly lit and generically carpeted room done up in ancient western motifs, but through a door to the proprietor's inner sanctum—it looked like he lived here—more music trickled out. He inspected the credit card I offered him.

"Dr. Dupree," he said, putting out his hand. "I'm Allen Fulton. Are you headed into Arizona?"

I told him I'd been bounced off the Interstate down by the border.

"I'm not sure you'll do any better on ten. Nights like this it seems like everybody in Los Angeles wants to move east. Like the flicker's some kind of earthquake or tidal wave."

"I'll be back on the road before long."

He handed me a key. "Get a little sleep. Always good advice."

"The card's okay? If you want cash—"

"Card's good as cash as long the world doesn't end. And if it does I don't suppose I'll have time to regret it."

He laughed. I tried to smile.

Ten minutes later I was lying fully clothed on a hard bed in a room that smelled of potpourri-scented antiseptic and too-damp air-conditioning, wondering whether I should have stayed on the road. I put the phone at the bedside and closed my eyes and slept without hesitation.

○ ○ ○

And woke less than an hour later, alert without knowing why.

I sat up and scanned the room, charting gray shapes and darkness against memory. My attention eventually settled on the pallid rectangle of the window, the yellow curtain that had been pulsing with light when I checked in.

The flicker had stopped.

Which should have made it easier to sleep, this gentler darkness, but I knew in the way one knows such things that sleep had become impossible. I had corralled it for a brief time but now it had jumped the fence, and there was no use pretending otherwise.

I made coffee in the little courtesy percolator and drank a cup. Half an hour later I checked my watch again. Fifteen minutes shy of two o'clock. The thick of the night. The zone of lost objectivity. Might as well shower and get back on the road.

I dressed and walked down the silent concrete walkway to the motel lobby, expecting to drop the key in a mail slot; but

Fulton, the owner, was still awake, television light pulsing from his back room. He put his head out when he heard me rattle the door.

He looked peculiar. A little drunk, maybe a little stoned. He blinked at me until he recognized me. "Dr. Dupree," he said.

"Sorry to bother you again. I need to get back on the road. Thank you for your hospitality, though."

"No need to explain," he said. "I wish you the best of luck. Hope you get somewhere before dawn."

"I hope so, too."

"Me, I'm just watching it on television."

"Oh?"

Suddenly I wasn't sure what he was talking about.

"With the sound turned down. I don't want to wake Jody. Did I mention Jody? My daughter. She's ten. Her mom lives in La Jolla with a furniture repairman. Jody spends the summers with me. Out here in the desert, what a fate, huh?"

"Yeah, well—"

"But I don't want to wake her." He looked suddenly somber. "Is that wrong? Just to let her sleep through it? Or as long as she can? Or maybe I *should* wake her up. Come to think of it, she's never seen 'em. Ten years old. Never seen 'em. I guess this is her last chance."

"Sorry, I'm not sure I understand—"

"They're different, though. They're not the way I remember. Not that I was ever any kind of expert . . . but in the old days, if you spent enough nights out here, you'd kind of get familiar with 'em."

"Familiar with what?"

He blinked. "The stars," he said.

o o o

We went out by the empty swimming pool to look at the sky.

The pool hadn't been filled for a long time. Dust and sand had duned at the bottom of it, and someone had tagged the walls with ballooning purple graffiti. Wind rattled a steel sign (NO LIFEGUARD ON DUTY) against the links of the fence. The wind was warm and from the east.

The stars.

"See?" he said. "Different. I don't see any of the old constellations. Everything looks kind of . . . scattered."

A few billion years will do that. Everything ages, even the sky; everything tends toward maximum entropy, disorder, randomness. The galaxy in which we live had been racked by invisible violence on a great scale over the last three billion years, had swirled its contents together with a smaller satellite galaxy (M41 in the old catalogs) until the stars were spread across the sky in a meaningless sprawl. It was like looking at the rude hand of time.

Fulton said, "You okay there, Dr. Dupree? Maybe you ought to sit down."

Too numb to stand, yes. I sat on the rubberized concrete with my feet dangling into the shallow-end declivity of the pool, still staring up. I had never seen anything as beautiful or as terrifying.

"Only a few hours before sunrise," Fulton said mournfully.

Here. Farther east, somewhere over the Atlantic, the sun must already have breached the horizon. I wanted to ask him about that, but I was interrupted by a small voice from the shadows near the lobby door. "Dad? I could hear you talking." That would be Jody, the daughter. She took a tentative step closer. She was wearing white pajamas and a pair of unlaced sneakers to protect her feet. She had a broad, plain-but-pretty face and sleepy eyes.

"Come on over, darlin'," Fulton said. "Get on up on my shoulders and have a look at the sky."

She clambered aboard, still puzzled. Fulton stood, hands on her ankles, lifting her that much closer to the glittering dark.

"Look," he said, smiling despite the tears that had begun to track down his face. "Look there, Jody. Look how far you can see tonight! Tonight you can see all the way to the end of practically everything."

o o o

I stopped back at the room to check the TV for news—Fulton said most of the cable news stations were still broadcasting.

The flicker had ended an hour ago. It had simply vanished, along with the Spin membrane. The Spin had ended as quietly as it had begun, no fanfare, no noise except for a crackle of uninterpretable static from the sunny side of the planet.

The sun.

Three billion years and change older than it had been when the Spin sealed it away. I tried to remember what Jase had told me about the current condition of the sun. Deadly, no question; we were out of the habitable zone; that was common knowledge. The image of boiling oceans had been mooted in the press; but had we reached that point yet? Dead by noon, or did we have until the end of the week?

Did it matter?

I turned on the motel room's small video panel and found a live broadcast from New York City. Major panic had not yet set in. Too many people were still asleep or had foregone the morning commute when they woke up and saw the stars and drew the obvious conclusions. The crew at this particular cable newsroom, as if in a fever dream of journalistic heroism, had set up a rooftop camera pointed east from the top of Todt Hill on Staten Island. The light was dim, the eastern sky brightening but still void. A pair of barely-holding-it-together anchors read to each other from freshly faxed bulletins.

There had been no intelligible link with Europe since the end of the flicker, they said. This might be due to electrostatic interference, the unmediated sunlight washing out aerostat-linked signals. It was too soon to draw dire conclusions. "And as always," one of the newscasters said, "although we don't have official reaction yet, the best advice is to stay put and stay tuned until we sort all this out. I don't think it would be inappropriate to ask people to remain in their homes if at all possible."

"Today of all days," his partner agreed, "people will want to be close to their families."

I sat on the edge of the motel-room mattress and watched until the sun rose.

The high camera caught it first as a layer of crimson cloud skimming the oily Atlantic horizon. Then a boiling crescent edge, filters sliding over the lens to stop down the glare.

The scale of it was hard to parse, but the sun came up (not quite red but ruddy orange, unless that was an artifact of the camera) and came up some more and kept coming up until it hovered over the ocean, Queens, Manhattan, too large to be a plausible heavenly body, more like an enormous balloon filled with amber light.

I waited for more commentary, but the image was silent until it cut to a studio in the Midwest, the network's fallback headquarters, and another reporter, too poorly groomed to be a regular anchor, who uttered more sourceless and futile cautions. I switched it off.

And took my med kit and suitcase to the car.

Fulton and Jody came out of the office to see me off. Suddenly they were old friends, sorry to see me go. Jody looked frightened now. "Jody's been talking to her mom," Fulton said. "I don't think her mom had heard about the stars."

I tried not to picture the early-morning wake-up call, Jody phoning from the desert to announce what her mother would have instantly understood as the approaching end of the world. Jody's mom saying what might be a final good-bye to her daughter while struggling not to scare her to death, shielding her from the onrushing truth.

Now Jody leaned into her father's ribs and Fulton put his arm around her, nothing but tenderness left between them.

"Do you have to go?" Jody asked.

I said I did.

"Because you can stay if you like. My dad said so."

"Mr. Dupree's a doctor," Fulton said gently. "He probably has a house call to make."

"That's right," I said. "I do."

o o o

Something near miraculous happened in the eastbound lanes of the highway that morning. Many people behaved badly in what they believed to be their final hours. It was as if the flickers had been merely a rehearsal for this less arguable doom. All of us had heard the predictions: forests ablaze, searing heat, the seas turned to scalding live steam. The only question was whether it would take a day, a week, a month.

And so we broke windows and took what appealed to us, any trinket life had denied us; men attempted to rape women, some discovering that the loss of inhibition worked both ways, the intended victim endowed by the same events with unexpected powers of eye-gouging and testicle-crushing; old scores were settled by gunshot and guns were fired on a whim. The suicides were legion. (I thought of Molly: if she hadn't died in the first flicker she was almost certainly dead now, might even have died pleased at the logical unfolding of her logical plan. Which made me want to cry for her for the first time in my life.)

But there were islands of civility and acts of heroic kindness, too. Interstate 10 at the Arizona border was one of them.

During the flicker there had been a National Guard detachment stationed at the bridge that crossed the Colorado River. The soldiers had disappeared shortly after the flicker ended, recalled, perhaps, or just AWOL, headed for home. Without them the bridge could have become a tangled, impassable bottleneck.

But it wasn't. Traffic flowed at a gentle pace in both directions. A dozen civilians, self-appointed volunteers with heavy-duty flashlights and flares out of their trunk emergency kits, had taken on the work of directing traffic. And even the terminally eager—the folks who wanted or needed to travel a long way before dawn, to reach New Mexico, Texas, maybe even Louisiana if their engines didn't melt first—seemed to understand that this was necessary, that no attempt to jump the line could possibly succeed and that patience was the only recourse. I don't know how long this mood lasted or what confluence of goodwill and circumstance created it. Maybe it was human kindness or maybe it was the weather: in spite of the doom roaring toward us out of the east the night was perversely *nice*. Scattered stars in a clear, cool sky; a quickening breeze that carried off the stench of exhaust and came in the car window gentle as a mother's touch.

○ ○ ○

I thought about volunteering at one of the local hospitals— Palo Verde in Blythe, which I had once visited for a consultation, or maybe La Paz Regional in Parker. But what purpose would it serve? There was no cure for what was coming.

There was only palliation, morphine, heroin, Molly's route, assuming the pharmaceutical cupboards hadn't already been looted.

And what Fulton had told Jody was essentially true: I had a house call to make.

A quest. Quixotic now, of course. Whatever was wrong with Diane, I wouldn't be fixing that, either. So why finish the journey? It was something to do at the end of the world, busy hands don't tremble, busy minds don't panic; but that didn't explain the urgency, the visceral need to see her that had set me on the road during the flicker and seemed, if anything, stronger now.

Past Blythe, past the uneasy gauntlet of darkened shops and the fistfights brewing around besieged gas stations, the road opened up and the sky was darker, the stars sparkling. I was thinking about that when the phone trilled.

I almost drove off the road, fumbling in my pocket, braking, while a utility vehicle in back of me squealed past.

"Tyler," Simon said.

Before he went on I said, "Give me a call-back number before you hang up or we get cut off. So I can reach you."

"I'm not supposed to do that. I—"

"Are you calling from a private phone or the house phone?"

"Sort of private, a cell, we just use it locally. I've got it now but Aaron carries it sometimes so—"

"I won't call unless I have to."

"Well. I don't suppose it matters." He gave me the number. "But have you seen the sky, Tyler? I assume so, since you're awake. It's the last night of the world, isn't it?"

I thought: *Why are you asking me?* Simon had been living in the last days for three decades now. He ought to know. "Tell me about Diane," I said.

"I want to apologize for that call. Because of, you know, what's happening."

"How is she?"

"That's what I'm saying. It doesn't matter."

"Is she dead?"

Long pause. He came back sounding hurt. "No. No, she's not dead. That's not the point."

"Is she hovering in midair, waiting for the Rapture?"

"You don't have to insult my faith," Simon said. (And I couldn't resist interpreting the phrase: *my* faith, he had said, not *our* faith.)

"Because, if not, maybe she still needs medical attention. Is she still sick, Simon?"

"Yes. But—"

"Sick how? What are her symptoms?"

"Sunrise is only an hour away, Tyler. Surely you understand what that means."

"I'm not at all sure what it means. And I'm on the road, I can be at the ranch before dawn."

"Oh—no, that's not good—no, I—"

"Why not? If it's the end of the world, why shouldn't I be there?"

"You don't understand. What's going on isn't just the world ending. It's a new one being born."

"How sick is she, exactly? Can I talk to her?"

Simon's voice became tremorous. A man on the brink. We were all on the brink. "She can only whisper. She can't get her breath. She's weak. She's lost a lot of weight."

"How long has she been like that?"

"I don't know. I mean, it started gradually . . ."

"When was it obvious she was ill?"

"Weeks ago. Or maybe—looking back on it—well—months."

"Has she had any kind of medical attention?" Pause. "Simon?"

"No."

"Why not?"

"It didn't seem necessary."

"It didn't seem *necessary*?"

"Pastor Dan wouldn't allow it."

I thought: *And did you tell Pastor Dan to go fuck himself?* "I hope he's changed his mind."

"No—"

"Because, if not, I'll need your help getting to her."

"Don't do that, Tyler. It won't do anybody any good."

I was already looking for the exit, which I remembered

only dimly but had marked on the map. Off the highway to-ward some bone-dry cienaga, a nameless desert road.

I said, "Has she asked for me?"

Silence.

"Simon? Has she asked for me?"

"Yes."

"Tell her I'll be there soon as I can."

"No, Tyler . . . Tyler, there are some troublesome things happening at the ranch. You can't just walk in here."

Troublesome things? "I thought a new world was being born."

"Born in blood," Simon said.

THE MORNING AND THE EVENING

I came up toward the low ridge overlooking the Condon ranch and parked out of sight of the house. When I switched off the headlights I was able to see the predawn glow in the eastern sky, the new stars washed out by an ominous brightening.

That's when I started to shake.

I couldn't control it. I opened the door and fell out of the car and picked myself up by force of will. The land was rising out of the dark like a lost continent, brown hills, neglected pastureland returned to desert, the long shallow slope down to the distant farmhouse. Mesquite and ocotillo trembled in the wind. I trembled, too. This was fear: not the pinched intellectual uneasiness we had all lived with since the beginning of the Spin but visceral panic, fear like a disease of the muscles and the bowels. End of term on Death Row. Graduation day. Tumbrels and gallows approaching from the east.

I wondered if Diane was this frightened. I wondered if I could comfort her. If there was any consolation left in me.

The wind gusted again, washing sand and dust down the dry ridge road. Maybe the wind was the first harbinger of the bloated sun, a wind from the hot side of the world.

I crouched where I hoped I couldn't be seen and, still trembling, managed to peck out Simon's number on the keypad of the phone.

He picked up after a few rings. I pressed the receiver into my ear to block the sound of the wind.

"You shouldn't be doing this," he said.

"Am I interrupting the Rapture?"

"I can't talk."

"Where is she, Simon? What part of the house?"

"Where are *you*?"

"Just up the hill." The sky was brighter now, brighter by the second, a bruised purple on the western horizon. I could see the farmhouse clearly. It hadn't changed much in the few years since I'd visited. The outlying barn looked a little spruced up, as if it had been whitewashed and repaired.

Far more disturbingly, a trench had been dug parallel to the barn and covered in mounded earth.

A recently installed sewer line, maybe. Or septic tank. Or mass grave.

"I'm coming to see her," I said.

"That's just not possible."

"I'm assuming she's in the house. One of the upper-floor bedrooms. Is that correct?"

"Even if you see her—"

"Tell her I'm coming, Simon."

Down below, I saw a figure moving between the house and the barn. Not Simon. Not Aaron Sorley, unless Brother Aaron had lost about a hundred pounds. Probably Pastor Dan Condon. He was carrying a bucket of water in each hand. He looked like he was in a hurry. Something was happening in the barn.

"You're risking your life here," Simon said.

I laughed. I couldn't help it.

Then I said, "Are you in the barn or the house? Condon's in the barn, right? How about Sorley and McIsaac? How do I get past them?"

I felt a pressure like a warm hand on the back of my neck and turned.

The pressure was sunlight. The rim of the sun had crossed the horizon. My car, the fence, the rocks, the scraggy line of ocotillo all cast long violet shadows.

"Tyler? Tyler, there *is* no way past. You have to—"

But Simon's voice was drowned in a burst of static. The full light of the sun must have reached the aerostat that was relaying the call, washing out the signal. I hit redial instinctively, but the phone was useless.

I crouched there until the sun was three quarters up, glancing at it and glancing away, as mesmerized as I was frightened. The disc was huge and ruddy orange. Sunspots crawled over it like festering sores. Now and again, gouts of dust rose from the surrounding desert to obscure it.

Then I stood up. Dead already, perhaps. Perhaps fatally irradiated without even knowing it. The heat was bearable, at least so far, but bad things might be happening on the cellular level, X-rays needling through the air like invisible bullets. So I stood up and began to walk down the pressed-earth road toward the farmhouse in plain sight, unarmed. Unarmed and unmolested at least until I had nearly reached the wooden porch, until Brother Sorley, all three hundred pounds of him, came hurtling through the screen door and levered the butt of a rifle against the side of my head.

○ ○ ○

Brother Sorley didn't kill me, possibly because he didn't want to meet the Rapture with blood on his hands. Instead he tossed me into an empty upstairs bedroom and locked the door.

A couple of hours passed before I could sit up without provoking waves of nausea.

When the vertigo finally eased I went to the window and raised the yellow paper blind. From this angle the sun was behind the house, the land and the barn washed in a fierce orange glare. The air was already brutally hot, but at least nothing was burning. A barn cat, oblivious to the conflagration in the sky, lapped stagnant water from a shady ditch. I guessed the cat might live to see sunset. So might I.

I tried to lift the ancient window frame—not that I could exactly leap down from here—but it was worse than locked; the sashes had been cut, the counterweights immobilized, the frame painted in place years ago.

There was no furniture in the room apart from the bed, no tool but the useless phone in my pocket.

The single door was a slab of solid wood and I doubted I had the strength to break it down. Diane might be only yards away, a single wall separating us. But there was no way to know that and no way to find out.

Even trying to think coherently about any of this provoked a deep, nauseating pain where the butt of the rifle had bloodied my head. I had to lie down again.

∘ ∘ ∘

By midafternoon the wind had stilled. When I staggered back to the window I could see the edge of the solar disc above the house and the barn, so large it seemed to be perpetually falling, almost near enough to touch.

The temperature in the upstairs bedroom had climbed steadily since morning. I had no way of measuring it, but I would have guessed at least an even hundred Fahrenheit and rising. Hot but not enough to kill, at least not at once, not immediately. I wished I had Jason here to explain that to me, the thermodynamics of global extinction. Maybe he could have drawn a chart, established where the trend lines converged on lethality.

Heat haze quavered up from the baked ground.

Dan Condon crossed to the barn and back a couple more times. He was easy to recognize in the sharp intensity of the orange daylight, something nineteenth-century about him, his squared beard and pocked, ugly face: Lincoln in blue jeans, long-legged, purposeful. He didn't look up even when I hammered on the glass.

Then I tapped the joining walls, thinking Diane might tap back. But there was no answer.

Then I was dizzy again, and I fell back on the bed, the air in the closed room sweltering, sweat drenching the bedclothes.

I slept, or lost consciousness.

○ ○ ○

Woke up thinking the room was on fire, but it was only the combination of stagnant heat and an impossibly gaudy sunset.

Went to the window again.

The sun had crossed the western horizon and was sinking with visible speed. High, tenuous clouds arched across the darkening sky, scraps of moisture drawn up from an already parched land. I saw that someone had rolled my car down the hill and parked it just left of the barn. And taken the keys, no doubt. Not that there was enough gas in the car to render it useful.

But I had lived through the day. I thought: *We* lived through the day. Both of us. Diane and I. And no doubt millions more. So this was the slow version of the apocalypse. It would kill us by cooking us a degree at a time; or, failing that, by gutting the terrestrial ecosystem.

The swollen sun finally disappeared. The air seemed instantly ten degrees cooler.

A few scattered stars showed through the gauzy clouds.

I hadn't eaten, and I was painfully thirsty. Maybe it was Condon's plan to leave me here to die of dehydration . . . or maybe he had simply forgotten about me. I couldn't even begin to imagine how Pastor Dan was framing these events in his mind, whether he felt vindicated or terrified or some combination of both.

The room grew dark. No overhead light, no lamp. But I could hear a faint chugging that must be a gasoline-power generator, and light spilled from the first-floor windows and the barn.

Whereas I owned nothing in the way of technology except my phone. I took it out of my pocket and switched it on, idly, just to see the phosphorescence of the screen.

Then I had another thought.

○ ○ ○

"Simon?"

Silence.

"Simon, is that you? Can you hear me?"

Silence. Then a tinny, digitized voice:

"You nearly scared the life out of me. I thought this thing was broken."

"Only during daylight."

Solar noise had washed out transmissions from the high-altitude aerostats. But now the Earth was shielding us from the sun. Maybe the 'stats had sustained some damage—the signal sounded low-band and staticky—but the bounce was good enough for now.

"I'm sorry about what happened," he said, "but I warned you."

"Where are you? The barn or the house?"

Pause. "The house."

"I've been looking all day and I haven't seen Condon's wife or Sorley's wife and kids. Or McIsaac or his family. What happened to them?"

"They left."

"Are you sure of that?"

"Am I sure? Of course I'm sure. Diane wasn't the only one to get sick. Only the latest. Teddy McIsaac's little girl took ill first. Then his son, then Teddy himself. When it looked like his kids were—well, you know, obviously really sick, sick and not getting better, well, that was when he put them in his truck and drove away. Pastor Dan's wife went along."

"When did this happen?"

"Couple of months ago. Aaron's wife and kids took off by themselves not long after. Their faith failed them. Plus they were worried about catching something."

"You saw them leave? You're certain about that?"

"Yes, why wouldn't I be?"

"Trench by the barn looks a lot like something's buried there."

"Oh, that! Well, you're right, something *is* buried there—the bad cattle."

"Excuse me?"

"A man named Boswell Geller had a big ranch up in the Sierra Bonita. Friend of Jordan Tabernacle before the shake-up. Friend of Pastor Dan. He was breeding red heifers, but the Department of Agriculture started an investigation late last year. Just when he was making progress! Boswell and Pastor Dan wanted to breed together all the red cattle varieties of the world, because that would represent the conversion of the Gentiles. Pastor Dan says that's what Numbers nineteen is all about—a pure red heifer born at the end of time, from breeds on every continent, everywhere the Gospel's been preached. The sacrifice is literal and symbolic, both. In the biblical sacrifice the ashes of the heifer have the power to clean a defiled person. But at the end of the world the sun consumes the heifer and the ashes are scattered to the four compass points, cleansing the whole Earth, cleansing it of death. That's what's happening now. Hebrews nine—'For if the blood of bulls and goats and the ashes of a heifer sanctifies for the purifying of the flesh, how much more shall the blood of Christ purge your conscience from dead works to serve the living God?' So of course—"

"You kept those cattle *here*?"

"Only a few. Fifteen breeders smuggled out before the Department of Agriculture could claim them."

"That's when people started getting sick?"

"Not just people. The cattle, too. We dug that trench by the barn to bury them in, all but three of the original stock."

"Weakness, unsteady gait, weight loss preceding death?"

"Yes, mostly—how did you know?"

"Those are the symptoms of CVWS. The cows were carriers. That's what's wrong with Diane."

There was a long ensuing silence. Then Simon said, "I can't have this conversation with you."

I said, "I'm upstairs in the back bedroom—"

"I know where you are."

"Then come and unlock this door."

"I can't."

"Why? Is somebody watching you?"

"I can't just set you free. I shouldn't even be talking to you. I'm busy, Tyler. I'm making dinner for Diane."

"She's still strong enough to eat?"

"A little . . . if I help her."

"Let me out. No one has to know."

"I can't."

"She needs a doctor."

"I couldn't let you out if I wanted to. Brother Aaron carries the keys."

I thought about that. I said, "Then when you take dinner to her, leave the phone with her—your phone. You said she wanted to talk to me, right?"

"Half the time she says things she doesn't mean."

"You think that was one of them?"

"I can't talk anymore."

"Just leave her the phone, Simon. Simon?"

Dead air.

○ ○ ○

I went to the window, watched and waited.

I saw Pastor Dan carry two empty buckets from the barn to the house and travel back with the buckets full and steaming. A few minutes later Aaron Sorley crossed the gap to join him.

Which left only Simon and Diane in the house. Maybe he was giving her dinner. Feeding her.

I itched to use the phone but I had resolved to wait, let things settle a little more, let the heat go out of the night.

I watched the barn. Bright light spilled through the slat walls as if someone had installed a rack of industrial lights. Condon had been back and forth all day. Something was happening in the barn. Simon hadn't said what.

The small luminosity of my watch counted off an hour.

Then I heard, faintly, a sound that might have been a closing door, footsteps on the stairs; and a moment later I saw Simon cross to the barn.

He didn't look up.

Nor did he leave the barn once he'd arrived there. He was inside with Sorley and Condon, and if he was still carrying the phone, and if he'd been idiotic enough to set it for an audible ring, calling him now might put him in jeopardy. Not that I was especially concerned for Simon's welfare.

But if he had left the phone with Diane, now was the hour. I pecked out the number.

"Yes," she said—it was Diane who answered—and then, inflection rising, a question, "Yes?"

Her voice was breathless and faint. Those two syllables were enough to beg a diagnosis.

I said, "Diane. It's me. It's Tyler."

Trying to control my own raging pulse, as if a door had opened in my chest.

"Tyler," she said. "Ty . . . Simon said you might call."

I had to strain to make out the words. There was no force behind them; they were all throat and tongue, no chest. Which was consistent with the etiology of CVWS. The disease affects the lungs first, then the heart, in a coordinated attack of near-military efficiency. Scarred and foamy lung tissue passes less oxygen to the blood; the heart, oxygen-starved, pumps blood less efficiently; the CVWS bacteria exploit both weaknesses, digging deeper into the body with every laborious breath.

"I'm not far away," I said. "I'm real close, Diane."

"Close. Can I see you?"

I wanted to tear a hole in the wall. "Soon. I promise. We need to get you out of here. Get you some help. Fix you up."

I listened to the sound of more agonized inhalations and wondered if I'd lost her attention. Then she said, "I thought I saw the sun . . ."

"It's not the end of the world. Not yet, anyway."

"It's not?"

"No."

"Simon," she said.

"What about him?"

"He'll be so disappointed."

"You have CVWS, Diane. That's almost certainly what McIsaac's family had. They were smart to get help. It's a curable disease." I did not add, *Up to a certain point* or *As long as it hasn't progressed to the terminal stage.* "But we have to get you out of here."

"I missed you."

"I missed you, too. Do you understand what I'm saying?"

"Yes."

"Are you ready to leave?"

"If the time comes . . ."

"The time is pretty close. Rest until then. But we might have to hurry. You understand, Diane?"

"Simon," she said faintly. "Disappointed," she said.

"You rest, and I—"

But I didn't have time to finish.

A key rattled in the door. I flipped the phone closed and pushed it into my pocket. The door opened, and Aaron Sorley stood in the frame, rifle in hand, huffing as if he'd run up the stairs. He was silhouetted in the dim light from the hallway.

I backed away until my shoulders hit the wall.

"Tag on your license says you're a doctor," he said. "Is that right?"

I nodded.

"Then come with me," he said.

∘ ∘ ∘

Sorley marched me downstairs and out the rear door toward the barn.

The moon, stained amber by the light of the gibbous sun, scarred and smaller than I remembered it, had risen over the eastern horizon. The night air was almost intoxicatingly cool. I took deep breaths. The relief lasted until Sorley threw open the barn door and a raw, animal stench gushed out—a slaughterhouse smell of excrement and blood.

"Go on in," Sorley said, and he gave me a push with his free hand.

The light came from a fat halide bulb suspended by its power cord over an open cattle stall. A gasoline generator rattled from an enclosure out back somewhere, a sound like someone revving a distant motorcycle.

Dan Condon stood at the open end of the pen, dipping his hands in a bucket of steaming water. He looked up when we entered. He frowned, his face a stark geography under the glaring single-point light, but he looked less intimidating than I remembered. In fact he looked diminished, gaunt, maybe even sick, maybe in the opening stages of his own case of CVWS. "Close that door back up," he said.

Aaron pushed it shut. Simon stood a few paces away from Condon, shooting me quick nervous glances.

"Come here," Condon said. "We need your help with this. Possibly your medical expertise."

In the pen, on a bed of filthy straw, a skinny heifer was try-ing to birth a calf.

The heifer was lying down, her bony rump projecting from the stall. Her tail had been tied to her neck with a length of twine to keep it out of the way. Her amniotic sac was bulging from her vulva, and the straw around her was dotted with bloody mucus.

I said, "I'm not a vet."

"I know that," Condon said. There was a suppressed hyste-ria in his eyes, the look of a man who's thrown a party but finds it spiraling out of control, the guests gone feral, neigh-bors complaining, liquor bottles flying from the windows like mortar rounds. "But we need another hand."

All I knew about brood stock and birthing I had learned from Molly Seagram's stories about life on her parents' farm. None of the stories had been particularly pleasant. At least Condon had set himself up with what I recalled as the neces-sary basics: hot water, disinfectant, obstetrical chains, a big bottle of mineral oil already stained with bloody handprints.

"She's part Angeln," Condon said, "part Danish Red, part Belarus Red, and that's only her most recent bloodline. But crossbreeding's a risk for dystocia. That's what Brother Geller used to say. The word 'dystocia' means a difficult la-bor. Crossbreeds often have trouble calving. She's been in la-bor almost four hours. We need to extract the fetus."

Condon said this in a distant monotone, like a man lectur-ing a class of idiots. It didn't seem to matter who I was or how I'd got here, only that I was available, a free hand.

I said, "I need water."

"There's a bucket for washing up."

"I don't mean for washing. I haven't had anything to drink since last night."

Condon paused as if to process this information. Then he nodded and said, "Simon. See to it."

Simon appeared to be the trio's errand boy. He ducked his head and said, "I'll fetch you a drink, Tyler, sure enough," still avoiding my eyes as Sorley opened the barn door to let him out.

Condon turned back to the cattle pen where the exhausted

heifer lay panting. Busy flies decorated the heifer's flanks. A couple of them lighted on Condon's shoulders, unnoticed. Condon doused his hands with mineral oil and squatted to expand the heifer's birth canal, his face contorting with a combination of eagerness and disgust. But he had barely begun when the calf crowned in another gush of blood and fluid, its head barely emerging despite the heifer's fierce contractions. The calf was too big. Molly had told me about oversized calves—not as bad as a breech birth or a hiplock, but unpleasant to deal with.

It didn't help that the heifer was obviously ill, drooling greenish mucus and struggling for breath even when the contractions eased. I wondered whether I should say anything about that to Condon. His divine calf was obviously infected, too.

But Pastor Dan didn't know or didn't care. Condon was all that was left of the Dispensationalist wing of Jordan Tabernacle, a church unto himself, reduced to two parishioners, Sorley and Simon, and I could only imagine how muscular his faith must have been to sustain him all the way to the end of the world. He said in the same tone of suppressed hysteria, "The calf, the calf is red—Aaron, look at the calf."

Aaron Sorley, who was posted on the door with his rifle, came over to peer into the pen. The calf was indeed red. Doused in blood. Also limp.

Sorley said, "Is it breathing?"

"Will be," Condon said. He was abstracted, seemed to be savoring it, this moment on which he genuinely believed the world was about to pivot into eternity. "Get the chains around the pasterns, quickly now."

Sorley gave me a look that was also a warning—*don't say a fucking word*—and we did as we were instructed, worked until we were bloody up to our elbows. The act of birthing an oversized calf is both brutal and ludicrous, a grotesque marriage of biology and crude force. It takes at least two reasonably strong men to assist at an outsized calving. The obstetric chains were for pulling. The pulls had to be timed to the cow's contractions; otherwise the animal could be eviscerated.

But this heifer was weak unto death, and her calf—its head lolled lifelessly—was now obviously a stillbirth.

I looked at Sorley, Sorley looked at me. Neither of us spoke. Condon said, "The first thing is to get her out. Then we'll revive her."

There was a movement of cooler air from the barn door. That was Simon, back with a bottle of spring water, staring at us and then at the half-delivered stillbirth, his face gone startlingly pale.

"Got your drink," he managed.

The heifer finished another weak, unproductive contraction. I dropped the chain. Condon said, "You take that drink, son. Then we'll carry on."

"I have to clean up. At least wash my hands."

"Clean hot water in buckets by the hay bales. But be quick about it." His eyes were closed, shut tight on whatever battle his common sense was conducting with his faith.

I rinsed and disinfected my hands. Sorley watched closely. His own hands were on the obstetrical chain, but his rifle was propped against a rail of the stall within easy reach.

When Simon handed me the bottle I leaned into his shoulder and said, "I can't help Diane unless I get her out of here. Do you understand? And I can't do that without *your* help. We need a reliable vehicle with a full tank of gas, and we need Diane inside it, preferably before Condon figures out the calf is dead."

Simon gasped, "It's truly dead?"—too loud, but neither Sorley nor Condon appeared to hear.

"The calf isn't breathing," I said. "The heifer's barely alive."

"But is the calf red? Red all over? No white or black patches? Purely red?"

"Even if it's a fucking fire engine, Simon, it won't do Diane any good."

He looked at me as if I'd announced his puppy had been run over. I wondered when he had traded his brimming self-confidence for this blank bewilderment, whether it had happened suddenly or whether the joy had drained out of him a grain at a time, sand through an hourglass.

"Talk to her," I said, "if you need to. Ask her whether she's willing to go."

If she was still alert enough to answer him. If she remembered that I'd spoken to her.

He said, "I love her more than life itself."

Condon called out, "We need you here!"

I drained half the bottle while Simon gazed at me, tears welling in his eyes. The water was clean and pure and delicious.

Then I was back with Sorley on the obstetric chains, pulling in concert with the pregnant heifer's dying spasms.

○ ○ ○

We finally extracted the calf around midnight, and it lay on the straw in a tangle of itself, forelegs tucked under its limp body, its bloodshot eyes lifeless.

Condon stood over the small body a little while. Then he said to me, "Is there anything you can do for it?"

"I can't raise it from the dead, if that's what you mean."

Sorley gave me a warning look, as if to say: Don't torture him; this is hard enough.

I edged to the door of the barn. Simon had disappeared an hour earlier, while we were still struggling with a flood of hemorrhagic blood that had drenched the already sodden straw, our clothing, our arms and hands. Through the open wedge of the door I could see movement around the car—my car—and a blink of checkered cloth that might have been Simon's shirt.

He was doing something out there. I hoped I knew what.

Sorley looked from the dead calf to Pastor Dan Condon and back again, stroking his beard, oblivious of the blood he was braiding into it. "Maybe if we burned it," he said.

Condon gave him a withering, hopeless stare.

"But maybe," Sorley said.

Then Simon threw open the barn doors and let in a gust of cool air. We turned to look. The moon over his shoulder was gibbous and alien.

"She's in the car," he said. "Ready to go." Speaking to me but staring hard at Sorley and Condon, almost daring them to respond.

Pastor Dan just shrugged, as if these worldly matters were no longer pertinent.

I looked at Brother Aaron. Brother Aaron leaned toward the rifle.

"I can't stop you," I said. "But I'm walking out the door."

He halted in midreach and frowned. He looked as if he were trying to puzzle out the sequence of events that had brought him to this moment, each one leading inexorably to the next, logical as stepping stones, and yet, and yet . . .

His hand dropped to his side. He turned to Pastor Dan.

"I think if we burned it anyway, that would be all right."

I walked to the barn door and joined Simon, not looking back. Sorley could have changed his mind, grabbed his rifle and taken aim. I was no longer entirely capable of caring.

"Maybe burn it before morning," I heard him say. "Before the sun comes up again."

○ ○ ○

"You drive," Simon said when we reached the car. "There's gas in the tank and extra gas in jericans in the trunk. And a little food and more bottled water. You drive and I'll sit in back and keep her steady."

I started the car and drove slowly uphill, past the split-rail fence and the moonlit ocotillo toward the highway.

SPIN

A few miles up the road and a safe distance from the Condon farm I pulled over and told Simon to get out.

"What," he said, "here?"

"I need to examine Diane. I need you to get the flashlight out of the trunk and hold it for me. Okay?"

He nodded, wide-eyed.

Diane hadn't said a word since we'd left the ranch. She had simply lain across the backseat with her head in Simon's lap, drawing breath. Her breathing had been the loudest sound in the car.

While Simon stood by, flashlight in hand, I stripped off my blood-soaked clothing and washed myself as thoroughly as I could—a bottle of mineral water with a little gasoline to strip away the filth, a second bottle to rinse. Then I put on clean Levi's and a sweatshirt from my luggage and a pair of latex gloves from the medical kit. I drank a third bottle of water straight down. Then I had Simon angle the light on Diane while I looked at her.

She was more or less conscious but too groggy to put together a fully coherent sentence. She was thinner than I had ever seen her, almost anorexically thin, and dangerously feverish. Her BP and pulse were elevated, and when I listened to her chest her lungs sounded like a child sucking a milk shake through a narrow straw.

I managed to get her to swallow a little water and an aspirin on top of it. Then I ripped the seal on a sterile hypodermic.

"What's that?" Simon asked.

"General-purpose antibiotic." I swabbed her arm and with some difficulty located a vein. "You'll need one, too." And me. The heifer's blood had undoubtedly been loaded with live CVWS bacteria.

"Will that cure her?"

"No, Simon, I'm afraid it won't. A month ago it might have. Not anymore. She needs medical attention."

"You're a doctor."

"I may be a doctor, but I'm not a hospital."

"Then maybe we can take her into Phoenix."

I thought about that. Everything I'd learned during the flickers suggested that an urban hospital would be swamped at best, a smoldering ruin at worst. But maybe not.

I took out my phone and scrolled through its memory for a half-forgotten number.

Simon said, "Who're you calling?"

"Someone I used to know."

His name was Colin Hinz, and we had roomed together back at Stony Brook. We kept in touch a little. Last I'd heard from him he was working management at St. Joseph's in Phoenix. It was worth a try—now, before the sun came up and scrubbed telecommunications for another day.

I entered his personal number. The phone rang a long while but eventually he picked up and said, "This better be good."

I identified myself and told him I was maybe an hour out of town with a casualty in need of immediate attention—someone close to me.

Colin sighed. "I don't know what to tell you, Tyler. St. Joe's is working, and I hear the Mayo Clinic in Scottsdale is open, but we both have minimal staff. There are conflicting reports from other hospitals. But you won't get quick attention anywhere, sure as hell not here. We've got people stacked up outside the doors—gunshot wounds, attempted suicides, auto accidents, heart attacks, you name it. And cops on the doors to keep them from mobbing Emerg. What's your patient's condition?"

I told him Diane was late-stage CVWS and would probably need airway support soon.

"Where the fuck did she pick up CVWS? No, never mind—doesn't matter. Honestly, I'd help you if I could, but our nurses have been doing parking-lot triage all night and I can't promise they'd give your patient any priority, even with a word from me. In fact it's pretty much a sure thing she wouldn't even be assessed by a physician for another twenty-four hours. If any of us live that long."

"*I'm* a physician, remember? All I need is a little gear to support her. Ringer's, an airway kit, oxygen—"

"I don't want to sound callous, but we're wading through blood here . . . you might ask yourself whether it's really worthwhile supporting a terminal CVWS case, given what's happening. If you've got what you need to keep her comfortable—"

"I don't want to keep her comfortable. I want to save her life."

"Okay . . . but what you described is a terminal situation, unless I misunderstood." In the background I could hear other voices demanding his attention, a generalized rattle of human misery.

"I need to take her somewhere," I said, "and I need to get her there alive. I need the supplies more than I need a bed."

"We've got nothing to spare. Tell me if there's anything else I can do for you. Otherwise, I'm sorry, I have work to do."

I thought frantically. Then I said, "Okay, but the supplies—anywhere I can pick up Ringer's, Colin, that's all I ask."

"Well—"

"Well, what?"

"Well . . . I shouldn't be telling you this, but St. Joe's has a deal with the city under the civil emergency plan. There's a medical distributor called Novaprod north of town." He gave me an address and simple directions. "The authorities put a National Guard unit up there to protect it. That's our primary source for drugs and hardware."

"They'll let me in?"

"If I call up and tell them you're coming, and if you have some ID to show."

"Do that for me, Colin. Please."

"I will if I can get a line out. The phones are unreliable."

"If there's a favor I can do in return . . ."

"Maybe there is. You used to work in aerospace, right? Perihelion?"

"Not recently, but yes."

"Can you tell me how much longer all this is going to last?" He half whispered the question, and suddenly I could hear the fatigue in his voice, the unadmitted fear. "I mean, one way or the other?"

I apologized and told him I simply didn't know—and I doubted anyone at Perihelion knew more than I did.

He sighed. "Okay," he said. "It's just galling, the idea that we could go through all this and burn out in a couple of days and never know what it was all about."

"I wish I could give you an answer."

Someone on the other end of the line began calling his name. "I wish a lot of things," he said. "Gotta go, Tyler."

I thanked him again and clicked off.

Dawn was still a few hours away.

Simon had been standing a few yards from the car, staring up at the starry sky and pretending not to listen. I waved him back and said, "We have to get going."

He nodded meekly. "Did you find help for Diane?"

"Sort of."

He accepted the answer without asking for details. But before he bent to get in the car he tugged at my sleeve and said, "*There* . . . what do you suppose that is, Tyler?"

He was pointing at the western horizon, where a gently curving silver line arced through five degrees of the night sky. It looked as if someone had scratched an enormous, shallow letter *C* out of the blackness.

"Maybe a condensation trail," I said. "A military jet."

"At night? Not at night."

"Then I don't know what it is, Simon. Come on, get in— we don't have time to waste."

o o o

We made better time than I expected. We reached the medical supply warehouse, a numbered unit in a dreary industrial park, with time to spare before sunrise. I presented my ID to the nervous National Guardsman posted at the entrance; he handed me over to another Guardsman and a civilian employee who walked me through the aisles of shelving. I found what I needed and a third Guardsman helped me carry it to the car, though he backed off quickly when he saw Diane gasping in the backseat. "Luck to you," he said, his voice shaking a little.

I took the time to set up an IV drip, the bag jury-rigged to the jacket hanger in the car, and showed Simon how to monitor the flow and make sure she didn't snag the line in her sleep. (She didn't wake even when I put the needle in her arm.)

Simon waited until we were back on the road before he asked, "Is she dying?"

I gripped the wheel a little tighter. "Not if I can help it."

"Where are we taking her?"

"We're taking her home."

"What, all the way across country? To Carol and E.D.'s house?"

"Right."

"Why there?"

"Because I can help her there."

"That's a long drive. I mean, the way things are."

"Yes. It might be a long drive."

I glanced into the backseat. He stroked her head, gently. Her hair was limp and matted with perspiration. His hands were pale where he had washed off the blood.

"I don't deserve to be with her," he said. "I know this is my fault. I could have left the ranch when Teddy did. I could have gotten help."

Yes, I thought. You could have.

"But I believed in what we were doing. Probably you don't

understand that. But it wasn't just the red calf, Tyler. I was certain we'd be raised up imperishable. That in the end we'd be rewarded."

"Rewarded for what?"

"Faith. Perseverance. Because from the very first time I set eyes on Diane I had a powerful feeling we'd be part of something spectacular, even if I didn't wholly comprehend it. That one day we'd stand together before the throne of God—no less than that. 'This generation shall not pass away till all be fulfilled.' *Our* generation, even if we took a wrong turn at first. I admit, things happened at those New Kingdom rallies that seem shameful to me now. Drunkenness, lechery, lies. We turned our backs on that, which was good; but it seemed like the world got a little smaller when we weren't among people who were trying to build the chiliasm, however imperfectly. As if we'd lost a family. And I thought, well, if you look for the cleanest and simplest path, that should take you in the right direction. 'In your patience possess ye your souls.' "

"Jordan Tabernacle," I said.

"It's easy to set prophecy against the Spin. Signs in the sun and in the moon and in the stars, it says in Luke. Well, here we are. The powers of heaven shaken. But it isn't—it isn't—"

He seemed to lose the thought.

"How's her breathing back there?" But I didn't really need to ask. I could hear every breath she took, labored but regular. I just wanted to distract him.

"She's not in distress," Simon said. Then he said, "Please, Tyler. Stop and let me out."

We were traveling east. There was surprisingly little traffic on the interstate. Colin Hinz had warned me about congestion around Sky Harbor airport, but we'd bypassed that. Out here we'd encountered only a few passenger cars, though there were a good many vehicles abandoned on the shoulder. "That's not a good idea," I said.

I looked in the mirror and saw Simon knuckling tears out of his eyes. At that moment he looked as vulnerable and bewildered as a ten-year-old at a funeral.

"I only ever had two signposts in my life," he said. "God

and Diane. And I betrayed them both. I waited too long. You're kind to deny it, but she's dying."

"Not necessarily."

"I don't want to be with her and know I could have prevented this. I would as soon die in the desert. I mean it, Tyler. I want to get out."

The sky was growing light again, an ugly violet glow more like the arc in a malfunctioning fluorescent lamp than anything wholesome or natural.

"I don't care," I said.

Simon gave me a startled look. "What?"

"I don't care how you feel. The reason you should stay with Diane is that we have a difficult drive ahead of us and I can't take care of her and steer at the same time. And I'm going to have to sleep sooner or later. If you take the wheel once in a while we won't have to stop except for food and fuel." If we could find any. "If you drop out it'll double the travel time."

"Does it matter?"

"She may not be dying, Simon, but she's exactly as sick as you think she is, and she will die if she doesn't get help. And the only help I know about is a couple of thousand miles from here."

"Heaven and earth are passing away. We're all going to die."

"I can't speak for heaven and earth. I refuse to let her die as long as I have a choice."

"I envy you that," Simon said quietly.

"What? What could you possibly envy?"

"Your faith," he said.

○ ○ ○

A certain kind of optimism was still possible, but only at night. It wilted by daylight.

I drove into the Hiroshima of the rising sun. I had stopped worrying that the light itself would kill me, though it probably wasn't doing me any good. That any of us had survived the first day was a mystery—a miracle, Simon might have said. It encouraged a certain rough practicality: I pulled a pair of sunglasses out of the glove compartment and tried to keep

my eyes on the road instead of on the hemisphere of orange
fire levitating out of the horizon.

The day grew hotter. So did the interior of the car, despite
the overworked air-conditioning. (I was running it hard in an
effort to keep Diane's body temperature under control.)
Somewhere between Albuquerque and Tucumcari a great
wave of fatigue washed over me. My eyelids drifted closed
and I nearly ran the car into a mile marker. At which point I
pulled over and turned off the engine. I told Simon to fill the
tank from the jericans and get ready to take the wheel. He
nodded reluctantly.

We were making better time than I'd anticipated. Traffic
had been light to nearly nonexistent, maybe because people
were afraid of being on the road by themselves. While Simon
put gas in the car I said, "What did you bring for food?"

"Only what I could grab from the kitchen. I had to hurry.
See for yourself."

I found a cardboard box among the dented jericans and
packaged medical supplies and loose bottles of mineral water
in the trunk. It contained three boxes of Cheerios, two cans
of corned beef, and a bottle of Diet Pepsi. "Jesus, Simon."

He winced at what I had to remind myself he considered a
blasphemy. "That was all I could find."

And no bowls or spoons. But I was as hungry as I was
sleep deprived. I told Simon we ought to let the engine cool
off, and while it did we sat in the shade of the car, windows
rolled down, a gritty breeze coming off the desert, the sun
suspended in the sky like high noon on the surface of Mercury. We used the torn-off bottoms of empty plastic bottles as
makeshift cups and ate Cheerios moistened with tepid water.
It looked and tasted like mucilage.

I briefed Simon on the next leg of the trip, reminded him
to turn on the air-conditioning once we were underway, told
him to wake me if there seemed to be trouble on the road
ahead.

Then I tended to Diane. The IV drip and the antibiotics
seemed to have bolstered her strength, but only marginally.
She opened her eyes and said, "Tyler," after I helped her
drink a little water. She accepted a few spoonfuls of Cheerios

but turned her head away after that. Her cheeks were sunken, her eyes listless and inattentive.

"Bear with me," I said. "Just a little longer, Diane." I adjusted her drip. I helped her sit up, legs splayed out of the car, while she passed a little brownish urine. Then I sponged her off and switched her soiled panties for a pair of clean cotton briefs from my own suitcase.

When she was comfortable again I stuffed a blanket into the narrow gap between the front and back seats to make a space where I could stretch out without displacing her. Simon had napped only briefly during the first leg of the trip and must have been as exhausted as I was . . . but he hadn't been beaten with a rifle butt. The place where Brother Aaron had clubbed me was swollen and rang like a bell when I put my fingers anywhere near it.

Simon watched all this from a couple of yards away, his expression sullen or possibly jealous. When I called him he hesitated and looked longingly across the salt-pan desert, deep into the heart of nothing at all.

Then he loped back to the car, downcast, and slid behind the wheel.

I compressed myself into my niche behind the front seat. Diane seemed to be unconscious, but before I slept I felt her press her hand against mine.

o o o

When I woke it was night again, and Simon had pulled over to trade places.

I climbed out of the car and stretched. My head still throbbed, my spine felt as if it had cramped into a permanent geriatric gnarl, but I was more alert than Simon, who crawled into the back and was instantly asleep.

I didn't know where we were except that we were on I-40 heading east and the land was less arid here, irrigated fields stretching out on either side of the road under crimson moonlight. I made sure Diane was comfortable and breathing without distress and I left the front and rear doors open for a couple of minutes to air out the stink, a sickroom smell overlaid with hints of blood and gasoline. Then I took the driver's seat.

The stars above the road were distressingly few and impossible to recognize. I wondered about Mars. Was it still under a Spin membrane or had it been cut loose like the Earth? But I didn't know where in the sky to look and I doubted I'd know it if I saw it. I did see—couldn't help seeing—the enigmatic silvery line Simon had pointed out back in Arizona, the one I had mistaken for a contrail. It was even more prominent tonight. It had moved from the western horizon almost to the zenith, and the gentle curve had become an oval, a flattened letter *O*.

The sky I was looking at was three billion years older than the one I had last seen from the lawn of the Big House. I supposed it could harbor all kinds of mysteries.

Once we were in motion I tried the dashboard radio, which had been silent the night before. Nothing digital was coming in, but I did eventually locate a local station on the FM band—the kind of small-town station usually devoted to country music and Christianity, but tonight it was all talk. I learned a lot before the signal finally faded into noise.

I learned, for one thing, that we had been wise to avoid big cities. Major cities were disaster areas—not because of looting and violence (there had been surprisingly little) but because of catastrophic infrastructure collapse. The rising of the red sun had looked so much like the long-predicted death of the Earth that most people had simply stayed home to die with their families, leaving urban centers with minimally functioning police and fire departments and radically understaffed hospitals. The minority of people who attempted death by gunshot, or who dosed themselves with extravagant amounts of alcohol, cocaine, OxyContin, or amphetamines, were the inadvertent cause of the most immediate problems: they left gas stoves running, passed out while driving, or dropped cigarettes as they died. When the carpet began to smolder or the drapes burst into flames nobody called 911, and in many cases there would have been no one there to pick up. House fires quickly became neighborhood fires.

Four big plumes of smoke were rising from Oklahoma City, the newscaster said, and according to phone reports much of the south side of Chicago had already been reduced to embers. Every major city in the country—every one that had been heard from—was reporting at least one or two large-scale uncontrolled fires.

But the situation was improving, not deteriorating. Today it had begun to seem possible that the human race might survive at least a few days longer, and as a result more first-responders and essential-service personnel were back at their posts. (The downside was that people had begun to worry how long their provisions might last: grocery-store looting was a growing problem.) Anyone who was *not* an essential-service provider was being urged to stay off the roads—the message had gone out before dawn over the emergency broadcast system and through every radio and TV outlet still functioning, and it was being repeated tonight. Which helped to explain why traffic had been reasonably scarce on the interstate. I had seen a few military and police patrols but none of them had interfered with us, presumably because of the plates on my car— California and most other states had begun issuing EMS license plate stickers to physicians after the first flicker episode.

Policing was sporadic. The regular military remained more or less intact despite some desertions, but Reserve and National Guard units were at fractional strength and couldn't fill in for local authorities. Electrical power was sporadic, too; most generating stations were understaffed and barely functional, and blackouts had begun to cascade through the grid. There were rumors that nuclear plants at San Onofre in California and Pickering in Canada had come close to terminal meltdowns, though that was unconfirmed.

The announcer went on to read a list of designated local food depots, hospitals still open for business (with estimated waiting times for triage), and home first-aid tips. He also read a Weather Bureau advisory cautioning against prolonged exposure to the sun. The sunlight seemed not to be immediately deadly, but excessive UV levels could cause "long-term problems," they said, which was about as sad as it was funny.

o o o

I caught a few more scattered broadcasts before dawn, but the rising sun obscured them all with noise.

The day dawned overcast. I did not, therefore, have to drive directly into the glare of the sun; but even this muted sunrise was dauntingly strange. The entire eastern half of the sky became a churning soup of red light, as hypnotic in its way as the embers of a dying campfire. Occasionally the clouds parted and fingers of amber sunlight probed the land. But by noon the overcast had deepened and within the hour rain began to fall—a hot, lifeless rain that coated the highway and mirrored the sickly colors of the sky.

I had emptied the last jerican of gasoline into the tank that morning, and somewhere between Cairo and Lexington the needle on the gas gauge began to sag alarmingly. I woke Simon and explained the problem and told him I'd pull into the next gas station . . . and each one after that, until we found one that would sell us some fuel.

The next station turned out to be a little four-pump mom-and-pop gas-and-snack-food franchise a quarter mile off the highway. The store was dark and the pumps were probably dead, but I rolled up anyhow and got out of the car and took the nozzle off its hook.

A man with a Bengals cap on his head and a shotgun cradled in his arms came around the side of the building and said, "That's no good."

I put the nozzle back, slowly. "Your power out?"

"That's correct."

"No backup?"

He shrugged and came closer. Simon started to get out of the car but I waved him back in. The man in the Bengals cap—he was about thirty years old and thirty pounds overweight—looked at the Ringer's drip rigged up in the backseat. Then he squinted at the license plate. It was a California plate, which probably didn't win me any goodwill points, but the EMS sticker was plainly visible. "You're a doctor?"

"Tyler Dupree," I said. "M.D."

"Pardon me if I don't shake your hand. That your wife in there?"

I said yes, because it was simpler than explaining. Simon shot me a look but didn't contradict me.

"You have identification to prove you're a medical doctor? Because, no offense, there's been some auto theft happening these past couple of days."

I took out my wallet and tossed it at his feet. He picked it up and looked at the card folder. Then he fished a pair of eyeglasses out of his shirt pocket and looked at it again. Finally he handed it back and offered me his hand. "Sorry about that, Dr. Dupree. I'm Chuck Bernelli. If it's just gas you need, I'll turn on the pumps. If you need more than that, it'll only take me a minute to open the store."

"I need the gas. Provisions would be nice, but I'm not carrying a lot of cash."

"The heck with cash. We're closed to criminals and drunks, and there's no lack of those on the road right now, but we're open all hours to the military and the highway patrol. And medical men. At least as long as there's gas to pump. I hope your wife's not too badly off."

"Not if I can get where I'm headed."

"Lexington V.A.? Samaritan?"

"A little farther than that. She needs special care."

He glanced back at the car. Simon had rolled down the windows to let some fresh air in. Rain spackled down on the dusty vehicle, the puddled oily asphalt. Bernelli caught a glimpse of Diane as she turned and began to cough in her sleep. He frowned.

"I'll get the pumps going, then," he said. "You'll want to be on your way."

Before we left he put together some groceries for us, a few cans of soup, a box of saltine crackers, a can opener in a plastic display pack. But he didn't want to get close to the car.

○ ○ ○

A racking, intermittent cough is a common symptom of CVWS. The bacteria is almost canny in the way it preserves its victims, preferring not to drown them in a catastrophic pneumonia, though that's the means by which it eventually kills—that, or wholesale cardiac failure. I had taken an oxygen canister, bleeder valve, and mask from the wholesaler outside Flagstaff, and when Diane's cough began to interfere with her breathing—she was on the verge of panic, drowning in her own sputum, eyes rolling—I cleared her airway as best I could and held the mask over her mouth and nose while Simon drove.

Eventually she calmed down, her color improved, and she was able to sleep again. I sat with her while she rested, her feverish head nestled into my shoulder. The rain had become a relentless downpour, slowing us down. Big plumes of water rooster-tailed behind the car every time we hit a low place in the road. Toward evening the light faded to hot coals on the western horizon.

There was no sound but the beating of rain on the roof of the car and I was content to listen to it until Simon cleared his throat and said, "Are you an atheist, Tyler?"

"Pardon me?"

"I don't mean to be rude, but I was wondering: do you consider yourself an atheist?"

I wasn't sure how to answer that. Simon had been helpful—had been invaluable—in getting us this far. But he was also someone who had hitched his intellectual wagon to a team of lunatic-fringe Dispensationalists whose only argument with the end of the world was that it had defied their detailed expectations. I didn't want to offend him because I still needed him—Diane still needed him.

So I said, "Does it matter what I consider myself?"

"Just curious."

"Well—I don't know. I guess that's my answer. I don't claim to know whether God exists or why He wound up the universe and made it spin the way it does. Sorry, Simon. That's the best I can do on the theological front."

He was silent for another few miles. Then he said, "Maybe that's what Diane meant."

"Meant about what?"

"When we talked about it. Which we haven't done lately, come to think of it. We disagreed about Pastor Dan and Jordan Tabernacle even before the schism. I thought she was too cynical. She said I was too easily impressed. Maybe so. Pastor Dan had the gift of looking into Scripture and finding knowledge on every page—knowledge solid as a house, beams and pillars of knowledge. It really is a gift. I can't do it myself. As hard as I try, to this day I can't open the Bible and make immediate sense of it."

"Maybe you're not supposed to."

"But I wanted to. I wanted to be what Pastor Dan was: smart and, you know, always on solid ground. Diane said it was a devil's bargain, that Dan Condon had traded humility for certainty. Maybe that's what I lacked. Maybe that's what she saw in you, why she clung to you all these years—your humility."

"Simon, I—"

"It's not anything you have to apologize for or make me feel better about. I know she called you when she thought I was asleep or when I was out of the house. I know I was lucky to have her as long as I did." He looked back at me. "Will you do me a favor? I'd like you to tell her I'm sorry I didn't take better care of her when she got sick."

"You can tell her yourself."

He nodded thoughtfully and drove deeper into the rain. I told him to see if he could find any useful information on the radio, now that it was dark again. I meant to stay awake and listen; but my head was throbbing and my vision wanted to double, and after a while it seemed easier just to close my eyes and sleep.

∘ ∘ ∘

I slept hard and long, and miles passed under the wheels of the car.

When I woke it was another rainy morning. We were parked at a rest stop (west of Manassas, I learned later) and a woman with a torn black umbrella was tapping on the window.

I blinked and opened the door and she backed off a pace, casting cautious looks at Diane. "Man said to tell you don't wait."

"Excuse me?"

"Said to tell you good-bye and don't wait for him."

Simon wasn't in the front seat. Nor was he visible among the trash barrels, sodden picnic tables, and flimsy latrines in the immediate neighborhood. A few other cars were parked here, most of them idling while the owners visited the potties. I registered trees, parkland, a hilly view of some rain-soaked little industrial town under a fiery sky. "Skinny blond guy? Dirty T-shirt?"

"That's him. That's the one. He said he didn't want you to sleep too long. Then he took off."

"On foot?"

"Yes. Down toward the river, not along the road." She peered at Diane again. Diane was breathing shallowly and noisily. "Are you two okay?"

"No. But we don't have far to go. Thank you for asking. Did he say anything else?"

"Yes. He said to say God bless you, and he'll find his own way from here."

I tended to Diane's needs. I took a last look around the rainy parking lot. Then I got back on the road.

○ ○ ○

I had to stop several times to adjust Diane's drip or feed her a few breaths of oxygen. She wasn't opening her eyes anymore—she wasn't just asleep, she was unconscious. I didn't want to think about what that meant.

The roads were slow and the rain was relentless and there was evidence everywhere of the chaos of the last couple of days. I passed dozens of wrecked or burned-out cars pushed to the side of the road, some still smoldering. Certain routes had been closed to civilian traffic, reserved for military or emergency vehicles. I had to double back from roadblocks a couple of times. The day's heat made the humid air almost unbearable, and although a fierce wind came up in the afternoon it didn't bring relief.

But Simon had at least abandoned us close to our destination, and I made it to the Big House while there was still some light in the sky.

The wind had grown worse, almost gale force, and the Lawtons' long driveway was littered with branches torn from the surrounding pines. The house itself was dark, or looked that way in the amber dusk.

I left Diane in the car at the foot of the steps and pounded on the door. And waited. And pounded again. Eventually the door opened a crack and Carol Lawton peered out.

I could barely make out her features through that crevice: one pale blue eye, a wedge of wrinkled cheek. But she recognized me.

"Tyler Dupree!" she said. "Are you alone?"

The door opened wider.

"No," I said. "Diane's with me. And I might need some help getting her inside."

Carol came out onto the big front porch and squinted down at the car. When she saw Diane her small body stiffened; she drew up her shoulders and gasped.

"Dear God," she whispered. "Have *both* my children come home to die?"

THE ABYSS IN FLAMES

Wind rattled the Big House all that night, a hot salt wind stirred out of the Atlantic by three days of unnatural sunlight. I was aware of it even as I slept: it was what I rose to in moments of near-wakefulness and it was the soundtrack for a dozen uneasy dreams. It was still knocking at the window after sunrise, when I dressed myself and went looking for Carol Lawton.

The house had been without electrical power for days. The upstairs hallway was dimly illuminated by the rainy glow from a window at the end of the corridor. The oaken stairway descended to the foyer, where two streaming bay windows admitted daylight the color of pale roses. I found Carol in the parlor, adjusting an antique mantel clock.

I said, "How is she?"

Carol glanced at me. "Unchanged," she said, returning her attention to the clock as she wound it with a brass key. "I was with her a moment ago. I'm not neglecting her, Tyler."

"I didn't think you were. How about Jason?"

"I helped him dress. He's better during daylight. I don't

know why. The nights are hard on him. Last night was . . . hard."

"I'll look in on them both." I didn't bother asking whether she had heard any news, whether FEMA or the White House had issued any fresh directives. There would have been no point; Carol's universe stopped at the borders of the property. "You should get some sleep."

"I'm sixty-eight years old. I don't sleep as much as I used to. But you're right, I'm tired—I do need to lie down. As soon as I finish this. This clock loses time if you don't tend to it. Your mother used to adjust it every day, did you know that? And after your mother died Marie wound it whenever she cleaned. But Marie stopped coming about six months ago. For six months the clock was stuck at a quarter after four. As in the old joke, right twice a day."

"We should talk about Jason." Last night I had been too exhausted to do more than learn the basics: Jason had arrived unannounced a week before the end of the Spin and had fallen ill the night the stars reappeared. His symptoms were an intermittent, partial paralysis and occluded vision, plus fever. Carol had tried calling for medical help but circumstances had made that impossible, so she was caring for him herself, though she hadn't been able to diagnose the problem or provide more than simple palliative care.

She was afraid he was dying. Her concern didn't extend to the rest of the world, however. Jason had told her not to worry about that. *Things will be back to normal soon,* he said.

And she had believed him. The red sun held no terrors for Carol. The nights were bad, though, she said. The nights took Jason like a bad dream.

○ ○ ○

I looked in on Diane first.

Carol had put her in an upstairs bedroom—her room from the old days, done over as a generic guest bedroom. I found her physically stable and breathing without assistance, but there was nothing reassuring in that. It was part of the etiology of the disease. The tide advanced and the tide ebbed, but each cycle carried away more of her resilience and more of her strength.

I kissed her dry, hot forehead and told her to rest. She gave no sign of having heard me.

Then I went to see Jason. There was a question I needed to ask.

According to Carol, Jase had come back to the Big House because of some conflict at Perihelion. She couldn't remember his explanation, but it had something to do with Jason's father ("E.D. is behaving badly again," she said) and something to do with "that little black wrinkly man, the one who died. The Martian."

The Martian. Who had supplied the longevity drug that had made Jason a Fourth. The drug that should have protected him from whatever was killing him now.

○ ○ ○

He was awake when I knocked and entered his room, the same room he had occupied thirty years ago, when we were children in the compassed world of children and the stars were in their rightful places. Here was the rectangle of subtly brighter color where a poster of the solar system had once shaded the wall. Here was the carpet, long since steam-cleaned and chemically bleached, where we had once spilled Cokes and scattered crumbs on rainy days like this.

And here was Jason.

"That sounds like Tyler," he said.

He lay in bed, dressed—he insisted on dressing each morning, Carol had said—in clean khaki pants and a blue cotton shirt. His back was propped against the pillows and he seemed perfectly alert. I said, "Not much light in here, Jase."

"Open the blinds if you like."

I did, but it only admitted more of the sullen amber daylight. "You mind if I examine you?"

"Of course I don't mind."

He wasn't looking at me. He was looking, if the angle of his head meant anything, at a blank patch of wall.

"Carol says you've been having trouble with your vision."

"Carol is experiencing what people in your profession call denial. In fact I'm blind. I haven't been able to see anything at all since yesterday morning."

I sat on the bed next to him. When he turned his head toward me the motion was smooth but agonizingly slow. I took a penlight from my shirt pocket and flashed it into his right eye in order to watch the pupil contract.

It didn't.

It did something worse.

It glittered. The pupil of his eye glittered as if it had been injected with tiny diamonds.

Jason must have felt me jerk back.

"That bad?" he asked.

I couldn't speak.

He said, more somberly, "I can't use a mirror. Please, Ty. I need you to tell me what you see."

"This . . . I don't know what this is, Jason. This isn't something I can diagnose."

"Just describe it, please."

I tried to muster a clinical detachment. "It appears as if crystals of some kind have grown into your eye. The sclera looks normal and the iris doesn't seem to be affected, but the pupil is completely obscured by flakes of something like mica. I've never heard of anything like this. I would have said it was impossible. I can't treat it."

I backed away from the bed, found a chair and sat in it. For a while there was no sound but the ticking of the bedside clock, another of Carol's pristine antiques.

Then Jason draw a breath and forced what he seemed to imagine was a reassuring smile. "Thank you. You're right. It isn't a condition you can treat. But I'm still going to need your help during—well, during the next couple of days. Carol tries, but she's way out of her depth."

"So am I."

More rain beat at the window. "The help I need isn't entirely medical."

"If you have an explanation for this—"

"A partial one, at best."

"Then please share it with me, Jase, because I'm getting a little scared here."

He cocked his head, listening to some sound I hadn't heard or couldn't hear, until I began to wonder whether he had forgotten me. Then he said, "The short version is that my nervous system has been overtaken by something beyond my control. The condition of my eyes is just an external manifestation of it."

"A disease?"

"No, but that's the effect it's having."

"Is this condition contagious?"

"On the contrary. I believe it's unique. A disease only I can develop—on this planet, at least."

"Then it has something to do with the longevity treatment."

"In a way it does. But I—"

"No, Jase, I need an answer to that before you say anything else. Is your condition—whatever it is—a direct result of the drug I administered?"

"Not a *direct* result, no . . . you're not at fault in any way, if that's what you mean."

"Right now I couldn't care less who's at fault. Diane is sick. Didn't Carol tell you?"

"Carol said something about flu—"

"Carol lied. It's not flu. It's late-stage CVWS. I drove two thousand miles through what looks like the end of the world because she's dying, Jase, and there's only one cure I can think of, and you just threw that into doubt."

He rolled his head again, perhaps involuntarily, as if he were trying to shake off some invisible distraction.

But before I could prompt him he said, "There are aspects of Martian life Wun never shared with you. E.D. suspected as much, and to a certain extent his suspicions were well founded. Mars has been doing sophisticated biotechnology for centuries. Centuries ago, the Fourth Age was exactly what Wun told you it was—a longevity treatment and a social institution. But it's evolved since then. For Wun's generation the Fourth was more like a *platform,* a biological operating system capable of running much more sophisticated software applications. There isn't just a four, there's a 4.1, 4.2—if you see what I mean."

"What I gave you—"

"What you gave me was the traditional treatment. A basic four."

"But?"

"But . . . I've supplemented it since."

"This supplement was also something Wun transported from Mars?"

"Yes. The purpose—"

"Never mind the purpose. Are you absolutely certain you're not suffering from the effects of the original treatment?"

"As certain as I can be."

I stood up.

Jason heard me moving toward the door. "I can explain," he said. "And I still need your help. By all means take care of her, Ty. I hope she lives. But keep in mind . . . my time is also limited."

○ ○ ○

The case of Martian pharmaceuticals was where I had left it, unmolested, behind the broken wallboard in the basement of my mother's house, and when I had retrieved it I carried it across the lawn through the gusting amber rain to the Big House.

Carol was in Diane's room administering sips of oxygen by mask.

"We need to use that sparingly," I said, "unless you can conjure up another cylinder."

"Her lips were a little blue."

"Let me see."

Carol moved away from her daughter. I closed the valve and set the mask aside. You have to be careful with oxygen. It's indispensable for a patient in respiratory distress, but it can also cause problems. Too much can rupture the air sacs in the lung. My fear was that as Diane's condition worsened she would need higher doses to keep her blood levels up, the kind of oxygen therapy generally delivered by mechanical ventilation. We didn't have a ventilator.

Nor did we have any clinical means of monitoring her blood gases, but her lips looked relatively normal when I took the mask away. Her breathing was rapid and shallow, however, and though she opened her eyes once she remained lethargic and unresponsive.

Carol watched suspiciously as I opened the dusty case and extracted one of the Martian vials and a hypodermic syringe. "What's that?"

"Probably the only thing that can save her life."

"Is it? Are you sure of that, Tyler?"

I nodded.

"No," she said, "I mean, are you *really* sure? Because that's what you gave Jason, isn't it? When he had AMS."

There was no point in denying it. "Yes," I said.

"I may not have practiced medicine for thirty years, but I'm not ignorant. I did a little research on AMS after the last time you were here. I looked up the journal abstracts. And the interesting thing is, there *isn't* a cure for it. There is no magic drug. And if there were it would hardly be cross-specific for CVWS. So what I'm assuming, Tyler, is that you're about to administer a pharmaceutical agent probably connected with that wrinkled man who died in Florida."

"I won't argue, Carol. You've obviously drawn your own conclusions."

"I don't want you to *argue*; I want you to *reassure* me. I want you to tell me this drug won't do to Diane what it seems to have done to Jason."

"It won't," I said, but I think Carol knew I was editing out the caveat, the unspoken *to the best of my knowledge*.

She studied my face. "You still care for her."

"Yes."

"It never fails to astonish me," Carol said. "The tenacity of love."

I put the needle into Diane's vein.

○ ○ ○

By midday the house was not merely hot but so humid I expected moss to be hanging from the ceilings. I sat with Diane to make sure there were no immediate ill effects from the injection. At one point there was a protracted knocking at the front door of the house. *Thieves,* I thought, *looters,* but by the time I got to the foyer Carol had answered and was thanking a portly man, who nodded and turned to leave.

"That was Emil Hardy," Carol said as she pulled the door

closed. "Do you remember the Hardys? They own the little colonial house on Bantam Hill Road. Emil printed up a newspaper."

"A newspaper?"

She held up two stapled sheets of letter-sized paper. "Emil has an electrical generator in his garage. He listens to the radio at night and takes notes, then he prints a summary and delivers it to local houses. This is his second issue. He's a nice man and well meaning. But I don't see any point in reading such things."

"May I look at it?"

"If you like."

I took it upstairs with me.

Emil was a creditable amateur reporter. The stories mainly concerned crises in D.C. and Virginia—a list of official no-go zones and fire-related evacuations, attempts to restore local services. I skimmed through these. It was a couple of items lower down that caught my attention.

The first was a report that solar radiation recently measured at ground level was heightened but not nearly as intense as predicted. "Government scientists," it said, "are perplexed but cautiously optimistic about chances for long-term human survival." No source was credited, so this could have been some commentator's fabrication or an attempt to forestall further panic, but it jibed with my experience to date: the new sunlight was strange but not immediately deadly.

No word on how it might be affecting crop yields, weather, or the ecology in general. Neither the pestilential heat nor this torrential rain felt especially *normal*.

Below that was an item headlined LIGHTS IN SKY SIGHTED WORLDWIDE.

These were the same C- or O-shaped lines Simon had pointed out back in Arizona. They had been seen as far north as Anchorage and as far south as Mexico City. Reports from Europe and Asia were fragmentary and primarily concerned with the immediate crisis, but a few similar stories had slipped through. ("Note," Emil Hardy's copy said, "cable news networks only intermittently available but showing recent video from India of similar phenomenon on larger scale." Whatever that meant.)

○ ○ ○

Diane woke for a few moments while I was with her.

"Tyler," she said.

I took her hand. It was dry and unnaturally warm.

"I'm sorry," she said.

"You have nothing to be sorry about."

"I'm sorry you have to see me like this."

"You're getting better. It might take a while, but you'll be all right."

Her voice was soft as the sound of a falling leaf. She looked around the room, recognizing it. Her eyes widened. "Here I am!"

"Here you are."

"Say my name again."

"Diane," I said. "Diane. Diane."

○ ○ ○

Diane was gravely ill, but it was Jason who was dying. He told me as much when I went to see him.

He hadn't eaten today, Carol had informed me. Jase had taken ice water through a straw but otherwise refused liquids. He could barely move his body. When I asked him to raise his arm he did so, but with such exquisite effort and torpid speed that I pressed it down again. Only his voice was still strong, and he anticipated losing even that: "If tonight is anything like last night I'll be incoherent until dawn. Tomorrow, who knows? I want to talk while I still can."

"Is there some reason your condition deteriorates at night?"

"A simple one, I think. We'll get to that. First I want you to do something for me. My suitcase was on the dresser: is it still there?"

"Still there."

"Open it. I packed an audio recorder. Find it for me."

I found a brushed-silver rectangle the size of a deck of playing cards, next to a stack of manila envelopes addressed to names I didn't recognize. "This it?" I said, then cursed myself: of course he couldn't see.

"If the label says Sony, that's it. There ought to be a package of blank memory underneath."

"Yup, got it."

"So we'll have a talk. Until it gets dark, and maybe a little after. And I want you to keep the recorder running. No matter what happens. Change the memory when you have to, or the battery if the power gets low. Do that for me, all right?"

"As long as Diane doesn't need urgent attention. When do you want to start?"

His turned his head. The diamond-specked pupils of his eyes glittered in the strange light.

"Now would not be too soon," he said.

ARS MORIENDI

The Martians, Jason said, were not the simple, peaceful, pastoral people Wun had led (or allowed) us to believe they were.

It was true that they weren't especially warlike—the Five Republics had settled their political differences almost a millennium ago—and they were "pastoral" in the sense that they devoted most of their resources to agriculture. But nor were they "simple" in any sense of the word. They were, as Jase had pointed out, past masters of the art of synthetic biology. Their civilization had been founded on it. We had built them a habitable planet with biotech tools, and there had never been a Martian generation that didn't understand the function and potential uses of DNA.

If their large-scale technology was sometimes crude—Wun's spacecraft, for instance, had been almost primitive, a Newtonian cannonball—it was because of their radically constrained natural resources. Mars was a world without oil or coal, supporting a fragile water- and nitrogen-starved ecosystem. A profligate, lush industrial base like the Earth's could never have existed on Wun's planet. On Mars, most human effort was devoted to producing sufficient food for a strictly controlled population. Biotechnology served this purpose admirably. Smoke-stack industries did not.

"Wun told you this?" I asked, as rain fell continuously and the afternoon ebbed.

"He confided in me, yes, though most of what he said was already implicit in the archives."

Rust-colored light from the window reflected from Jason's blind, altered eyes.

"But he could have been lying."

"I don't know that he ever *lied*, Tyler. He was just a little stingy with the truth."

The microscopic replicators Wun had carried to Earth were cutting-edge synthetic biology. They were fully capable of doing everything Wun promised they would do. In fact they were more sophisticated than Wun had been willing to admit.

Among the replicators' unacknowledged functions was a hidden second subchannel for communicating among themselves and with their point of origin. Wun hadn't said whether this was conventional narrowband radio or something technologically more exotic—the latter, Jase suspected. In any case, it required a receiver more advanced than anything we could build on Earth. It required, Wun had said, a *biological* receiver. A modified human nervous system.

o o o

"You *volunteered* for this?"

"I would have. If anyone had asked. But the only reason Wun confided in me was that he feared for his life from the day he arrived on Earth. He harbored no illusions about human venality or power politics. He needed someone he could trust to take custody of his pharmacopoeia, if anything happened to him. Someone who understood the purpose of it. He never proposed that I become a receiver. The modification only works on a Fourth—remember what I said? The longevity treatment is a platform. It runs other applications. This is one of them."

"You did this to yourself *on purpose*?"

"I injected myself with the substance after he died. It wasn't traumatic and it had no immediate effect. Remember, Tyler, there was no way for communication from the replicators to penetrate a fully functioning Spin membrane. What I gave myself was a *latent* ability."

"Why do it, then?"

"Because I didn't want to die in a condition of ignorance. We all assumed, if the Spin ended, we'd be dead within days or hours. The sole advantage to Wun's modification was that in those last days or hours, as long as I lasted, I would be in intimate contact with a database almost as large as the galaxy itself. I would know as nearly as anyone on Earth *could* know who the Hypotheticals were and why they had done this to us."

I thought, *And do you know that now?* But maybe he did. Maybe that was what he wanted to communicate before he lost the ability to speak, why he wanted me to make a recording of it. "Did Wun know you might do this?"

"No, and I doubt he would have approved . . . although he was running the same application himself."

"Was he? It didn't show."

"It wouldn't. Remember: what's happening to me—to my body, to my brain—that's not the application." He turned his sightless eyes toward me. "That's a malfunction."

o o o

The replicators had been launched from Earth and had flourished in the outer solar system, far from the sun. (Had the Hypotheticals noticed this, and had they blamed the Earth for what was in fact a Martian intervention? Was that, as E.D. had implied, what the sly Martians had intended all along? Jason didn't say—I presumed he didn't know.)

In time the replicators spread to the nearest stars and beyond . . . eventually far beyond. The replicator colonies were invisible at astronomical distances, but if you had mapped them onto a grid of our local stellar neighborhood you would have seen a continually expanding cloud of them, a glacially slow explosion of artificial life.

The replicators were not immortal. As individual entities

they lived, reproduced, and eventually died. What remained in place was the network they built: a coral reef of gated, interconnected nodes in which novel data accumulated and drained toward the network's point of origin.

"The last time we talked," I reminded Jase, "you said there was a problem. You said the replicator population was dying back."

"They encountered something no one had planned for."

"What was that, Jase?"

He was silent a few moments, as if gathering his thoughts.

"We assumed," he said, "that when we launched the replicators we were introducing something new to the universe, a wholly new kind of artificial life. That assumption was naive. We—human beings, terrestrial or Martian—weren't the first sentient species to evolve in our galaxy. Far from it. In fact there's nothing particularly unusual about us. Virtually everything we've done in our brief history has been done before, somewhere, by someone else."

"You're telling me the replicators ran into other replicators?"

"An *ecology* of replicators. The stars are a jungle, Tyler. Fuller of life than we ever imagined."

I tried to picture the process as Jason described it:

Far beyond the Spin-sequestered Earth, far beyond the solar system—so deep in space that the sun itself is only one more star in a crowded sky—a replicator seed alights on a dusty fragment of ice and begins to reproduce. It initiates the same cycle of growth, specialization, observation, communication, and reproduction that has taken place countless times during its ancestors' slow migrations. Maybe it reaches maturity; maybe it even begins to pump out microbursts of data; but this time, the cycle is interrupted.

Something has sensed the replicator's presence. Something hungry.

The predator (Jase explained) is another kind of semiorganic autocatalytic feedback system—another colony of self-reproducing cellular mechanisms, as much machine as biology—and the predator is plugged into its own network, this one older and vastly larger than anything the terrestrial replicators have had time to construct during their exodus from Earth. The predator is more highly evolved than its prey: its subroutines for nutrient-seeking and resource-utilization have been honed over billions of years. The terrestrial replicator colony, blind and incapable of fleeing, is promptly eaten.

But "eaten" carries a special meaning here. The predator wants more than the sophisticated carbonaceous molecules of which the replicator's mature form is composed, useful as these might be. Far more interesting to the predator is the replicator's *meaning,* the functions and strategies written into its reproductive templates. It adopts from these what it considers potentially valuable; then it reorganizes and exploits the replicator colony for its own purposes. The colony does not die but is absorbed, ontologically devoured, subsumed along with its brethren into a larger, more complex, and vastly older interstellar hierarchy.

It is not the first nor the last such device to be so absorbed.

"Replicator networks," Jason said, "are one of the things sentient civilizations tend to produce. Given the inherent difficulty of sublight-speed travel as a way of exploring the galaxy, most technological cultures eventually settle for an expanding grid of von Neumann machines—which is what the replicators are—that costs nothing to maintain and generates a trickle of scientific information that expands exponentially over historical time."

"Okay," I said, "I understand that. The Martian replicators aren't unique. They ran into what you call an ecology—"

"A von Neumann ecology." (After the twentieth-century mathematician John von Neumann, who first suggested the possibility of self-reproducing machines.)

"A von Neumann ecology, and they were absorbed by it. But that doesn't tell us anything about the Hypotheticals or the Spin."

Jason pursed his lips impatiently. "Tyler, no. You don't understand. The Hypotheticals *are* the von Neumann ecology. They're one and the same."

o o o

At this point I had to step back and reconsider exactly who was in the room with me.

It looked like Jase. But everything he'd said was casting that into doubt.

"Are you communicating with this . . . entity? Now, I mean? As we speak?"

"I don't know if you'd call it communication. Communication works two ways. This doesn't, not in the sense you're implying. And real communication wouldn't be quite so overwhelming. This *is*. Especially at night. The input is moderated during daylight hours, presumably because solar radiation washes out the signal."

"At night the signal is stronger?"

"Maybe the word 'signal' is misleading, too. A signal is what the original replicators were designed to transmit. What I receive is coming in on the same carrier wave, and it does convey information, but it's active, not passive. It's trying to do to me what it's done to every other node in the network. In effect, Ty, it's trying to acquire and reprogram my nervous system."

So there *was* a third entity in the room. Me, Jase—and the Hypotheticals, who were eating him alive.

"Can they do that? Reprogram your nervous system?"

"Not *successfully,* no. To them I look like one more node in the replicator network. The biotechnology I injected into myself is sensitive to their manipulation, but not in the ways they anticipate. Because they don't perceive me as a biological entity, all they can do is kill me."

"Is there any way to screen this signal or interfere with it?"

"None that I know of. If the Martians had such a technique they neglected to include the information in their archives."

The window in Jason's room faced west. The roseate glow now penetrating the room was the waning sun, obscured by clouds.

"But they're with you now. Talking to you."

"They. *It.* We need a better pronoun. The entire von Neumann ecology is a single entity. It thinks its own slow thoughts and makes its own plans. But many of its trillions of parts are also autonomous individuals, often competing with each other, quicker to act than the network as a whole and vastly more intelligent than any single human being. The Spin membrane, for instance—"

"The Spin membrane is an *individual*?"

"In every important sense, yes. Its ultimate goals are derived from the network, but it evaluates events and makes autonomous choices. It's more complex than we ever dreamed, Ty. We all assumed the membrane was either *on* or *off,* like a light switch, like binary code. Not true. It has *many* states. *Many* purposes. Many degrees of permeability, for instance. We've known for years that it can transit a spacecraft and repel an asteroid. But it has subtler capabilities even than that. That's why we haven't been overwhelmed with solar radiation in the last few days. The membrane is still giving us a certain level of protection."

"I don't know the casualty numbers, Jase, but there must be thousands of people in this city alone who have lost family since the Spin stopped. I would be very reluctant to tell them they're being 'protected.'"

"But they are. In general if not in particular. The Spin membrane isn't God—it can't see the sparrow fall. It can, however, prevent the sparrow from being cooked with lethal ultraviolet light."

"To what end?"

At that he frowned. "I can't quite grasp," he began, "or maybe I can't quite *translate*—"

There was a knock at the door. Carol entered with an armful of linen. I switched off the recorder and set it aside. Carol's expression was grim.

"Clean sheets?" I asked.

"Restraints," she said curtly. The linen had been cut into strips. "For when the convulsions start."

She nodded at the window, the lengthening daylight.

"Thank you," Jason said gently. "Tyler, if you need a break, this would be the time. But don't be too long."

o o o

I looked in on Diane, who was between episodes, sleeping. I thought about the Martian drug I had administered to her (the "basic Fourth," as Jase had called it), semi-intelligent molecules about to do battle with her body's overwhelming load of CVWS bacteria, microscopic battalions mustering to repair and rebuild her, unless her body was too weakened to withstand the strain of the transformation.

I kissed her forehead and said gentle words she probably couldn't hear. Then I left her bedroom and went downstairs and out onto the lawn of the Big House, stealing a moment for myself.

The rain had finally stopped—abruptly, completely—and the air was fresher than it had been all day. The sky was deep blue at the zenith. A few tattered thunderheads cloaked the monstrous sun where it touched the western horizon. Raindrops stood on every blade of grass, tiny amber pearls.

Jason had admitted that he was dying. Now I began to admit it to myself.

As a physician I had seen more of death than most people ever see. I knew how people died. I knew that the familiar story of how we face death—denial, anger, acceptance—was at best a gross generalization. Those emotions might evolve in seconds or might never evolve at all; death could trump them at any instant. For many people, facing death was never an issue; their deaths arrived unannounced, a ruptured aorta or a bad decision at a busy intersection.

But Jase knew he was dying. And I was bewildered that he seemed to have accepted it with such unearthly calm, until I realized that his death was also an ambition fulfilled. He was on the brink of understanding what he had struggled all his life to understand: the meaning of the Spin and humanity's place in it—*his* place in it, since he had been instrumental in the launch of the replicators.

It was as if he had reached up and touched the stars.

And they had touched him in return. The stars were murdering him. But he was dying in a state of grace.

o o o

"We have to hurry. It's almost dark now, isn't it?"

Carol had gone off to light candles throughout the house.

"Almost," I said.

"And the rain stopped. Or at least, I can't hear it."

"Temperature's dropping, too. Would you like me to open the window?"

"Please. And the audio recorder, you turned it back on?"

"It's running now." I raised the old frame window a few inches and cool air infiltrated the room.

"We were talking about the Hypotheticals. . . ."

"Yes." Silence. "Jase? Are you still with me?"

"I hear the wind. I hear your voice. I hear . . ."

"Jason?"

"I'm sorry . . . don't mind me, Ty. I'm easily distracted right now. I—*uh!*"

His arms and legs jerked against the restraints Carol had tied across the bed. His head arched into the pillow. He was having what looked like an epileptic seizure, although it was brief: over before I could approach the bed. He gasped and took a deep lungful of air. "Sorry, I'm sorry . . ."

"Don't apologize."

"Can't control it, I'm sorry."

"I know you can't. It's all right, Jase."

"Don't blame them for what's happening to me."

"Blame who—the Hypotheticals?"

He attempted a smile, though he was clearly in pain. "We'll have to find a new name for them, won't we? They're not as hypothetical as they used to be. But don't blame them. They don't know what's happening to me. I'm under their threshold of abstraction."

"I don't know what that means."

He spoke rapidly and eagerly, as if the talk were a welcome distraction from the physical distress. Or another symptom of it. "You and I, Tyler, we're communities of living cells, yes? And if you damaged a sufficient number of my cells I would die, you would have murdered me. But if we shake hands and I lose a few skin cells in the process neither of us even notices the loss. It's invisible. We live at a certain level of abstraction; we interact as bodies, not cell colonies. The same is true of the Hypotheticals. They inhabit a larger universe than we do."

"That makes it all right to kill people?"

"I'm talking about their perception, not their morality. The death of any single human being—*my* death—might be meaningful to them, if they could see it in the correct context. But they can't."

"They've done this before, though, created other Spin worlds—isn't that one of the things the replicators discovered before the Hypotheticals shut them down?"

"Other Spin worlds. Yes. Many. The network of the Hypotheticals has grown to encompass most of the habitable zone of the galaxy, and this is what they do when they encounter a planet that hosts a sentient, tool-using species of a certain degree of maturity—they enclose it in a Spin membrane."

I pictured spiders, wrapping their victims in silk. "Why, Jase?"

The door opened. Carol was back, carrying a tea candle on a china saucer. She put the saucer on the sideboard and lit the candle with a wooden match. The flame danced, imperiled by the breeze from the window.

"To preserve it," Jason said.

"Preserve it against what?"

"Its own senescence and eventual death. Technological cultures are mortal, like everything else. They flourish until they exhaust their resources; then they die."

Unless they don't, I thought. Unless they continue flourishing, expand into their solar systems, transplant themselves to the stars . . .

But Jason had anticipated my objection. "Even local space travel is slow and inefficient for beings with a human life span. Maybe we would have been an exception to the rule. But the Hypotheticals have been around a very long time. Before they devised the Spin membrane they watched countless inhabited worlds drown in their own effluvia."

He drew a breath and seemed to choke on it. Carol turned to face him. Her mask of competence slipped, and in the moment it took him to recover she was plainly terrified, not a doctor but a woman with a dying child.

Jase, perhaps fortunately, couldn't see. He swallowed hard and began to breathe normally again.

"But why the Spin, Jase? It pushes us into the future, but it doesn't change anything."

"On the contrary," he said. "It changes everything."

○ ○ ○

The paradox of Jason's last night was that his speech grew awkward and intermittent even as his acquired knowledge seemed to expand exponentially. I believe he learned more in those few hours than he could begin to share, and what he did share was momentous—sweeping in its explanatory power and provocative for what it implied about human destiny.

Pass over the trauma, the agonized groping after appropriate words, and what he said was—

Well, it began with, "Try to see it from their point of view."

Their point of view: the Hypotheticals.

The Hypotheticals—whether considered as one organism or many—had evolved from the first von Neumann devices to inhabit our galaxy. The origin of those primal self-replicating machines was obscure. Their descendants had no direct memory of it, any more than you or I can "remember" human evolution. They may have been the product of an early-emerging biological culture of which no trace remains; they may have migrated from another, older galaxy. In either case, the Hypotheticals of today belonged to an almost unimaginably ancient lineage.

They had seen sentient biological species evolve and die on planets like ours countless times. By passively transporting organic material from star to star they may even have helped seed the process of organic evolution. And they had watched biological cultures generate crude von Neumann networks as a byproduct of their accelerating (but ultimately unsustainable) complexity—not once, but many times. To the Hypotheticals we all looked more or less like replicator nurseries: strange, fecund, fragile.

From their point of view this endless stuttering gestation of simple von Neumann networks, followed by the rapid ecological collapse of source planets, was both a mystery and a tragedy.

A mystery, because transient events on a purely biological time scale were difficult for them to comprehend or even perceive.

A tragedy, because they had begun to conceive of these progenitor cultures as failed *biological* networks, akin to themselves—growing toward real complexity but snuffed out prematurely by finite planetary ecosystems

For the Hypotheticals, then, the Spin was meant to preserve us—and dozens of similar civilizations that had arisen on other worlds before and since—in our technological prime. But we weren't museum pieces, frozen in place for public display. The Hypotheticals were reengineering our destiny. They had suspended us in slowtime while they put together the pieces of a grand experiment, an experiment formulated over billions of years and now nearing its ultimate goal: to build a vastly expanded biological landscape into which these otherwise doomed cultures could expand and in which they would eventually meet and intermingle.

o o o

I didn't immediately grasp the meaning of this: "An expanded biological environment? Bigger than the Earth itself?"

We were courting full darkness now. Jason's words were interrupted by convulsive movements and involuntary sounds, edited out of this account. Periodically I checked his heartbeat, which was rapid and growing weaker.

"The Hypotheticals," he said, "can manipulate time and space. The evidence of that is all around us. But creating a temporal membrane is neither the beginning nor the end of their abilities. They can literally connect our planet through spatial loops to others like it . . . new planets, some artificially designed and nurtured, to which we can travel *instantaneously* and *easily* . . . travel by way of links, bridges, structures, structures assembled by the Hypotheticals, assembled from—if this is truly possible—the matter of dead stars, neutron stars . . . structures literally dragged through space, patiently, patiently, over the course of millions of years—"

Carol sat beside him on one side of the bed and I sat on the other. I held his shoulders when his body convulsed and Carol stroked his head during the intervals in which he could not speak. His eyes sparked in the candlelight and he stared intently at nothing at all.

"The Spin membrane is still in place, working, thinking, but the temporal function is finished, complete . . . that's what the flickers were, the byproduct of a detuning process, and now the membrane has been made permeable so that something can enter the atmosphere through it, something *large*. . . ."

Later it became obvious what he meant. At the time I was bewildered and I suspected he might have begun to pass into dementia, a sort of metaphorical overload governed by the word "network."

I was, of course, wrong.

Ars moriendi ars vivendi est: the art of dying is the art of living. I had read that somewhere in my postgraduate days and remembered it as I sat at his side. Jason died as he had lived, in the heroic pursuit of understanding. His gift to the world would be the fruits of that understanding, not hoarded but freely distributed.

But the other memory that sprang to mind, as the substance of Jason's nervous system was transformed and eroded by the Hypotheticals in a way they could not have known was lethal to him, was of that afternoon, long ago, when he had ridden my thrift shop bicycle down from the top of Bantam Hill Road. I thought of how adroitly, almost balletically, he had controlled that disintegrating machine, until there was nothing left of it but ballistics and velocity, the inevitable collapse of order into chaos.

His body—and he was a Fourth, remember—was a finely tuned machine. It didn't die easily. Sometime prior to midnight Jason lost the ability to speak, and that was when he began to look both frightened and no longer entirely human. Carol held his hand and told him he was safe, he was at home. I don't know if that consolation reached him in the strange and convolute chambers his mind had entered. I hope it did.

Not long after that his eyes rolled upward and his muscles

relaxed. His body struggled on, drawing convulsive breaths almost until morning.

Then I left him with Carol, who stroked his head with infinite gentleness and whispered to him as if he could still hear her, and I failed to notice that the sun when it rose was no longer bloated and red but as bright and perfect as it had been before the end of the Spin.

I stayed on deck as the *Capetown Maru* left its berth and made for the open sea.

No less than a dozen container ships abandoned Teluk Bayur while the oil fires were burning, jostling for position at the harbor mouth. Most of these were small merchant ships of dubious registry, probably bound for Port Magellan despite what their manifests said—vessels whose owners and captains had much to lose from the scrutiny that would follow an investigation.

I stood with Jala and we braced ourselves against the rails, watching a rust-spackled coastal freighter veer out of a bank of oil-fire smoke alarmingly close to the *Capetown*'s stern. Both ships sounded alarms and the *Capetown*'s deck crew looked aft apprehensively. But the coastal freighter sheered off before it made contact.

Then we were out of the protection of the harbor into high seas and rolling swells, and I went below to join Ina and Diane and the other émigrés in the crew lounge. En sat at a trestle table with Ibu Ina and his parents, all four of them looking unwell. In deference to her injury Diane had been given the only padded chair in the room, but the wound had stopped bleeding and she had managed to change into dry clothes.

Jala entered the lounge an hour later. He shouted for attention and delivered a speech, which Ina translated for me: "Setting aside his pompous self-congratulation, Jala says he went to the bridge and spoke to the captain. All deck fires are out and we're safely underway, he says. The captain apologizes for the rough seas. According to forecasts we ought to be out of this weather by late tonight or early tomorrow. For the next few hours, however—"

At which point En, who was sitting next to Ina, turned and vomited into her lap, effectively finishing her sentence for her.

○ ○ ○

Two nights later I went up on deck with Diane to look at the stars.

The main deck was quieter at night than at any time during the day. We found a safe space between the exposed forty-foot containers and the aft superstructure, where we could talk without being overheard. The sea was calm, the air was pleasantly warm, and stars swarmed over the *Capetown*'s stacks and radars as if they had tangled in the rigging.

"Are you still writing your memoir?" Diane had seen the assortment of memory cards I was carrying in my luggage, alongside the digital and pharmaceutical contraband we had brought from Montreal. Also various paper notebooks, loose pages, scribbled notes.

"Not as often," I said. "It doesn't seem as urgent. The need to write it all down—"

"Or the fear of forgetting."

"Or that."

"And do you *feel* different?" she asked, smiling.

I was a new Fourth. Diane was not. By now her wound had closed, leaving nothing but a strip of puckered flesh that followed the curvature of her hip. Her body's capacity for self-repair still struck me as uncanny. Even though, presumably, I shared it.

Her question was a little mischievous. Many times I had

asked Diane whether she felt different as a Fourth. The real question, of course, was: did she seem different *to me*?

There had never been a good answer. Obviously she was a different person after her near-death and resurrection at the Big House—who wouldn't be? She had lost a husband and a faith and had awakened to a world that would make even the Buddha scratch his head in perplexity.

"The transition is only a door," she said. "A door into a room. A room you've never been in, though you might have caught a glimpse of it from time to time. Now it's the room where you live; it's yours, it belongs to you. It has certain qualities you can't change—you can't make it bigger or smaller. But how you furnish it is up to you."

"More a proverb than an answer," I said.

"Sorry. Best I can do." She turned her head up toward the stars. "Look, Tyler, you can see the Arch."

We call it an "arch" because we're a myopic species. The Archway is really a ring, a circle a thousand miles in diameter, but only half of it rises above sea level. The rest of it is underwater or buried in the crust of the Earth, perhaps (some have speculated) exploiting the suboceanic magma as a source of energy. But from our ant's-eye point of view it was indeed an arch, the peak of which extended well above the atmosphere.

Even the exposed half of it was completely visible only in photographs taken from space, and even those photographs were usually doctored to emphasize detail. If you could take a cross-section of the ring material itself—in effect, the wire that bends into a hoop—it would be a rectangle a quarter mile on its short side and a mile on the long. Immense, but a tiny fraction of the space it enclosed and not always easy to see at a distance.

Capetown Maru's route had taken us south of the ring, parallel to its radius and almost directly beneath its apex. The sun was still shining on that peak, no longer a bent letter *U* or *J* but a gentle frown (a Cheshire frown, Diane called it) high in the northern sky. Stars rotated past it like phosphorescent plankton parted by the prow of a ship.

Diane put her head against my shoulder. "I wish Jason could have seen this."

"I believe he did see it. Just not from this angle."

○ ○ ○

There were three immediate problems at the Big House following Jason's death.

The most pressing was Diane, whose physical condition remained unchanged for days following the injection of the Martian drug. She was nearly comatose and intermittently feverish, her pulse beating in her throat like the flutter of an insect wing. We were low on medical supplies and I had to coax her to take an occasional sip of water. The only real improvement was in the sound of her breathing, which was incrementally more relaxed and less phlegmatic—her lungs, at least, were mending.

The second problem was distasteful, but it was one we shared with too many other households across the country: a family member had died and needed burying.

A great wave of death (accidental, suicidal, homicidal) had swept over the world in the last few days. No nation on Earth was equipped to deal with it, except in the crudest possible fashion, and the United States was no exception. Local radio had begun to announce collection sites for mass burials; refrigerated trucks had been commandeered from meat packing plants; there was a number to call now that phone service had been restored—but Carol wouldn't hear of it. When I broached the subject she drew herself into a posture of fierce dignity and said, "I won't do that, Tyler. I *will not* have Jason dumped into a hole like a medieval pauper."

"Carol, we can't—"

"Hush," she said. "I still have a few contacts left from the old days. Let me make some calls."

She had once been a respected specialist and must have had an extensive network of contacts before the Spin; but after thirty years of alcoholic seclusion, whom could she possibly know? Nevertheless she spent a morning on the phone, tracking down changed numbers, reintroducing herself, explaining, coaxing, begging. It all sounded hopeless to me. But not more than six hours later a hearse pulled into the driveway and two obviously exhausted but relentlessly kind and professional men came inside and put Jason's body on a wheeled stretcher and carried him out of the Big House for the last time.

Carol spent the rest of the day upstairs, holding Diane's hand and singing songs she probably couldn't hear. That night she took her first drink since the morning the red sun rose—a "maintenance dose," she called it.

Our third big problem was E. D. Lawton.

○ ○ ○

E.D. had to be told that his son had died, and Carol steeled herself to perform that duty, too. She confessed she hadn't talked to E.D. except through lawyers for a couple of years now and that he had always frightened her, at least when she was sober—he was big, confrontational, intimidating; Carol was fragile, elusive, sly. But her grief had subtly altered the equation.

It took hours, but she was finally able to reach him—he was in Washington, within commuting distance—and tell him about Jason. She was carefully vague about the cause of his death. She told him Jason had come home with what looked like pneumonia and that it had turned critical shortly after the power died and the world went berserk—no phone, no ambulance service, ultimately no hope.

I asked her how E.D. had taken the news.

She shrugged. "He didn't say anything at first. Silence is E.D.'s way of expressing pain. His son died, Tyler. That might not have surprised him, given what's happened in the last few days. But it hurt him. I think it hurt him unspeakably."

"Did you tell him Diane's here?"

"I thought it would be wiser not to." She looked at me. "I didn't tell him you're here, either. I know Jason and E.D. were at odds. Jason came home to escape something that was happening at Perihelion, something that frightened him. And I assume it's connected somehow with the Martian drug. No, Tyler, don't explain it to me—I don't care to hear and I probably wouldn't understand. But I thought it would be better if E.D. didn't come bulling out to the house, trying to take charge of things."

"He didn't ask about her?"

"No, not about Diane. One odd thing, though. He asked me to make sure that Jason . . . well, that Jason's body is pre-

served. He asked a lot of questions about that. I told him I'd
made arrangements, there would be a funeral, I'd let him
know. But he didn't want to leave it at that. He wants an autopsy. But I got stubborn." She regarded me coolly. "Why
would he want an autopsy, Tyler?"

"I don't know," I said.

But I set about finding out. I went to Jason's room, where
his empty bed had been stripped of sheets. I opened the window and sat in the chair next to the dresser and looked at
what he'd left behind.

Jason had asked me to record his final insights into the nature of the Hypotheticals and their manipulation of the Earth.
He had also asked me to include a copy of that recording in
each of a dozen or so fat padded envelopes, stamped and addressed for mailing if and when mail service was restored.
Clearly Jase had not expected to produce such a monologue
when he arrived at the Big House a few days before the end
of the Spin. Some other crisis had been dogging him. His
deathbed testament was a late addendum.

I leafed through the envelopes. They were addressed, in Jason's hand, to names I didn't recognize. No, correct that; I
did recognize the name on one of the envelopes.

It was mine.

Dear Tyler,

*I know I've burdened you unconscionably in the past.
I'm afraid I'm about to burden you again, and this time the
stakes are considerably higher. Let me explain. And I'm
sorry if this seems abrupt, but I'm in a hurry, for reasons
that will become clear.*

*Recent episodes of what the media call "the flicker"
have set off alarm bells in the Lomax administration. So
have several other events, less well publicized. I'll cite just
one example: since the death of Wun Ngo Wen, tissue samples taken from his organs have been under study at the Animal Disease Center on Plum Island, the same facility
where he was quarantined when he arrived on Earth. Martian biotechnology is subtle, but modern forensics is stubborn. It recently became clear that Wun's physiology,*

particularly his nervous system, had been altered in ways even more radical than the "Fourth Age" procedure outlined in his archives. For this and other reasons, Lomax and his people have begun to smell a rat. They invited E.D. out of his reluctant retirement and they're giving new credence to his suspicions about Wun's motives. E.D. welcomed this as an opportunity to reclaim Perihelion (and his own reputation), and he's wasting no time capitalizing on the paranoia in the White House.

How have the authorities chosen to proceed? Crudely. Lomax (or his advisors) conceived a plan to raid the existing facilities at Perihelion and seize whatever we had retained of Wun's possessions and documents, as well as all our records and working notes.

E.D. hasn't yet connected the dots between my recovery from AMS and Wun's pharmaceuticals; or, if he has, he's kept it to himself. Or so I prefer to believe. Because if I fall into the hands of the security services the first thing they'll do is a blood assay, rapidly followed by making me a captive science experiment, probably in Wun's old cell at Plum Island. And I don't believe E.D. actually wants that to happen. As much as he may resent me for "stealing Perihelion" or collaborating with Wun Ngo Wen, he's still my father.

But don't worry. Even though E.D. is very much back in the loop at Lomax's White House, I have resources of my own. I've been cultivating them. These are generally not powerful people, though some are powerful in their own way, but bright and decent individuals who choose to take a longer view of human destiny, and thanks to them I was warned in advance of the raid on Perihelion. I've effected my escape. Now I'm a fugitive.

You, Tyler, are merely a suspected accessory, though it may come to the same thing.

I'm sorry. I know I bear some responsibility for putting you in this position. Someday I'll apologize face-to-face. For now all I can offer is advice.

The digital records I put into your hands when you left Perihelion are, of course, highly classified redactions from the archives of Wun Ngo Wen. For all I know you may have burned them, buried them, or tossed them into the Pacific Ocean. No matter. Years designing spacecraft taught me the virtue of redundancy. I've parceled out Wun's contraband wisdom to dozens of people in this country and across the world. It hasn't been posted on the Internet yet—no one is that feckless—but it's out there. This is no doubt a profoundly unpatriotic and certainly criminal act. If I'm captured I'll be accused of treason. In the meantime I'm making the most of it.

But I don't believe knowledge of this kind (which includes protocols for human modifications that can cure grave diseases, among other things, and I should know) ought to be corralled for national advantage, even if releasing it poses other problems.

Lomax and his tame Congress clearly disagree. So I'm dispersing the last fragments of the archive and making myself scarce. I'm going into hiding. You might want to do the same. In fact you may have to. Everyone at the old Perihelion, anyone who was close to me, is bound to fall under federal scrutiny sooner or later.

Or, contrarily, you may wish to drop in at the nearest FBI office and hand over the contents of this envelope. If that's what you think is best, follow your conscience; I won't blame you, though I don't guarantee the outcome. My experience with the Lomax administration suggests that the truth will not, in fact, set you free.

In any case, I regret putting you in a difficult position. It isn't fair. It's too much to ask of a friend, and I have always been proud to call you my friend.

Maybe E.D. was right about one thing. Our generation has struggled for thirty years to recover what the Spin stole from us that October night. But we can't. There's nothing in this evolving universe to hold on to, and nothing to be gained by trying. If I learned anything from my "Fourthness," that's it. We're as ephemeral as raindrops. We all fall, and we all land somewhere.

Fall freely, Tyler. Use the enclosed documents if you need them. They were expensive but they're absolutely reliable. (It's good to have friends in high places!)

The "enclosed documents" were, in essence, a suite of spare identities: passports, Homeland Security ID cards, driver's licenses, birth certificates, Social Security numbers, even med-school diplomas, all bearing my description but none bearing my correct name.

○ ○ ○

Diane's recovery continued. Her pulse strengthened and her lungs cleared, although she was still febrile. The Martian drug was doing its work, rebuilding her from the inside out, editing and amending her DNA in subtle ways.

As her health improved she began to ask cautious questions—about the sun, about Pastor Dan, about the trip from Arizona to the Big House. Because of her intermittent fever, the answers I gave her didn't always stick. She asked me more than once what had happened to Simon. If she was lucid I told her about the red calf and the return of the stars; if she was groggy I just told her Simon was "somewhere else" and that I'd be looking after her a while longer. Neither of these answers—the true or the half-true—seemed to satisfy her.

Some days she was listless, propped up facing the window, watching sunlight clock across the valleyed bedclothes. Other days she was feverishly restless. One afternoon she demanded paper and a pen . . . but when I gave it to her all she wrote was the single sentence *Am I not my brother's keeper,* repeated until her fingers cramped.

"I told her about Jason," Carol admitted when I showed her the paper.

"Are you sure that was wise?"

"She had to hear it sooner or later. She'll make peace with it, Tyler. Don't worry. Diane will be all right. Diane was always the strong one."

○ ○ ○

On the morning of the day of Jason's funeral I prepared the envelopes he had left, adding a copy of his last recording to each one, stamped them, and dropped them into a randomly selected mailbox on the way to the local chapel Carol had reserved for the service. The packages might have to wait a few days for pickup—mail service was still being restored—but I figured they'd be safer there than at the Big House.

The "chapel" was a nondenominational funeral home on a suburban main street, busy now that the travel restrictions had been lifted. Jase had always had a rationalist's disdain for elaborate funerals, but Carol's sense of dignity demanded a ceremony even if it was feeble and *pro forma*. She had managed to round up a small crowd, mostly longtime neighbors who remembered Jason as a child and who had glimpsed his career in TV sound bites and sidebars in the daily paper. It was his fading celebrity status that filled the pews.

I delivered a brief eulogy. (Diane would have done it better, but Diane was too ill to attend.) Jase, I said, had dedicated his life to the pursuit of knowledge, not arrogantly but humbly: he understood that knowledge wasn't created but discovered; it couldn't be owned, only shared, hand to hand, generation to generation. Jason had made himself a part of that sharing and was part of it still. He had woven himself into the network of knowing.

E.D. entered the chapel while I was still at the pulpit.

He was halfway down the aisle when he recognized me. He stared at me a long minute before he settled into the nearest empty pew.

He was more gaunt than I remembered him, and he had shaved the last of his white hair into invisible stubble. But he still carried himself like a powerful man. He wore a suit that had been tailored to razor-tight tolerances. He folded his arms and inspected the room imperially, marking who was present. His gaze lingered on Carol.

When the service ended Carol stood and gamely accepted the condolences of her neighbors as they filed out. She had wept copiously over the last few days but was resolutely dry-eyed now, almost clinically aloof. E.D. approached her after the last guest had left. She stiffened, like a cat sensing the presence of a larger predator.

"Carol," E.D. said. "Tyler." He gave me a sour stare.

"Our son is dead," Carol said. "Jason's gone."

"That's why I'm here."

"I hope you're here to mourn—"

"Of course I am."

"—and not for some other reason. Because he came to the house to get away from you. I assume you know that."

"I know more about it than you can imagine. Jason was confused—"

"He was many things, E.D., but he was not confused. I was with him when he died."

"Were you? That's interesting. Because, unlike you, I was with him when he was alive."

Carol drew a sharp breath and turned her head as if she'd been slapped.

E.D. said, "Come on, Carol. I was the one who raised Jason and you know it. You may not like the kind of life I gave him, but that's what I did—I gave him a life and a means of living it."

"I gave birth to him."

"That's a physiological function, not a moral act. Everything Jason ever owned he got from me. Everything he learned, I taught him."

"For better or worse . . ."

"And now you want to condemn me just because I have some practical concerns—"

"*What* practical concerns?"

"Obviously, I'm talking about the autopsy."

"Yes. You mentioned that on the telephone. But it's undignified and it's frankly impossible."

"I was hoping you'd take my concerns seriously. Clearly you haven't. But I don't need your permission. There are men outside this building waiting to claim the body, and they can produce writs under the Emergency Measures Act."

She took a step back from him. "You have that much power?"

"Neither you nor I have any choice in the matter. This is going to happen whether we like it or not. And it's really only a formality. No harm will be done. So for god's sake let's preserve some dignity and mutual respect. Let me have the body of my son."

"I can't do that."

"Carol—"

"I can't give you his body."

"You're not listening to me. *You don't have a choice.*"

"No, I'm sorry, *you're* not listening to *me*. Listen, E.D. I *can't* give you his body."

He opened his mouth and then closed it. His eyes widened.

"Carol," he said. "What have you done?"

"There *is* no body. Not anymore." Her lips curled into a sly, bitter smile. "But I suppose you can take his ashes. If you insist."

o o o

I drove Carol back to the Big House, where her neighbor Emil Hardy—who had given up his short-lived local news sheet when the power was restored—had been sitting with Diane.

"We talked about old times on the block," Hardy said as he was leaving. "I used to watch the kids ride their bikes. That was a long time ago. This skin condition she's got—"

"It's not contagious," Carol said. "Don't worry."

"Unusual, though."

"Yes. Unusual it is. Thank you, Emil."

"Ashley and I would love to have you over for dinner sometime."

"That sounds lovely. Please thank Ashley for me." She closed the door and turned to me. "I need a drink. But first things first. E.D. knows you're here. So you have to leave, and you have to take Diane with you. Can you do that? Take her somewhere safe? Somewhere E.D. won't find her?"

"Of course I can. But what about you?"

"I'm not in danger. E.D. might send people around to look for whatever treasure he imagines Jason stole from him. But he won't find anything—as long as you're *thorough*, Tyler— and he can't take the house away from me. E.D. and I signed our armistice a long time ago. Our skirmishes are trivial. But he can hurt *you,* and he can hurt Diane even if he doesn't mean to."

"I won't let that happen."

"Then get your things together. You may not have much time."

○ ○ ○

The day before *Capetown Maru* was due to cross the Archway I went up on deck to watch the sun rise. The Arch was mostly invisible, its descending pillars hidden by horizons east and west, but in the half hour before dawn its apex was a line in the sky almost directly overhead, razor sharp and gently glowing.

It had faded behind a haze of high cirrus cloud by midmorning, but we all knew it was there.

The prospect of the transit was making everyone nervous—not just passengers but the seasoned crew, too. They went about their customary business, tending to the needs of the ship, mending machinery, chipping and repainting the superstructure, but there was a briskness in the rhythm of their work that hadn't been there yesterday. Jala came on deck lugging a plastic chair and joined me where I sat, protected from the wind by the forty-foot containers but facing a narrow view of the sea.

"This is my last trip to the other side," Jala said. He was dressed for the warmth of the day in a billowing yellow shirt and jeans. He had opened the shirt to expose his chest to the sunlight. He took a can of beer from the topside cooler and cracked it. All these actions announced him as a secularized man, a businessman, equally disdainful of Muslim *sharia* and Minang *adat*. "This time," he said, "there's no coming back."

He had burned his bridges behind him—literally, if he'd had anything to do with orchestrating the riot at Teluk Bayur. (The explosions had made a suspiciously convenient cover for our getaway, even if we had almost been caught in the conflagration.) For years Jala had been running an emigrant-smuggling brokerage trade far more lucrative than his legitimate import/export business. There was more money in people than in palm oil, he said. But the Indian and Vietnamese competition was stiff and the political climate had soured; better to retire to Port Magellan now than spend the rest of his life in a New Reformasi prison.

"You've made the transit before?"

"Twice."

"Was it difficult?"

He shrugged. "Don't believe everything you hear."

By noon many of the passengers were up on deck. In addition to the Minangkabau villagers there were assorted Acehnese, Malay, and Thai emigrants aboard, perhaps a hundred of us in all—far too many for the available cabins, but three aluminum cargo containers in the hold had been rigged as sleeping quarters, carefully ventilated.

This wasn't the grim, often deadly, human-smuggling trade that used to carry refugees to Europe or North America. Most of the people who crossed the Arch every day were overflow from the feeble U.N.-sanctioned resettlement programs, often with money to spend. We were treated with respect by the crew, many of whom had spent months in Port Magellan and who understood its blandishments and pitfalls.

One of the deck hands had set aside part of the main deck as a sort of soccer field, marked off with nets, where a group of children were playing. Every now and then the ball bounced past the nets, often into Jala's lap, much to his chagrin. Jala was irritable today.

I asked him when the ship would make the transit.

"According to the captain, unless we change speed, twelve hours or so."

"Our last day on Earth," I said.

"Don't joke."

"I meant it literally."

"And keep your voice down. Sailors are superstitious."

"What will you do in Port Magellan?"

Jala raised his eyebrows. "What will I do? Fuck beautiful women. And quite possibly a few ugly ones. What else?"

The soccer ball bounced past the net again. This time Jala scooped it up and held it against his belly. "Damn it, I warned you! This game is over!"

A dozen children promptly pressed against the nets, shrieking protest, but it was En who summoned the courage to come around and confront Jala directly. En was sweating, his rib cage pumping like a bellows. His team had been five points ahead. "Give it back, please," he said.

"You want this back?" Jala stood up, still clutching the ball, imperious, mysteriously angry. "You want it? Go get it." He kicked the ball in a long trajectory that took it past the deck rails and out into the blue-green immensity of the Indian Ocean.

En looked astonished, then angry. He said something low and bitter in Minang.

Jala reddened. Then he slapped the boy with his open hand, so hard that En's heavy glasses went skittering across the deck.

"Apologize," Jala demanded.

En dropped to one knee, eyes squeezed shut. He drew a few sobbing breaths. Eventually he stood up. He walked a few steps across the deck plates and collected his eyeglasses. He fumbled them into place and walked back with what I thought was an astonishing dignity. He stood directly in front of Jala.

"No," he said faintly. "*You* apologize."

Jala gasped and swore. En cringed. Jala raised his hand again.

I caught his wrist in midswing.

Jala looked at me, startled. "What is this! Let go."

He tried to pull his hand away. I wouldn't let him. "Don't hit him again," I said.

"I'll do what I like!"

"Fine," I said. "But don't hit him again."

"*You*—after what I've done for you—!"

Then he gave me a second look.

I don't know what he saw in my face. I don't know exactly what I was feeling at that moment. Whatever it was, it appeared to confuse him. His clenched fist went slack. He seemed to wilt.

"Fucking crazy American," he muttered. "I'm going to the canteen." To the small crowd of children and deck hands that had gathered around us: "Where I can have *peace* and *respect*!" He stalked away.

En was still staring at me, gap-jawed.

"I'm sorry about that," I said.

He nodded.

"I can't get your ball back," I said.

He touched his cheek where Jala had slapped him. "That's okay," he said faintly.

Later—over dinner in the crew mess, hours away from the crossing—I told Diane about the incident. "I didn't think about what I was doing. It just seemed . . . obvious. Almost reflexive. Is that a Fourth thing?"

"It might be. The impulse to protect a victim, especially a child, and to do it instantly, without thinking. I've felt it myself. I suppose it's something the Martians wrote into their neural rebuild . . . assuming they can really engineer feelings as subtle as that. I wish we had Wun Ngo Wen here to explain it. Or Jason, for that matter. Did it feel forced?"

"No . . ."

"Or wrong, inappropriate?"

"No . . . I think it was exactly the right thing to do."

"But you wouldn't have done it before you took the treatment?"

"I might have. Or wanted to. But I probably would have second-guessed myself until it was too late."

"So you're not unhappy about it."

No. Just surprised. This was as much *me* as it was Martian biotech, Diane was saying, and I supposed that was true . . . but it would take some getting used to. Like every other transition (childhood to adolescence, adolescence to adulthood) there were new imperatives to deal with, new opportunities and pitfalls, new doubts.

For the first time in many years I was a stranger to myself again.

○ ○ ○

I had almost finished packing when Carol came downstairs, a little drunk, loose-limbed, carrying a shoebox in her arms. The box was labeled MEMENTOS (SCHOOL).

"You should take this," she said. "It was your mother's."

"If it means something to you, Carol, keep it."

"Thank you, but I already took what I wanted from it."

I opened the lid and glanced at the contents. "The letters." The anonymous letters addressed to Belinda Sutton, my mother's maiden name.

"Yes. So you've seen them. Did you ever read them?"

"No, not really. Just enough to know they were love letters."

"Oh, God. That sounds so saccharine. I prefer to think of them as tributes. They're quite chaste, really, if you read them closely. Unsigned. Your mother received them when we were both at university. She was dating your father then, and she could hardly show them to *him*—he was writing her letters of his own. So she shared them with me."

"She never found out who wrote them?"

"No. Never."

"She must have been curious."

"Of course. But she was already engaged to Marcus by that time. She started dating Marcus Dupree when Marcus and E.D. were setting up their first business, designing and manufacturing high altitude balloons back when aerostats were what Marcus called 'blue sky' technology: a little crazy, a little idealistic. Belinda called Marcus and E.D. 'the Zeppelin brothers.' So I guess we were the Zeppelin sisters, Belinda and I. Because that's when I started flirting with E.D. In a way, Tyler, my entire marriage was nothing more than an attempt to keep your mother as a friend."

"The letters—"

"Interesting, isn't it, that she kept them all these years? Eventually I asked her why. Why not just throw them away? She said, 'Because they're sincere.' It was her way of honoring whoever had written them. The last one arrived a week before her wedding. None after that. And a year later I married E.D. Even as couples we were inseparable, did she ever tell you that? We vacationed together, we went to movies together. Belinda came to the hospital when the twins were born and I was waiting at the door when she brought *you* home for the first time. But all that ended when Marcus had his accident. Your father was a wonderful man, Tyler, very earthy, very funny—the only person who could make E.D. laugh. Reckless to a fault, though. Belinda was absolutely devastated when he died. And not just emotionally. Marcus had burned through most of their savings and Belinda spent what was left servicing the mortgage on their house in Pasadena. So when E.D. moved east and we made an offer on this place it seemed perfectly natural to invite her to use the guest house."

"In exchange for housekeeping," I said,

"That was E.D.'s idea. I just wanted Belinda close by. My marriage wasn't as successful as hers had been. Quite the opposite. By that time Belinda was more or less the only friend I had. Almost a confidante." Carol smiled. "Almost."

"That's why you want to keep the letters? Because they're part of your history with her?"

She smiled as if at a slow-witted child. "*No,* Tyler. I told you. They're *mine.*" Her smile thinned. "Don't look so dumbfounded. Your mother was as uncomplicatedly heterosexual as any woman I have ever met. I simply had the misfortune to fall in love with her. To fall in love with her so abjectly that I would do anything—even marry a man who seemed, even in the beginning, a little distasteful—in order to keep her close. And in all that time, Tyler, in all those silent years, I never told her how I felt. Never, except in these letters. I was pleased she kept them, even though they always seemed a little dangerous, like something explosive or radioactive, hidden in plain sight, evidence of my own foolishness. When your mother died—I mean the very day she died—I panicked a little; I tried to hide the box; I thought about destroying the letters but I couldn't, I couldn't bring myself to do it; and then, after E.D. divorced me, when there was no one left to deceive, I simply took them for myself. Because, you see, they're *mine.* They've always been mine."

I didn't know what to say. Carol saw my expression and shook her head sadly. She put her fragile hands on my shoulders. "Don't be upset. The world is full of surprises. We're all born strangers to ourselves and each other, and we're seldom formally introduced."

○ ○ ○

So I spent four weeks in a motel room in Vermont nursing Diane through her recovery.

Her physical recovery, I should say. The emotional trauma she'd suffered at the Condon ranch and after had left her exhausted and withdrawn. Diane had closed her eyes on a world that seemed to be ending and opened them on a world without compass points. It was not in my power to make this right for her.

So I was cautiously helpful. I explained what needed to be explained. I made no demands and I made it clear that I expected no reward.

Her interest in the changed world awoke gradually. She asked about the sun, restored to its benevolent aspect, and I told her what Jason had told me: the Spin membrane was still in place even though the temporal enclosure had ended; it was protecting the Earth the way it always had, editing lethal radiation into a simulacrum of sunlight acceptable to the planet's ecosystem.

"So why did they turn it off for seven days?"

"They turned it *down,* not entirely *off*. And they did it so something could pass through the membrane."

"That thing in the Indian Ocean."

"Yes."

She asked me to play the recording of Jason's last hours, and she wept as she listened. She asked about his ashes. Had E.D. taken them away or had Carol kept them? (Neither. Carol had pressed the urn into my hands and told me to dispose of them any way I deemed appropriate. "The awful truth, Tyler, is that you knew him better than I did. Jason was a cipher to me. His father's son. But you were his friend.")

We watched the world rediscover itself. The mass burials finally ended; the bereaved and frightened survivors began to understand that the planet had reacquired a future, however strange that future might turn out to be. For our generation it was a stunning reversal. The mantle of extinction had fallen from our shoulders; what would we do without it? What would we do, now that we were no longer doomed but merely mortal?

We saw the video footage from the Indian Ocean of the monstrous structure that had embedded itself in the skin of the planet, seawater still boiling to steam where it came into contact with the enormous pillars. The Arch, people began to call it, or the Archway, not only because of its shape but because ships at sea had returned to port with stories of lost navigational beacons, peculiar weather, spinning compasses, and a wild coastline where no continent should have been. Various navies were promptly dispatched. Jason's testament hinted at the explanation, but only a few people had the advantage of having heard it—myself, Diane, and the dozen or so who had received it in the mail.

She began to exercise a little every day, jogging a dirt path behind the motel as the weather cooled, coming back with the scent of fallen leaves and woodsmoke in her hair. Her appetite improved, and so did the menu in the coffee shop. Food delivery had been restored; the domestic economy was creaking back into motion.

We learned that Mars, too, had been un-Spun. Signals had passed between the two planets; President Lomax, in one of his rally-'round-the-flag speeches, even hinted that the manned space program would be resumed, a first step toward establishing ongoing relations with what he called (with suspicious exuberance) "our sister planet."

We talked about the past. We talked about the future.

What we did not do was fall into each other's arms.

We knew each other too well, or not well enough. We had a past but no present. And Diane was wracked with anxiety by Simon's disappearance outside Manassas.

"He very nearly let you die," I reminded her.

"Not intentionally. He's not vicious. You know that."

"Then he's dangerously naive."

Diane closed her eyes meditatively. Then she said, "There's a phrase Pastor Bob Kobel liked to use back at Jordan Tabernacle. 'His heart cried out to God.' If it describes anyone, it describes Simon. But you have to parse the sentence. 'His heart cried out'—I think that's all of us, it's universal. You, Simon, me, Jason. Even Carol. Even E.D. When people come to understand how big the universe is and how short a human life is, their hearts cry out. Sometimes it's a shout of joy: I think that's what it was for Jason; I think that's what I didn't understand about him. He had the gift of awe. But for most of us it's a cry of terror. The terror of extinction, the terror of meaninglessness. Our hearts cry out. Maybe to God, or maybe just to break the silence." She brushed her hair away from her forehead and I saw that her arm, which had been so perilously thin, was round and strong once more. "I think the cry that rose up from Simon's heart was the purest human sound in the world. But no, he's not a good judge of character; yes, he's naive; which is why he cycled through so many styles of faith, New Kingdom, Jordan Tabernacle, the Condon ranch . . . anything, as long as it was plainspoken and addressed the need for human significance."

"Even if it killed you?"

"I didn't say he's wise. I'm saying he's not wicked."

Later I came to recognize this kind of discourse: she was talking like a Fourth. Detached but engaged. Intimate but objective. I didn't dislike it, but it made the hair on my neck stand up from time to time.

○ ○ ○

Not long after I declared her completely healthy Diane told me she wanted to leave. I asked her where she meant to go.

She had to find Simon, she said. She had to "settle things," one way or another. They were, after all, still married. It mattered to her whether he had lived or died.

I reminded her she didn't have money to spend or a place of her own to stay. She said she'd get by somehow. So I gave her one of the credit cards Jason had supplied me, along with a warning that I couldn't guarantee it—I had no idea who was paying the premium, what the credit limit might be, or whether someone might eventually track it to her.

She asked how she could get in touch with me.

"Just call," I said. She had my number, the number I had paid for and preserved these many years, attached to a phone I had carried even though it seldom rang.

Then I drove her to the local bus depot, where she vanished into a crowd of displaced tourists who had been stranded by the end of the Spin.

○ ○ ○

The phone rang six months later, when the newspapers were still running banner headlines about "the new world" and the cable channels had begun to carry video footage of a rocky, wild headland "somewhere across the Archway."

By this time hundreds of vessels large and small had made the crossing. Some were big-science expeditions, I.G.Y. and U.N. sanctioned, with American naval escorts and embedded press pools. Some were private charters. Some were fishing trawlers, which came back to port with their holds full of a catch that could pass for cod in a dim light. This was, of course, strictly forbidden, but "arch cod" had infiltrated every major Asian market by the time the ban came down. It proved to be edible and nutritious. Which was, as Jase might have said, a clue: when the fish were subjected to DNA analysis their genome suggested a remote terrestrial ancestry. The new world was not merely hospitable, it seemed to have been stocked with humanity in mind.

"I found Simon," Diane said.

"And?"

"He's living in a trailer park outside Wilmington. He picks up a little money doing household repairs—bikes, toasters, that kind of thing. Otherwise he collects welfare and attends a little Pentecostal church."

"Was he happy to see you?"

"He wouldn't stop apologizing for what happened at the Condon ranch. He said he wanted to make it up to me. He asked if there was anything he could do to make my life easier."

I gripped the phone a little more tightly. "What did you tell him?"

"That I wanted a divorce. He agreed. And he said something else. He said I'd changed, that there was something different about me. He couldn't put his finger on it. But I don't think he liked it."

A whiff of brimstone, perhaps.

"Tyler?" Diane said. "Have I changed that much?"

"Everything changes," I said.

o o o

Her next important call came a year later. I was in Montreal, thanks in part to Jason's counterfeit ID, waiting for my immigrant status to be officialized and assisting at an outpatient clinic in Outremont.

Since my last conversation with Diane, the basic dynamics of the Arch had been worked out. The facts were confounding to anyone who conceived of the Archway as a static machine or a simple "door," but look at it the way Jason had—as a complex, conscious entity capable of perceiving and manipulating events within its domain—and it made more sense.

Two worlds had been connected through the Arch, but only for manned ocean vessels transiting from the south.

Consider what that means. For a breeze, an ocean current, or a migrant bird the Arch was nothing more than a couple of fixed pillars between the Indian Ocean and the Bay of Bengal. They all moved unimpeded around and through the Arch space, as did any ship traveling from north to south.

But cross the equator by ship from the south at ninety degrees east of Greenwich and you'd find yourself looking back at the Arch from an unknown sea under a strange sky, untold light-years from the Earth.

In the city of Madras an ambitious if not quite legal cruise service had produced a series of English-language posters announcing EASY TRAVEL TO FRIENDLY PLANET! Interpol closed the business down—the U.N. was still trying to regulate passage in those days—but the posters had it just about right. How could such things be? Ask the Hypotheticals.

Diane's divorce had been finalized, she told me, but she was out of work and out of prospects. "I thought if I could join you . . ." She sounded tentative and not at all like a Fourth, or what I imagined a Fourth ought to sound like. "If that would be all right. Frankly I need a little help. Finding a place and, you know, getting settled."

So I arranged a clinic job for her and submitted the immigration paperwork. She joined me in Montreal that autumn.

o o o

It was a nuanced courtship, slow, old-fashioned (or semi-Martian, perhaps), during which Diane and I discovered each other in wholly new ways. We were no longer straitjacketed by the Spin nor were we children blindly seeking solace. We fell in love, finally, as adults.

These were the years when the global population topped

out at eight billion. Most of that growth had been funneled into the expanding megacities: Shanghai, Jakarta, Manila, coastal China; Lagos, Kinshasa, Nairobi, Maputo; Caracas, La Paz, Tegucigalpa—all the firelit, smog-shrouded warrens of the world. It would have taken a dozen Archways to dent that population growth, but crowding drove a steady wave of emigrants, refugees, and "pioneers," many of them packed into the cargo compartments of illegal vessels and more than a few of them delivered to the shores of Port Magellan already dead or dying.

Port Magellan was the first named settlement in the new world. By now much of that world had been at least crudely mapped, largely by air. Port Magellan was at the eastern tip of a continent some were calling "Equatoria." There was a second and even larger land mass ("Borea") that straddled the northern pole and extended into the temperate zone of the planet. The southern seas were rich with islands and archipelagos.

The climate was benign, the air was fresh, the gravity was 95.5 percent of Earth's. Both continents were bread-baskets-in-waiting. The seas and rivers teemed with fish. The legend circulating in the slums of Douala and Kabul was that you could pick dinner from the giant trees of Equatoria and sleep among their sheltering roots.

You couldn't. Port Magellan was a U.N. enclave policed by soldiers. The shantytowns that had grown up around it were ungoverned and unsafe. But functional fishing villages dotted the coastline for hundreds of miles; there were tourist hotels under construction around the lagoons of Reach Bay and Aussie Harbor; and the prospect of free fertile land had driven settlers inland along the White and New Irrawaddi river valleys.

But the most momentous news from the new world that year was the discovery of the second Arch. It was located half a world away from the first, near the southern reaches of the boreal land mass, and beyond it there was yet another new world—this one, according to first reports, a little less inviting; or maybe it was just the rainy season there.

○ ○ ○

"There must be other people like me," Diane said, five years into the post-Spin era. "I'd like to meet them."

I had given her my copy of the Martian archives, a first-pass translation on a set of memory cards, and she had pored over them with the same intensity she'd once brought to Victorian poetry and New Kingdom tracts.

If Jason's work had been successful, then, yes, there were surely other Fourths on Earth. But announcing their presence would have been a first-class ticket to a federal penitentiary. The Lomax administration had put a national security lid on all things Martian, and Lomax's domestic security agencies had been granted sweeping police powers in the economic crises that followed the end of the Spin.

"Do you ever think about it?" she asked, a little shyly.

Becoming a Fourth myself, she meant. Injecting into my arm a measured dose of clear liquid from one of the vials I kept in a steel safe at the back of our bedroom closet. Of course I'd thought about it. It would have made us more alike.

But did I want that? I was aware of the invisible space, the gap between her Fourthness and my unmodified humanity, but I wasn't afraid of it. Some nights, looking into her solemn eyes, I even treasured it. It was the canyon that defined the bridge, and the bridge we had built was pleasing and strong.

She stroked my hand, her smooth fingers on my textured skin, a subtle reminder that time never stood still, that one day I might need the treatment even if I didn't especially want it.

"Not yet," I said.

"When?"

"When I'm ready."

o o o

President Lomax was succeeded by President Hughes and then by President Chaykin, but they were all veterans of the same Spin-era politics. They saw Martian biotech as the new atomic bomb, at least potentially, and for now it was all theirs, a proprietary threat. Lomax's first diplomatic dispatch to the government of the Five Republics had been a request to withhold biotech information from uncoded Martian broadcasts to Earth. He had justified the request with plausible arguments about the effect such technology might have on a politically divided and often violent world—he cited the death of Wun Ngo Wen as an example—and so far the Martians had been playing along.

But even this sanitized contact with Mars had sewn some discord. The egalitarian economics of the Five Republics had made Wun Ngo Wen a sort of posthumous mascot to the new global labor movement. (It was jarring to see Wun's face on placards carried by garment workers in Asian factory zones or chipsocket fillers from Central American *maquiladoras*— but I doubt it would have displeased him.)

○ ○ ○

Diane crossed the border to attend E.D.'s funeral eleven years almost to the day after I rescued her from the Condon ranch.

We had heard of his death in the news. The obituary mentioned in passing that E.D.'s ex-wife Carol had predeceased him by six months, another sad shock. Carol had stopped taking our calls almost a decade ago. Too dangerous, she said. It was enough just knowing we were safe. And there was nothing, really, to say.

(Diane visited her mother's grave while she was in D.C. What saddened her the most, she said, was that Carol's life had been so incomplete: a verb without an object, an anonymous letter, misunderstood for the want of a signature. "I don't miss her as much as I miss what she might have been.")

At E.D.'s memorial service Diane was careful not to identify herself. Too many of E.D.'s government cronies were present, including the attorney general and the sitting vice president. But her attention was drawn to an anonymous woman in the pews, who was sneaking reciprocal glances at Diane: "I knew she was a Fourth," Diane said. "I can't say exactly how. The way she held herself, the sort of ageless look she had—but more than that; it was like a signal went back and forth between us." And when the ceremony was over Diane approached the woman and asked how she had known E.D.

"I didn't know him," the woman said, "not really. I did a research stint at Perihelion at one time, back in Jason Lawton's day. My name is Sylvia Tucker."

The name rang a bell when Diane repeated it to me. Sylvia Tucker was one of the anthropologists who had worked with Wun Ngo Wen at the Florida compound. She had been friendlier than most of the hired academics and it was possible Jase had confided in her.

"We exchanged e-mail addresses," Diane said. "Neither of us said the word 'Fourth.' But we both *knew*. I'm certain of it."

No correspondence ensued, but every once in a while Diane received digital press clippings from Sylvia Tucker's address, concerning, for instance:

An industrial chemist in Denver arrested on a security writ and detained indefinitely.

A geriatric clinic in Mexico City closed by federal order.

A University of California sociology professor killed in a fire, "arson suspected."

And so on.

I had been careful not to keep a list of the names and addresses to which Jason had addressed his final packages, nor had I memorized them. But some of the names in the articles seemed plausibly familiar.

"She's telling us they're being hunted," Diane said. "The government is hunting Fourths."

We spent a month debating what we would do if we attracted the same kind of attention. Given the global security apparatus Lomax and his heirs had set up, where would we run?

But there was really only one plausible answer. Only one place where the apparatus failed to operate and where the surveillance was wholly blind. So we made our plans—these passports, that bank account, this route through Europe to South Asia—and set them aside until we needed them.

Then Diane received a final communication from Sylvia Tucker, a single word:

Go, it said.

And we went.

o o o

On the last flight of the trip, coming into Sumatra by air, Diane said, "Are you sure you want to do this?"

I had made the decision days ago, during a layover in Amsterdam, when we were still worried that we might have been followed, that our passports might have been flagged, that our supply of Martian pharmaceuticals might yet be confiscated.

"Yes," I said. "Now. Before we cross over."

"Are you sure?"

"As sure as I'll ever be."

No, not sure. But willing. Willing, finally, to lose what might be lost, willing to embrace what might be gained.

So we rented a room on the third floor of a colonial-style hotel in Padang where we wouldn't be noticed for a while. We all fall, I told myself, and we all land somewhere.

Half an hour before the transit of the Arch, an hour after dark, we came across En in the crew dining room. One of the crewmen had given him a sheet of brown paper and a few stubby crayons to keep him busy.

He seemed relieved to see us. He was worried about the transit, he said. He pushed his glasses up his nose—wincing when his thumb brushed the bruise Jala had left on his cheek—and asked me what it would be like.

"I don't know," I said. "I've never crossed."

"Will we know when it happens?"

"According to the crew, the sky gets a little strange. And just when the crossing happens, when we're balanced between the old world and the new world, the compass needle swings around, north for south. And on the bridge they sound the ship's horn. You'll know."

"Traveling a long way," En said. "In a short time."

That was undeniably true. The Arch—our "side" of it, anyway—had been physically dragged across interstellar space, presumably at something less than the speed of light, before it was dropped from orbit. But the Hypotheticals had had eons of Spin time to do the dragging. They could conceivably have bridged any distance shy of three billion light-years. And even a fraction of that would be a numbing, barely comprehensible distance.

"Makes you wonder," Diane said, "why they went to so much trouble."

"According to Jason—"

"I know. The Hypotheticals want to preserve us from extinction, so we can make something more complex of ourselves. But it just begs the question. Why do they want that? What do they expect from us?"

En ignored our philosophizing. "And after we cross—"

"After that," I told him, "it's a day's cruise to Port Magellan."

He smiled at the prospect.

I exchanged a look with Diane. She had introduced herself to En two days ago and they were already friends. She had been reading to him from a book of English children's stories out of the ship's library. (She had even quoted Housman to him: *The infant child is not aware* . . . "I don't like that one," En had said.)

He showed us his drawing, pictures of animals he must have seen in video footage from the plains of Equatoria, long-necked beasts with pensive eyes and tiger-striped coats.

"They're beautiful," Diane said.

En nodded solemnly. We left him to his work and headed up on deck.

○ ○ ○

The night sky was clear and the peak of the Arch was directly overhead now, reflecting a last glimmer of light. It showed no curvature at all. From this angle it was a pure Euclidean line, an elementary number (1) or noun (I).

We stood by the railing as close as we could get to the prow of the ship. Wind tugged at our clothes and hair. The ship's flags snapped briskly and a restless sea gave back fractured images of the ship's running lights.

"Do you have it?" Diane asked.

She meant the tiny vial containing a sample of Jason's ashes. We had planned this ceremony—if you could call it a ceremony—long before we left Montreal. Jason had never put much faith in memorials, but I think he would have approved of this one. "Right here." I took the ceramic tube out of my vest pocket and held it in my left hand.

"I miss him," Diane said. "I miss him constantly." She nestled into my shoulder and I put an arm around her. "I wish I'd known him as a Fourth. But I don't suppose it changed him much—"

"It didn't."

"In some ways Jase was *always* a Fourth."

As we approached the moment of transit the stars seemed to dim, as if some gauzy presence had enclosed the ship. I opened the tube that contained Jason's ashes. Diane put her free hand on mine.

The wind shifted suddenly and the temperature dropped a degree or two.

"Sometimes," she said, "when I think about the Hypotheticals, I'm afraid . . ."

"What?"

"That we're their red calf. Or what Jason hoped the Martians would be. That they expect us to save them from something. Something *they're* afraid of."

Maybe so. But then, I thought, we'll do what life always does—defy expectations.

I felt a shiver pass through her body. Above us, the line of the Arch grew fainter. Haze settled over the sea. Except it wasn't haze in the ordinary sense. It wasn't weather at all.

The last glimmer of the Arch disappeared and so did the horizon. On the bridge of the *Capetown Maru* the compass must have begun its rotation; the captain sounded the ship's horn, a brutally loud noise, the bray of outraged space. I looked up. The stars swirled together dizzyingly.

"Now," Diane shouted into the noise.

I leaned across the steel rail, her hand on mine, and we upended the vial. Ashes spiraled in the wind, caught in the ship's lights like snow. They vanished before they hit the turbulent black water—scattered, I want to believe, into the void we were invisibly traversing, the stitched and oceanless place between the stars.

Diane leaned into my chest and the sound of the horn beat through our bodies like a pulse until at last it stopped.

Then she lifted her head. "The sky," she said.

The stars were new and strange.

○ ○ ○

In the morning we all came up on deck, all of us: En, his parents, Ibu Ina, the other passengers, even Jala and a number of off-duty crewmen, to scent the air and feel the heat of the new world.

It could have been Earth, by the color of the sky and the heat of the sunlight. The headland of Port Magellan had appeared as a jagged line on the horizon, a rocky promontory and a few lines of pale smoke rising vertically and tailing to the west in a higher wind.

Ibu Ina joined us at the railing, En in tow.

"It looks so familiar," Ina said. "But it feels so different."

Clumps of coiled weeds drifted in our wake, liberated from the mainland of Equatoria by storms or tides, huge eight-fingered leaves limp on the surface of the water. The Arch was behind us now, no longer a door out but a door back in, a different sort of door altogether.

Ina said, "It's as if one history has ended and another has begun."

En disagreed. "No," he said solemnly, leaning into the wind as if he could will the future forward. "History doesn't start until we land."

ACKNOWLEDGMENTS

I invented a couple of diseases for dramatic purposes in *Spin*. CVWS is an imaginary cattle-borne disease with no real-world counterpart. AMS is also wholly imaginary, but its symptoms mimic the symptoms of multiple sclerosis, unfortunately a very real disease. Although MS is not yet curable, a number of promising new therapies have been introduced or are on the horizon. Science fiction novels shouldn't be mistaken for medical journals, however. For readers concerned about MS, one of the best Web sources is www.nationalmssociety.org.

The future I extrapolated for Sumatra and the Minangkabau people is also very much my own invention, but the matrilineal Minangkabau culture, and its coexistence with modern Islam, has attracted the attention of anthropologists—see Peggy Reeves Sanday's study, *Women at the Center: Life in a Modern Matriarchy*.

Readers interested in current scientific thought about the evolution and future of the solar system might want to check out *The Life and Death of Planet Earth* by Peter D. Ward and

Donald Brownlee or *Our Cosmic Origins* by Armand Delsemme for information not refracted through the lens of science fiction.

And once again, of all the folks who helped make possible the writing of this book (and I thank them all), the MVP award goes to my wife, Sharry.

Look for Robert Charles Wilson's

AXIS

Available now from Tom Doherty Associates

Turk sat back in his chair. True to his prediction, the lights in the restaurant began to dim. A couple of waiters rolled back the glass wall that separated the indoor dining room from the patio. The sky was starry and deep, slightly washed out by the lights of the Port but still crisper than any sky Lise had known back in California. Had the meteor shower begun? She saw what looked like a few bright flashes across the meridian.

Turk hadn't spared it a glance. "I'll have to think about this."

"I'm not asking you to violate any confidences. Just—"

"I know what you're asking. And it's probably not unreasonable. But I'd like to think it over, if that's okay with you."

"All I can do is ask," she said.

"Appreciate it if you would. So. Business attended to? At least for now?"

"For now," she said reluctantly.

"Then what do you say we take our coffee out on the patio while we can still find a table?"

The crowd on the patio began to react to the meteor shower. Lise looked up as three scaldingly-bright white lines scribed across the meridian. The meteors emanated from a point well above the horizon and almost directly due east, and before she could look away there were more of them— two, then one, then a spectacular cluster of five.

She was reminded of a summer in Idaho when she had gone stargazing with her father—she couldn't have been more

Copyright © 2007 by Robert Charles Wilson

than ten years old. Her father had grown up before the Spin and he had talked to her about the stars "the way they used to be," before the Hypotheticals dragged the Earth a few billion years down the river of time. He missed the old constellations, he said, the old star names. But there had been meteors that night, dozens of them, the largest intercepted by the invisible barrier that protected the Earth from the swollen sun, the smallest incinerated in the atmosphere. She had watched them arc across the heavens with a speed and brilliance that left her breathless.

As now. The fireworks of God. "Wow," she said, lamely.

Turk pulled his chair around to her side of the table so they were both facing the sea. He didn't make any kind of an overt move and she guessed he probably wouldn't. Navigating the high mountain passes must have been simple compared to this. She didn't make any moves either, was careful not to, but she couldn't help feeling the heat of his body inches from hers. She sipped her coffee without tasting it. There was another flurry of falling stars. She wondered aloud whether any of them ever reached the ground.

"It's just dust," Turk said, "or that's what the astronomers say. What's left of some old comet."

But something new had caught her attention. "So what about that?" she asked, pointing east, lower on the horizon, where the dark sky met the darker sea. It looked to Lise like something was actually falling out there—not meteors but bright dots that hung in the air like flares, or what she imagined flares would look like. The reflected light of them colored the ocean a streaky orange. She didn't remember anything like that from her previous time in Equatoria. "Is that part of it?"

Turk stood up. So did a few others among the crowd on the patio. A puzzled hush displaced the talk and laughter. Here and there, phones began to buzz or chatter.

"No," Turk said. "That's not part of it."

○ ○ ○

It was like nothing Turk had seen during his ten years in the New World.

But, in a way, that was exactly typical. The New World had

a habit of reminding you it wasn't Earth. Things happened differently here. It ain't Kansas, as people liked to say, and they probably said the same thing in a dozen different languages. It ain't the Steppes. It ain't Kandahar. It ain't Mombassa.

"Do you think it's dangerous?" Lise asked.

Some of the restaurant's clientele evidently thought so. They settled their bills with barely-disguised haste and made for their cars. Within a few minutes there were only a few stalwarts left on the broad wooden patio. "You want to leave?" Turk asked.

"Not if you don't."

"I guess we're as safe here as anywhere," Turk said. "And the view is better."

The phenomenon was still hanging out at sea, though it seemed to move steadily closer. What it looked like was luminous rain, a rolling gray cloud shot with light—the way a thunderstorm looked when you saw it from a long way off except that the glow wasn't fitful, like lightning, but seemed to hang below the billowing darkness and illuminate it from beneath. Turk had seen storms roll in from sea often enough, and he estimated this one was approaching at roughly the local wind speed. The brightness falling from it appeared to be composed of discrete luminous or burning particles, maybe as dense as snow, but he could be wrong about that—it didn't snow in this part of Equatoria and the last snow he had seen was off the coast of Maine many years back.

His first concern was fire. Port Magellan was a tinderbox, crowed with sub-code housing and shacks; the docklands housed countless storage and transport facilities and the bay was thick with oil and LNG tankers, funneling fuel to the insatiable Earth. What looked like a dense squall of lit matches was blowing in from the east, and he didn't want to think about the potential consequences of that.

He said nothing to Lise. He imagined she had drawn many of the same conclusions, but she didn't suggest running— was smart enough, he guessed, to know there was no logical place to run to, not at the speed this thing was coming. But she tensed up as the phenomenon visibly approached the point of land at the southern extremity of the bay.

"It's not bright all the way down," she said.

The staff at Harley's started dragging in tables from the patio, as if that was going to protect anything from anything, and urged the remaining diners to stay indoors until someone had some idea what was going on. But the waiters knew Turk well enough to let him alone. So he stayed out a while longer with Lise and they watched the light of the flares, or whatever they were, dancing on the distant sea.

Not bright all the way down. He saw what she meant. The shifting, glittering curtains trailed into darkness well before they reached the surface of the ocean. Burned out, maybe. That was a hopeful sign. Lise took out her phone and punched up a local news broadcast, relaying bits of it to Turk. They were talking about a "storm," she said, or what looked on radar like a storm, the fringes of it extending north and south for hundreds of miles, the heart of it more or less centered on the Port.

And now the bright rain fell over the headlands and the inner harbor, illuminating the decks and superstructures of cruise ships and cargo vessels at anchor. Then the silhouettes of the cargo cranes grew misty and obscure, the tall hotels in the city dimmed in the distance, the souks and markets vanished as the shining rain moved up the hillsides and seemed to grow taller as it came, a canyon-wall of murky light. But nothing burst into flame. That was good, Turk thought. Then he thought: But it could be toxic. It could be any fucking thing. "About time to move indoors," he said.

Tyrell, the headwaiter at Harley's, was a guy Turk had briefly worked with on the pipelines out in the Rub al-Khali. They weren't big buddies or anything but they were friendly, and Tyrell looked relieved when Turk and Lise finally abandoned the patio. Tyrell slid the glass doors shut and said, "You got any idea—?"

"No," Turk said.